27 Stories

27 Stories

FEATURING

The winning entries

FROM THE

Owl Canyon Press
Short Story Hackathon No. 2
Challenge

CHOSEN FROM 950+ ENTRIES
RECEIVED FROM OVER 45 COUNTRIES

Edited by Gene Hayworth
With a foreword by David Greenson

OWL CANYON PRESS
BOULDER COLORADO
USA

First Edition, 2019

All Rights Reserved

Library of Congress Cataloging-in-Publication Data

27 Stories —1st ed.

p. cm.

ISBN: 978-0-9985073-7-8

2019

Owl Canyon Press

Boulder, Colorado

CONTENTS

CONTENTS (CONT.)

Introduction

Everybody runs into obstacles. Writers get blocked, runners hit the wall, and criminals fleeing the scene of a crime run into roadblocks (at least in the movies). Most of the time, these kinds of obstructions come into play once you are underway with whatever it is you are doing, and perhaps that momentum helps you persevere. It's much harder to run into a big hindrance right at the very beginning.

But that's exactly what each of the writers in this anthology had to contend with. As entrants in the Owl Canyon Press' Winter 2018 Hackathon, they had to start their stories with the same first paragraph, one which described an ominous concrete wall with a bizarre bit of graffiti. They had to write stories that were fifty paragraphs, no more and no less, and each paragraph had to be at least forty words. Oh, and then at roughly the halfway point in their story, just when they thought they might break free from all these constraints, they had to incorporate another pre-written paragraph, this time choosing between two options. Sounds impossibly hard, right? How could anyone find their way through that kind of a thicket of snags and come out with a compelling short story?

The twenty-seven authors on the pages that follow not only made their way through this carefully constructed obstacle course, they did so with such grace and wit and heart that you'll soon forget that they are dancing with stacks of plates delicately balanced atop their heads. From the common beginning point I described above, each author was able to craft a thoroughly unique and delightful piece of fiction.

The anthology starts with "Random and Small Redemptions," Rita Sommers-Flanagan's top-prize winning entry, which will introduce you to a handful of memorable characters whose lives intersect in unpredictable ways across a desolate parking lot. You'll meet Suzy Q, who likes to scream her angst out the window of her apartment, and Capricorn, a pizza delivering philosopher and would-be orator. Then there is Malachi, a grizzled truck driver haunted by a feeling he can neither articulate nor dismiss, who crosses paths with Rainbow, an ownerless dog who remains optimistic in spite of her tragically poor luck. The world that Sommers-Flanagan creates is both real and magical, and her story is both poignant and surprisingly uplifting.

Virginia Brackett creates an entirely different world for her second-place winning story, "The Final Word." You'll be captivated by the saga of the Anderson kid, rendered mute by tragedy and taken on by the passionate Preacher Main. Then in "Galop," Donald Ryan's tale that rounds out the top-three, you'll feel the reverberations of a single day in the life of a young man, a day miraculous with beauty and connection, and simultaneously weighed down by a soul-crushing loss.

Of course, these three spectacular stories are just the beginning. As you read on, you'll discover a wide range of genres and styles, stories that will frighten you and make you laugh and pierce your heart; stories that will transport you to frightening futures alongside stories that will explore the hidden corners of our modern world. In the pages that follow, dear reader, there is something for everyone, and once you have hungrily digested them all, I am confident that you will join me in raising a glass to salute these authors and what they have accomplished. I am honored to present you with the winners and finalists of the Owl Canyon Press Winter 2018 Hackathon. Rejoice!

David Greenson

Random and Small Redemptions

RITA SOMMERS-FLANAGAN

-♦-

Beyond the cracked sidewalk, and the telephone pole with layers of flyers in a rainbow of colors, and the patch of dry brown grass there stood a ten-foot high concrete block wall, caked with dozens of coats of paint. There was a small shrine at the foot of it, with burnt out candles and dead flowers and a few soggy teddy bears. One word of graffiti filled the wall, red letters on a gold background: Rejoice!

It took being murdered to attain any kind of attention around here. The choice of colors and the word on the wall were a bit unusual, but the creation of a shrine was not. This time, the shrine had lasted for weeks, but Suzy Q could not remember when, exactly, it arose and she could not remember why. She herself arose like smoke and drifted into the wee hours of the day, sleep residue obscuring her path. Without full consciousness, she found herself in the bathroom and turned the shower on hot. To make sure it was her image in the mirror, she cut a few divots in her bangs with the manicure scissors. Small shards of straight black hair peppered the sink. The roommates would find them later, and wash them away.

A pre-dawn chorus of blaring horns and revving engines echoed from the parking lots below. Delivery trucks fought for space, their trailers engorged with excesses that make the world go round. Sometimes, Suzy would throw open the moldy bathroom window and scream at them but it was chilly this morning. She doubted that her screams of protest made it down the three flights anyway. Today she would substitute aggressive indoor soprano trills she liked to think of as opera. Renee Fleming in La Traviata, if anyone asked.

Her roommates slept on. Suzy Q helped herself to three partially-filled boxes of Thai food abandoned on the filthy counter in the slapped together cave of cabinetry that passed as a kitchen. She finished off the wine in glasses marked with greasy prints and in one case, pink lipstick. Hidden inside her cozy robe, she floated to the safety of her bed, and peeked through her curtains at the wall. It still said "Rejoice." *Nice*, she thought. *I like that word.*

Capricorn delivered pizza in his rusted Honda Civic. The kid was invisible, and he knew it. Sometimes, he welcomed the urban cloak of invisibility—even relied on it to shelter himself. In their blinding anticipation of slabs of tomato-daubed dough dripping in cheap cheese and overdone spices, his customers saw only the red, insulated pizza box and began to salivate. They may have glimpsed his shaded face as they flung a tip his way. That's all. They didn't see the car either. Just the light on top declaring his pizza-centric identity. If the kid had a creed, it came from the old paperback copy of "Watership Down" he'd read long ago. He didn't remember much about the book, but he remembered the final price of being caged and fattened up. Capricorn was temporarily caged and he knew it. But he would not be harvested anytime soon. He wore his clothing tight. He was plenty thin and intended to stay that way. But his complete invisibility burdened him. He had things to say, and he wanted someone to listen.

What the fuck? Capricorn asked himself, time and again. He had no answer, but asking the question comforted him. *What the fuck?* he'd say, driving along, the Honda humming, the aroma of oregano so heavy he could hardly breathe. Capricorn hated oregano. He drove with the window open, but sometimes, he had to stop the car, get out, and breathe in a gulp of alley shit or exhaust fumes just to keep from puking.

The women in his life ate pizza. His mother. His older sisters, Aquarius and Libra. They were an overbearing trio in Capricorn's world.

Random and Small Redemptions

He fed them mistakes and hung out on the plywood floor he'd attached to the rafters of the garage, safe above the hoarded accumulations of nothing stacked on nothing; clothes no one would wear again, torn books, broken dishes. There, he practiced speeches he would make someday, and dreamed of a better life. A better world.

Rainbow didn't bark much. After the last of the die-hard partiers dissipated, a dismissive shrug settled over the city. She liked this hiatus in the chaos that otherwise surrounded her. It was the best time to prowl, looking for scraps and a bit of connection to other living beings. Rainbow had once had people. They'd chosen her from among her litter mates left in a box on the street. But it didn't last. They dumped her in a parking lot a few months later, and sped away. She'd found shelter under a navy blue futon disintegrating at the bottom of three flights of metal stairs, partially sheltered by a thick cement wall. The futon was crumpled in a way that made a mildewed cave, warm and hidden, not far from a pizza shop where occasional scraps of crust or cheese would fall from the over-filled trash. Sometimes, even in broad daylight, it was worth a dash.

Malachi compulsively checked the tires on his rig. He wore the cab around himself like shelter, loose and comfortable—a cushion against the road. Mal owned his truck–a fine hunk of baby blue. He called her Babe. The interior was saturated with the smell of him. After he checked the tires, he climbed in for the next long haul. The wall caught his eye, the gold background catching the predawn light and throwing it down into the parking lot where it scattered and was lost. The wall was a fleeting distraction. He couldn't see the teddy bears or the candles, but if he had seen them, he would've shook his head. That's all. He also didn't see Rainbow dashing under the last set of tires on the extended trailer which somehow caught her back left leg. The high-pitched dog screams went unnoticed in the bellicose din of the street and the roar of the engine.

The leg was crushed flat but it didn't detach. Rainbow ran three-legged, dragging the flat appendage, yipping in pain and terror. Instinctively, she ran along the back of the wall, aiming for the futon, but the panic-driven adrenalin was short-lived, and she dropped in the rough grass before she got to the futon.

The next haul was to Wichita. Truck loaded and ready, Malachi glanced at himself in his rearview mirror and rubbed away a thin line of tobacco juice that had dribbled down one side of his jaw, completely unaware that he had nearly killed a dog. He'd hoped to be on the road earlier. It was time to roll. "Sing to me, darling," he said as he rubbed his hands on his oily Wranglers. He couldn't remember the last time he'd had a good night's sleep or a meal that he hadn't selected by pointing at something rotating on a spick behind cracked glass. Didn't matter. It was all the same to him. He considered grabbing a pizza before pulling out, but decided against it. Sometimes the smell of pizza made him remember better times. He stepped on the gas. That raging rumble of kick-ass diesel squared his shoulders. His face split into a grin, revealing dark gaps and inflamed gums. He knew he'd be eating the miles to Kansas with whatever teeth he had left.

Suzy Q's roommates were hungry. They ordered pizza for breakfast. The Thai food leftovers were gone; they knew they could get a contribution out of Suzy later. They dumped change purses and counted enough for a large meat-lover's plus a generous tip. They always tipped.

Capricorn clanked his boots up three flights of metal steps, meat-lover's pizza balanced perfectly, senses assaulted by the dank backwash of humanity that festers on the surface of meaningless mornings like this one. Before he pushed the buzzer, he scratched himself and scanned the surroundings below. The wall still had the gold and red, the mangled teddy bears, the burned out candles. Oh, what a speech he could make at the base of that wall. He imagined what he'd say. How he'd finally make people see they needed to see.

These girls ordered often, and it was a short walk across a few parking lots to deliver. This made the kid happy, as the oregano odor could float into the ozone instead of leaching into his skin. Where was that futon dog? Little bitch always there this time of the morning, all sly-eyed and skinny. Capricorn carried dog biscuits and often tossed the wary ones a freebie. He especially liked the futon dog. She was wary but polite. Sometimes, she even licked his hand.

Suzy Q slept fitfully in a golden fog of synthetic fabric and warm oregano. She jerked and drooled on the faux-satin pillow case. Her uneven bangs were plastered to her forehead, her forearm and wrist curled in a hook. Her nightmare momentarily expanded to explain the high-pitched yelps that had intruded into her sleep, but then she woke up. She rolled over. In the distance, a semi driver used his Jake brake, spewing sound like a machine gun spraying the street. Suzy Q hated that noise. It was like truck ejaculation. She flung open the window, howled her protest from the shelter of the twisted bedding and cried a while before she fell back to sleep.

What the fuck? Capricorn muttered a second time, as Suzy Q's maniacal wail miraculously made it all the way to the street. This was not an especially good morning. The wall and its declaration, the wall and the littered tributes—it was eating at him. And where was that dog?

On his third trip back to the pizza place, Capricorn took a few minutes to walk around. He peered into the moldy futon, shouting, *Here doggie. C'mere.* He clapped his hands. Miraculously, he heard a whimper and found the dog in tall weeds behind the wall. The close up view of the deteriorating teddy bears and candle stubs upset him, but the sight of Rainbow's mangled back leg bent him over, and he threw up on his steel-toed boots. She raised her head to watch and sniff the air. The bleeding had been minimal but the exposed bone gleamed iridescent white and the meat around it was drying a dull crackling burgundy.

Shoulda died, little bitch, he thought. *Shoulda died. What the fuck. This ain't any good at all.* He backed away as he pulled his loose hood up around his head, wiping his mouth with his sleeve. She watched him go. Her tail slapped a few automatic friendly beats, stirring dust from the dry brown grass.

Suzy Q found the missing shoe by accident. It was under her roommate's coat which had disappeared behind the couch. Two days ago, she'd given up the search for this very shoe, and angry to the point of despair, she'd thrown away the mate. But now, here it was, made single and irrelevant by her own reactivity. Tears of self-reproach began. She sobbed uncontrollably, stroking the remaining black velvet slip-on as if it were a pet. When she wasn't high, Suzy Q relived the rape. The jagged memory was always there, waiting for her attention. Defining her reality. Even the smallest losses shredded her coping capacity and reduced her to raw emotion.

Evening came. Rainbow sensed the return of the vomit-breathed kid. He leaned over her. His tentative, soothing touch sent a convoluted surge of both alarm and relief through her. Humans this close usually meant trouble. The noise that came out of her throat was a garbled sigh of resignation. The noise that came out of his sounded vaguely like *What the fuck?* but it was garbled too. The kid slipped an open pizza box under her body and tried to lift her with the least movement possible. The flap bent and she yipped in pain, but he didn't drop her. Somehow, once again, Rainbow was in the back seat of a human car. Last time, this hadn't ended well.

When the ride ended, she was lifted again. The kid slid her body onto a soft pile of clothing among the boxes in the garage. He pulled an old coat over the top, creating a cave that emanated the sweetness of old ladies who frequently powdered themselves—a light rose motif that played ironically well in the deep recesses of Rainbow's ancestral brain. The pizza kid lifted her head to help her lap water from a hubcap. He broke bits of pepperoni and crust into bite-sized pieces and left them where her tongue could reach them. Much later, she would heard him practicing his orations like songs. Like monks chanting in the distance, they were a comfort.

Capricorn's chance came before he was ready. The morning after he took Rainbow home, he pulled his Honda into the parking lot later than usual. The lot was partly filled with a crowd, focused on a tall, silver-haired man who was standing at the base of the wall. "Repent and rejoice," the man was shouting. He'd obviously delivered some kind of sermon. The kid stood transfixed. The crowd was mostly white and well-dressed. Not native to this neighborhood.

"This wall is the barrier we need to live proud," the man continued, bullhorn blaring his message to the outer limits of the parking lot. "We need walls that declare the way to salvation. Walls that protect and guide. We must build the walls and choose to live on the right side of them." People clapped and shouted their agreement.

"Who among you has a testimony?" the man shouted and then waved the bullhorn above his head. "Tell us what this wall, this glorious wall, means to you. The wall of redemption. Rejoicing in the name of Jesus, oh dear ones. Rejoice."

His heart in his throat, fury in his veins, Capricorn knew this was his chance. Sick to death of easy answers and privileged people, car-struck dogs, and no way forward. This was his parking lot, his ground, his wall. But it had been invaded, made into some kind of funky shrine, and smeared with cheap gold and ugly red. He clenched his fists tight and made his way through the crowd, which parted like the Red Sea for this angry-looking kid who'd appeared out of nowhere.

The kid got up onto a milk crate and raised his hand. A murmur went through the crowd and then it fell silent, except for a few people shouting words of encouragement at him. The kid acknowledged them with a nod and a shy smile. In the full light of day, he looked less angry and more beautiful. He waited until people stopped shouting. A siren could be heard, maybe five or ten blocks away. The kid raised the bullhorn, pressed the button, and began to speak.

"A dog got run over in this parking lot and left for dead," he said. "It could've been me." The crowd looked puzzled, quieting, waiting for a testimonial of some sort. "Could've been you," Capricorn continued, his voice growing stronger. "We creatures on this good earth, we're afraid of anything different than us. The fear makes us invisible to each other until it's too late. A shrine and candle won't fix it. Sermons won't fix it. Walls will definitely not fix it. When we all can finally see each other, when we serve each other, when we wash each other's feet, then we can put this word on this wall. But we won't need to. We don't need walls. They are a cheap, self-defeating defense." He stopped, surveyed the crowd, and realized he'd said all he wanted to say. The kid was done. He'd given his first speech in a world that he was sure needed to hear from him.

Capricorn gave the bullhorn back to the silver-haired man, stepped off the milk crate, and walked quietly to his Honda. His face was glowing with sweat, but also with pride. He'd done it. He'd stepped out of the deep shadow of nothing and insisted, if only for a moment, on being seen. It felt good.

The Kansas State Trooper that pulled Malachi over wore his uniform proud. The dark blue authority covered him in glory. He jawed his gum in slow circles, reminding Malachi of the family milk cow chewing her cud back in the day. Speeding. It was four in the morning. Not the usual time to get caught, but Malachi always drove over the limit. He budgeted for it. It usually took very little time. But this brash little jackass was apparently bored, fishing for a rise out of Malachi. The trooper's half-lidded eyeballs flashed mean and cold as a snake, his smart mouth drawling out suggestions about Malachi's lineage that got all the way under Mal's thick, rashy skin. Mal flipped him off, which earned him a pants-down crotch search for drugs, a probe, and finally, a hard grab that dropped Malachi from straddle to knees to fetal curl. Rocks flew as the trooper peeled out, taking Mal's money and dignity with him.

The first light of day licked at the underbelly of the receding night as Malachi eased through the gears. So many things about life had to either be swallowed whole or bit in two and spit out. If you kept it anywheres near you, if chewed on it at all, you'd grind the shit out of whatever teeth you had left. Mal cranked up Linda Ronstadt, stroked the steering wheel and let the rumble of the road sooth him like a baby, cradled in the arms of a diesel-Jesus. It wasn't until he was a hundred mile past Topeka that he even realized he was hungry. His stomach ached like a foreign object someone had stuck in his gut. He pulled in and fed himself grudgingly, slapping down the greasy fare with self-loathing and intense impatience. Malachi didn't have time to waste. He didn't have anything to waste.

A few days before his spontaneous oration, Capricorn had noticed a nice, velvet shoe when he lifted the lid of the parking lot dumpster. It was late, and he was tired. The streetlight lit up the golden embroidery threaded through the pliant toe. It shimmered like Christmas. He rummaged for a mate, but found none. Single shoes, gloves, stockings: these unsettled Capricorn. How could such obvious pairings come apart? And why?

The sparkle of this shoe brought Cinderella to mind. Capricorn had stood for a moment, imagining a black Cinderella, his secret sister, someone his real sisters would torment, like they tormented him. Then he shook it off. What a dumbass story. Glass slippers. As if moving through the world wasn't precarious enough. But in this lily white story, Cinderella's lost shoe was ultimately redemptive. *Now that's the fairy-tale part*, Capricorn thought. *Loss is loss. No fucking way any happily-ever-after shit*

23

happens to the mateless adornments of human appendages littered around this city. He had slammed the dumpster lid down, leaving the shoe to settle further in the sludge of all things cast aside. But the image of that little shoe held fast, as unwelcome as the smell of oregano.

Suzy Q had cried herself to sleep again, this time on the couch, clinging to her found but now mateless shoe. The roommates worked around the situation by draping a small towel over her head and a satin comforter over the rest of her. They were a thoughtful and patient lot. They eased themselves down the flights of metal steps. Each of them stepped lightly in stylish leather boots. Nothing clanked until they were nearly on the ground.

The dream world was not kind to Suzy Q. She jerked and punched and fought her way through the murky world of Nod. She invariably awoke famished. This time, she drifted to consciousness among the long shadows that draped the room with street-light gloom, hours after her shiny roommates had slipped away. There was absolutely nothing to eat anywhere. With puffy eyes unfocused, her cell phone almost automatically dialed for pizza. Tonight, plain cheese would do. She paced the perimeter of the known world, hungry, sleek as a yearling leopard, slapping the single shoe on her thigh. She fed the three goldfish on one of her rounds, wondering vaguely how they would taste fried in bacon grease.

Rainbow had always been a clean dog, shy about her inner workings and quick with it all. But when the human returned, held her down, and dumped nasty orange liquid over her wound, she'd dirtied herself and the soft pile of clothing under her. As her bowels moved, she readied her body for a punishing kick. But none came. What came was a fire that lit itself as the liquid splashed over her open flesh. It was the kind of fire that cleans the soul and sharpens the spirit for a final escape. She moaned as she began the long wait for death. But death didn't come either.

The next morning, the haze lifted and she ate and drank what was offered. The return from hell made her giddy, ready to caper about. But the human had built a restraining cave of boxes that kept her from doing much more than a very slight wiggle. Even that snapped her back to real time, real body, real dislocation. The weak smell of dusty rose was overtaken by dog shit and iodine. But not a whiff of rotting flesh. The exposed strips were drying like jerky. The useless mass of matted hide, frayed sinew, and tenuously connected muscle had begun to shrivel.

Malachi stored most of what he knew in the marrow of his bones, with a smattering of fact tucked in the folds of his mind. He worked out the details of life as they presented themselves. Habit took care of the rest. But lately, something nagged at him. Neither a fully formed idea nor an articulated longing. But something. It was an itch that, for the life of him, he could not scratch. Or a color he knew he'd like if he could just pick it out from the stream of colors that flowed along beside him. He actually turned his head sometimes, hoping to catch a glimpse of this mocking phantom, flickering just out of his line of vision. His own image stared back, slack skin swaying from his jaw, frayed collar of his western shirt askew.

He was almost back. A round trip that crossed eight states in four days. Did this matter? After his sister died some time back, there was no one who paid one bit of attention to the circles he drove in, or the time it took him, or the small victories or defeats along the way. He rubbed his chin and slapped himself to stay awake. When he got back, he promised himself a nice motel, a long shower, and a very, very long nap.

Suzy Q met pizza boy at the door with a single shoe in one hand and exact change in the other. His eyes widened, fixated on the shoe. Neither of them had ever spoken a complete sentence to the other. To reach across such an obvious chasm took more intention that either of them wanted to muster. Suzy Q put the shoe down beside her as she took the pizza box. His eyes followed the shoe.

Pizza kid clattered down the stairs. Suzy Q turned the dead-bolt and leaned against the door. She ate in big gulps. Her mouth went dry. Reluctantly, she moved away from the door and took a drink of the lukewarm city water that dribbled from the tap. The she began an insistent search through discarded wine bottles in the recycling corner. Her faith was rewarded. She ignored the solids floating in the purple liquid. Probably just broken cork.

By the beginning of the third day, Rainbow expected the routine: a change of rags, douse of iodine, food, water. The boy had cut away the extraneous parts of what had been a leg—strands so withered the removal was more ceremonious than substantive. Rainbow accepted her lot in life like an old soul flitting through a twisted and temporary world. In her dark cave, she repositioned herself and stood. Her energy was returning. She was ready to reclaim what was left of herself and the kid was ready to let her go. He remembered his aversion to captivity.

One more ride in the backseat of the rusty Honda. Back to the futon cave at the base of the stairs. The boy filled the hub caps he'd brought along with food and water. Rainbow situated herself in her futon cave. She was free to come and go. Free to learn a new, three-legged stride.

Malachi was busting butt to get out of Kansas, not by driving over the limit but by crawling precariously close to that place where mind detaches from all things related to the earthly body. He stocked up on No-Doz, Red Bull, Baby Ruths, and chocolate milk. He powered through the hours, legs bouncing, music blaring, and synapses misfiring like fireworks lit too close to the ground. It wouldn't have been so bad if the unloading and reloading hadn't gotten all screwed up so he stood around, twiddling his God damned thumbs, waiting to leave. Each police cruiser that drove by flipped his stomach and all he saw was the face of that State Trooper with his ironed uniform and malignant eyes. Mal felt shrunk up and dusty.

Capricorn's way of thinking had bends and loops that sometimes distorted the sheen of everyday life. He liked it that way. It gave him material for his imagined speeches. But delivering pizza to the owner of the other shoe? The shoe that he'd stared at, floating on the junk in the dumpster just two days ago? Too weird. How could she stand there, slant-eyed and sleep-faced, holding that shoe? After he gave her the pizza, he went straight to the dumpster, and miraculously found the other shoe, buried under everything he hated about humanity. But now, it was his shoe, like the dog's leg which he'd carefully detached. These were trophies in a war between meaninglessness and coherence. The kid was doing what he could to hold the universe together.

Good God, Suzy Q's roommates said in unison when they saw the dog limp-running across the parking lot that evening. It was Rainbow's maiden voyage as a three-legged creature. *Gross.* They started to tell Suzy Q about it but she wasn't listening (as usual). So they examined their purchases, like quarreling squirrels. They sometimes considered how they might rid themselves of Suzy Q, but she was like an interesting piece of furniture or an exotic, dangerous pet. They kept their distance. She kept hers.

Suzy Q planned to move as soon as she found the last few parts of herself and got them reattached. She knew her former configuration by heart, but her body had been invaded. She'd been dismembered–a thousand-piece jigsaw was child's play compared to the complexities Suzy Q faced when she saw her reflection. Some days, she seemed almost ordinary by the end of the day, but night would come and unravel the strands, and she'd start the next stretch of consciousness enraged or diminished. No one had picked her up and wrapped her in rose-scented rags. No one had done anything.

When Malachi rolled into the parking lot, his guard was down, his mind blown. He slid out of his small world to take a leak and breathe the dark city air. His body was rag-dolling on him and he fought to stay upright and not piss himself. Thus, he was easy prey for a quick heist. They took his wallet. He didn't protest. They shoved him. He staggered stupidly, spinning in slow motion, out of control. They hit him with something hard. He fell to his knees, crawled a few yards, looking for knee-level shelter. The futon came into focus long enough for him to fall on it before he passed out and they lost interest. There he slept, under the golden wall with the bright red word. It was the sleep of the irredeemably innocent, the fatally flawed, the invisibly dead.

When Rainbow returned from her pre-dawn tour, she that found a stinking human had flattened her cave. She stood for a long while, frozen. Then she circled it. The body didn't move. She moved in closer. Sniffed the boots, jeans, crotch, arms, head. Blood was still oozing from the wound above his ear. She licked it, cautiously at first, but then with instinctual fervor.

Malachi dreamed the dog's tongue lapping away his shame, the gash across his skull closing. But he didn't move. After cleaning the wound, Rainbow stood guard for a while, but finally eased down beside the immobile intruder and tucked three legs under herself to rest. Both bodies radiated warmth against the chill that seeps into the bones of anything exposed that time of the morning.

The kid knew it was time to reunite the shoes. He didn't want to, but something told him there was no other option. He'd imagined a number of scenarios in his head. Some had included words and explanations. But in the end, he decided to slip back into his familiar invisibility. He crept up the steps, very early, shoe in hand, and hung it from the doorknob by the toe. The lights weren't on, but inside, he could hear someone singing in a terrible falsetto. It was almost a shriek, but not the kind that pulled you in to help—the kind that made you back away. Which he did.

On his way up the stairs, he'd been so focused on his mission that he hadn't noticed the futon flattened at the base of the wall—no longer a cave, but a bed. He hadn't seen the dog stretched out next to the sprawled human body. His eyes had been looking down, calculating how to make each step noiseless. But as he came back down the stairs, the gold paint caught his eye as it reflected light and curved it downward, casting a golden halo around the nestled bodies. Capricorn froze. Wonderment raised the hair on the back of his neck as he stared at the futon and that unlikely pair of God's creatures, side by side, apparently warm and at peace. *What the fuck* seemed inadequate. But it was all he had.

The Final Word

VIRGINIA BRACKETT

⠌⠌⠌

Beyond the cracked sidewalk, and the telephone pole with layers of flyers in a rainbow of colors, and the patch of dry brown grass there stood a ten -foot high concrete block wall, caked with dozens of coats of paint. There was a small shrine at the foot of it, with burnt out candles and dead flowers and a few soggy teddy bears. One word of graffiti filled the wall, red letters on a gold background: Rejoice!

Rejoice! That word first appeared years ago, painted by young Alice. She's long gone now, of course, but we all keep it refreshed. The wall was first used to protest the plant closing, then to advertise Sunbeam bread, then repainted to remind us that we all needed to deposit into First National any pennies that weren't tithed to the church, and then – well, you get my drift. If you need to know more, the whole list is in my notebook, because I'm a born observer. Chances are good that Rejoice! will be the final word. The penultimate call to action had been Repent! Alice covered that word that marked the history of our community's sorrow and its sin – that last bit according only to some, present company excluded.

We had been called to repent by Preacher Main a couple of years after the sole tragedy to have taken place in our community. Part of our sorrow was that it didn't have to happen, not really, as the perp, John James Soda had bragged beforehand about the arson. Problem is when dealing with someone who talks out of his ass all his life, and then of a sudden he's telling the truth, how is one to know. Johnny – which is how we all knew him, but the state paper took to using his full name – Johnny was short a few cards from a full deck. He was known to like a fire and would sneak into other folks' camps or bonfire gatherings just to stare into the flames, which if it brought him joy, we didn't mind. At that time, we were still a live-and-let-live kind of place. The law – that is to say Chief Darnley – correctly figured Johnny's father's tool shed as the source of the gasoline and the rags, and that was all plain - no outside investigator required. But Johnny's choice of the Anderson house at 1:00AM was not so plain – what did they ever do to him? And him out on a snowy night with the once-in-a-decade frozen pipes and all – that family did not stand a chance. Our community did not like unanswered questions. The out-of-town news people were sent to me, as I was the closest thing to a reporter – more like a recorder, really - for our town.

Following that terrible occurrence, the wall was officially declared "in memorium" and bears and silk flowers and toys of all sorts appeared, now long gone, except for a few bedraggled remembrances. Before that sad co-opting of the space, we had been exposed to non-stop advertising on a wall of many colors. Words came and went, colors came and went, but not much really changed until the fire, which later became a sign as well as a regret for all.

And the Anderson kid, ten or so at the time of the fire, who escaped by the grace of God and the family dog who dragged him out and then died itself, was the lone survivor, with seven dead of smoke – eight counting the dog. Johnny was sent downstate in haste, but he was not there for long, because he was found swinging by the neck in his prison cell. The state paper said suicide, but others had their theories, and suicide was not among them. School children made up a song: "Poor Johnny, poor Johnny, where have you gone? Send ashes, ashes, to cover your grave," and so on. None of us would have thought to pray for his soul. Prayer was cheap but also a personal matter. That soul might have been lost in sad circumstance, but we did not see it as a black mark on the community. That would come later.

And the Anderson boy was cared for by everyone over time. Like if he was in Piggly Wiggly, someone would say "Hey, kid, do you like fudge," or "Hey, kid, how about this truck." Even if he didn't answer, because he spoke not at all, he would end up with candy or a toy. Or people would leave a basket in front of his Aunt Junie's house with food or clothes or marbles and a tag "For the kid." That was believed to be doubly useful, as Junie had raised no children of her own, and may have had few clues as to how to go about it.

So, after a while we all got used to seeing him around. Kenneth K. Anderson was his name, but we all just called him the kid. By that time he was about eleven, maybe closer to twelve, and no one had heard him speak since the fire. He was schooled by his Aunt Junie, who didn't want to fight him outside of the school house to go in. The elementary principal once asked, "Where's the proof," but no one could answer, and, truthfully, no one cared that much. When we thought of the terrible things he might say, we just let it lay.

I tried to remember my eleven going on twelfth year. No details will come, but I remember being confused. That was because I got my height before my friends. The boys were mad and the girls more interested in me than ever before, and I didn't know how to act. The kid couldn't relate to that, as he was still on the short side and had no friends that I could see – no one ever with him. Not until young Alice May Curts got him in her sights.

I'd be in the hardware store and see him ride by on the bike someone bought him at J.C. Penney. He did not look right or left. However, if someone was to yell, "Hey, kid," he might nod at them. You wouldn't say he was rude or anything – sometimes he managed a little smile. There was nothing there to make us think he'd ever been, or would ever be, trouble. We still regarded sin, when we cared to regard it at all, as an external condition resulting in an undesirable act, rather than internal. We could not see it reflected anywhere in our town.

Someone had put a bell on the bike handle and clothes-pinned playing cards to the kid's bike wheels, so we heard that click, click, click the cards made as they licked the spokes. And he had taken to stopping to pick up rocks and dropping them into the basket on the front of the bike. I worried about that basket as it was more fitting for a girl, but no one gave the kid any trouble about it.

Then we started to see the rocks in front of the memorial wall. They were in stacks; some just heaps without any order, some more by design, like four, then three, then two, then one on top, and some in a row that stretched the length of the wall. Next we saw some rocks that had been painted and laid out in patterns. You might have your red, green, green, red, or your white, speckle green, white, speckle green, each group flanked with plain stones. You couldn't call it art exactly, but it did catch the eye. I guess that was the beginning of the shrine.

I took to driving by the wall more regular, like on my way to the P.O., to see what I could see. I remember the first time I saw the kid with red-haired Alice. She had a brush and paint and at that moment was painting a streak down one of the kid's cheeks, war-paint like. I heard her say, "Please, kid, just once. Just say my name one time." The kid stood silent as ever, not a smile or a twitch to even show that he heard young Alice. She blew a curl away from her left eye and applied another stripe. I drove on by, but watched them in my rearview until I couldn't see them anymore.

When the end-of-summer revival came to the dirt lot, a lot of us were there. We always helped with the speaking platform by hauling in crates. Back then the preacher couldn't afford a tent and politely refused the invitation into the local church, feeling it would be too small. A picnic followed the stage building, which had become a tradition, with lunch provided to that year's revival preacher, Purdy Main. I ate with my kin, never having to fix anything myself. Like I said, it was a close community.

Most everyone knew me, and I knew all of the families. The kid wasn't there that day, but I saw Alice, and I knew she was looking for him, wanting to share her apple pie. Everyone came back for the first night, standing around the makeshift stage, food crates with boards stretched across and an extra stack in the middle. Some had young ones on their shoulders; others put the children by their feet. As a rule, the service started in the heat of the afternoon and lasted on past dark. Businesses locked up early, and much of the town was in attendance.

The first night, the preacher climbed up on the stage and offered a welcome. Then he commenced in the normal way, with a focus on evil, the sin it begats, and the dirty souls that result. We all knew the lines, but then he said something that quieted us right down, about the dirt that likely filled our town. He followed up with, "This is not a personal charge, my friends, for we all bear the mark of the Devil. He treads acrost our souls, straight from his fiery den – we can trace his footsteps, dark and sooty. And they cannot be scrubbed clean, my friends, no, they cannot. The Devil's soot cancels us, like the lines the U.S. government places across a postage stamp. That postage is useless underneath that stamp" - at which point he slammed his hand down on the bible – "used up, never to serve again." I couldn't quite make out the parallel, but I appreciated picturing the many stamp possibilities in my mind.

I can't say that I thought a lot of Preacher Main. He was enthusiastic about the fires of hell as preachers usually are, but I didn't see much color in his words. Color is important to making a point about hell. In the past, hell was sketched out by the preachers in oranges, reds, yellows, even greens – all colors of fire, if you take my point. But his focus on the soot, which is the leftover after all, didn't inspire much fear in the community's heart.

The truth of the matter is, no one got too excited about sin in our parts. After the Anderson tragedy, which everyone chalked up to human imperfection on Johnny's part, sin didn't come along much. There was a few broken Commandments about, like a bit of thieving, and I'm sure some was lying with others outside their commitments. But we didn't own enough to covet of one another, honoring of our parents came natural, and our church was so poor that we couldn't afford graven images, even if we wanted them. We only saw the more spectacular sins once in a blue moon. And so we accepted Preacher's word that his charge was not personal, and we all focused on the production and went home knowing we would return.

But not far into the second afternoon, Preacher Main was winding up again. This followed some loud singing on our own and the passing of the plate, which came back around much the way it started – empty. Most folks were moved to give on the first night, following which they were pretty much tapped out. But after a few minutes, we forgot all about the plate and the coins that weren't in it. Preacher stood up to the tip of his lanky height and reached one skinny arm to the sky, waving his bible. "Lord," he called out. Then he went silent for a minute, waiting for the crowd to do the same, as some were still in the throes of the praise hymns.

"Forgive me, Lord!" Preacher Main cried, with one eye to the crowd. That got us curious to see what he had that needed forgiving, and everyone quieted down. So quiet, that I heard the clack of the kid's bicycle tire cards, getting louder by the moment, but I did not turn around to spot him. Then Preacher started in again. "Forgive me, Lord, for not coming sooner! Not coming sooner to this corner in the wilderness of sin where love for one's neighbor and one's god has been abandoned! Abandoned I say!"

I could see folks in front of me and feel folks behind me moving about and looking at each other. Abandonment of our neighbors and our god? No one was going to take kindly to a charge like that. My sometime neighbor, Will Faithful – a sometime neighbor because he preferred camping in the woods to sleeping under a roof – yelled out, "Them is dastardly accusations, Preacher!" Others then added their "Yeahs!," mostly the men, and the women tried to quieten them down without much luck. I saw Ruby Smith head for the gas station down the road. She had been instructed by Chief Darnley, who quite publicly never attended a revival, to phone him if any sign of trouble was to arise.

"You may believe that you have been faithful, but how can it be so, when you allow sin to fester in your midst." Fester seemed to really trip the wire, and those sitting in the dirt jumped to their feet. "I speak of the hellish sight you viewed not long ago, the hell that arose to the sky not two blocks from this vacant lot! Did you not see the flames leaping, did you not hear the victims crying for help!" It suddenly came to us that he was talking about the burning of the Anderson house, although factually speaking, there had been no cries for help. I swung around and saw the kid standing at the back of the group and noted that others had done the same. Alice appeared beside him while I and the rest of humanity stared.

"Had the Lord lived here, would he have allowed such a tragedy?" We turned back to regard Preacher Main, who by this time looked like a bomb for which the spark had started to burn up the wick. He produced a bullhorn from somewhere he'd kept at the ready. Then he blasted us, although we could already hear pretty well. He went up on his toes, balancing on the edge of those crates who knows how, and yelled, "And more importantly, most importantly, my good friends," he paused there for effect and for a breath. "Had the Lord lived in that house, would not lives have been spared? That was a house of sin, my friends, a house of pure-dee sin that required repentance and purification!" As if that wasn't shock enough, he went on to part three: "And had the Lord been with you all, would not the fire starter have found a way to resist the Lord's nemesis, who is the Devil? To resist his temptation? Where were you when he needed help?" He paused to wipe at his forehead with a rag already pretty useless, due its soaked condition.

Then Will Faithful yelled, "But Johnny paid the price! The Lord himself exacted revenge!" The preacher looked Will Faithful straight in the eye, disregarding what Will said and all the noise around him, and asked, "And where were you, my good man? Did you offer that perpetrator the path to repentance?" He answered his own question, while several around Will laid their hands on his shoulders. "No, not you, nor your brethren." He paused his beat, and some of the hands slid off of Will. "The proof is that the perpetrator took his own life!" Voices began to rise again, so Preacher Main notched his volume up as well. "Satan had to burn that house to the ground to show you the devil in your days! He had to double that sin in your midst! That fire was but a taste of what awaits you in hell should you not repent! Do not disregard the signs, my friends. Repent, I say!"

Folks were shaking their fists at Preacher and at one another. I thought back to some of the talk about the kid right after the fire. We were so glad someone had survived. Wasn't that a sign? A good sign amidst all the darkness of undeserved death? I thought about such theories of signs as we all watched the kid walk toward the stage. The crowd parted, making an aisle for him to navigate. His aunt tried to grab him, but he shrugged her hands away, and did the same with Alice. He did let Alice walk him to the podium, looking small as ever, but anger burning his eyes. Preacher's eyes were wide open, like he was seeing something for the first time. Then it seemed like we were all seeing it with him. He handed the bullhorn to the kid, showed him the button to push. Then he licked his lips and stepped back.

The kid got up onto a milk crate and raised his hand. The crowd fell silent, except for a few people shouting words of encouragement at him. The kid acknowledged them with a nod and a shy smile. In the full light of day, he looked less angry and more beautiful. He waited until people stopped shouting. A siren could be heard, maybe five or ten blocks away. The kid raised the bullhorn, pressed the button, and began to speak.

Or thus was our hope. Everyone leaned in and inhaled, all in one breath. We held it a good ten, fifteen seconds, willing that boy to say a word, any word. Then he said, "Unhhhh." And once again, "Unhhh." He made more sounds, animal-type sounds, amplified by the unnecessary bullhorn. Many who had leaned forward shifted backward. The air went out of them like a bellows. We exchanged wary glances as we watched the kid struggle to make his words. We wanted bad to hear them, but also did not want to. It was like wishing, but not wishing, for relief from summer and the first fall day, because you knew winter would follow. Preacher Main's eyes took on what some might have called an unholy gleam, and he looked like he might eat the kid then and there. Chief Darnley had driven into the field, parked and jumped out of his car. He walked to the front of the crowd to look us over, then looked at the kid, then back at us. He crossed his arms and spread his legs into a stance of authority, but he did not speak either. The gulf of silence that had filled with hope emptied right out again.

But in the next moment, Preacher Main reclaimed his bullhorn. "What additional proof do we need here?" he asked, then set the bullhorn down and let his words sink in. "This child" - he now laid hands on the kid's shoulders - "this child is possessed, silenced by Lucifer himself. He is the devil's instrument in your midst." Some looked doubtful, and Preacher Main continued, "No medical explanation exists for this child's silence, does it?" He looked directly at Junie who shook her head, and it occurred to me that he had all the details of the story down pat. And the problem was the kid did look some crazy at that moment. His hair was sticking out everywhere, and he had dirt splotched around on his T-shirt – he was also barefoot. Of course, he pretty much looked like that every day, but not everyone saw him regular like me. Thus, Preacher's words were somewhat validated. The kid stepped down from the podium, but stayed on the stage, all hangdog like. This time, he let young Alice slip her arm in his. The Chief's eyes flickered about looking for trouble, but he still did not speak.

Preacher then startled us all by displacing young Alice from the kid's side and putting that long lanky arm over the kid's skinny shoulders. "Do not despair, my son," he said, speaking to the kid, but looking at us. "Do not despair that Satan has singed your speaking parts and stolen your voice. On the day that you turn to the Lord, it will return." Then Preacher pushed the kid forward a bit, so that we all looked him over pretty good. I remember his raising his head, inch by inch as it were, and then locking his eyes on the crowd. It was a tense moment, when he seemed to look at no one but at everyone. Preacher Main looked at us again and pronounced, "I declare today that I will take this child with me. I take him with me, and he will seek repentance until the glory of the Lord shines around him and moves his tongue again." He then stepped in front of the kid with his quivering shoulders to the crowd, but made sure we could hear what followed. "Will you trust me, son? Will you trust the Lord Almighty and come with me?" Then, Preacher Main slowly turned back to face us.

When the kid's Aunt Junie tried to push in front of the others to make it to the aisle, Preacher Main held his flat palm toward her, and she froze still. "Fear not, good lady. I will care for him as if he was one of my own, for he is one of the Lord's flock and as the Lord's shepherd, I pledge to do so. And you will have the sin of his father removed from you and yours forever." By way of defending against those who might criticize Junie, most murmured approval. The whole crowd then began to nod its heads. I heard Pride Jones say, "Perhaps it was not to be," and such comments followed 'til Junie didn't appear exactly convinced, but stepped back and took her place again among us. We all looked at the kid and we all stood witness that he nodded his head "yes." Tears ran down the face of Alice May Curt, as the preacher stepped aside. "Now, let us contribute to the care of this young sinner, one of your own, soon to be cleansed," he said, and he handed the plate to Rose. Then he began to sing softly.

"Alright, folks," Chief Darnley said, ignoring Preacher Main's endeavors. "Alright, now." I thought he might speak to the kid going off with the Preacher, but he only frowned and clearly considered his duty done. "Let's have a quiet finish, and then you find your way home quick like." The Chief dismissed us with a nod, and walked through the crowd to depart. At that point it seemed both of the laws that we held dear – that of the people and that of the Lord - had put a stamp of approval on Preacher's plan. Many joined him in a repeat of "Shall We Gather at the River," and the plate made the rounds, reappearing in the front row considerably more blessed than during the first pass.

On the third night, the crowd had grown quite a bit, and by the fourth and fifth may have set a revival record for our community. Word had got around to the surrounding towns that we had something special, our own local Innocent branded by sin. Preacher Main had assembled a new crate stack for the kid to stand on, but had not cleaned him up at all, that being more to his purpose. Because young Alice refused to leave the kid's side, Preacher had given her a tambourine to shake at times that he indicated, and all in all, it was an interesting night. I could not begrudge Preacher Main his moment.

We kept showing up again, because no one wanted to miss when the kid would speak. Cause if he spoke, he would be redeemed and we would be redeemed and he wouldn't have to leave. But the Lord did not so choose, a fact the Preacher told us we must accept, and that the kid's silence was a sign that he had not yet repented. I think he saw that some of us did not buy into children in sin, so he repeated the sins of the father line and pulled us all in to share the guilt for the kid's silence. And on the last night, Alice laid down her tambourine and led all of us, the kid right behind her and Preacher bringing up the rear, into a solemn pre-arranged 20-minute foot parade to the wall. We knew it to be pre-arranged, because the wall had been painted a color not yet seen there - a glittery gold.

We all stood silent, and then young Alice picked up a paint brush and took the paint can handed to her by Preacher. She painted the word "Repent" big as the world on our wall and recorded our shame. That action closed the revival, and most went home, likely feeling unrest in their gut. Some of us lingered to see the kid step up to the wall and touch the paint and his hand come away red. Who could know his thoughts, but something about the way he stared at "Repent," took a couple of steps back, then stopped and stared again made us uncomfortable. Of course, who were we to feel uncomfortable compared to all of the emotions the kid must have jammed up over time. Young Alice took his red hand and the two walked back to his Aunt Junie's house to gather his belongings. My own comfort over the Preacher's plan was not strong, but I was not a relation and could not speak to the matter.

When Preacher Main, his bullhorn and tambourine, and the kid moved out on the sixth morning, most watched them drive the road in the preacher's black pick-up. Young Alice, of course, had to stay behind. Her family had not been moved by the spirit as had Junie. However, none judged Junie, in respect for which the gifts continued appearing outside her door, being the mystery in which the Lord moves.

We heard word about the kid, the revival, and the preacher from time to time. The kid became a curiosity, and we heard Preacher Main bought himself a tent and a new trailer to carry it, so respectable had become his audience and their giving. The kid had taken over tambourine duties and was a regular on the stage. He was labeled "the miracle kid," which some in the bigger world thought strange, his not having spoken yet. But some of us — me included — held onto the idea that his initial survival was the miracle, full and sign enough.

That fall, we made the usual harvest and watched the leaves turn, then felt the chill of the change. Young Alice visited the wall regular, keeping the red color fresh. I once saw her with her rake, cleaning the ground around that ten-foot high wall. She seemed to take up the mantle of silence the kid left in his wake. She took to staying in her house except for school and not attending any school festivities.

As the months rolled around, we had a lot to do, and most minds did not go to the kid or his circumstances. Sometime in the holidays we heard that the revival had moved further south to winter in Florida. It had settled in with the circus troupes, and made regular appeals to the animal keepers and high-wire folks and also the farm day laborers there about. Some said that, according to the postmaster, Young Alice did receive a postcard stamped "Sarasota Florida," maybe more than once. That same postmaster put about that he did not read the contents, which was right, according to his charge. News being news, it traveled on its own legs, it seems – yet another miracle one might say.

With the first spring came the time to prepare the fields, as that was our main activity now that the factory had closed. But a drought settled over our county that would not break all through the summer months, and we knew we'd have a slim harvest. "It's the kid," some were heard to grumble, "it's his curse abiding on our fields, another sign." Some resisted at first, but falling in step with the get-along made for a simple choice, and bad luck demanded someone to blame. I didn't know that I agreed with that idea, but I did not dismiss the possibility.

The revival did not return to our town that year, as it was hitting big venues now, or so we heard, with the popularity of the kid. Will got hold of a bright yellow flyer that advertised the revival and dropped by to see me and say, "Durned if the kid is not featured front and center." Even though his picture was hand-drawn, it was clearly him. He wore a shirt with flames painted on the front, and the tambourine he held high had orange flames as well. Eventually it was lost under other flyers for bake sales, school events and the like. I looked for it one day, but it had disappeared, gone as a souvenir, I suspected.

The drought lingered the next spring, and at first everyone hoped aloud and then prayed silently for rain, but it did not come. Our town

The Final Word

turned bitter in mood as the second summer approached following the kid's departure. It was clear that the take from the field would be only about half normal. When fall passed by, no one felt like celebrating the holidays much that year. The only time we all came together was in church, and not only for Christmas service. The kid's Aunt Junie died at the end of December. The weather was cold and the land dry but not froze, so the grave digging was not a challenge. We wondered that the kid did not show up, and I think most just wanted to see him in that flaming shirt.

A panic arose when young Alice disappeared for several hours, but she was later located in Junie's house, just sitting in a front room chair. When I drove by the wall the next spring – must have been about April - I saw some newly painted stones arranged on top of the shrine, and I pulled over. I could see the letters A-L-I-C-E, painted in red. The stack of course soon collapsed, the letter stones scattered on the ground. And young Alice, for who the rocks were namesake, kept "Repent" bright and hard to miss on the wall. No one else paid much attention to the makeshift shrine, or memorial as called by some. I think they all just lacked the energy. Even the daffodils, trusted harbingers of spring and good times ahead, had hardly bothered to show their faces.

The next time I saw a flyer, I decided to go see the revival. I was curious how the kid was getting along and how he might have changed. I bought a bus ticket, slipped out of town, and walked two miles from the terminal to the fairgrounds, where the white tent was pitched. When Preacher Main came on stage, he looked pretty much the same, except for bigger bags under his eyes. He began to sweat right away, and I could see that was still appreciated by the crowd. When he spoke, he started right out with the kid, and this is where I could see a difference. "Look upon sin!" he said softly at first, but then louder. "Look upon sin made manifest before you!" He pointed to the kid who jerked a bit and stepped back, and I could see this was all planned. They moved around the stage like they was dancing, or maybe Preacher was the hunter and the kid the hunted. It was then I noticed the fringe that swung from the hem of the kid's shirt. And I wondered for the first time why he would do it.

Throughout his sermon, Preacher kept coming back to the kid, and once he even struck him with his bible and yelled, "Be gone, Satan!," but I could see it was a glancing blow and all-in-all good theater. The kid looked my way once, but not even a flicker of recognition appeared on his face. Then of a sudden, he stopped still in the middle of the stage, and the crowd quieted. He opened his mouth and worked his face, like trying to let a sound slip from between his lips. It was then he locked eyes with mine, and I knew he saw me there. In the end he said nothing, the Preacher made hay out of Satan's continued grip, and when the plate passed, it was filling nicely. The kid slipped off the stage during Preacher's rap-up, and I did not see him again.

And so it went, as a couple more years rolled by with flyers and drought that surely must end soon. We had no daffodils at all – I figure the bulbs had hunkered down to save each drop of water. We did have the occasional postcard from places like Milwaukee in the state of Wisconsin. My curiosity got the best of me, so I caught the bus one spring day and went to the library in the city to read about the wintering of the circus. I found a helpful librarian who pointed me to the stacks where I found copy from some old newspapers, yellowed by time and finger-turning. They told me that some circus folks used to winter in a place called Delavan, Wisconsin, and I put that down in my notepad. I saw photos in the old newspapers with elephants walking down the street. And it appeared that a well-known member of the local pop was a former circus performer, who came to found the biggest church in Delavan. That all happened a long time ago, but it gave me lots to consider on my return trip and during the months that followed. Then one day young Alice disappeared in the early summer. There was hardly a mystery about where she would go, as a recent flyer had touted the revival in Cloverdale, just over the county line. Some of us offered to go get her. But her ma, a slight woman with a frail mind following the passing of Alice's pa, said, "She is of age," so the group stayed put. A month passed, and not a word came from young Alice, not even a postcard.

Well, me being me and still among the few undecided as to the kid's guilt and its true effect on the community, toward summer's end I decided to go to Preacher Main's show to see what I could see. I hitched to Cloverdale, and the driver offered to take me to the site, him having heard of the revival and being curious. We spotted the dust clouds before we arrived, the local drought making itself well known. He parked his car, and I got out, and stood in line, noticing the rules had changed. This time, all who entered dropped their coins in the basket first. It was called a donation and was necessary to enter the tent. Folding chairs now filled the area, and I parked myself in the fourth row, close enough to see the stage pretty well, but not close enough to call attention to myself. It wasn't long before the music began, and I could see Preacher Main had brought in a real piano player. He led the crowd - respectable in size as a first night crowd should be, but seeming smaller than before - in song. Then the kid appeared. He had come into his growth, and his shirt had grown with him, the flames still there, the collar now standing high around his neck, and his haircut fresh. He moved around quite a bit, swaying to the beat. From time to time, he would mouth the words, no sound emitted of course. I was not surprised to see young Alice, tambourine in hand. She never took her eyes off the kid.

I saw a movement behind the stage, and then Preacher Main jumped up during the final chords of "Be Still My Soul." It didn't take long for me to see something was not right. Young Alice for the first time moved her gaze from the kid to Preacher Main. Her lips drew a thin line across her face, pale and ringed by auburn frizz, and I had a sick stab in my gut. "I am so grateful," Preacher told the audience, "to have returned to your fair city," which no one found a strange reference to this ramshackle town. "I welcome you all again into our fold. And as you can see, all of you good folk, our fold has increased by one." As he pointed to young Alice, I would swear she shuddered. Then she looked at the kid who licked his lips. "This young woman and her bloom of Christian youth will surely bring the miracle for which we have long prayed." He slid more than walked across the stage and took Alice's hand. "Would you good folks like that? Would you like to see the Lord's will be done right here, this night, on this stage?" The crowd murmured their yes sirs. "And if the Lord found suitable to loose this young man's tongue, why could not that same tongue call for another miracle? Another miracle that be of rain?" This time the crowd responded more loudly, and I could see Preacher had their attention. They all hoped the kid would choose this place, their town, for his miracle and second to follow. One miracle could follow another, after all, as the Scriptures had shown time and again.

Then Preacher Main laid hands on both the kid, his eyes fixed on the back of the room, and on young Alice. Her eyes showed too much white, and the crowd clapped to the piano, slightly out of tune. I thought Preacher was moving fast, pressing for the climax when he had barely begun. We all waited and watched, but nothing happened. I felt the shift in feeling that crowds are known to make, and the promise of sweet seemed to have gone sour. Preacher could feel it too, and I could see that he decided time was nigh. He signaled the piano player and led the crowd in song, although he was met with little enthusiasm. But then, mid-verse of "Oh, How I Love Jesus," Preacher Main took Alice firmly by the hand and led her to the kid. The singing trailed away with the piano music, and a murmur rippled through the group. The Preacher raised both of Alice's hands and placed them on the kid's shoulders and in exhortation cried, "Repent, my son, repent! Beneath these innocent hands find the Lord's peace!" It was a beautiful moment, like the final brush stroke to a piece of art. They posed there, the three of them, a triangle of perfect balance, and the crowd waited.

My notepad account differs a bit from the widely-spread reports of what happened next. With Preacher's back to the crowd, the kid and young Alice were partially shielded from view, but some claimed the word "Repent!" came from the kid's lips. Others said it may have came from a too-anxious audience member, who jumped the gun out of enthusiasm. "It's the miracle!" someone else yelled, and everyone broke into a round of "Hallelujahs," at which point others way in the back of the tent yelled, "It's lightning – rain is coming!" But the light behind the stage was no lightning. Within a couple of minutes, we could see flames going up the back of the tent. People ran for the exit, but I held firm, dodging the chairs some pushed over as they made a path through the once-neat rows. The piano player fled the stage and ducked out under the side of the tent, but the three main players did not much move. Alice's hands had slipped from the kid's shoulders, and she grabbed his hand to pull him toward escape. The smoke was thickening, and I knew I had to go, but before I turned away, I saw the kid's lips move as he looked straight into Preacher Main's face. I heard – muffled over the noise of the fire and yelling, but distinct – the single word "Alice." When Alice pulled on his hand again, I heard, stronger this time, "Alice!"

The kid and young Alice leaped from the stage and followed the piano player, and Preacher was still standing there when I ran through the back opening along with some stragglers who had stayed to watch. It went up fast, but everyone got out, and then darned if rain didn't fall and help douse the flames. Word went out from a few who had been in the back of the tent that the kid had finally spoken. Some argument ensued over the word "Alice" when he should have said "Repent." But in the end, all agreed that a word was a word and "Alice" qualified as miracle one, which likely brought on miracle two in the form of rain. So everyone got their miracle – the thirsty county folks, Preacher Main, the kid, and young Alice. Accounts speculated on the source of the fire, but the locals agreed the kid had lit it for balance – meeting fire with fire for personal absolution. So we got our miracle, too, being this precisely: a once rumored source of sin purified by fire and washed clean by rain had lifted the heavy hand of that same sin from our community. The next day, more folks than could be counted were at the wall, freshening the paint and bringing new items in memoriam to leave behind. This time, it was for celebration instead of tragedy and making a proper shrine to normalcy. Although the kid and young Alice did not return, the harvest did.

That time has long passed, and we heard Preacher Main still winters in Florida, drawing big crowds from folks seeking post-holiday entertainment, he having been both recipient and provider of multiple miracles. The daffodils have come back, along with regular community meet-ups. As for me, I'm thinking of retiring as postmaster and community reporter. I've never made much money, but I own my good reputation and a tidy collection of postcards sent by the kid and young Alice now and again, and I might make a trip to Delavan, Wisconsin to see what I can see. Until then, I have my notepad to keep me company. I especially like reviewing details from Miracle Night at the Tent Revival, as the state paper had labeled it. I read my own account to remind myself of Preacher Main's actions before he jumped on the back of the stage, when I saw him drop a match into a bucket in the back of that tent. But I did not record his intentions in doing so, as those I cannot know. I remain an observer and a recorder of events, pure and simple.

Galop

Donald Ryan

-♦-

Beyond the cracked sidewalk, and the telephone pole with layers of flyers in a rainbow of colors, and the patch of dry brown grass there stood a ten -foot high concrete block wall, caked with dozens of coats of paint. There was a small shrine at the foot of it, with burnt out candles and dead flowers and a few soggy teddy bears. One word of graffiti filled the wall, red letters on a gold background: Rejoice!

This was what the kid knew, his basis for all knowledge within his few years of wisdom. There had always been cracks in sidewalks, rainbows on poles, walls revitalized and neglected then revitalized and neglected. There was always a shrine somewhere in view, flowers, candles, teddy bears. No matter where you looked in the city, there was always an artist with a message. The kid liked this message. It didn't boast, like most tags, but praised.

His Uncle Alfonzo didn't share this sentiment. His childhood was a different time, I tell you what. The city was a different place, a place to be, he said many times on the porch or in front of the game's half-static reception, the can in hand as consistent as the story. It was a great place, the place, a community where families wanted to raise their children knowing they'd be taken care of good. Yes, sir, I tell you what. This neighborhood, this block, was a family and we were taken care of good. But now look at it, all pissed on to hell and back. Ain't no respect in sight through all the shit. I'll tell you what, P, if they call it a turf then it ain't family. If you got to initiate then it ain't family. And that's what this place was, yes sir, a place with open arms, where you just stepped up and were accepted. That's what they're missing, what they need to make a vigil for, what this place used to be, I'll tell you what. But this wasn't Uncle Al's story, so the kid knew none of this. The kid only knew his world.

And a big part of his world was the local library. Where they kept it air conditioned in the summers and toasty in the winters, and once they started stocking up on comics, where he started liking some of the books. And there was Hannah. She was the one who snuck in the Sega and not so subtly yelled Booyah when she'd get her little blue hedgehog all the gold rings. She was the one who would bring in pop and chips, just don't get your greasy digits all over the pages. She was the one with the skin that glowed, with the braids just touched the top of the ass the kid was starting to pay more and more attention to, the one who could be anywhere in the world with that smile and that giggle, but worked behind the counter with the stuffy old women, the ones who hated comics, blue hedgehogs, and pop. She lived with some boyfriend named Derrick. And the kid didn't know why, but decided vehemently he didn't like the name Derrick. She didn't talk about him too too much, which was good because when she did the name was an intrusion to his ears, even if Hannah was the only one to make a name like that roll off a tongue. But thank God this wasn't a story about Derrick. It could have been about Hannah, however. The kid didn't understand this. It was new. And he wouldn't mind knowing. Wouldn't have minded Hannah being the world.

This story was more in tune with a cello as much as it was about Hannah. She let the kid do odd jobs from time to time around the library, talk them up like they were prizes, volunteering's its own reward, but work was work. But anything she'd ask him to do he already knew his fool ass would be doing because all she ever had to do was ask, always ever only once. One time was all some things ever took. Or as Uncle Al would say, a three pointer still ain't nothing but one shot. So when Hannah saw the kid breezing through that Batman comic with the demon bride, again, with what should be his homework notebooks sprawled out in front of him, not again, she asked for his help for one minute, just this once, one time, shifting a few boxes in the back storage. He was beginning to notice how her eyelashes fluttered over favors, sweeping him into volunteering because you know, it's good for the community, it's good for character. He was more interested in Batman. As a character. And it would have stayed that way if Hannah hadn't asked.

So that was how he came across the cello, or the why is this guitar on a stick so big? It's because it's not a guitar, Hannah said swatting the dust from her face looking over his shoulder into the case. It's a cello. Smaller than an upright bass, played like a violin. On your shoulder? Hannah cut her eye at him with her patented half-cocked smile. He was beginning to notice the little shadowed dimple in the glow of her cheek. He hoped the back room was dark enough to keep his face from visibly burning. Yes, prop that bad boy up there. He pulled the instrument from the case by the neck. It had weight but still lighter than he anticipated. Here it is, it's played with this. Hannah handed him a stick with frayed hair. It a wand? He took it like it might bite. Close, a bow. But music is magic, she said, still dimpled. He noticed how his heart began to race.

He plucked the thickest string. The vibration a wobble, thud clunking wire against wood, loose under his finger, slacked from time and neglect, something the kid didn't quite understand yet but one day would. What do you do with it? he asked. Play it, silly. I mean, why is it here? I didn't know it was here, she said, shifting a box across the floor, the cardboard scraping concrete more melodious than the next string he plucked. But you should learn to play it. I'll get right on that, he said.

Which, of course, he didn't. He helped Hannah with the boxes, caught himself sneaking glimpses down her shirt, knew she caught him but was cool enough not to say anything, and went back to Batman with a pop from the fridge, in clear violation of the no food or drink policy. Hannah gave it to him, anyway, which kept the old jokers off his back. It wasn't until a week later she pulled him aside, I got you something. The kid froze suspicious. He never got nothing for free, that's because there ain't nothing in this Godforsaken world for free, as Uncle Al would yell to the man by way of himself, Freddy M., or the television. Even he was accustomed to having to work for a bit of reward, and all he'd done worth a damn so far today was step into the library. It more volunteering? No, she said with that smile, but there's always a need for volunteering if you're interested. Tell me what you got first. He stepped up like a stray wary of a treat to where she was hunched at the counter. So, if anything, he at least got to sneak a peek down the V of her shirt. All rewards came with a risk.

Hannah held up a single finger and one moment later came back with a long rectangular box and a floppy ass book. What's this? he asked even though he could clearly see *Tipbook's Guide for Beginning Cellists* typed in a look at me font atop its green boarder, a little happy ass Asian kid, with his big ass instrument and oversized glasses, seemed way too excited to see him. It's not perfect, but it's a start, Hannah said sliding the book across the counter. Same goes with this. The kid undid the folded cardboard clasp and the stick with strands rattling inside slid into his hand. The thin hairs, where they hairs, they looked like hairs, so they had to be hairs, were no longer frayed as bad as his neighbor Mrs. Jackson's why should I give a damn do, but now straight and tight as Billie Dee Williams'. When you leave, take the cello with you, see what you can do with it. Polish it up. Tune it. And if I refuse? he said. You won't. That smile.

And he didn't, luging that dusty ass case down the five blocks and across the seven to Uncle Al's, who was sitting on the porch, talking mostly to his can and whoever else would listen. What you got there, Young P? he called out, breaking conversation with Freddy M., not to be confused with Freddy D., the gangbanger, who loved listening to Uncle Al when there was an extra can for himself involved. It look like his guitar swolled up. Freddy M. had that creaky too old for his age voice and followed it with that creaky too old for his age laugh. That's because it ain't a guitar. It's a cello, the kid said over the sound of the case dragging the pavement. And what you planning to do with that old swolled up guitar, Uncle Al jumping on the bandwagon. I guess I'm gonna learn to play it, the kid said, too winded and unsure to sound confident. And after dragging it this far, that's what he guessed he was setting out to do. He fumbled it the last few steps, both horizontal and vertical, past the old men and their devices, into the house. The case along the bulbous edge scratched up like a cat attack from the sidewalk. But inside the instrument looked all right—even if it wasn't, he wouldn't know the difference. He plucked one of the strings with his finger that clanked like throwing one of those scratchy cats down an elevator shaft. He figured he'd start with the book.

So you want to play the cello? Excellent! We're sure that's why you bought this book. Amongst these pages we will do our best to teach you all you need to know to master, in our humble but correct opinion, the finest of the stringed instruments. And how could it be considered anything but? The cello, like a fine underappreciated rosé, is able to maintain a full body like the deep red double bass AND be light and fresh as a chilled white violin. If you can find a better stringed instrument we highly recommend you learn that instead, but you won't, we promise, so we wrote this book. As you take on the wonderful world of the cello, we will do what we can to guide your journey, from fingering to vibrato (more on these later), but these pages lacking sound can only take you so far, but we promise to take you as far as we can if you promise to practice, practice, practice, because together we are harmony.

He closed the book. What the actual fuck? Uncle Al came into the living room. Freddy M. must have run out of beer since he never runs out of conversation. How's the rock n' rolling coming? The kid held out the book like proof of ignorance: About as good as Mrs. Jackson's haircut.

That good, huh, Uncle Al said. Then all we got to do is straighten that shit out. Uncle Al strutted off to his room, and the kid thought that was that. He flipped back to the book in defense of calling it quits, at least for today. The cello, of all instruments, shares closest in range to the human voice. With this book you can make your cello sing! he read. And yes, that was enough for now. He threw down the book in lieu of checking for any snack cakes left in the cabinet. They didn't always have snack cakes, Uncle Al prizing his feet over temptation, so when they did the kid cherished them like rations when lost at sea. But he didn't make it too far when Uncle Al stormed in with a purpose, that Uncle Al's got something on his mind so you best get comfy because you're about to be in for it determination, lugging a case, boxy unlike the kid's. If you starting a band then I got a treat for you. He plopped it down on the couch, unlatched it with a click click, and lifted the lid. I didn't know we had a record player, the kid said. We don't, I do. Uncle Al strained but managed to plug it in. Get comfy, cause we about to go for a ride. And he wasn't kidding the kid because a ride it was. The needle scratched onto the record to pick out a soft rattle like the tempo of tires, a horn scooting across like a siren, more horns clashing jammed like traffic, before smoothing out into a joy ride between stop lights, cool like the reflections of neon across the windows of a Caddy at night. And all this transported the kid in the first two minutes. What is this? he asked. This, young squire, is The Black Saint and the Sinner Lady. Uncle Al mellowed and swayed, eyes closed, to whoever they were. The kid leaned back, followed the lead, eyes closed, and went where the horn through the crackly speaker took him: through the city, into the country, potholes to a smooth ride. He couldn't yet drive, but dammit if he wasn't crusin'. Eyes tight, he looked over and saw Hannah smiling back, hand out the down window. His heart kept up with the beat, with the speed, they were coasting. Coasting on chaos. They were never going back, this world all melody. He made the mistake of opening his eyes but glad he couldn't close his ears. He never quite understood passion, but he was sure this could be it. Why you never play this before? Kid, you'll come to learn as the world turns there's so much more you ain't know. This is just the tip of the pen. So take it in. Cause you got to write your legacy.

I need a book on Charles Mingus, he said, first thing, like a mad dash as soon as he saw Hannah at the service desk. Well, hello to you too. Was she speaking slower on purpose? That would be a subtle aggravation she'd find funny. Hi, so are there any books on Charles Mingus? He spoke fast to make up the balance. That I don't know. I'd have to do some digging. In the meantime, I'm glad you're here. I got something for you. Came across them like fortune. He was immediately apprehensive— the last time she had something for him it involved dusty ass work in the dusty ass back and then lugging a dusty ass case all them blocks to the house. That wasn't light work either. Okay, he stalled out the word, his urgency dialed back to a two. Come to the back, she motioned a nod sideways. NOOOOOOOOOO. But of course he went. It was Hannah's request. She pulled out a boom box, much smaller than Radio Raheem's, and put it on their foldout lunch table. Here. She hands him two cassettes. One was green, had a cello on it, yellow font: *Tune Your Cello From A to C*. The other might have been the dumbest case he'd ever seen. There was what he assumed to be a cello, since that seemed to be the theme for the evening, and a piano, hella wonky in a wonky ass kitchen making a cake: well, the piano was mixing a batter which didn't make no damn sense since the cello was icing the already finished two tiered baked good. But what did he know about baking? Thank you? he said, holding the case like it might pop off in his hand. The one, she said, was the closest thing to a tuner I could get my hands on, so you'll just have to listen real close and match the sounds. But it should help you train your ear, or at least that's what the back of the case promises. He flipped over the green one, sure enough: Helps train your ear to the cello's four notes. The other one, she continued, is all cued up to track three. He flipped the other hand: 3: Galop. What's a Yo Yo Ma cello? That the kind I got? Close, so very close, Yo Yo Ma is a cellist. World renowned. Then why I ain't never heard of him? Oh, you're about to. She pressed play on the box:

If what Uncle Al played was a cool ride through the city, then what fired out of the speakers in the library was like having a rocket strapped to his ass and being blasted. Ok: so the kid, growing up in the city and all, when he looked up at the night sky he didn't get the luxury of stars, mainly associating that above with endless blacks and grays, so the little he did know about the whatever out there he learned from comic books. And right now, from the speakers, those vibrant colors on black backgrounds made the most sense. The twinkling piano was like the stars. Even when not seen, the night needed stars. But the whooshing, the reds and the oranges and the yellows, all that fire, all that propelled, that came from the other instrument. That a cello at work? he asked. That's a cello at its finest, she said and smiled and was beautiful. The kid didn't know what a muse was, but he had one. And she picked him up on some angel wings and off they went, into the mellows of nebulas before taking off again on a burst of energy, like that spark between two people when shit just clicks like a lighter. Yes, he was ignited. He didn't know the word passion, but he felt it. He would learn the cello, if for no other reason then to write her a song. If he had any reason, he would take her away from here.

A: The A string is the highest, therefore is the furthest away. It sounds plucky, like a giggle, the tenor to your quartet of strings, he read from his book, but that sure as hell didn't help him tune the damn thing. So he played the tape again and again, matching the rub of the bow to the underlying drone of the tape's consistent sigh, twisting the top knob (the peg on the scroll, according to the book's technicalities) when he had too, those suckers stiff, mainly messing with what the book called the fine tuners until the squeals of joy were the same. D and G: He carried on

56

with these middle bad boys, tightening the top knobs then twisting the bottom twisters, till they hummed like a conversation between the lower toned Uncle Al and the higher (wetter) Freddy M. C: And finally, what has it been, like an hour? He got to the C string, that rumbly like a king leader string. And he rewound the tape and rubbed the string and rewound the tape and rubbed the string, Uncle Al spending some extra time on the porch so he didn't lose his damn mind in the monotony. But finally the kid got it, he thought. He didn't have the knowledge to be sure. But it felt right. So it had to be.

He flipped further into his book, little shit doodles of how to hold the cello, how to sit up straight, how to arch the fingers. He peeked ahead to the little arms and hands grasping up and down a ladder, notes in a language he didn't yet know. A visual representation of sounds. Physically in place like the melodies through the city: the car horns, the train rolling through, the singsong excitement in Uncle Al's voice when a neighbor gets him on the right topic, the crescendo of joy when Mrs. Jackson called out to feed the strays (the occasional gunshot in the distance he hoped was only an echo, the tempo of police sirens more angry and shrill than the ambulance, the howl of praises from the man who found himself a bottle). Like a montage set to an infusion of classical and jazz, order and chaos, the melody of life whether you dig the groove or not: it played on and played it did.

And in that montage the kid got quite good. Not great or nothing. Not like that Yo Yo Ma guy on the tape with the dumb ass cover. But he knew how to finger a few chords and he got quite comfortable with the bow and his fingers began to stretch, the tips going from sore to calloused. Progress was progress. He even learned to appreciate some of those songs on the tape he wasn't feeling at first, those slower ones, preferring his music lively since he himself was young and alive. Though, he still didn't quite understand the emotion behind music. He was just glad to get Twinkle Twinkle Little Star down, but in his own way, with a bow to make it his own. That's what made sense to him—playing for himself, those seeds of emotion there sprouting little holy shit I'm doing it put into the strings. And this, too, took time to grow. Uncle Al helped water this whether he knew it or not. And not with his front porch philosophies, which he still spewed out to whoever would listen, neighbors and the television—so mostly the television—but with his records. He had so many records the kid never knew about, in their tangible existence and the music on them. They'd spend their nights, the game turned down in the background—Uncle Al wasn't about to miss a game—and go from Bitches Brew to cello sonata on a tape back to Blue Train and that one with the lame ass white dude on the cover looking the exact opposite of the sounds coming from the piano he played. Uncle Al occasionally detailed interjections on how any given player should be playing—the music and the game—forming in the kid a collection, a collage of the world, disjointed and sporadic and coming together, individual pieces into an individual when he didn't even know he was the mold. He'd listen real close, starting to hear emotions within himself, new music new to him.

What's a sonata? he asked, flipping over the tape case with another crusty portrait of a crusty white dude, and why he look so angry? He hadn't made it to the library as often as he used to. Hannah said that was okay, as long as he was learning the location was inconsequential (we don't force people to read all their books here), and as long as he didn't completely abandon them, which obviously he didn't if she was telling him all this—even though I've been hanging on to this tape for like a week and a half for you. A sonata is what I drive, she said. What? His response was as muted as the case. I'm joking, I mean I'm serious, but I'm joking. A sonata is basically a certain type of music that apparently Bach wrote and is performed on this tape, she said while flipping through a book about the size of a city block, which according to this dictionary is a piece composed for a soloist often accompanied by a piano. If it's with a piano that ain't a solo, is it? he asked. Someone cranked up the sass this afternoon, she said looking up from the tome. Just listen to it. You don't have to like it. But at least keep expanding so you can keep asking the tough questions.

As it turned out the tape, the sonata, had a piano. Uncle Al said he could appreciate all types of music but they should kick it up a notch. The kid was inclined to agree. But it was smooth, they said, both agreeing. Sometimes it was nice to swallow something easy. So the spectrum continued, the infusion of the classical and the jazz they took turns playing, his embarkation into the world around him, the layers of sights and sounds, the university in diversity of things noticed, things he felt, but things he couldn't put words to while knowing they were empirically there. Like when the news cut into the regularly scheduled programming, LIVE never leaving the screen, all the screens from all the channels from all the way across the country, where he tried understanding the why: some people who are supposed to be good people did some bad shit to one of our brothers and some more people who are supposed to be just didn't serve no justice, so I'd be mad as all hell too, I am mad as all hell too, as his Uncle Al explained. But he definitely understood the what: the protests in the square, peaceful in the daylight turning to confrontation in the night, a volley of words into a wall of officers' shields, turning physical with fists in the air, feet stomping cars, weapons blazed, if one man's not safe then ain't nothing safe, their anger palpable as the fires started. Uncle Al sent him to bed. He hadn't had a bed time since, well, he couldn't remember—that's how long. It ain't going nowhere, Uncle Al said. There's only so much a brain can process in a day.

And it didn't go nowhere. How could it when it was everywhere? For the next five days. Interviews. Analyses. From fires to looting, gunfights in the streets like the not ok corral. The kid began playing the records and the tapes simultaneously. As his ear was training, it was the only way he could make sense of what he saw. There was still melody. There was still noise. He would tune his cello then he would bang the strings. And once out of tune enough for his practicing ear to notice, he'd ever so softly bow Ode to Joy. Like sitting between the record player and the boom box, like disorienting the strings to retain the sweetest melody, he sat in the middle, finding the balance, of what on screen seemed so distant and how every person, from here to there, was in some way effected personally. He didn't understand this yet. But it was there on and in the air. It was on the strings. Fear.

I want to do something, he said to Hannah. The sweetness of your greetings is going to give me a cavity, she said—that smile. What? Nothing, what is it you want to do? She braces her elbows on the desk, that full attention stance, that one that compelled him to glance down her shirt and learn things at the library. I want to put on a concert. She stood (session over): I think that's a wonderful idea, showcase your skills, you must be getting good. No, not really—honest not modest—but with some other people, like one person can't make all the sounds, but with other people, I don't know, it could be something. She nodded to calibrate, like a metaphor for life? No, he said, like a concert in the streets. Do you have a song picked out? No, he said matter of fact, too young to understand the embarrassment of unprepared but wise enough at his age to have his mind set on an idea. Well then, she said, that's where we should start.

Every couple of poles or so the kid added to the collage of flyers of wants and engagements. They had decided on Canon in D. Like the old ass gun thing? he asked when Hannah mentioned it would be the perfect song to bridge the community. In a canon, everyone plays the same song over a melody, but they start at different times, so as they start and stop a chain is formed so people can join in whenever to create new versions of the same song. Order and chaos, the kid thought, seemed like jazz to him. So Hannah made up a set of flyers on neon colored papers, a piece of sheet music and a time and a place—three weeks, the Rejoice! wall—a spot of his choosing—and the kid went pole to pole with the industrial stapler Hannah "borrowed" from the library's toolbox (a drawer left with a screwdriver and a few bent nails). All welcome, it said. All instruments. Any portion of the song. Come play. Come listen. So along with the flyers and the stapler, he took Hannah's word for this. He'd yet to hear the song himself.

But when he did, like the idea, it all came together. In his mind, like the sound in his ears. Hannah could only find a record, in such short notice as she put it, but he said that worked for him. And work for him it did, from the inside out. He knew she made the right choice. I got you these too, she said, sliding a bullhorn and the sheet music she copied and he was still learning to read across the desk. What I need a bullhorn for? he said. It felt heavy, heavier than they looked on the TV. Crowd control, she said with that smile. Won't you be there? he asked. I wouldn't miss this for the world. Not even the riots could stop me. So back at Uncle Al's he picked up his cello (let's be honest, after he first played with the bullhorn, how the speaker made his voice scratchy and his laugh shrill) to teach himself the underlying melody. Someone had to control the crowd.

In what seemed like no time, like another montage, the day arrived. The kid knew what nervous was, but he didn't start feeling it until that morning, and it didn't start taking over until he headed for the wall: cello, Uncle Al, Freddy M. and even cranky ass never leaves her house Mrs. Jackson in tow. And when their little promenade hit that block there was the same wall covered in the same paint with the same candles and the same soggy teddy bears, the same rejoice smiling down its mostly ignored encouragement—the same he only ever knew. Except now there was a crowd on that same old patch of brown grass. Not a large crowd, maybe twenty people or so, about half of them holding instruments, a trumpet, an electric guitar, harnessed drums used for marching. But the kid noticed this secondary—not in the crowd was Hannah. Now's your moment, son, Uncle Al said, I'm proud of you. He'd never said anything like this before, and while the kid didn't pay too much heed to his opinions on most things, this one made his back straighten a little tighter. He didn't know to call it pride. And he didn't know how to balance it with the annoyance of Hannah's unfound promise and his conscious attempts to stall. But don't keep these folks waiting no more, Uncle Al continued. Now's not the time to keep people in heat riled up. But he too was getting riled up, unable to quite rationalize being upset, so he went with mad as hell. He gave one last stall to search the crowd for Hannah before his Uncle Al said get on up there now, because like previously mentioned, this story's in tune with Hannah as much as the cello.

The kid got onto a milk crate and raised his hand. A murmur went through the crowd and then it fell silent, except for a few people shouting words of encouragement at him. The kid acknowledged them with a nod and a shy smile. In the full light of day, he looked less angry and more beautiful. He waited until people stopped shouting. A siren could be heard, maybe five or ten blocks away. The kid raised the bullhorn, pressed the button, and began to speak.

Uh, thank you for coming. He scanned the small crowd. Still didn't see her. His anger, his nerves, his annoyance, he wasn't sure what he was doing, not yet knowing no one has any idea what they're doing, but smiled composure because what other choice was there when oration wasn't your thing? Freddy M. kept shouting what? encouragements? It was after noon but still too early for him to be tilting back into this much excitement. Uh, community is a place, no, uh, a people. Community is people that, you know, come together. There are tragedies in communities, sure, you know—the bullhorn took on weight, his grip slickening—we've seen it here—he meant the candles and teddies but didn't know if he pointed enough with the horn to clarify—and we've seen it on TV, but, uh, we're here, I'll start, join in, and we'll, uh, you know, add melody to the chaos—Freddy M. encouraged again and the small crowd clapped. The kid sat on the crate, propped his cello between his knees, and began the single progression he practiced and practiced and practiced for this moment, a repetition that would take them, where? He didn't know.

But sure enough, they started going. A clarinet and a woman with her hands knotted at her stomach joined in with low hums and ahhs. A trombone joined in like the bass line. A keytar, the size of a child's toy, joined the trombone player, sprinkling a note one key at a time. The trumpet and harmonica rode in along the small amplifier of the electric guitar. And the whole thing, full circle, rounded out with the drums rattling steady, bleating sticks. Every man and woman, young and old, in the orchestra came in as natural as breathing, knowing their fit in the scaled creation of something so random and beautiful. The sirens in the background drew closer against the melody. Classical and jazz. Harmony and chaos. It was the song of relative strangers. Their parts, their songs, their city. Rejoicing.

The patrol cars pulled up, dousing the revelers with their blues and reds, as the song was spinning into its third rotation. The kid continued the melody. The orchestra continued their progressions. Without direction, emotions rose hot in the air. The sonification of joy. Strangers working together to create a whole, to create a smile, like those the kid saw when he looked out at the audience who gathered or passed. The only faces not smiling—or in Freddy M.'s case, hollering—were the officers. No amount of music could level their anxieties from their high rise. They saw a crowd. They saw a riot. No matter what they heard. The leader, the largest in his blues, his bald head shining in tune with the makeshifters called out for who was in charge and for an explanation of what was going on here. Which was fine: it didn't stop the melody, it couldn't, fueling the emotions of the instrumentations wider. Uncle Al stepped in. The kid had no idea what they were saying—how could he?— until he heard Uncle Al all amped up, open palm towards the crowd, when did anyone ever need a permit to come together for something beautiful? The large officer stood tall. Uncle Al wasn't short but sure as hell seemed it. He pushed a riled Freddy M. back like an apology. The officer pointed. Freddy M. kept at his escalating notations. Uncle Al tried keeping the harmony. There was no use. Please disperse, the car amplified louder than their ode to joy. The canon fired back by continuing. Please disperse or actions will be taken, arrests will be made. But the kid played on, so the orchestra followed. They needed to see their measure out to completion. This is your final warning. C'mon, P, Uncle Al leaned to his ear. You did good. You did damn good. But what'll happen next ain't worth it. The kid lifted his bow from the sting.

The music stopped in a wave extinguishing a fire with a hiss. Please disperse was louder now. The kid leaned his cello towards Uncle Al who took it out of reflex, leaving no time to react to the kid standing on his milk crate. The bullhorn was to his lips. P, don't be stupid, Uncle Al said. Thank you for coming, said the kid. That was better than I could have imagined. Better than I did. And for those not here, he dug, missed a moment. Because what else could he have said when it, like all moments at a given time, was over. This wasn't a moral stand, a social issue, justice, whatever things the kid didn't understand embedded in the officers' fear. This was something good and beautiful, and like all things good and beautiful was misunderstood so was destroyed. Disperse now, crackled with exclamation, this is your final warning. The kid didn't understand the role of the martyr. All he knew was what had happened and what was directly before him. Bigger still seemed out of reach, even when he was touching it. Thank you, he said and dropped the horn to his side. He got off the crate, the crowd clapped, unprovoked to walk away without a bass line to follow. Let's go home, Uncle Al said. So that's where they went.

And that's where he stayed the next day, waking up early still pumped on the excitement of accomplishment but staying in bed from the heartache he didn't know wasn't a tummy ache. Nerves, he said. And like most kids, he was in a way right. He figured, too, if he told himself his tummy hurt then he wouldn't need any other justification for not going to the library. He wouldn't have to practice his cello, could feign disinterest. He'd find a new hobby. A new interest. A new instrument. And, with a tummy ache came the perk of daytime television. Always a treat like ice cream. He was trying to get into some talk show hosted by some old white dude named Murry (if that was even what they kept saying?) talking to another old white couple, the dude looking way too goofy and the woman looking way more goofy. No one under God's sun needed that much makeup on. And those that did probably didn't need to be on television. But the host was hosting (he kept talking about bakers?) and the couple was talking or bickering or whatever: he couldn't get into it. Even ice cream melts before the last spoonful. But, lucky him, the phone rang on commercial break. Alfonzo Alvarez residence, he answered like he should, not having to put on an act with school out and all (otherwise, he would have coughed a little bit into the greeting, made his voice a little creaky, you know, cause we've all done it). Hi, this is Dolores Fry from the Bull Street Public Library, and it was, too, he recognized the sounds of the shusher having heard it plenty of times before, may I speak with a Mr. Paco Black? His tummy dropped even further into the ache of what the fuck. Okay, fine, he wasn't always consistent with bringing shit back on time, but they had never called his house. Maybe she was cranky about the cello, but it was Hannah that gave it to him, he ain't ask for it. For better or far worse, he was just glad he'd answered the phone. This is he, I'm P. Can you come down to the library, said ol' cranky, but the voice sounded distant, and from the distance seemed sad, at your own convenience. There's no hurry, but I feel the sooner the better. Uncle Al would kick his ass if he had an overdue book. Did he lose a book? No, there was no way. Money wasn't something to fuck around with. Even ten cents. And even when he did fuck around, Hannah usually slid those dimes under the rug. I don't feel well, he said keeping that up. No, this wasn't about no book. This was about his broken heart and not keeping a promise. This was about Hannah not having the gall to call him herself but wanting to face him about not showing up. Well, when you feel better, please come, the voice said, but like I said, sooner would be better if possible. Maybe she wanted to say sorry, say it while it still mattered, which she should. She should be forced to defend her lack of action in person. Yes, ma'am, he said.

Why did the air hang heavy? Not crushing, but enough difference to register a change, like the difference between ninety-nine cents and a dollar. He didn't see Hannah at the desk, which was fine, he wasn't sure if he was even ready for that. He brought his books and the bullhorn just in case, even if the card stamps said they weren't overdue. Mrs. Dolores had the only private desk out in the open by the only window near the big checkout desk. She was at it behind piles of—what else but—books. She made eye contact in his direction, put her pen down, visibly sighed. She waved him over. Now: conversations with Mrs. Dolores Shusher generally didn't go well, either being about something he need not be doing, there is no food or drinks allowed in the library, or something he ought to be doing, if you must cackle please go to the park where the wind can carry it away. My books aren't overdue, he said unable to conceal the apprehensiveness in his voice. Please, Mr. Black, take a seat, your books are fine. He pulled out the chair, the legs scraping the tiled floor, and he braced for scorn but she didn't shoot the look. Still, he remained braced for the he had no idea what was going on that was coming. Well, Mr. Black, it appears it has fallen to me to inform you of a situation that isn't easy to, she paused, forever the librarian looking for the right word, convey, one that's as difficult to comprehend as it is to speak as this new reality, but yesterday morning, a deep breath towards the desk, which she focused on even though he stared at her intently, their general roles of eye contact in the reverse, and we don't know all the details, but yesterday morning, Hannah had an accident. Well, that's a half -truth. Hannah was murdered—oh, but that came out too harsh, her voice quivered with the shock and sadness of her words—Hannah is no longer with us, even if that's too faux pas. The kid sat silently, watching the woman so stoic—what he'd call mean—fumble through emotions. But her boyfriend, there was some sort of altercation, which was him, him and his temper, she didn't know what to describe, didn't know how, doesn't matter, what matters cannot be reversed, but he is in custody. Are you okay? He heard the question but didn't hear the question. But he nodded he was, slowly, in that slack jawed way that said he wasn't. I'm sorry, she said. His nod continued. The funeral will be in a few days, here, she held up a slip of ripped paper, the arrangements have been made. I'll place it in this book, she had it for you, though it isn't a library book, so I don't know where she got it, so there must be some importance there. She marked a random page with the time and address and added the book to his pile.

He doesn't remember how his feet carried him out of the library, or how they traversed the blocks back to his Uncle's, if he subconsciously avoided the Rejoice wall or if life just didn't take him that way, going forward how it wants to, not really giving a damn about how its directions can change the course. He didn't notice the weather, sunny and warm, with the type of breeze that would be described in some other story as to set and perfect that feel good mood. It, the world, the whole wide world was a blur of sunshine and blue skies and people, so many people it seemed, experiencing the same day in the way life chose this day to be. All the people sans one. So for him it was he and the hollow. And if he opened his mouth he was afraid of the sounds that would strike a chord. There was no jazz, no sir, not this trip. Nor classical to carry on. There was only loud silence. Life equaled loud silence.

What he did feel was numb. Anger. And hate. Madness. Sadness. And love. He wouldn't have been able to tell you this. Especially when he couldn't even process that which was in front of him. These feelings boiling in him volatile. He'd sit on the edge of his bed. He'd lay down, fetal. He'd sit back up. In unspoken terms, he understood how all those people on the television felt. Empathy wouldn't come to mind, per say. No. Only Hannah would occupy that space. And the empty desk. And her fucking asshole boyfriend. And that smile. That smile fading. Not frowning. F A D I . . . But he was feeling how things festered in the heat of rage. He wanted to destroy. No. Enough had already been destroyed. No. Even that didn't stop him from wanting to tear and burn. He was in a phase of sitting on the edge. When he lifts his head from his hands, he'll see the cello case, a casket full of so many songs left to play sitting silent against his dresser. He'll let a tear fall. Then he'll stop himself from crying.

So this story is as much about the cello as it is Hannah and the kid. What it's not is some lean on me shit, where everyone comes together at the end, the music swells, emotions surge, difficulties in life embody the warm fuzzies. This story is just as much about after. Because things resort into a sort of normalcy. Never the same. But a new normal for the day to day. Stories are like the memories you didn't know you were making. Where sometimes, even when things aren't profound, the way things were at a given point are called back in a disorganized mesh of who said what and what happened was. Memories are chaos ordered as they come.

Good. Now you know a bit about the parts of a cello, the strings and the bow, it's time to make the magic of music. But like any good magic trick, we need to learn to be slight with our hands. Hold the cello between your thighs, bracing the cello in the needle. Good. Feels strange? If it doesn't you're already ahead and if it does you'll get used to it (and even welcome it once you start hearing the beauty coming from you). Hold the bow in your right hand. Excellent. And with your free hand turn the page—> Did you feel that motion? That dynamic range of the fingers? That's because this is your fingering hand. Fingering is how we press the strings with, what else, but our fingers, and each place you hold a string down corresponds with a note. The cello has at least 32 positions, depending on where you place your left hand. We know what you're thinking. That's a lot of positions. Where do I start? Well, we're going to start with number 1. Hold your left hand out like you're holding a beverage, a cup or a can, nothing bigger than a mug. Now place the fingerboard where the beverage should be, your thumb roughly in the middle of the neck's backside, not too high because too close to the scroll would be half position, nor too low which would be second, but that sweet spot in between. Go ahead, give it a try (we'll wait). Great! As you hold down the string, just enough to touch the string to the board, each note held by each finger corresponds with a note on the sheet music…

He'll go to the funeral. Sit in the back. Won't know nobody else there. Not really, at least. He'll recognize a few folks from the library, like Mrs. Fry, but he'll do just fine avoiding most folk on a day like today. As long as he's there. It'll be best he's there. Showing his love for Hannah like he always did, silently looking on from a distance. He'll choose the spot he wants to sit—like stated, this isn't lean on me shit with an emotional swell of cello playing, this is a time for him to try and understand this why is he so sad inside, this grieving he doesn't know to call as such—and Uncle Al will sit next to him in his best suit. He'd never seen Uncle Al so stoic. He'll respect Uncle Al's respect. And he'll only cry a tear or two when he thinks no one is looking.

Eventually, he'll learn Derrick, the boyfriend, is in prison, where he'll be and should be, as Freddy M. will say on Uncle Al's porch. They won't talk about what happened, only the details, how he got 15 years for manslaughter, possibility of parole in 10. That boy has a depraved heart, Freddy M. will say and take a sip from a can Uncle Al gave him, like nothing under the sun ever changes. The kid will find out, mostly through city news, official rumors, the Derrick had an anger problem, one of those opposites attract sort of bullshit with Hannah the angel to the devil, the pair on and off since high school, they thinking it was the only way it should be, so every time Derrick would go fucking up, like that time he fucked Kym Hansen in the bushes against Reggie Rodrick's momma's house, the sweet angel could only punish him with the cold shoulder for so long. For what? Now her shoulder knows nothing but the cold. He'll learn from someone who heard it from one of the neighbor's God's honest truths that Derrick was in one of his moods, how this neighbor heard that boy firing off at the lip again, ain't nothing new, but did think it was strange when she heard the crash and didn't hear either the door slamming or the making up as she normally did, not putting the 2 with the 2 together until the ambulance came for her—another neighbor apparently sick and tired or suspicious—and came out with a bag on the stretcher. Her neck broke when she fell to the backhand, her body spinning just right for her head to crack against the counter. Or something. The person he'll hear this from will drone on into details. The devil's always in the details. But the kid won't want to hear no more about it, blocking out enough while thinking back on the casket, how soft her neck looked in her sleep, how smooth her cheek had been, how at peace her lips. They caught Derrick, this being where he'll tune back in, down at Reggie's, banging on the door like a bitch, Reggie not letting him in, apparently sick of his shit and still not quite over him disrespecting his momma's bushes.

And he'll stick with the cello for a while longer. Uncle Al will pitch in to get him some lessons. And he'll get halfway decent, too. Never as quick as that tape Hannah played for him, but enough to hold his own with Beethoven and Chopin. Create his own rhythms and stops like Mingus. Although, his favorite piece will always be the melody of Canon in D. The one he won't play.

That said, he'll never return the cello, one of those they never asked for it back so they must not have missed it. And even when he grows out of playing it, which in time will happen, as do most things during the experiment of childhood, he will still care for the cello, take it out from time to time, caress it with a soft rag, tighten the bow, tune the strings, then return it before his fingers quiver a melody as if it's a secret that never was. He'll also hang onto the book Dolores Fry had given him that day. Again, they never asked, even long after he returned the beginner's guide for the last time. Turns out, it's a book about Charles Mingus. An autobiography. *Beneath the Underdog.* And he hasn't read it yet, this prized possession. But he will. And he'll swallow every vulgar word pounded out like jazz. And he'll love it and hate it so much he'll read it again. Even a third time. Not for Mingus, who he'll remain a fan of, or why he even asked for it in the first place, but for the bookmark, a ripped slip of lined paper with a date, a time, and an address. He'll hate this fucking bookmark he cherishes. Keeping it safe where it only feels right, beneath the pages of this underdog.

Now: this isn't to say he'll quit going to the library. He will for a time, and who can blame him. The presence of the desk and the ghost of a smile. So he'll return his books, sometimes early in fact, but will forgo going back in until the wound can handle the revenant. Which will come. It will. In time. Like time: repeating but never as it used to be. They will hire someone new. Some white boy with a sense of humor who the kid will get to know at a distance, despite the nametag, not even in name only. A friendship in stamps of strict transactions. And Mrs. Fry will not shush him. Not because some connection they feel they share. Because they won't. Their distance will remain the same: as far from her desk as he can stay. She'll not shush him because she'll have no reason. The library for him will become a place of reverence. A sacred holder of memories. Ones he'll branch into. Ellison, Wright, Faulkner, O'Connor. But best believe he'll still read comic books—here he will assume a connection, old Dolores seeming to stay current in the collection of the most recent issues. He'll respect this and hide the drinks he'll sneak in from her view (after learning to open the initial hiss outside or in the restroom). He will never again be asked to volunteer on a whim. Nor will he ask to.

So this—all this—this is what the kid knew, the kid knows, and the kid will come to know. At least for a measure of time: some things remembered, some forgotten, all a beat in between. He'll eventually meet Janice, then Monica, then Destiny, then Chenylle, but Destiny will stick around. And one day, long after he gives up on the cello but while he's still good with his hands, he'll get a job at Mr. Pelicano's Resterante Italiano run by a Mr. Dupox. They'll teach him to toss dough and gawk at the fact this high school kid ain't rippin' the shit. You see that shit, fuckin' natural. Gots marinara in his blood. Ignorant shit like that, but he'll laugh and hate the hours but love the work and learn to fire back with ignorant shit of his own. And he'll earn a paycheck, and with that paycheck he'll ask Destiny on a date, just the two of them as opposed to a pairing in a social gathering, an actual I'll call on you at eight date. She'll giggle, say yes, then giggle. This will be his first. So they'll go to dinner because he'll figure that's just how it's done. And he'll be smart enough not to take her to Pelicano's because those guys aren't the kind of impression she needs at first. He'll want this to go well—no, perfect. And it will. It will be awkward, but they'll have fun, their company kept well received. So they'll walk a little slower after dinner—what's the rush— well, besides his nerves (having had to force down bites of food, his empty stomach too full)—as they wander the long way to Destiny's house. And they'll walk past the wall, no more candles, no more bears, no more Rejoice!, the word painted with smooth gray to match the buildings on either side. He'll pause for a moment: he can still see the word. He'll listen to cars not far off and hear the rumble of a canon. She'll ask, you ok? Couldn't be more perfect, he'll attempt to say boldly into her eyes, but look down from the weight of his smile, and he'll tell her a story about the time he organized a concert, for shits and giggles, and how people actually showed and somehow played the same song as if it was all meant to be, and how the cops came and broke them up, and how he never saw those people again, wouldn't even notice them if they walked past right now, but how he'll never forget them. That'll be the truth. He won't mention Hannah. She'll come to mind but she won't be a part of this version of the story. That'll also be the truth. You played the cello? Destiny'll laugh. They'll hold hands the rest of the walk home.

And Uncle Al will still be Uncle Al, still spending his evenings on the front porch with Freddy M. or in front of his static sprinkled TV, giving his commentaries on how his teams ain't been shit since so-and-so played such-and-such, and how the city been going to shit, I'll tell you what, this city used to bring people together, now everyone locks themselves behind their doors. Not Alfonzo Alvarez, no sir, I'll sit my happy ass right here on this porch because I knew what it used to be, and if it was once it will be again. That's in the Bible. And so is the wisdom of these gray hairs. So in order to see what it was someone's got to find it, and that someone might as well be someone who's got some common sense about a thing or two. So that's exactly what he'll do, because if he wasn't true to what came out of his mouth then he wasn't Uncle Al. Long after Mrs. Jackson. Long after Freddy M. He'll keep his eye on the city, the keeper of its history. And the kid won't be there as much—he'll grow as kids tend to do—but he'll be there on the holidays and the weekends he can be and he'll bring his family, his wife Laila, his sons Charles and "Duke." Uncle Al will tell them his stories, usually the same ones, and the kid will pretend he never head them when they're actually a part of him. Uncle Al will keep teaching the new generation about how it was the way it ought to be and if that ref opened his eyes maybe he'd stop making bullshit calls—don't repeat that to your father.

They'll live close to Uncle Al's but not close enough where they won't need to drive. Their car will be filled with the appreciation of music, pop and R&B—middle ground for the family. The speakers will tell them the call and response of how hot it is in here and what they should do with all their clothes. His family will enjoy the beat, Laila bobbing in the passenger seat will giggle and turn it up, this takes me back to the day. The boys dance to imitate their mother. He'll smile at her, smile at them in the mirror. Okay, so maybe the message won't be the best for the children, the implications not fully realized but oft repeated, but he won't lie: the song had always been catchy. Hell, the song's basically a classic. He won't bob but the beat gets him. And how could he not love the voices he loves chiming in to the ceiling about the girl who thinks her butt's getting big. This will make them laugh. This will warm him.

And one day he'll come upon an image he hadn't seen since he was a little older than his eldest. It'll be a square version fitted for a jewel case: that awkward looking piano awkwardly cooking a cake with an awkward looking cello. So, of course, he'll justify the memory and buy it. And on an evening driving home from Uncle Al's he'll spring it on the unsuspecting family, slide the disc into the mechanical whirl, and skip ahead straight to track number 3. The sounds he once knew so well, a sound that was once a part of him, his melody, his fingers, his bow, his heart, will rush into the car. He'll enjoy songs on the radio, sure—and more importantly he'll enjoy his family's enjoyment of those songs, how music never loses its God given ability to simultaneously be personal and collective—an instrument and an orchestra, a solo and a melody, live and recorded—but those songs on the radio will be out there on the air waves, external. Like the wind, he'll feel them outside himself, not deep within like a breath. But as the cello calls its response to the piano's first note, this music will transport him: his family sedan the Caddie he imagined as a kid, and he'll lean back into the seat as the sky above him spins like a fisheyed lens from day to night to sunrise to stars to clouds to clarity, and all lights will turn green and buildings will smile down upon them and the city'll be slick without a drop of rain, so they'll have the windows down to hear the music play on the streets, the makeshift orchestra lining the sidewalks the once was version of what it will become. At the corner, he'll wave two fingers up off the wheel at the beautiful librarian conducting the memory. And she'll smile that smile he'd at times wish to forget. This memory carrying him forward for at least a city block, not even enough time for the drummer to chime in, when his son will bring him back from the ineffable asking why are there no words?

They'll make it home, watch some TV, get ready for bed: normal family shit. He won't give the kids a bed time if they'll follow the rule: once the TV's off they can stay up as late as they want as long as they're reading. This rule will apply to the whole family (with the exception of the mother more often than naught, who on Thursday nights goes back to back with them Shonda Rhimes shows which he's just fine doing without—but moms get to break rules like that). He'll learn to wear out his library card like frequent flyer miles, see the changes in the world: stacks, the collection, the staff—Mrs. Dolores retiring (?) sometime between when he wasn't going and started going again—the technology. He'll make sure his family has the ability to go anywhere often. Learn anything. Do anything. Tonight, he will not read in bed. He'll kiss Laila goodnight then stay on the couch, read his book about the airborne toxic event but have trouble concentrating, the words staying on the page like the white noise of the title. He'll have an idea. No. It'll actually be a plan that strikes a chord with reverberation that'll echo till carried out. The house will be quiet, so it may be asleep. He won't check, not to disturb, just in case. He'll use the arm of the couch as a bookmark and head to the 24-hour mart a city over so he can buy paint where no one knows his name.

So now you've learned the basics of the most wonderful of the stringed instruments, if not all the instruments. Therefore, this book has taken you as far as we can because we are merely a book with words on a page that guides where it can whereas the cello is life set to music. So don't give up!

You didn't give up on your first steps and now you can run. Or if you can ride a bike, we're willing to bet you've had a few spills. Ever baked cookies? Well, sometimes even they burn. So yes, even for us, once upon a time even the cello was awkward. But like us, you will get there! We want to say we promise, we do. But that's on you. With these basic fundamentals provided in these pages and practice, practice, practice (are you tired of us saying that? Because that just means practice some more!) you'll be able to master any song. And who know? Maybe one day in the future edition, your songs will be what inspires those future cellist who haven't a clue when they pick up the instrument to start their own adventure into the brave new world. Yours truly, the authors of this book, Meghan Jorndson and Charles Glenlock.

The city will go through periods of prosperity and periods of neglect. Like any other place, like any other life. Freddy D. will lose control of his bangers by losing his mind from years in a closed circuit of hate and fear and drugs and paranoia. He'll mistrust all in his path, those closest to him the most, so much so he'll be taken out in mutiny by two of his crew. They'll literally stab him in the back. In a room full of motherfuckers he'll die alone. Or, at least that'll be how the legend goes. It won't be talked about much. Not since the election of Mayor Manning with her community projects like public art and parks, her clean up the street initiatives (the city is our home and it's time to clean house—used for both crime and litter), her revitalization of run down spots, shiny and new for the next generation of pockets. She'll basically get to do whatever she wants, despite what Uncle Al will have to say about it all—we used to be able to go out on a Friday night with ten dollars in our pocket and not return home till Sunday morning and now, hell, I can't even afford to think about eating in any of them snazzy ass joints, but I'll tell you what, a steak is a steak no matter how you cut it, and I'll get mine just fine from the market—will be valued by most, seeing how they'll keep her around till she chooses not to run. Yes, say what you will about either Freddy D. or the mayor, but they breathed business. Money the music to their ears. So, like any politician, there will be good (taking out Freddy D.'s fractions) and bad (don't get Uncle Al started again), but at least somewhere in the middle Mayor Manning will be a supporter of the library, and sometimes something that small makes the biggest deal.

So in this new city, this same city he's always known, there will be a cracked sidewalk lined with newly refurbished metallic telephone poles, black and sleek, modern with the comfort of classic. And just beyond the small community garden of wildflowers will stand a ten-foot high concrete black wall kept up with coats of gray paint to match the exteriors on either side. The streets on the side of town will have been cleaned up. But a lone figure, under the light of the streetlamps, will move his fingers with diligent accuracy along the wall with bottles of spray paint, one red, one gold.

And in the morning he'll wake everyone up an hour earlier so they can take the long way to church. The sun will have risen by the time they reach the other side of town, with only the faintest hints of it Rayleigh scattering in the distance. He'll pull the car over, and point to a single word: Rejoice! And he'll tell his kids about when he was a little bit older than them that word was on that wall, not exactly like that but close enough to what they see now. And he'll tell them about how he used to play the cello—to which they'll ask what's a cello?—and how he made an impromptu concert—what's impromptu?—that was broken up by the police, but not before people, strangers really, came together to play a single song a single time. And for a moment nothing in the world mattered and everything in the world mattered. And how he learned that during this concert, while this most amazing thing was transpiring—what's transpiring?—the worst thing at the time happened when a friend of his, a very important person, was taken away from him—where did they go? Laila, who'd never heard this story, will rub his arm propped on the center consol. She won't interrupt him even when she doesn't understand. Which is kind of ironic, he'll say—what's ironic?—since there used to be a bunch of drive-bys in this spot. There were candles and teddy bears, little monuments. But this is where we picked to create, a place where so much was taken away. I don't know why this spot. I think it was the word. It's been away so long, but there it is. Sprawled out like a memory for the world to see. And, the way things go, it'll get painted over like it did once before, so it'll happen again, and under that new layer of paint will be the vestige of what's also there—what's vestige? See, hang on to that boys, hang on to all you can, cause even when it ain't on the surface your memories are who you are. And his boys, without disdain but with love, will look at him like he's gone crazy. I don't know, I guess I'm just trying to say don't ever forget those things, those people that are important to you. As you grow, as layers and layers are added, they'll always be underneath there somewhere because they'll always be a part of who you are. And he'll be thankful their blank expressions are still filled with love. And he'll reciprocate this with words before they wonder where they are: I love you. We love you, too, Daddy, they'll say, a sincere imitation of his melody. Rejoice! And if (when) Laila sees the paint stains on his fingers, she won't say a word. Nor will this stop her from squeezing the hand of the man she loves do dearly, the father of her two beautiful boys. The same two beautiful boys who will excitedly tell Uncle Al about how there was an impromptu painting on a wall that Daddy showed them and how it's transpiring towards ironic to become a vestige, and Uncle Al won't know what the hell they're talking about but will tell them if they don't hush up while the game's on they won't be able to impromptu transpire ironic whatever, that so-and-so was on the court and he was the best player since such-and-such. And they'll sit around the TV drinking (soda) from their cans (games with Uncle Al a once week special treat). But at some point the kid will sneak off to search for exactly what he knows will be exactly where to find it: the old record player that hadn't moved in years. He'll blow off the dust and set it up for after the game. Something new for his kids, the way it used to be.

But no. Right now the kid knew none of this. All he knew was the pain in his heart. In his being. In his core. This story not yet about the wall as it is the cello and himself. And Hannah. A present that shouldn't already be a memory. A place he was stuck in when Uncle Al called him to dinner—even if you ain't hungry you got to eat something, you ain't got to taste it, just swallow it. So he sat on the couch, plate in his lap, occasionally putting small forkfuls to his mouth. What will happen to that city? he asked during a commercial. What city? The one out there with the riots. Uncle Al chewed, mouth closed, swallowed. They'll rebuild, I guess. Cause hell, there ain't much else they can do.

All Things Hang on Our Possessing

ANDREA AVERY

⋅❧⋅

Beyond the cracked sidewalk, and the telephone pole with layers of flyers in a rainbow of colors, and the patch of dry brown grass there stood a ten-foot high concrete block wall, caked with dozens of coats of paint. There was a small shrine at the foot of it, with burnt out candles and dead flowers and a few soggy teddy bears. One word of graffiti filled the wall, red letters on a gold background: Rejoice!

On the way from her car to the rear of the building and the wall where she now stood, Michelle noticed that someone had left a computer on in the tire shop, a turquoise screen saver rippling like a fish tank. Even from behind the tire shop, Michelle could see the street-lights on Pico Boulevard unfurling banners of light into the sky, which glowed quiet and pale silver, like a snowy night might some-where else—even though this was Los Angeles, the first Saturday in May.

As she stood at the wall, Michelle didn't feel like rejoicing. No, the command felt like a dentist's instructions to open wide, a thing she did only because she'd been commanded to do it by a strip of eyes between a cap and a mask, a bandit with glinting instruments. Her jaw knew what to do at the command, thanks to a lifetime of unhinging itself to breathe and scream and sing and pray, and so when the order came, muffled from behind a rampart of pleated blue paper—open, it said—Michelle's body could do it. If she could do it twice a year in that slick, putty-colored recliner, she could do it here, now, before this wall. She unhinged her heart then, mechanically, before that wall, and she waited to feel something. It had only been six hours since David had dropped her off at her apartment right after dinner and told her they were done. Maybe, she thought as she stared at the freshly painted wall, the paint wasn't dry on their breakup. If she could feel what he'd always wanted her to, see what he was able to see, maybe she could still get him back.

She hadn't been back to this wall since she and David painted it together a year earlier. It was David's idea. It was their first date after meeting in an acting class in Studio City; they'd been at dinner at some twinkle-light café in West Hollywood. David was halfway through a bottle of wine even before he'd finished his fennel ravioli, and the flush from his cheeks extended down his neck under a silver chain that hung inside the collar of his white shirt. Michelle was thinking more about how he probably smelled just there, where the ruddy hollow of his throat met the soap-white pique of his shirt, than about what he was saying, which didn't ultimately matter because as it turned out he was saying something he'd repeat over and over for almost exactly a year. He was talking about what he believed.

At the end of dinner, after an inscrutable dessert featuring anise seed and rosewater, David grabbed Michelle's waist in the parking lot and pulled her to him. "I have an idea," he said, his breath a hot, welcome towel on her neck. He tossed Michelle the keys to his BMW since she'd barely finished a glass of wine before he finished off the rest of the bottle, and as she drove slowly through the wide streets of Los Angeles, he held one wide palm on her right thigh and gave her directions—not to his place, as she expected, but to Ace Hardware. The paint aisle. He picked the colors.

And then he directed her back through the streets to the wall behind the tire shop on Pico Boulevard, and the whole way he gave her a primer on his faith, stopping only to tell her where to go. Once we accept that we cannot ultimately control the behavior of others, we are free. Freed of our unreasonable expectations of them. I mean, think about it—take a left at the next light—when was the last time you were angry at someone? What if you accepted that you were angry at them not because of what they did but because of your selfish expectation of what they would do?

"Why do we paint the wall pink?" she'd asked, whispering because the wall, stretching as it did across the back of a tire shop on Pico Boulevard, was not theirs to paint—in fact, it was already painted with a labored, amateurish portrait of a brown-skinned boy holding a basketball and the words "Gone but Not Forgotten, Hermano"—and also because they had not yet been fully undressed with one another so everything they said to one another was laced with flirtation, with the possibility of nudity, of revelation. The template for their whole yearlong relationship, Michelle saw now, was formed in the journey from the café to the hardware store to the wall behind the tire store: David was the tutor and Michelle his student, not because of the age difference (13 years, Michelle calculated, doing math from scraped-together clues while David talked) but because David believed things—ardently—and Michelle just, well, didn't. She was clean and empty, ready to be scribbled and filled. At the wall, as they covered the boy and his basketball and the words, she asked David only "Why do we paint the letters green?" and it was downright Socratic, the pattern they'd fallen into already.

"These are springtime colors," David hushed. "In springtime, we offer our thanks for the Word and for all words." "Why the word 'rejoice'?" she asked, and he shrugged. "I don't know, really. It's a word, and it came to me!" He kissed Michelle then, filling her with breath. Her pelvis roiled; she was going to sleep with David when they were done painting the wall, she knew. She wondered what was attached to the chain he wore around his neck, which even now glinted in the streetlight, and what it would look like swinging free above her against the white scrim of his chest, and whether sex with an older man with so many beliefs would be different from the sober, well-matched peer sex she'd always had.

It's not that Michelle had ever stopped being Lutheran; rather, it was that she'd never really started. Her parents' rule had been that she had to go to church up until she was confirmed, when they could recuse themselves from responsibility for her soul "or somesuch," as her dad said. Michelle wore for her confirmation a stiff-skirted dress and pantyhose. It was a special occasion, this last day of church as a whole family. When they got home and she rolled the nylons and her cotton underpants down her legs, intending to shrug off the dress clothes along with any pretense of religiosity, looking forward to spending all the Sunday mornings between confirmation and college in corduroy pants, luxuriating at home with her parents who were now off the hook for her spiritual well-being, she discovered she'd gotten her first period. Her heart sinking, she stuffed the stained underthings in the little round trashcan and when the next Sunday came around, she asked her parents to take her to the 9:30 service.

Michelle knew that the arrival of her period and her would-be emancipation from church were connected, but she'd never quite figured out how. She felt certain the connection wasn't about blood or wounds or marrying the church—in fact, she'd learned in Sunday School that Martin Luther sough to shutter convents during the Reformation. Women, in the original Lutheran view, were to be homely, not holy, and in Michelle's own modern Lutheran upbringing, it appeared that women's most crucial contributions to ministry were domestic: they played the organ and mended the choir robes and made the casseroles. So perhaps the connection was as simple as this: Michelle's period heralded the arrival of adulthood and, as her parents often said, being an adult means doing all kinds of things you don't feel like doing.

But as David clutched her under the streetlight behind the tire store and filled her with his breath that May night, holding his paint brush aloft so he didn't drip any green paint in her hair, Michelle also knew that being an adult, at least being a 23-year-old adult, meant doing a lot of things you really, suddenly, felt like doing, too. Not just first-date sex with an older man from your acting class, but also graffiti.

And it did make sense what he said, a lot of it, not so much the part about changing the molecular structure of water by praying over it, if she'd heard that right, but the stuff about adjusting your expectations when people made you angry. When David first explained that part, Michelle pictured interpersonal conflict—even world wars?! —like millions of glinting marbles and instead of violently catapulting them at one another or filling their pockets with tons of them and threatening to drown themselves as martyrs in the nearest lake as people—yes, if she was honest, as Michelle herself—had always done, what if we instead gobbled them up like Hungry Hungry Hippos, fighting not with one another but only to claim more responsibility for the conflict itself?

Michelle swept one foot across the gravel before the wall to clear a spot, and she sat down. She leaned back, stretched one leg out straight from her body, and pushed one thin finger into the front pocket of her jeans to pull out the black plastic trash bag she'd stuffed down there. She stood and scooped all the trash into the bag, and as she did she realized that the wall had been repainted, that what had been pink was now yellow, that what had been green was now red. The paint was still wet. She held the bag by in one fist and used the flat of her other hand to send the heft of it spinning. When its neck was narrowed and twisted, she knotted the bag and tossed it to the left of the wall. She'd get it on her way out, on her way back to Pico Boulevard and her car. Once the wall told her where to go. Now, with the holy garbage gone, she could focus on the letters in red against the gold background. Michelle folded her legs in toward her body. She rested her hands palms up on her knees, straightened her spine, and she waited for the letters on the wall to do their thing. Why David had chosen these colors, she didn't know. They weren't spring-like at all. The color scheme called to mind Chinese New Year, or McDonald's. Michelle had read somewhere once that fast-food places used red and green color schemes to induce people to eat fatty, salty, mouth-feely foods. She didn't know if that was true, and even if it was true, did her knowing about it make her less susceptible to manipulation? The restaurant he'd taken her to tonight, right before breaking up with her, was a far cry from the twinkle lights and anise seed of their first date.

Tonight, Michelle had reached her hand across the table to try to touch David's hand, and he'd pulled it away, leaving her extended lamely across the sticky red-checkered tablecloth, the chintzy kind with the flocked backing, staring over David's shoulder at a copse of plastic yellow flowers in a planter by the door. She should have known she was getting dumped after they ate, that this was their last supper.

As it turned out, Michelle and David did sleep together that night they first painted the wall together, but not promptly after finishing that single word, that command in green—Rejoice!—against a background of pink. When they were done with the wall, David pulled out of his pocket what appeared to be a pair of concert tickets, and these he flashed in the shape of a V with one paint-splattered hand. "Join me?"

Painting the wall—and the way David held her around the waist and kissed her each time Michelle returned to the paint can to dip her brush—had made Michelle delirious, but it seemed to have sobered David up. So when they returned to the BMW on Pico, David still brandishing the tickets while Michelle carried the brushes and the nearly empty paint cans, David said he would drive. He drove them not to the Hollywood Bowl or the Troubador but to a nonde-script three-story office building in Culver City. The building was totally dark except for a tiled elevator lobby on the ground floor that glowed, artificially bright and nearly green.

Inside, he kissed her again in the grimy, ceramic-tiled lobby under fluorescent lights, and then he pushed the down button for the eleva-tor. In the basement, David took Michelle by the hand and led her down a narrow hallway carpeted in royal blue, and when they got to the end of the hallway, he handed their tickets to an angry-looking kid with a curtain of hair over one eye, a cash box and a half-drunk coffee at his elbow on the table, which was draped in blue linen to match the carpet. "Great to see you, David," he said, his eyes low-ered, as he tore off the ticket stubs to hand back to him. "Who's this?" David circled his left arm tightly around Michelle's waist. She looked down at it and saw a splotch of green paint drying into a smothering plaster over his golden hairs. Her face felt hot. "This is Michelle," David said quietly.

"It's nice to meet you," Michelle said, feeling strange in her clothes. It had to be 11 o'clock?, midnight?, maybe later. Michelle couldn't call to mind what the digital display in David's BMW had read. The kid at the table was framed perfectly by a pair of closed doors behind him, both blue, one over his left shoulder and one over his right. David let his arm fall from around Michelle's waist, stuffed the ticket stubs into his breast pocket, and made for the door on the right. When Michelle went to follow him, the surly kid sprung from the table, his knees jarring it, his half-drunk coffee spilling an inky continent on the blue linen. "Whoa, hey," he said. "Hey, David?"

David turned back to Michelle then and put his paint-splattered hands on her shoulders. "Women go that way," he said, jutting his chin toward the other door behind her. "Wait until I come for you." Because Michelle could still call to mind precisely the feel of his square chin fitting into the nook above her clavicle, and because of how her insides had felt at the wall, she did what he wanted: She crossed back past the blue-draped table, where the kid was settling himself back into his chair, and she went through the door for women. Only after she'd passed through the door did she realize David had lifted her purse strap from her shoulder, wrapped it a few times around the small bag, which contained only her phone, a lipstick, and her wallet, and handed it to the kid at the table.

Inside the windowless room, two dozen women sat silently in nubby upholstered banquet chairs. Around the entire perimeter of the otherwise empty room, up near the ceiling, hung a series of posters, each of them a blank white field with a letter, number, or symbol on it. Michelle tried to discern some logic to the arrangement of these ordinary computer-keyboard symbols, but she couldn't: it wasn't alphabetic, it wasn't QWERTY. As Michelle settled into a chair to await the beginning of what she was still hoping was a concert, she realized that all of the women were staring intently at the symbols. One had her eyes trained fixedly on F; another was in deep contemplation of &.

Michelle found H and looked at it. She found all the letters of her first name, and then all the letters of her last name. When the concert still wasn't beginning—the other women were still meditating on the same letters and symbols—Michelle tried picking out all of her passwords, for Amazon.com and LoseIt.com and Netflix and UnitedHealthcare. When she'd finished that, she looked around. The other women were unmoved, unmoving. Michelle understood then that there was no concert. That until David came for her, she would remain in this silent room in the basement of this indistinct building with these strange women staring at an exploded computer keyboard. She didn't feel unsafe, exactly. Being an adult means doing a lot of things you don't want to do, she reminded herself. Michelle developed a system. She picked a poster and quickly picked a song it reminded her of, a song from deep inside her brain—something from elementary school, like "The Big Rock Candy Mountain" for the B poster—and she stared at the poster for as long as it took to silently mouth the words to the song. When she finished, she picked a new letter, a new song.

When the door was flung open eight hours later, Michelle had just woken up, had just addressed the garland of drool draped from her chin to her chest. Her eyes had been open for only moments when David appeared above her, radiant, stroking her cheek with one hand. The room was empty of women. Even the posters were gone. Michelle was alone on an uncomfortable chair in the cold room. It had to be Sunday morning by now. "Hey," David whispered, kneeling in front of her. "Wasn't that amazing?" He took Michelle by the hand and led her out of the room, out past the empty table—where was the angry kid?—back into the elevator, where he kissed her again and handed her her purse. Michelle was shy about her mealy morning breath, but David's mouth tasted inexplicably like maple syrup and so she gave herself over to his lips and his hands for the short ride up to ground floor.

As they walked through the tiled lobby and pushed their way through the double doors to the parking lot, Michelle could barely see David's BMW through the throng of people. Half of them were the women from her room; the others were men. Among them was the angry-looking kid from the check-in desk, his swatch of hair now pushed back on his head as he worked his way through the crowd, clasping men in handshake-hugs, kissing women on one cheek. Along the edge of the parking lot, a row of folding table boasted chafing dishes of scrambled eggs, sausages, and pancakes, their fragrant steam smogging the otherwise clear morning. David held Michelle from behind, tucked his chin into that space above her clavicle, and whispered, "I bet you're ready for a big breakfast. After the sermon." He kissed the side of her neck and moved their bodies together so they could see what was going on at the front of the parking lot.

The kid got up onto a milk crate and raised his hand. A murmur went through the crowd and then it fell silent, except for a few people shouting words of encouragement at him. The kid acknowledged them with a nod and a shy smile. In the full light of day, he looked less angry and more beautiful. He waited until people stopped shouting. A siren could be heard, maybe five or ten blocks away. The kid raised the bullhorn, pressed the button, and began to speak.

"Good morning!" he called to the crowd. "I hope this morning finds you refreshed, restored, and rejuvenated." A smattering of applause went up from the crowd, and a few people called out, "The word is good!" David was one of them, and his voice boomed in her ear and she also felt it on her back, which was pressed tight up against his chest. "Isn't it?" he asked her, pulling her to him. She turned her head to the side, catching the scent of the breakfast foods wafting over the crowd. "So good," she said.

Later, as they lay in bed together, her first-date dress, which had been crisp and newly selected at dinner the night before, lay in a pile on the floor, wilted from the driving and the painting and eight hours of sex-segregated alphanumeric meditation and the parking lot breakfast sermon. She had the fingers of one hand tangled up in the chain that hung around his neck, which turned out to be anchored only by a zodiac pendant: Gemini, his sign. "So what did you think?" he asked her, nuzzling her hair. "Of the service?"

"Those pancakes were amazing," she said, kissing his chest. But when she looked up at him, he wore a serious expression. He pulled his head away and looked at her carefully. "I don't mean the pancakes," he said. "What did you think of the service?"

"I liked what the kid—the guy. Sorry, what is he? A pastor?—said about thinking carefully about how we use words. Understanding their power." She wasn't lying; when she set aside the part of the night that took place in that silent basement, and just thought about certain things the kid shouted at the crowd with his bullhorn as her stomach went crazy with wanting for breakfast—which, as it turned out, was the second breakfast served that morning, as the men had done all the cooking and served themselves first—this religion, this faith, whatever it was, seemed reasonable. Appealing, even. "Do you all do that every Saturday night?" Michelle wasn't sure she could sign up for that experience weekly.

"Oh, God no," David said, laughing. "It's a holiday. You know? Like Christmas? It happens the first Saturday in May. It's called Say Day." Michelle thought that a holiday devoted to words, followed by a giant, all-you-can-eat camping breakfast, was not a bad thing. It was at least as cozy as Christmas, and twice as plausible as the resurrection and candy-colored eggs of Easter. "It's our biggest holiday."

"So why did you ask me out for Say Day? I mean, if it's such a big deal. It's a lot of pressure for a first date. Especially since I just thought we were going to dinner. I didn't know about the wall, or the service."

"I don't know. I guess, well, to be honest, I wasn't a hundred percent sure I was going to take you to the service. I figured dinner for sure, and then if I had to I could just drop you off. But then something you said at the restaurant made me sure I wanted you to come with me."

"What was it?" Michelle asked. "What did I say at the restaurant?" In her own recollection, she hadn't said much. Almost immediately after they'd ordered, David had started in on the wine and the gesticulating, his impassioned monologue. As far as she could recall, Michelle hadn't said much.

"It was when we were ordering. He was reading the specials, and he described something as 'artesian,' and you asked him if he meant 'artesian' or 'artisan.' That's when I knew you'd love the service. That you'd get it." He pulled himself out of the knot of arms and legs and rolled over onto his stomach, propping himself up on his elbows. "You did, didn't you? You got it?"

"I think so," Michelle said, still lying on her back, the sheets a tangled shroud around her torso. She'd almost told David that she'd fallen asleep during the meditation, that she'd woken up just before he barged into the women's room, but the way he was looking at her now, she knew she couldn't tell him that. "It was really interesting. I've never been to anything like that before."

Once, when Michelle was about 15, just a couple years after her confirmation, she'd spent the night at the Lutheran church. It was a youth group activity called a lock-in. After a pizza dinner on the lawn, everyone went inside and the doors to the church were locked with the twelve teenagers and the hapless pastor inside. There was a movie in the fellowship hall, then bowling in the corridor outside the sanctuary, then ice cream sundaes in the kitchen. But the bleary-eyed pastor retired to his office for a nap around 11 and Michelle and her friends explored their church in the dark.

They got into the communion wine in the sacristy and sat on the counters burning through books of matches, just lighting them and blowing them out as they played a loosely organized game of Truth or Dare. In the middle of the night, Michelle and a pink-cheeked boy named Mark peeled off from the group and found their way to a pew in the sanctuary, where the pastor, refreshed from his nap, found them making out. "I'm going to pretend this didn't happen," the pastor told her that morning, as Michelle waited for her parents to pick her up. "You're a good kid. This isn't who you are."

That seemed fair to Michelle. The pastor tuned out the parts of

Michelle that didn't work for him, just as she tuned out the parts of church that didn't work for her, keeping the parts that did: the songs, mostly. Now, though, she chose not to tell David that story, or her theory of devotion—to faith, and to work, and to most people— which entailed a whole lot of patiently overlooking any parts that didn't quite work for her as long as there were enough parts that did. That was exactly what she was doing in bed with David that first Sunday morning, ignoring her dawning awareness of his brand of piety in favor of admiring the shape of his shoulders against her poplin sheets.

And even earlier tonight, that had been her plan as she got dressed in the same dress that she'd worn to the twinkly dinner and her first (albeit unwitting) Say Day. She planned to quietly endure the hours in the women's room, staring at the letters on the wall, looking forward to maple-syrup kissing in the elevator and a Chinet plate heavy with eggs and sausage in the parking lot and a long, sweet Sunday morning in bed.

Now, though, she sat in front of the freshly repainted wall alone even as she knew David was in the basement of the office building in Culver City without her, observing Say Day in whatever way the men did while the women sat in their uncomfortable chairs in that bright room and stared at symbols ringing the walls. No doubt David himself had repainted the wall tonight, but Michelle didn't know if he'd done it before taking her to that chintzy restaurant—in which case he knew he was going to break up with her that night—or after he'd dropped her off at her apartment.

She tried to summon a transcript of their evening. Had she said something to the waiter tonight, some inverse of the artisan/artesian exchange, that made David certain he didn't want to take her to her first official Say Day? Something that made him pull his hand from her across the checkered table and drive her promptly home, saying only, "I'm sorry, I can't share my life with someone who doesn't share my beliefs."

"But I—I do," Michelle said as David idled in the parking lot of her apartment complex. And even if she didn't—and she didn't—how did he know? Hadn't she been compliant? Hadn't she listened attentively whenever he talked about what he believed? Hadn't she been good?

But David just shook his head. "No, Michelle, don't, OK? I can tell you don't get it." And then he was gone, to paint the wall red and gold without her, or to do whatever men did in the basement in Culver City, while she stood stupidly in her own living room on the first Saturday in May in a dumb first-date dress, wondering what ever happened to his Hungry Hungry Hippos theory of conflict resolution. If she wasn't devout enough for him, if she disappointed him, wasn't that his own fault, by the logic of his precious faith? Hadn't he spent a year training her to adjust her expectations of him? And now, when she disappointed him, he just blinked plasticly at her and expected her to scoop up all the marbles. She'd sat on the edge of her bed in that silly dress before pulling on a pair of jeans and heading to the wall.

Now, she sat in the dirt before the wall and she waited for the letters—Rejoice!—to either mean something or change themselves. If the letters danced for her the way they seemed to dance for David, and for those silent women, then she would give herself over. She would rush to David while it was still Say Day, she would intercept him at the parking lot in Culver City while he forked eggs into his maple mouth and declare that she—finally, for the first time in her life—believed something holy, wholly.

She was still sitting there when morning came and, with it, a skinny boy in a knit beanie who placed a lit candle—the tall Mexican kind with a picture of a lady on it, or a saint—on the ground in front of the wall before sitting down next to Michelle. "How did you know him?" he asked. The boy was 20, maybe. Young, but not for long.

"Who?" Michelle asked. The boy pulled the ends of his sleeves over his hands, puffed his cheeks out like it was winter somewhere else. He laughed sadly, jutting his chin at the wall. "Duh, lady. Joe. How did you know Joe?" The boy wasn't looking at her; he was squinting at the wall, at the candle he'd placed there, like it was farther away than it was.

"I guess I didn't," Michelle said, remembering the portrait of the boy with the basketball who had graced this wall before she and David painted it last Say Day. She thought she could almost see the outline of the boy's head and the words, "Gone but not forgotten, Hermano" behind the blocky letters he'd instructed Michelle to form, kissing her each time she returned to dip her brush. She realized then that the boy with the basketball was a dead boy, that they had repainted his shrine.

"True that," the boy said, shaking his head like Michelle had said something wise. "Don't think much of anybody really knew my man Joe Rice," he said. "Bro's been gone four years and we're still learning shit about him no one knew. Like, who knew he was homies with a white lady like you? Bro was a mystery or like a—what do you call it?—an enema."

"Enigma," Michelle said. "A riddle wrapped in a mystery inside an enigma." She kept her eyes on the wall, but she felt the boy turn his big eyes on her. She could feel it on her cheek, him looking at her, or maybe the sun was coming up, or maybe both. "Damn, lady," the boy said. "You get it. I see why you and Joe was friends."

Michelle pulled her eyes from the wall, from its command, and looked at the boy, who continued to stare at her even as he lit a cigarette and passed it to her. "Joe Rice died here?" she asked, and when the boy simply stared at her, she repeated it. But this time, she made it sound less like a question than an intonation. "Joe Rice died here," she said. And when they had finished their cigarette, Michelle and the boy went wordlessly in her car to breakfast near the ocean. On this, the first Sunday in May.

Basic Repairs

DOMINIC BREITER

.♦.

Beyond the cracked sidewalk, and the telephone pole with layers of flyers in a rainbow of colors, and the patch of dry brown grass there stood a ten-foot high concrete block wall, caked with dozens of coats of paint. There was a small shrine at the foot of it, with burnt out candles and dead flowers and a few soggy teddy bears. One word of graffiti filled the wall, red letters on a gold background: Rejoice!

That kind of desperate elation, which always felt incongruous to the grief at hand, reminded Pastor Kim of his mother's funeral. Specifically, the directive in her will forbidding anyone from wearing black. What had resulted was a bouquet of mourners looking uncomfortable and self-conscious until the sky over the cemetery eventually turned overcast, as if to restore a natural austerity to the occasion. No such sartorial request, in fact no will of any kind, was expected to manifest in this instance, given the deceased's young age. "Another year," Pastor Kim thought. "Another year and he could've been away from this place. Like we discussed so many times."

He approached the shrine as one approaches the rotting carcass of an animal, drawing that careful curvature with his yellow footprints in the dead grass. Close enough to observe, but far enough away where the smell won't carry. The wall was in fact the rear of a dugout, and Kim could hear the knell of a ball against a metal bat, boyish outcries of support and mockery on the other side. Life swirled on without Buddy Tenpas, Jr. Feeling that he was being spied upon, like a sentry tower kept watch over the shrine, Kim kept walking. Besides, he had brought nothing to contribute, no sentimental totems of remembrance. He watched the shiny tops of his loafers and was caught unawares, having heard no one approach, when a new set of feet entered his field of vision. These shoes, plain white trainers flecked with grass stains, were attached to pale denim jeans. Above that was a white sweatshirt bearing an airbrushed tableau of two cats at play, and then, poking from the elastic collar, perhaps the single most despondent face Kim had ever seen.

"Marianne," he murmured. "My sympathies." She was still Mrs. Tenpas in his head, not Ms. Kaminsky. The divorce had been finalized with Bud, Sr. in absentia, communicating via his lawyer from some unknown pocket of America. Well, presumably America. Kim wondered if he'd bother to make it home. How had Marianne even gone about informing the callow man of their son's tragedy? It was possible he did not know, and this revelation struck Kim as unforgivably sad. She offered a kind word in response, something about how much Buddy had respected him, that she knew how hard Kim had fought to prevent something like this from happening. "I have to believe," Marianne said, "that this is what God wanted."

Kim carried the remark home. He oscillated between feeling humbled and mortified by its import. Not even forty-eight hours had passed and here she was making peace with the tyranny of fate, the tyranny which had calculated Buddy, Jr. out of her life with a few cold keystrokes. He passed up the freezer-box chicken pot pie his wife Gracie had heated for dinner, could not even look his daughter Amelia in the eye, just three years Buddy's junior. Was life already so complicated for her? He did not like to think of her as having the capacity to suffer, at least not in a grownup sense. Suffering was something a child should pay reverence to but never know in the flesh. It should remain an abstraction, an effigy above the altar or portrayed in stained glass. But suffering had come to Hargrove, worming its tendrils into every home, holding up a mirror to every unsullied child and showing them an image of the cosmos that not even the strongest minds among us can help wincing away from. Pastor Kim sat on the toilet for three quarters of an hour mulling this all over in his head, massaging the salt-and-pepper sideburns that carpeted his temples. Only then did a concerned Gracie summon the nerve to knock.

2

Buddy had made peace with what everyone called his "white boy fro." As long as he used extra conditioner in the shower and limited shampoo to once a week, he could retain some semblance of luster instead of walking around with a lump of steel wool on his head. All the same, he would've loved to have known what it felt like to flip his bangs. Guys always looked so cool doing that shit. Maybe during his stay in Milwaukee he'd pick up some new fashion trend he could smuggle back to Hargrove. Maybe he'd inspire envy in the bang-flippers and be invited into their higher echelon of dopeness. His plane landed at General Mitchell International twenty-five minutes late. From there he did as Bud told him. Flag a cab, or better yet an Uber, out by the bus depot. His destination was 1114 S 23rd in Walker's Point. Dad liked everyone calling him Bud, even his own son. The separation was still upsetting, sure, but Mom and Dad were too indoctrinated by the Confessional Lutherans to ever get a divorce, so Buddy held out hope they would make amends before long. Pastor Kim had already confided that he shared this optimism.

Dad's place wasn't a dump, but it was janky compared to what he'd left behind. No yard, shared laundry appliances with the other tenants - plus you had to stick quarters in the machines! - and his view was primarily of smokestacks feeding dijon-colored smog into the atmosphere. All the same, it held a certain bachelor appeal. Buddy intuited at once that there were far less rules here. He wondered if they'd drink a beer together, or catch a Brewers game. As it turned out, Milwaukee rent kept Bud punched in more often than not, so Buddy found himself with giant swaths of time to kill. When he had memorized the flat (Fleetwood Mac record sleeves mounted on the wall like trophy kills, bobbleheads amassed on the entertainment center's bottom shelf) Buddy wandered the streets, only half trusting himself not to get lost. The first two days were exciting. Not that anything momentous happened but they were fresh. Buddy was getting the lay of the land. After that, it sunk in that there was nothing so romantic about the city. People were just living their lives, and they were stacked on top of each other while doing it. He got sick of eating lunch at the same old greasy taquería just because it was dirt cheap and decided to walk farther than he had ever walked before. Clear to the harbor, a mooring basin where the Kinnickinnic River fed into Lake Michigan.

During this jaunt he scrolled through his phone and kept track of goings-on in Hargrove. "Stagnant" was a word he often used to describe his hometown, but he wondered now if that was fair. Was it an attribute strictly assigned to Ohio shipping hamlets, or to every human terrarium big and small? What did they have here in the city that was so great? More options, more distractions, more clutter and fervor and noise. But none of that rubbed off on the people and made them glow. Lives were unfurling at the same tedious rate all over the world. It was a lie perpetuated by the entertainment industry that just over the next hill the grass was greener, every day ending in a romantic hookup or a valiant achievement. Standing at the end of a jetty buttoned on all sides by rubber tires, watching the great barges encumbered with shipping containers (like the coffins of gods) be loaded and unloaded by cranes whose necks seemed to soar on forever, Buddy was reminded of his own marina back home, only taken to a grander scale. Dad was over there right now, sweating in his hard hat and polyurethane gloves, cussin' and talking game with his fellow longshoremen. He'd said the pay hike was so generous that he would've been daft not to go, but Mom wouldn't hear of leaving Hargrove. Things had already been volatile between them for awhile and this final straw - Buddy guiltily thought - was just the excuse each of them had privately wanted. But where did that leave him? Caught between two worlds, learning hard truths too early, or maybe just early enough to have a leg-up on his peers when it came time to raise anchor on that great lonesome voyage called Adulthood.

3

In between all his other roles as pastor - overseeing financial matters; coordinating staff meetings and fundraising ventures; performing special services such as baptisms, confirmations, weddings, and funerals; and then of course writing sermons - the role Kim took most seriously, the one he saw as being most integral to his leadership position in the community, was serving as counselor to his parishioners in times of crisis. At seminary he'd gone out of his way to take numerous courses centered on psychology, deeming the human propensity for confusion and self-harm to be his greatest adversary, second only to Satan. He attended seminars nationwide given by experts who had written books on "faith-forward" healing and mentorship. And every day he was learning from sundry interactions with people around him, their different hues of fallibility and torment. He found them all the more beautiful for it and was inspired to trace the complicated fretwork of his own soul, the tender fleshy parts never before prodded. New pains flooded him as water floods a sponge, but through God he could wring himself out each time to flood anew with the blood of his beloved flock.

When Buddy Tenpas, Jr. first entered his office, it was at the behest of his mother. She had phoned Kim two days earlier in a fit of distress, confiding that she'd snooped around on Buddy's bedroom computer because he had been spending so much time on it lately, getting more withdrawn and less cheerful. All her friends told her this was textbook teen behavior, but the alarm bell in her head wouldn't quit sounding. Minimized on his desktop was a Facebook Messenger chat window. The other party was a name Marianne had never heard before, it meant nothing to her, but upon scrolling through the history of this dialogue, she found it certainly meant something to her son. Now she didn't know how to confront him about it. Buddy still had no idea she was behind Pastor Kim's asking to speak with him that day, though Kim knew he would have to divulge as much before long.

They started by discussing the primacy of faith in Buddy's life. Did he feel it was essential to who he was? Did God cross his mind on a regular basis - daily, hourly? When he communed with God, what was his approach and what feelings did it evoke? Was he appreciative in prayer, thanking God for the blessings He had bestowed? Was he penitent, spending a significant amount of time apologizing for his wrong-doings? After the Amen left his lips, did he rise feeling refreshed or weighed down? Buddy had an easy time with these questions at the outset, responding that his faith brought him only levity and purpose, that he couldn't imagine how one negotiated life without divine guidance. But then Pastor Kim kept asking. Throughout their untold discussions, he would pose the questions to Buddy in different ways, altering his syntax, finding new discreet angles from which to approach, applying his training as best he could and soliciting knowledge from the minds he respected most. Kim would never forget that turning point twelve sessions in when the boy abruptly broke down in his chair, sobbing.

Joseph Nicolosi, a clinical psychologist and founder of NARTH (National Association for Research and Therapy of Homosexuality) theorized that a gender-identity deficit can become inflamed when the subject feels rejected or alienated by other members of their sex. So Kim, once having breached Buddy's concrete shell of denial, inquired about his relationships with other male teens. As a freshman Buddy had played center-field on the school's baseball team. Following a wrist injury, which had been fully mended for two years now, he never returned. Buddy skirted the causation for this lapse in fraternity, saying he wasn't the competitive sort, wasn't a jock. He liked to have fun without all the pressure of championships and "school honor" dangling above his head. That was all good and fine - Kim could empathize, having never been too athletic during his own physical prime - but how had Buddy replaced this social outlet? Through what medium was he engaging his peers, whetting the communication skills that would buoy him in the workforce, observing the natural, healthy paradigm of interpersonal behavior firsthand? Buddy didn't have a good answer for this, so Kim took it upon himself pick up the slack where he felt Bud, Sr. had failed (though he never voiced this judgment aloud), guiding Buddy through the rigors and decorum of manhood.

He pressured Buddy to enroll in an extracurricular shop class taught after school by the laudable jack of all trades, Mr. Glarus. Kim would often sit in, both for moral support and also to try and glean a few lessons himself, oblivious as he was to the basics of carpentry and metallurgy. One field he did have some experience in, however, was auto repair, and on his own beta car, a 2004 Camry (used only when the Charger was out of commission), he mapped out for Buddy that formidable symbiosis of tanks, pumps, belts and hoses under the hood. He taught him how to change his oil, his tires; how to replace everything from filters to spark plugs to distributor caps; how to use a multimeter to test current, voltage, and resistance; the difference between those three things; and he even demonstrated - improvisationally - how to change a set of brake pads when just such a need arose on the Charger. It took an entire afternoon. At the end of it they sat on Pastor Kim's patio spattered with grease, enjoying the year's first pitcher of sun tea.

It was then that Buddy finally opened up about a circumstance which had affected him greatly, and which he had not spoken of to anyone before. It revolved around a trip taken the year prior to visit his father in Milwaukee. "I didn't really know what to do over there half the time. He was always working. So mostly I'd just walk around. I found this coffee shop over by the harbor one day and ended up, well, striking up a conversation with this other kid there . . ." Cole. Kim could guess the name before Buddy revealed it. It was the name of his secret Facebook correspondent who'd driven Marianne into such a tizzy. Cole. They'd hit it off so well that they agreed to meet again the next day in a park near Bud, Sr.'s place. Cole had taken Buddy to a cheap little arthouse production of Death of a Salesman that some of his theater friends were performing. Although Buddy did not dwell on description, Kim could imagine the two of them shoulder to shoulder in the rear of some dank, dilapidated theater stinking of marijuana and mildew, watching a troop of flamboyant thespians in feather boas make a mockery of Arthur Miller's classic. "We met up all nine days I was there," Buddy went on. "Except Sunday, when Bud - when Dad had off. But even then . . ." By losing himself in the confession, Buddy had veered off-script. Kim heard a vein of tenderness enter his delivery. Startled back into the present moment, and with a flush blooming across his face, Buddy concluded, "We've stayed in touch ever since."

Kim absorbed this intelligence with a physician's neutrality. All the books told him this was the proper way to view Buddy: as an afflicted patient. The boy was not willfully perverse like some of these queers depicted on TV. If anything it was that very media saturation, that over-representation on sitcoms and in movies, that was taking its toll on the impressionable minds of young people nowadays. Standards of gender and sexuality were being skewed beyond recognition. Kim didn't profess to know the reason: if it was some emasculating conspiracy of the liberal elite, as certain theorists claimed, or if it had to do with pollutants reducing testosterone levels exponentially in each successive generation. Kim's role was not to wake the world from this venal trance, merely to wake Buddy. But every individual is the sum of myriad inputs, so what Kim had to do was supplant those most pernicious inputs condoning homosexuality with others rooted in God, Church, and Family. He reached across the smoked-glass tabletop and took Buddy's hand, hoping to convey with a warm smile his salutary intentions. "You're not beyond help," he assured. "Not by a long shot. Everyone strays in their youth. When problems arise is when some stray so far that they disown God because it's too painful to know He's looking over their shoulder. Keep your humility, keep your perspective, and you'll keep your salvation, Buddy. This I can promise you."

4

Marianne stood fourth row, center wing, watching the muscles in her son's neck swell along with all the other tenors' in the Calvary Evangelical Men's Choir. She wore a salmon-colored short-sleeve shirt with a sort of lace bib tapering from the collar. It was one of two shirts she reserved for church and fancy occasions. The elastic waistband of her plus-size white slacks cut into her flesh. She couldn't wait to get home and back into her sweats. This was all too surreal anyway. Buddy out here in the spotlight, playing normal, putting on that self-conscious smile in front of everybody. It was his father's smile - that panicky way Bud smiled in public, too - like there was a muzzle aimed at the back of his head coercing him to play happy.

She didn't know what it was in their genetics that made them so miserable. They seemed to succor themselves on making life more complicated than it need be. If not for the blessed intervention of Pastor Kim, she might've started feeling her mind slip long ago, same as her ex-husband and son seemed to have let theirs slip without putting up much of a fight.

At the same time, Marianne had very real doubts about the effectiveness of this so-called "conversion" or "reparative" therapy. She could act like Jessica Lange all she wanted, it wouldn't make her a movie star. By the same token, dressing her boy up in a suit or a greasy set of coveralls or making him hit the gym, none of that was going to flip him into a real man by the power of suggestion. She felt the same nagging humiliation watching him sing as she did the other day when he got back from Jujutsu. Pastor Kim's brother-in-law, some Latin fella named Fonzo, apparently was an instructor, teaching the Japanese martial art primarily to children and other middle-age women who were still pretty enough to worry about getting raped. Buddy had been so excited: handing her that wooden spoon, saying "Pretend it's a knife," then striking some outrageous pose and telling her, "Come on, try 'n stab me." So she'd played along, indulgently letting herself be disarmed, but at the end of it when he stared at her so expectantly, like she was supposed to be proud or something, she was at a loss how to react, and he had seen it in her eyes. She regretted it now. She wanted to have greater faith in her boy. But the Lord, in His infinite wisdom, had seen fit to give her a dud.

Well, she would hold out hope for as long as Pastor Kim did. She loved Buddy of course. He was not the object of any of her scorn. No, that was reserved exclusively for the kid's father, that craven little self-centered man who didn't even have enough parental sense to make sure his offspring wasn't frollicking around with homos on a nine-day visit. Nine days, and he'd managed to screw up that badly.

Imagine the cumulative effect of his being around for most of Buddy's life. Defective genes, that's what she and Pastor Kim were up against. In light of Buddy's illness, it seemed clear to Marianne retrospectively that her husband bore a little homo in him as well. She could count on two hands the number of times they'd made love in the latter half of their marriage. He'd always wanted to be out around other men, burly barrel-armed longshoremen. No wonder. No wonder her life had fallen to shambles and here she was in this church wearing the same panicky smile as Buddy because he kept looking at her for affirmation while he sang and she didn't want to disappoint him again. No wonder she'd broken down crying in the hospital mailroom where she worked as a clerk - sorting and delivering all day long - disclosing everything when her closest friend and coworker Peggy found her like that. Another instant regret, but she was sure Peggy could keep a secret. Anyway it had felt better to tell somebody, to get that cancerous burden off her chest before it asphyxiated her.

Following the service, Marianne congratulated her son with as much earnesty as she could muster, which was a considerable amount, fueled by the shame she felt for having to muster it in the first place. Then together they joined the queue of congregants shaking Pastor Kim's hand on their way out the door. She hoped no one else beat her to the punch. She planned to invite him over for a nice home-cooked meal, her famous Kaminsky Family Pot Roast, a recipe passed down from her Lithuanian grandmother. The longer the juices simmered together the better, so it was already roiling away in her crock pot and had been since 8AM. As it happened, the pastor was able and willing to gormandize his fair share. He arrived promptly at six wearing a blue-gray checkered suit. The pleasing brine of his aftershave reminded Marianne of more chivalrous times. Much to her suppressed delight, he brought along a Sara Lee French silk pie. It went straight into the fridge. The pot roast was divvied in her good ceramic bowls. It almost felt like old times, having a man join the table with them. What she had failed to foresee, however, was the immediate chord of tension that would thrum throughout the visit like an endless fermata.

Buddy had not failed to foresee it, and he knew neither had Kim - something in how the old pastor's eyes flickered away from Marianne when she first extended the invitation, before crinkling into that crows-footed smile that said he would accept. Were they heckling this poor man, being too needy, hoarding all his time and resources? Grateful as he was for Kim's vested interest, Buddy sometimes wished he had more breathing room to try and process his own psychology. Like, when had it all started? When had he got his first inkling that something was off? In the boys locker room? At recess, chafing up against bodies on the basketball court? Or how about at Todd Boilen's birthday party, when a half dozen of them were huddled in the basement pawing through a magazine Todd had stolen from his dad - the hot draft of other boys whispering by his ear as they narrated what effects the images were having on them? It was puberty then, right around when all his peers started to have sex on the brain 24/7, that Buddy was forced to confront he was different. Discovering masturbation for the first time . . . blood flooded his cheeks even upon remembering it, shoveling Mom's pot roast into his mouth . . . lying on the floor flipping through a Batman comic. Wounded in battle, Bruce Wayne strips from the waist up to clean his wounds, every exaggerated muscle seeming to flex on the page as he twists this way and that. The pressure down in Buddy's groin while he reads the thought bubble a hundred times over, a pressure that tickles, building when he grinds himself a little tighter to the carpet. The thought bubble reads, "Nothing too terrible. Just a few basic repairs." And it's to this mantra that Buddy first experiences a wetness, the tickle gushing out of him on a tacky current he takes at first to be blood, and Buddy is so scared he almost cries because he figures he must have broken something. Popped an artery. Who knows. No one ever told him.

Would he have to relive this episode out loud to Pastor Kim? Did he get to have secrets anymore, private thoughts, or were they not really his thoughts but the Devil working through him and so that's why everything needed to be purged and laid on the table? He was trying to cooperate. He didn't want this evil in him. At his mom's command - and the pastor's more diplomatic urging - he had deleted Cole from his Facebook friends and ceased all contact, but not before letting on about his mother's snooping, about the therapy he was now forced to undergo. Cole had dropped all kinds of expletives in response, hadn't even stopped short of ridiculing Buddy's mother, calling her a dinosaur, a repressed, brainwashed little church mouse. He'd alleged that Buddy was in a cult, not a religion, and that the rest of the world was light years more evolved in their way of thinking. It'd almost seemed like he was making a pitch for Buddy to run away. To Milwaukee, presumably. To be with him. Buddy went cold with fear at the thought of it. But was it fear of a reckless prospect, its irresponsibility and ingratitude? Or was it fear of its appeal?

As Marianne chatted on about how she'd had to buy the matching curtains and valance in the dining room at two different stores, and what an improbable stroke of good fortune that had been because the design, in her estimation, was so unique, Pastor Kim nodded along affably, careful not to slurp his broth like he was wont to do when he ate alone, offering his two cents when he could but wondering privately if the discussion would ever turn to her son. Buddy was still a chaste, good-hearted boy. Kim felt a greater affinity for him each and every day, as he often confided to Gracie in bed while they sat up late reading biblical exegeses, in his case, or spiritual fiction in hers. According to the young parishioner - who Kim believed wholeheartedly - there had been only one kiss, one kiss and nothing more. Furthermore, it'd sounded in his retelling as if the kiss had been sprung on him, and Buddy, not knowing how to react, had failed to recoil. This Cole character was five years his senior, which cemented Kim's bias that Buddy had been predated upon. He became increasingly convinced as time went on that the boy's recovery was well within the realm of viability.

Marianne knew she was talking too much but couldn't help herself. The elephant in the room was the last thing she wanted to address. She couldn't address it, as she realized now, wishing she'd realized it before inviting the pastor for supper. Golly . . . and she still had that pie to serve. It would be rude not to. Maybe a little hiatus in between for digestion. That's surely when it would come up, certain to spoil everyone's appetite, hers especially. She couldn't even look at Buddy anymore without wondering what degraded thoughts were pouring through his mind. It was awful, awful to be repulsed by your own child. But she knew what she knew, what she'd been taught and what she'd read: that homosexuality was an abomination. So what did that say of the condition of her womb?

5

I looked out over a sea of picket signs, most of them alike. Red lettering against a gold background: Rejoice! That's what was blazoned on Darnell Winters' T-shirt in that famous picture of him gone viral, the one where he lay dead on the curb, beaten to a bloody pulp. The contrast of that shirt beneath his mangled face - shit had struck a chord with people. It'd struck a chord with me, which is what I was doing here, imbued in the picketers but not really participating, feeling a little bit lost and in over my head. Should've made a damn sign. Rejoice! I'd heard it was the slogan of some youth camp Darnell attended, but that didn't really matter now. The LGBTQ machine had requisitioned it, repurposed it into a bittersweet, defiant symbol, scathingly ironic like the picture itself had been. But if I'm being real, all that slogan really meant to most people was a traffic hindrance. The mob was constipating traffic on Wisconsin and 3rd, a major downtown intersection. It was dusk, the sky a cautionary orange, coloring the tinted commercial glass of high-rise façades. America had come to recognize this sight by now. This was what happened when a black fairy got stomped to death by a posse of drunken frat boys. This was what happened nowadays when hatred reared its familiar head. Just then a kid shoved past me, couldn't have been more than Darnell's age, nineteen or twenty, wielding a bullhorn. His glassy-smooth face danced with the angry, flailing shadows of the protesters, creating a grimace that may or may not have been real. Everyone else seemed to know him. They were clearing a path, clapping him on the back as he passed. Again I felt woefully uninformed, like I'd failed to read some pre-riot memo. Shit, I mean protest. Hopefully this didn't turn into no riot.

The kid got up onto a milk crate and raised his hand. A murmur went through the crowd and then it fell silent, except for a few people shouting words of encouragement at him. The kid acknowledged them with a nod and a shy smile. In the full light of day, he looked less angry and more beautiful. He waited until people stopped shouting. A siren could be heard, maybe five or ten blocks away. The kid raised the bullhorn, pressed the button, and began to speak.

Admittedly, I didn't stick around to hear much of what little man was saying. The approaching sirens just compounded my claustrophobic anxiety, so I backtracked out of that swarm as deftly as I could, telling myself I'd done my part. Besides, I'd received a couple of texts from Hannah saying she wanted to meet up at my place to "talk some shit over." When I was free and clear off the throng I shot her a text back, saying I'd be home in thirty minutes if I walked briskly. My apartment building was in a slummy neighborhood west of downtown called Martin Drive. She was already parked out front when I arrived. Baby Reese was in her carseat sucking and drooling on some big rubber ring, kicking her feet, smiling when she saw me and was transferred into my arms. As I peppered her cheeks with kisses, Hannah looked on wearing half a smile. We barely exchanged hellos. Upstairs I didn't waste much time on chit-chat either. I could tell she'd had a rough day and was jonesing pretty hard, though she didn't go into it. Like me, she preferred to suffer in silence, to sequester and repress. The downside was we would probably both die of matching brain tumors. We'd made a pretty good team once upon a time, back before I committed the judgment lapse of cheating on her - and with a man no less.

When everything was prepped, I gave her use of the bathroom, shutting the door for privacy. Reese and I went into the bedroom, me making airplane noises as I whooshed her through the air. All the turmoil and graveness of the demonstration felt far behind me. Seated at my computer, I bounced my little girl on my lap, enjoying how spellbound she became when a pigeon roosted on the fire escape outside my window. I logged onto Facebook just to see if anything about the protest had been posted, or if there were updates on the arraignment of Darnell's killers, or lastly, if Bob Ross had grown a fucking pair yet and re-added me as a friend. Bob Ross was the nickname I'd saddled him with when he confided that other kids liked to tease him about his "white boy fro."

Alas, dude was still incommunicado, stranded in that Ohio dead zone where I envisioned people wore bonnets and buckles on their shoes and still blamed seizures on demonic possession. My heart went out to him. I couldn't imagine being raised under such dogma. It felt like we came from two different worlds, the way he described every facet of life being tied up in the church, everyone being privy to each other's business. But then, my situation wasn't exactly the healthiest either. I looked around my small squalid space. Reese needed to be changed, I could smell it. How long had she stewed in a dirty diaper, the poor thing? Hannah, like most addicts, was single-minded when it came to securing a fix. Sheer tunnel vision. All other priorities eclipsed. I knew the feeling well. I stood up and laid Reese down on the floor, where she was happy to squirm like the cutest little inch worm you ever saw, sucking her fist in lieu of that rubber ring. I went to the bathroom door to ask Hannah if she'd bothered to bring any spare diapers along. If not, I was trying to think what I had around the flat that could substitute. An old dish towel, I guess. But Hannah wasn't responding, so I opened the door . . .

I tried for several minutes to resuscitate her, several painstaking minutes before accepting that her pulse was not coming back. Reese, with a kind of sixth sense, began to whine in the next room. It was time to cut through the panic and think rationally. What that ended up meaning was packing a backpack with some clothes and the re-mainder of my stash. Next I placed a call to 9-1-1, reported the OD, gave my address but not my name, and hung up as the operator tried in vain to extract more information. Before leaving the flat - for good, I imagined - I double-checked that there was nothing on the bedroom floor that could potentially harm Reese. She wasn't crawl-ing yet, so she would stay put until EMS arrived. I knelt down and kissed her doughy cheeks once more in parting, swearing to her and to myself it wouldn't be the last time. My own pulse stayed remarka-bly even-keel the entire time. As someone who worried nonstop when things were stable, it appeared the flipside was also true. This was a well-rehearsed contingency plan: fleeing my flat in the event of a client overdose. I just hadn't expected it to be a pro like Hannah. It wasn't until several blocks away, as I boarded the 35 transit line, that it all failed to feel like a drill anymore - and my chest muscles clenched with an iron grip around my now-stammering heart.

6

Pastor Kim was dismayed that he had to learn about the bullying through his daughter Amelia. She'd seen Buddy being pushed around in the parking lot of a drugstore near their school and distinctly heard him being called "the F word." When confronted about it, Buddy downplayed its severity, saying they called everyone that. He had not confided about his therapy sessions to anyone in Hargrove and there was no way anyone could know. Although, he tacked on casually, the main instigating bully did also happen to be the son of Marianne's friend and co-worker, Peggy Chandler. Kim took this insinuation without comment. He feared at times, in the solitude of his ongoing dialectic with God, that he had bitten off more than he could chew. There just weren't the same resources available to him as there had been in the past, not that he had ever tried anything like this before, or was adhering to some codified regimen. Kim derived guidance and expertise mainly from out-of-print books published by the now-disbanded Exodus International. Conversion therapy had a bad rap, many of the authors conceded. It was still a relatively new social science, and, as in all fields of science, mistakes had been made in the past. Combining electric shocks with gay porn stimuli was one major point of contention the liberals harped on about. What they failed to acknowledge, however, were the success stories, the lives that had been saved, the family units restored. No, their confirmation bias wouldn't allow it. Relapse and scandal, that's what was magnified and shoveled into the troughs of the waiting public.

Negative reinforcement was old hat. Kim knew that. The opposite was proven to be far more effective. And so this was how he found himself driving twenty miles outside of town late one night, his throat constricting, his palms turning sweaty on the wheel when he saw that first illuminated billboard like a beacon of sin along the shoulder. TOYS, DVDS, SO MUCH MORE!! He took the off-ramp and entered a gravel parking lot, which was thankfully sparse with only three other vehicles in attendance, one being a Mack truck. The next day, a patina of contamination seemed to cling to his body. Nightmarish scenarios played through his head of somebody, for some reason, rummaging through his office desk and finding the magazine slipped inside a manila folder. His next session with Buddy was scheduled for tomorrow, so he tried to banish the excursion from his head for that remaining window of time. (The fluorescent tube lighting inside that warehouse-like structure, the colorful packaging and DVD covers that he adamantly kept a peripheral blur, the trucker's attempt at small talk in that stale bower of magazine racks: "Seems like there's more and more tranny rags everytime you look.") Kim focused on prayer and conducting business inside the church. Then, at around 4PM, he received a call. He was just about to lock up his office and head home for supper when it came through. On the line was Marianne Tenpas - wait, Kaminsky - seeming breathless and distraught. "You've got to come over quick, Pastor, if you can. I don't know what to do. I've half a mind to call the police . . ." To Kim it sounded like she was making a weak attempt to keep her voice down, as if someone was in the next room who she didn't want overhearing. He asked her to slow down and explain herself clearly. Why did she want to call the police? She answered through clenched teeth, "He's here, Pastor. He just showed up. That boy from Milwaukee . . ."

When he pulled up at the house fifteen minutes later, Marianne was standing by the screen door and came outside to meet him. "He already left," she said. "He got wind of my police comment and that did it. Scared him off. He looked like a transient, Pastor. Some kind of junky." Tears glossed her eyes, which were darting around in an overwhelmed fashion, desperate for some solace to latch onto. Some answer. Kim tried to provide that by gripping her shoulders and harnessing her gaze inside his own. In a weepy voice she pleaded, "What would my Buddy want with someone like that?" There was only one person who could supply an answer, and he was seated on the tweed living room couch with his hands in his lap, staring straight ahead. Kim thought he looked dazed.

Buddy was indeed dazed, foggy-headed, entranced by a magic spell. He remained so for the rest of the night and well into the following day. He felt grateful to Kim for coming over and assuaging his mother's agitation, for staying calm and not persecuting Buddy but simply asking questions. As soon as he left, however, Marianne disappeared inside the thorny bramble of her own mind. She had no problem working herself back into a froth. How could he give out their address? How could he be so careless? Was he trying to get them robbed, or murdered? How many other indigents could she expect to come loiter on their stoop? He shut himself in his room, but that was no escape. Once an hour she would barge in with something new to say, some rehashing of her primary indignation, and the third time she took Buddy's computer, saying she should have confiscated it long ago but that she'd wanted to treat him with a degree of trust and respect. Where had that got her? He did feel guilty, even treacherous, but he had never in a million years expected Cole to show up in the flesh. He'd shared his address for correspondence purposes. Seeing Cole was like a seeing a fictional character appear from a movie, like two worlds which had nothing to do with each other were overlapping, a kind of wormhole effect that created a glitch in Buddy's cognition. He had not felt happy or panicked or anything in between. The numbness set in immediately. It was only as he lay in bed that night, reliving the bizarre confrontation, that it finally formatted to match his other memories, that its texture became defined and he could move through it like a lucid dream. Worry set in. Was he still out there, in Hargrove somewhere? Where had he gone? Would he be picked up by cops? Did he have any money? Before Buddy knew it, the sun was rising behind his curtains, painting them a dull blue, and his eyelids felt sore like their hinges were rusted.

Speaking of lucid dreams, that was his impression of the ensuing school day. Little shards of silver confetti sparkled in his periphery. Colors were dulled. Voices came echoing at him as if through a long brick tunnel. He did not comprehend a single word his teachers said. It was through sheer muscle memory that he made it from class to class, stopping at his locker in between, piling his plastic tray with syrupy peach halves and mini corn dogs come lunchtime. It never had much taste to begin with, but today it seemed even to lack substance, matter, like he was chewing on clouds. He did not think once about his upcoming session with Pastor Kim, so again it must have been muscle memory that conducted him there. For the first time in all the years he'd known this man, this Hargrove personage who was a fixture in Buddy's reality, he saw the pastor's face flush red with anger. It was in response to a quiet declaration made by Buddy himself: "I think, I love him." Kim did not lash out or even raise his voice. The color was subsumed back into his collar, but the tonal quality of his next words definitely took on a flintier, coarser grain. "That's the sickness talking, rest assured. Think, Buddy. Think in the most basic terms. Where would our species be if men married men and women other women? How long do you think that formula would bode well for the human race? Is there any plainer evidence that what you're feeling is wholly unnatural? I don't know how else to convey it to you, the implication of what you're saying . . ." With a trembling hand, the pastor smoothed back a strand of hair which had come loose from his parted bangs. Then he reached into a drawer beneath his desktop, and with visible trepidation, took out a manila folder.

Buddy emerged from the church an hour later, supposing that a small miracle had actually occurred. For a small window of time there, Cole had been evicted from his thoughts, replaced by burning shame and squirming discomfort. "Flip through the pages, Buddy. This is what normal boys your age are peeking at behind closed doors. Sure, it's sinful, vile even. Make no mistake. But God Himself engineered this curiosity so that His children might procreate. The same cannot be said for those aberrations in His kingdom marred by Satan." So that's what he was, Buddy thought. Marred by Satan. As good as possessed. He'd always envisioned those people as tied to bedposts, uttering monstrous depravities, getting showered with holy water by a Catholic priest. Maybe that was just Hollywood, papal propaganda. It stood to reason that Satan would be much sneakier. He crossed the Calvary parking lot and merged onto a wooded bike lane that cut straight through Hargrove, connecting the southern outskirts, downtown, and finally Lake Erie: the docks where Bud, Sr. once worked supporting his wife and son, who by all appearances was perfectly normal. As Buddy passed by a clearing that housed a giant igneous boulder, every square inch of it tagged with graffiti, from its shadow emerged a familiar face. Buddy froze in his tracks.

"–Aren't you happy to see me?" the man asked. They took a few mutual steps forward, until Buddy could smell the sourness of his breath, the staleness of his clothing, the endorphins in his sweat. Cole's eyes kept flitting around, constantly on alert. Then Buddy surprised them both by taking the other's head in his hands and kissing him, kissing him hard on the mouth before he dissolved into tears, pulling away, collapsing against the boulder where he sat cradling his head in his hands. Cole stood there and watched, unable to think or to move. How did he even find me? Buddy wondered, underestimating how much he'd divulged in the course of their DMing, such as the name of his church and what days he visited Kim after school. "I'm in big fucking trouble," Cole said, his voice a lifeless croak that Buddy might not have recognized over the phone. "There's nowhere else for me to go. I need you, Buddy. I wouldn't put you in this position if I didn't need you. I'm dead broke. Fucking homeless. Everything's gone to shit for me . . . What about you?" His words permeated Buddy's jumble of thoughts, but they took a moment to cohere into anything processible. Buddy blinked back hot, prickling tears. He scrubbed the sopping laminate from his cheeks with the back of his hand. The ground between his feet finally came back into focus. He gazed up into the somehow angelic face of this great disruptor who had shot like a meteor into his orbit and thought, the Devil would be this beautiful. But all he said aloud was, "I'll do anything I can to help."

7

Infomercials flashed across the screen, beaming photons into Marianne's haggard gaze. It was the dead of night and there were no other lights on in the house, just this severe bluish composite that swam through the room and at times seemed to assault her with its importunity. On her lap sat an open bag of off-brand sour cream and onion chips. On the cushion beside her, a plastic tray of Chips Ahoy cookies, its foil packaging flayed open like a cadaver in a coroner's office. When her phone began vibrating in her pocket, she had to wipe the grease and crumbs on her sweater before extracting it to read the screen. An unknown number from Wisconsin. She very nearly let it go to voicemail, but some switch inside her flicked at the last second, propelled by loneliness and desperation. She scrambled for the remote, muted the TV, and answered in the nick of time. "What do you want?" she all but whispered. "Thanks for answering," the voice on the line said, "I had a feeling you'd be up." Marianne, with the sharp corner of a chip caught in her throat, repeated her question. "I heard about Buddy," the man said. "Thanks for telling my lawyer."

She wanted in her heart of hearts to call him a scoundrel, a pathetic excuse for a father, a husband. She wanted to summon every scrap of rage she had yet to purge through prayer and lay it at this man's feet, make it his poison, as if pain could ever be that easily transferable. But she was tired, exhausted nearly to the point of transcendence, and hearing Buddy's name said aloud still brought a much -resented flood of tears to her eyes. "Well," she choked. "You didn't leave me much of a choice, did you? I couldn't have you reading about it in the goll-dang paper . . ." Bud, Sr. stayed on the phone and listened to the mother of his child sob for an unknowable stretch of time, because time is unknowable in a vacuum, and depression, especially at night, is a vacuum. The only condolence he could offer was to say her name now and again. It dripped into her like an IV after detouring to some satellite above, transmitting their shared grief. "Marianne . . ." By force of habit, her eyes were still glued on the TV. Mute smiling heads compared their product to lesser retail varieties. How very strange. The thought was in and out of her brain like a single pulse of blood, but there was something unaccountable in it that felt blasphemous.

8

Buddy strode toward the ball diamond in the pitch of night, certain he could feel whatever remained of his soul warring with itself, reducing into smaller and smaller tatters. $1000 was the maximum withdrawal amount per day of his mother's bank ATM. He knew the pin, since she often sent him to run errands with her debit card, like to the grocery store or pharmacy. He wished he could bring more, notwithstanding how great a burden $1000 already was on his con-science. Marianne was not a rich woman by any means, though she was better off now that the divorce had been finalized in her favor, with Bud, Sr. copping the majority of her legal fees and being forced to pay a year's alimony. Still, would she be able to take this betrayal, this icing on a cake baked of so many other disappointments? As he neared the dugout, Buddy could hear the hissss and rattle-rattle-rattle attributed to a spray can. Odd as that struck him, it was less discon-certing than the jocular, carefree voices drifting over from a play-ground fifty yards away. He knew teenagers liked to hang out there after curfew. Doing what exactly? That part was a mystery. Some rite into which Buddy had never been initiated. His shoes crunched over the dead carpet of grass, yet he was able to catch the vandal at the dugout by surprise. "–What are you doing?"

Cole whipped around, stumbled a little from the centrifugal force of this reflex, and balanced himself with his free hand against the block wall. He let out a nervous, wispy laugh that didn't sound to Buddy quite human, more wraith-like, a ghoul's impersonation of human laughter. "Scared the shit out of me, Buddy." "You're vandal-izing the dugout?" "In the city we call it street art." "Where'd you get the paint?" "Someone left their garage open." "I don't understand. Are you trying to get arrested?" This shadow-Cole, outlined in silver threads by the quarter moon, bore little resemblance to the Cole Buddy had known in Milwaukee, the Cole Buddy had kissed. Even earlier that day by the boulder, and yesterday when Cole shook the pillars of the Earth by showing up at his house, Buddy had registered somewhere in the thicket of all his own turmoil that an alteration had taken place. Hard, lean living is what he chalked it up to. After all, Cole did express how he'd fallen on hard times, but didn't much specify beyond that. It never dawned on Buddy until now - the arith-metic never quite fell into place - a certain vulnerable confession

Cole had made the year prior in Milwaukee. He was a recovering addict.

Suddenly Cole's offbeat behavior took on a whole new nefarious import. Buddy didn't know how to broach the issue, but he knew he owed it to his mother to broach it somehow before he handed off her hard-earned money. One of the teenagers at the park let out a woop and now it was Buddy's turn to whip around in surprise. He could see the faint, spectral outline of someone drawing figure-eights in the grass with their bicycle. Uncomfortably close. He hoped that he and Cole were invisible against the wall. Why wasn't Cole in the dugout? Why was he being so reckless? What was he, Buddy, going to do now that an out-of-body judgment of his own actions was focusing ever clearer? Now that he saw himself as naïve, youthful, and accordingly selfish? At the sound of Cole muttering, Buddy turned back to find him slumped against the wall, expounding unintelligibly about someone named Darnell. "Those fucks 're gonna get off scot-free, Buddy. Wait and see. Ain't no justice in this world. I done some bad things, shit, but I ain't ever - there ain't a hateful bone in my body. You feel me? I don't hate those frat fucks. Me, I'm praying for 'em. In my own way. Teach me how to pray, Buddy. Teach me how. Is it something like this?" And he dropped to his knees, pressed his palms together at chest level, tilted his head back, then launched the following statement at full volume toward the sky, "GOD WHY AIN'T THERE NO JUSTICE IN THIS WORLD?"

Buddy lunged forward, clapping a hand over his friend's mouth, but it was all for naught and he knew it. A voice carried back at them from the direction of the playground, "Fuck you!" Cole wrestled free, shoving Buddy in the process, hard enough that his head knocked against the block wall. A delayed pain response went spider-webbing into Buddy's skull. Cole, if he noticed at all, did not acknowledge what he'd done. His next words were, "Say. How much did you get off your old lady?" Reeling, Buddy got to his feet. He put a hand to his hair and it came away wet, but a sniff confirmed it was only paint. "A grand," he heard himself say, though he hadn't meant to answer. It was reflexive in him to be truthful with the people he cared about, even though in hindsight he couldn't think of a single good this had ever done him. "My man!" Cole exclaimed, dusting off his jeans. The spray can lay discarded at his feet. More jeers and taunts floated from the playground. Surely they would be over to investigate, a phalanx of adolescents on bicycles. Buddy hurried to backtrack, to put things right as best he could. He'd made up his mind. Getting his head knocked against concrete had sealed the deal. "You're on drugs again, aren't you?"

This made Cole fall silent for a moment. In fact, the whole world went quiet so simultaneously that Buddy did not trust his ears. He was straining to hear past some woolly obstruction, or so it seemed, until another voice loafing on the jungle gym mimicked Cole by bellowing, "God whyyyy?!" When Cole at last spoke up, it was in the form of a scrambled explanation, more like a leaked inner monologue than an actual response. Buddy tried to hang on. He caught snippets of something about a baby and an overdose and more about this mystery kid, Darnell . . . "You don't understand. How everything just sucks the life out of you, Buddy. This hick-shit town, at least it's quiet. At least I can hear myself think and I can walk down the street and I don't gotta worry about who's fucking turf I'm on, whether I should be selling here, whether I'm being set up. You meet a kid one day, he's dead the next, and most of the time there ain't no fucking candlelight vigil. Most of the time there's no campus-organized kumbaya protest, man, 'cause certain people just don't matter. Certain motherfuckers are lost causes and we all accept that. I accept it! Ma and my old man, they accept it. Hannah accepted it. Little Ree, sweet little Ree, she'll accept it too, quicker than most . . ." And so on in this fashion. Buddy could not make heads or tails of it. Half his attention was delegated to monitoring the approach of the playground crew. Though he couldn't see any indication they were nearing, he sensed them out there like gators in the bayou watching a bass boat trawl past.

Finally he had to interject, cut off Cole's stream of babble and put his foot down. "I can't give you this money. I'll help you all I can. I'll talk to the pastor about some NA or detox or whatever it is you need but I can't give you all this cash. I stole it from my mom. I never stole anything in my life, and I just . . ." But there it was: the whispering synchrony of tires cutting through dry grass, the creak of pedals, the breath of the riders spoiling for any mix-up in their bucolic routines, even if it be something as trite as a man screaming about God and justice at a baseball diamond. Buddy was so caught up in this ancillary dilemma that he almost didn't notice the shape of Cole rushing at him. By the time he did, the first thing he saw was moonlight gleaming on a metal object in Cole's hand.

9

Police were on the scene in ten minutes. A pack of teenagers on bicycles had flagged down an officer parked at a well known speed trap just four blocks away. They'd all told corroborating stories about having witnessed a murder, the first in Hargrove's long peaceful history for as long as anyone could remember. The next day, morning commuters were treated to the sight of police tape encircling the Majerle Park dugout. By the following day it was removed. The killer had been apprehended. Out of reverence, complete strangers to the deceased came and paid their respects, leaving behind candles and flowers and teddy bears and the like. State news crews filmed the touching vigil, interviewed passersby on the street, asked what sort of lessons the people of Hargrove were gleaning from this heinous crime. One interviewee by the name of Peggy Chandler commented, "This awful thing here just validates what we in Hargrove already knew down in our bones. The world is changing and changing fast. Things ain't as innocent as they used to be. We liked to think we were sealed off from it here, that it was just something you watch on the nightly news and think, oh my gosh. But I guess the world's finally caught up to little old Hargrove. Or I don't know, maybe it's the other way around."

A storm swept through later that evening and saturated the baseball diamond, turning it into a mudflat. Pastor Kim tossed and turned in bed, listening to the rain drum on his roof and sluice through his gutters. So as not to wake Gracie with his restlessness, he moved to the living room, cinching his bathrobe tighter, and a brewed a mug of chamomile with a dash of NyQuil to help him sleep. In the meantime he prayed, watching the darkness beyond his picture window, the intermittent pulses of lightning that exposed his neighbor's house like a flasher throwing back his trenchcoat. Thunder seemed to emanate from the bowels of bedrock beneath him rather than the sky above. He made up his mind then and there, which served to ease some of the unconscious tension he was carrying in his neck and shoulders. The next morning, after leaving a message with his secretary that he would be unavailable for much of the morning, he climbed into his Charger and drove west to the Ottawa County Justice Center in Port Clinton.

The process for signing in was quite simple, and he was surprised when an affable sheriff led him to a private room, albeit one monitored by closed-circuit cameras, then asked him to wait while the inmate was delivered. What elapsed was easily the longest five minutes of Kim's life. He'd been allowed to bring in chewing gum and so crammed a tab of Juicy Fruit in his mouth, working it over furiously until his jaw ached, catching a whiff of armpit that notified him he'd sweated through his deodorant. His stiff plastic chair was bolted to the floor, as was the table, so he could not even busy himself with meaningless adjustments. He imagined what it was like being an inmate, to be sitting here waiting for someone to visit him. The walls were cinder block painted butterscotch, the floor an ugly gray mock terrazzo. No exterior windows, just the blue metal door with its little gridwire pane. Wringing his hands beneath the table, he solicited strength and wisdom from his savior. Last night while watching the rain it had seemed so obvious what he would say, but now in the cruel overlit dimensions of this room his tongue was a dry biscuit, his brain a radio caught between frequencies, airing only static. Some commotion outside. The affable sheriff's face was now framed in the window as she opened the door. She ushered inside a young man wearing a navy jumpsuit whose head was slung low, wrists cuffed together.

Kim got to his feet. What he meant to be a full-throated greeting came out as a plea and a whisper. "Buddy." The disparity of seeing a life-long acquaintance, one who had always been mild-mannered, generous, and even a bit pitiful, now done up like prisoner, it reminded Kim of Halloween. After an unrequited embrace owing to the cuffs, they sat across from each other. Buddy didn't say a word beyond "thank you" for the gum, unwrapping the foil from his sweetened strip of food-grade polymers like it was the most precious thing in the world, like he was opening a love letter, taking time to cherish even the rip of the envelope. He was wan in complexion, undernourished, after just two days of cell life. Marianne's divorce lawyer had put them in touch with a Toledo counterpart who specialized in criminal defense. He'd be arriving later that day just in time for Buddy's arraignment where the bail would be set fantastically high. Kim was more or less certain he would be called upon to testify, once the sordid business of articulating the killer's link to the victim was underway. The whole town would be agog. It was sure to be a mortifying fiasco.

"What happened, Buddy? Start to finish. Please. Tell me what you told the police." Buddy allowed himself a few more ruminations of Juicy Fruit before giving the self-evident answer, "It was self-defense. Just like in Jujutsu. I saw the knife and took it away from him." Then he added, with a wry grimace meant to resemble a smile, "Tell Fonzo he saved my life, indirectly." Kim swore he'd pass the message along, trying to summon a degree of warmth, but the obvious follow-up question chilled his bones too badly, stunting the full measure of compassion he wanted to extend. "Why didn't it stop there?" One jab of the knife might have been explained away as knee-jerk, but there were two more to follow. The bicycle teens had reached the juncture where their eyes could focus just in time to see one male driving a knife three times into another, and letting out a wail as he did so. No one saw the disarming. No one could confirm that Cole wielded the knife first. It was Buddy's word against theirs for the time being. Maybe an autopsy report could substantiate his claims, maybe his defense would be able to trace ownership of the knife back to Cole, but none of that would undo the egregiousness of the act itself. And worse yet, Buddy could give no answer. He said he scarcely remembered the attack, that a kind of fog or blind posses-sion had taken hold. Kim believed this, but deep down he knew a jury would not be swayed, that this amnesia would strike them as all too convenient. The two of them sat there wanting to encourage the other but lacking the tools.

"How's Mom?" Buddy asked before the pastor left, when the sheriff outside knocked and flashed them five fingers through the window. "Struggling. But she has her faith. She has the whole church supporting her." "Make sure everyone knows she tried with me." Kim carried those words with him back to his car. Their objectivity compounded their effect. He could smell Buddy's jailhouse musk on his clothes from their opening and closing one-sided embraces. Beneath that he could smell Buddy per se, or the irreducible essence people carry from cradle to grave. Only after observing someone's life in aggregate can it really be disentangled what about them was essential and what about them was social graffiti, so to speak. Only after a flood comes along and purges all but the indelible. Kim already had a fair idea what Buddy's flood would reveal, whether or not it corresponded with how the jury eventually ruled. He sat there in the jail parking lot watching a breeze from nowhere gently rock the silver cross hooked on his rearview mirror. As for his own flood, he worried its verdict might also hinge on the trial to come.

Missed

ARAMIS CALDERON

⁓❖⁓

Beyond the cracked sidewalk, and the telephone pole with layers of flyers in a rainbow of colors, and the patch of dry brown grass there stood a ten-foot high concrete block wall, caked with dozens of coats of paint. There was a small shrine at the foot of it, with burnt out candles and dead flowers and a few soggy teddy bears. One word of graffiti filled the wall, red letters on a gold background: Rejoice!

I knew the pastor meant well but it was spin. The community church was trying to make a shitty situation look like good news. The plain fact was Terry, barely seven, got shot by a stray bullet here in broad daylight. His father, Sergio, was my friend and he hadn't re-joiced.

Sergio had been missing for three days now. His lady, Karla, was bereft and in a deep depression; worried sick over the father of her dead boy. The gas station where he worked as a mechanic didn't know where he was. We'd given up and some of us prayed for him to return, but then at a Recovery meeting this morning Sergio's spon-sor, Gee, had said he heard one of the old dealers saw him here in Little Havana, around Seventeenth Avenue Southwest. This made sense to us because it's where his son was killed and his old stomping ground. Addicts usually came back to the places they used to get high.

Gee gently placed a fresh teddy bear next to the old ones. The stuffed animal had a soft baseball glove stitched to its left hand. He took out a pack of Newports from his pocket and placed one on his lips. His lighter had the NA emblem and the tattoo on his smoking arm had the serenity prayer written in an elegant script. Terry had loved baseball.

I took out my phone and took a picture of the place where Terry was murdered senselessly. I had taken an interest in watching the toys and graffiti grow around this spot. He was a popular boy in the neighborhood.

After a deep drag Gee turned to me and said, "Alright Scooter, across the street is where he was spotted crossing, after going to the liquor store," he shook his head and the minty smoke blew out of his nostrils. It was understandable he had relapsed, but difficult for me to hear. I needed to make sure Sergio was OK and let him know we would help.

I looked around the busy street. Humidity and heat made everyone drive with their windows up and the AC on. There was already traffic this late in the morning, but it was a Saturday, and Miami after all. The storefronts, pawn shops and bodegas, had old graffiti. In this town, there were at least five liquor stores on the way to any halfwayhouse. I said, "Let's go."

I ran in front of the slow-moving cars to get across. Car horns blared, and Gee flipped them all off. He had a majestic middle finger, easily as thick and long as a Cuban cigar. When Gee gave you the finger, you felt it in your soul.

Coming from the south side of Chicago, Gee's real name was Gordon, but his street name had been G-Money. In his recovery he went by Gee, and he'd been clean and sober for close to nine years. He'd been a crack addict and a pimp before becoming a manager at a McDonald's. He said there wasn't much difference between managing a fast food joint and managing a stable of whores. This man was also the most devout Christian I knew.

Together we moved west, towards Twenty-Second Avenue in a section of run down single-family homes. The style of construction was old art deco, faded turquoise paint decorated windows and doorframes, all blocky and tacky. I was looking for one that was two stories high and found it. The address numbers were missing and a post without a mailbox stood like a decapitated man. There was a condemned notice visible from the street. I knew this was the place Sergio would go because he told me he grew up in the tallest house of this neighborhood. "We're here Gee."

The property had a rusted chain link fence surrounding it no taller than the average Cuban. Gee pointed at the broken lock hanging limp on the gate, "How'd Serg open that lock?" He threw the butt of his cigarette on the cracked sidewalk.

I opened the gate and stepped through the invisible property line. "His boss said some tools were missing since he took off. Probably took a bolt cutter with him." I was worried about some nosy old lady calling the cops on a pair of guys, a black guy and a trashy looking gringo trespassing.

Gee said, "He probably sold the rest for a rock," but Sergio was a capital H kind of guy and not crack. Gee disappeared around the corner of the house to check out the sides. My phone buzzed in my pocket. It was Karla, but I didn't want to answer her right away.

After checking the next-door houses and across the street for anyone looking, I judged this was probably not the place with a neighborhood watch captain. Every house in sight was also abandoned and boarded up. I went for the door, but it was locked and wasn't busted in by Sergio.

Gee came back and said, "There's a broken window," and he moved back away. I followed him and checked the text message from Karla. Scooter have you seen him? It was the same message she had sent twenty times before since we told her we were looking for him.

We came in through the window. The sour stench of mold overpowered us. It was dark and took us a long second to get our phones out. Roaches the size of hamsters scurried from my phone's flashlight. The paint, where there wasn't missing drywall, was peeling, and the humidity had rusted every piece of visible metal.

Gee's phone illuminated a staircase in the back of what used to be the living room. He covered his mouth with a durag and marched forward. I followed him, and we looked at each other and the moldy wood boards. I put some weight on the first step, and it felt sturdy. I went up and Gee followed a few seconds behind.

At the top of the landing, a collapsible ladder lay on its side. It was too new to belong here; the plastic sleeve of the aluminum steps was barely scratched. Gee pointed at the ceiling and where the roof access was. It was rimmed with black mold. We set up the ladder and I went up first again.

The hot sunlight and street smells of car exhaust and stagnant puddles came as a welcome relief. The roof had pigeon shit and sagged in some parts, but otherwise looked safe enough to walk on. I stood, let my eyes adjust and helped Gee up.

There were no vents or antenna dishes. Sergio was laying on his back and looked to be asleep. "Sergio, wake up," I said as I walked carefully towards him. In a few steps I saw that his usual tanned leather skin was a pale grey. There wasn't going to be another time to watch a ball game or talk about my sobriety with him again. The world was emptier now. Gee was calling out the Lord's name over and over.

Sergio had no pulse. He was not breathing. His skin was dirty and cold. I was startled by the vibration of a text notification in my pocket. Gee started to pray in words I did not hear. I ignored Karla's message.

Sergio was still wearing what he wore at his son's wake, but his shoes were missing. The soles of his feet were black from walking the streets. The clothes were tattered and dirty from the he time spent in the street. His hand clutched an iodine colored bottle of Oxycontin that had a mangled label. I pried it from his fingers and realized stiffness from death hadn't set in. He's only been dead a few hours.

Around and below us the neighborhood reminded me of Sergio's dead body. Marlins Park loomed two blocks away. Tomorrow it would be packed with fans rooting for the team and drinking and fighting and shouting. Not one will realize what happened to my friend so close by or wonder why there is a state of the art ball park next to condemned and rotted houses.

Near the ballpark I saw the community church that had made the shrine for Terry. There was a crowd gathered in front. Everyone looked so small from here, far away. The pastor was bringing what looked like a kid to the front of the crowd. I could tell it was his boy, because they both wore matching suits. The pastor's son was a bully of Terry's.

The kid got up onto a milk crate and raised his hand. A murmur went through the crowd and then it fell silent, except for a few people shouting words of encouragement at him. The kid acknowledged them with a nod and a shy smile. In the full light of day, he looked less angry and more beautiful. He waited until people stopped shouting. A siren could be heard, maybe five or ten blocks away. The kid raised the bullhorn, pressed the button, and began to speak.

I understood nothing. The crowd held their arms up as if receiving deliverance. I felt the phone again, Karla was waiting for an answer. I held the phone in one hand, Sergio's pill bottle in the other. I said, "Gee, what do we do now?"

He took out his phone and stopped dialing to look at the church crowd. "We gotta call the paramedics, Scooter. They take the body to the morgue. I'll tell Karla," his eyes were red, and his thick silver bracelet rattled from the shakes in his hands, "Damn. Shit. I don't want to tell her…"

"I'll do it." I typed out we found him but didn't hit send yet. Gee was sniffing real hard, but he kept cool. I put my away my phone and searched Sergio's body for anything else. His wallet was gone, but he had a picture in his right pocket. It was from the last NA picnic. Sergio, Karla, and Terry were smiling and happy in front of the picnic table in Haulover Beach park.

Gee cleared his throat and spoke to the 911 operator. "Yes hello, I found someone. He's my friend. He's dead. He OD'd." A subwoofer from a car pounded a low hum followed by a heavy vibrating sound. "No, we didn't do CPR…we found him like this…he was in recovery…yes ma'am." He placed his hand on the body's chest and grabbed his shirt in his fist. Gee's face was contorted into a grimace and his eyes shut hard.

I hit send on the message to Karla. She's lost everything now. She's going to relapse I think for the first time since she got sober, fifteen years last Christmas. There's nothing to be done about it, and I don't believe anyone could blame her. She messaged back, how is he?

Gee took his hand slowly from Sergio's still chest and rubbed it on his. He continued to speak to the operator, "We're at 1433 Northwest Fourteenth Court, on the roof…where we found him… yes we'll stay right here…no thank you, have a blessed day."
He got up and walked to the edge of the roof, facing Marlins Park. Gee lit up another Newport. I could barely hear him because he didn't turn to look at me. "They'll be here in thirty minutes. Probably be more like forty-five."

I put the picture in my pocket. I checked him again. His wedding ring was gone. All his things were gone. All he had was an empty prescription bottle and the anchor tattoo he had on his hand. Karla had a matching one on her hand.

My phone rang. It was her. An arm's length away I saw a pebble that looked too perfect. It was one of Sergio's pills. It had somehow remained dry and must have fallen out of the bottle when he had downed the whole monthly prescription. Gee was still turned away. I put it in my pocket and turned my phone off.

Gee's phone rang a minute later. He still didn't look to me. He said, "It's Karla. Scooter I thought you were going to tell her," my stomach fluttered, and I focused on what to do next. I tried to forget what I just did without thinking.

I said, "We can't leave him up here." Gee's puffed up face finally turned to me, flicked his half-finished smoke over the ledge, and he turned his phone off. I said, "Let's at least take him down to the front yard." I stood and hooked my hands under Sergio's arms to drag him to the access hole.

My old friend Sergio was not small. He was a stocky Cuban man. He made his living before sobriety going to sea, fishing for marlins. Gee came to his legs and lifted. Together we carried him around the soft spots of the roof to where we had come up.

We sat his body, his legs dangled over the moldy edge of the entrance. Of the two of us, Gee was the strongest, so he went down first into the dark house. I held Sergio upright in an embrace. He smelled like his cologne and street and death.

When Gee was ready I lowered him as best I could. I have never been strong, and I was a legal clerk in my dark days, so I didn't have the muscles to make this easy. I tried but I had to drop Sergio and hope he was caught.

I heard a thud and a curse from the darkness below. Gee was pissed. I said, "I'm sorry." It was quiet down there for a long pause and then I heard, "Don't be sorry, be careful." That was what Sergio used to say to us.

I came down the ladder and I couldn't even see my hand if it was in front of my face. A brightness came from Gee and his phone light was strong enough to glow from within his shirt pocket. It was in his left pocket and he looked like those pictures of Jesus with the flame coming from his heart.

He pushed me out of the way a little roughly and lifted Sergio from his upper half. This time I grabbed his legs. I went down the stairs first and I heard the wood of the steps moan. We breathed through our mouths. I heard a crunch from under my foot, and I knew that was from a roach.

When we got to the bottom, we headed for the window we came in through. I said, "Why don't we go out the front door?" Gee shrugged and didn't know which way was the front. I peered at the darkness of the hallway we had just come from; the light of the phone was unable to break through. I moved toward that part. "I think it's this way."

We walked in the dark surrounded by decay and rot; two addicts, one dead friend, and one opioid pill. I bumped into the door just before I was going to lose my nerve. The deadbolt was sticky, but it turned and when I opened the door my eyes hurt.

Together we stepped into the sun and laid our friend down. We took deep breaths and leaned on each other. Sergio looked somehow better now away from the house. Sirens interrupted our moment of rest, but it wasn't the ambulance for us.

Gee said, "I'm going to go and look out for the paramedics." He lit up another cigarette and went to the corner of the street to look for the emergency personnel. His tightly braided hair was frazzled from the exertion of moving Sergio.

I turned my phone back on. Messages, voice, text, and missed calls flooded my display. She was freaking out. Is he okay? and call me now. Even while I was reading them, more came. I gave up and called her. I hung up before the first ring.

Sergio's shirt was opened from the carrying and his hairy chest still had faint tan lines, light grey and slightly lighter grey. I reached into my pocket for a half empty pack of Camel Wides and felt the pill. The one he had missed.

Gee was still smoking on the corner of the street looking out. The neighborhood street was still empty, and the houses were locked up tight. No one lived here anymore. Just roaches and addicts. My friend here told us in meetings how unhappy he was in this home and how he wanted very much for his son to have a happier childhood. He said this thought kept him sober.

In one hand I had one of the pills that killed my friend, in the other the desperate messages of a widow and mother of a dead son. It was just one pill. I needed it. Just one. I took it and waited for the tired calm it provided. I called Karla.

Greysteel

KYLE CALDWELL

⁌

Beyond the cracked sidewalk, and the telephone pole with layers of flyers in a rainbow of colors, and the patch of dry brown grass there stood a ten-foot high concrete block wall, caked with dozens of coats of paint. There was a small shrine at the foot of it, with burnt out candles and dead flowers and a few soggy teddy bears. One word of graffiti filled the wall, red letters on a gold background: Rejoice!

A small crowd of Catholics stood silent before the wall, their faces held still and bitter beneath the stinging October wind. For the third morning in a row they had awoken to this identical provocation scrawled in red across the narrow portion of wall that divided the Lower Falls from the neighboring Shankill Road. Before the Troubles, a one-lane road had there connected the Catholic and Protestant neighborhoods, but since its construction last summer, the wall had turned the road into a shallow dead-end. And since the events of last week, the dead-end had become a roadside memorial to a murdered six-year-old boy.

The old shopkeeper made towards his store across the way to collect a bucket of paint and return to once again cover over the morning's graffiti. But before he had gone a step, the young mother at the front of the crowd raised her hand and signaled him to stop. He watched with the rest of the crowd as she stepped forward and approached the small shrine at the foot of the wall. She knelt down and removed the dead flowers that leaned against the letters and prayer cards and replaced them with the fresh ones she had in her hand. She retrieved a matchbook from the apron pocket beneath her coat and relit the burnt out candles and said a silent prayer as she made the sign of the cross in front of her chest.

Her boy had been dribbling a football on that shallow drive in front of the wall when a regiment of Royal Ulster Constabulary arrived in Shorland armored cars and opened fire on a block of adjacent flats with Browning machine guns. They were retaliating against the bombing of a loyalist pub on Shankill that they claimed Lower Falls nationalists had been responsible for. When the shooting had finished, the boy had been struck through the neck by a ricochet and, staring up at a sheet metal sky, had died alone on the cold and wet concrete of that dead-end street.

The mother rose from the shrine and turned to face the crowd. Wisps of hair, dark honey and barley, escaped from underneath her wool shawl and fell across her face. Cherrywood irises sat behind sharp angular features like a blooming orchard out of reach behind an iron gate. She had clear skin and pouty lips and a few light freckles dusted the end of her nose. She was still quite young, despite having mothered four boys.

The priest watched the mother from the back of the crowd and thought she resembled some kind of Hellenic marble sculpture. Smooth and cool and stoic almost to the point of vacancy. It was the same expression he had offered guidance to when he presided over her husband's wake last winter. But the face held more depth today. More scope. A simmering rage, silent and nihilistic. Like a burnt out wick bleeding black smoke.

"Leave it be," the mother finally said to the shopkeeper. "'Tis a talisman now. Always pointing north. These loyalists..." She stared off. "First me husband. Now me youngest. Both ends of me life cut short." She raised her head tall and searched the eyes of the crowd. "I'm going to find the Orangie bastard who did this and I'm going to kill 'im meself. And if any of yous know a damn thing about it, you had best come clean or so help me God, I'll be coming for yous when I'm done. Three nights in a row and not a peeper on this Proddy? Impossible."

The mother turned around and stared into the blood red graffiti, the dead flowers of yesterday still hanging from her hand. The morning slid into a lighter shade of grey and a faint police siren rang out beyond the horizon, the echo of muted gunfire close behind it.

The mother turned back around and faced the neighborhood. "They want me to rejoice?" She stared up into the dim Belfast skyline beyond the crowd, cut straight and clean by the uniform brickwork of the rooftops and chimneys and telephone poles that held dead power lines. "Well, then, so be it. God as me witness and true as me aim, I shall rejoice yet."

Over a breakfast of porridge and marmalade toast, the mother asked her three eldest boys if they had heard any rumors over the past few days or thought any classmates at school responsible for the vandalism of their departed brother's shrine. They ate by candlelight, the small kitchen window letting in little of the grey morning light and the fixtures providing none at all due to the Lower Falls power outage.

Her oldest was a shy and thoughtful boy, now twelve, who avoided confrontation at all costs, but the mother believed him when he said he had not heard anything nor suspected anyone in his class of the vandalism. She stared at her other two boys from across the table. Nine-year-old twins, their faces softly lit by the candles in front of them, their bright sweet eyes retreating with guilt. "Out with it," said the mother and the twins sheepishly glanced over at their older brother. "Papa told us never to sell out yer own," said one of the twins. The mother looked at her oldest with bated disappointment, but he stared back at her with genuine confusion about what his little brothers were getting at.

The mother reassured the twins that they were not in any trouble and after a moment, taking comfort in one another, the twins took turns explaining that they had seen their older brother walking a 'Proddy' girl home to Shankill Road two days ago, carrying her schoolbooks for her. The mother softened and asked her oldest if it was true. "She came to the wake last week," he said, lowering his head and talking into his chest. "Her name is Greta. She wouldn't do that."

The mother recalled the dusk so many years ago when she had kissed their father for the first time. Plum and tangerine streaked the sky, the two lovers lost in each other in the tall grass of the moorland on the slope of Divis. He had brushed back the hair that blew over her face and held her cheek, the air between them electric, their shallow breath sharp with Bushmill's. The mother smiled and looked across the table at her oldest and hoped his first kiss would be as sweet.

After walking her boys to school, the mother stopped by the grocery to pick up a few items. She greeted the old shopkeeper and a dockworker he was chatting with as she entered the store and noticed the dockworker had a large bruise under his eye and a freshly split lip. "Still having donnybrooks down at the yard, then?" asked the mother, disinterested. The dockworker glanced at her over his shoulder as she passed, his eyes sullen and defeated. "Something like that, mum." He threw a few quid on the counter, bid farewell to the shopkeeper, and quickly exited the store with his bag of groceries under his arm. The mother watched him as he passed by the shop window outside, his face fragile and ashamed, and she turned to the shopkeeper. "What the hell was that?" The shopkeeper cleared his throat and began wiping down the spotless countertop. "It's nothing, mum. Leave the man be."

The mother stormed out of the shop and called down the street for the dockworker to return. The man glanced back at her, but continued on, disappearing down a street corner. "Mum, please. There's no need for that," said the shopkeeper, following her out of the store. "What's with all the cloak and dagger then?" asked the mother. "He looked like he swallowed the god damn canary." The shopkeeper held up his arms in a gesture of peace. "It's got nothing to do with your boy, mum. I promise. I know the man." The mother narrowed her eyes and searched the shopkeeper's face and saw that he was true. She exhaled and calmed herself and looking off, noticed a bullhorn standing upright on one of the overturned milk crates in front of the store. The shopkeeper looked at it and shrugged and said that an RUC officer had left it behind after a regiment came through the neighborhood a few weeks ago while enforcing the curfew. He thought it best to leave it out, lest the Ulster's come back looking for it. After a moment, he held out his arm and followed behind the mother as she made her way back into the store to complete her shopping.

The chandelier fixtures above the nave of the dark cathedral strobed weakly with the struggling power and it was several minutes after she arrived before the mother realized that she was not alone. Sitting upon the chancel, the kid from Greysteel read the Catechism by candlelight, studying for a potential life with the church. But feeling the mother's eyes upon him, he raised his head and stared hard at her from across the cathedral. From where she stood, his eyes shone malevolent, white points of light hiding within twin black alcoves.

She knew very little about him, only that the priest of the cathedral had brought him back to Belfast after visiting the small village of Greysteel last month. But the kid had nevertheless impressed upon the mother that he was an angry and distrustful boy, if only by the joyless expression he constantly wore.

The priest emerged from the vestibule and greeted the mother at the votive stand and joined her in lighting a candle for her boy. She closed her eyes and made the sign of the cross and said a silent prayer. The priest glanced up at the murals painted on the ceiling of the ancient cathedral, one of the oldest buildings in the city, and asked the mother to sit with him a moment. "I have not seen you here in some time," said the priest. The mother did not respond. "I'd have supposed you'd be in need of guidance, mum. Has your faith not been shaken?" "It's a sin to doubt God," said the mother. The priest smiled. "Tis no sin at all. Tis the requisite of a good Catholic." The mother looked to the front of the cathedral. Candlelight cast an exaggerated shadow of the kid from Greysteel over the massive crucifix on the altar behind him. Christ shrouded in darkness.

"Perhaps you are unaware the depths of your faith, mum. You light a candle so that God may receive your boy." The mother looked over at the votive stand. "I was asking for me boy's forgiveness," she said. The priest felt a deep pity in his heart, but looking up into the mother's eyes, seeing them flicker hotly in the candlelight, unrepentant, he realized he had misunderstood her and became unnerved. "What deed are you planning, mum?" She did not respond. "You mustn't set down a path you can't come back from. Nihilism be the road to ruin. You must align yourself with the path though you cannot see the way." The mother rose from the pew and stared at the colossal crucifix above the altar, and at the vacant chancel the kid from Greysteel had disappeared from. "Look around ye, Father," she said, pulling her wool shawl over her head, recalling her dead husband once intimating that the IRA was storing weapons in the basement of the cathedral. "Belfast be the road to ruin."

In just a few days, paranoia had swept through the Lower Falls. The mother had begun launching accusations at everyone she encountered, trying to provoke a telling response, and becoming extremely belligerent with anyone she suspected of hiding anything. A toxic atmosphere of anxiety and dread rolled through the streets like a fog and as the centre-piece to it all, the blood-red "Rejoice!" remained, an accusatory finger perpetually pointing at any neighbor brave enough to glance at it. But despite the mother's passionate and thorough inquest, nothing of consequence had been unearthed. Nothing until a midwife came knocking upon her door.

The midwife had heard a rumor at the Mater Hospital where she worked that a local Lower Falls millwright had been spotted in the vicinity of the shrine on all three nights prior to the vandalism. The midwife was bashful and timid and did not want to get involved with the mother's witch hunt, but felt that the best way to extricate herself was to come clean with what she had overheard. The mother, in fact, knew the millwright the midwife spoke of. A large burly man with a thick chestnut beard streaked evenly with grey that lived just two streets over from her. More importantly, the mother knew that the millwright came from a Protestant family. That evening, the mother tracked the millwright to a crowded nationalist pub off of Falls Road and watched as the man ordered a shot of Irish and a pint of porter and drank alone at the end of the bar. And as the millwright lit a cigarette and took a drag, the mother saw on the sleeve of his olive-green parka the unmistakable stain of red paint.

Dawn lingered beneath the horizon and bruised the sky a Prussian blue. The millwright locked his small loft, greasy coveralls beneath his parka, metal lunch pail in hand, and began on his way to work. He walked through the streets slick with morning frost and sang "The Wind That Shakes the Barley" under his breath, the cold air crisp in his lungs. He passed by the shopkeeper's grocery and by the dead-end street and glanced at the graffiti still bright on the concrete wall whereupon he heard the mother call out his name. The mill-wright turned around and saw the young mother standing in the mid-dle of the street with a Webley .38 revolver at her side. The mother had risen while it was still dark in order to catch the millwright be-fore work and had made no effort to conceal the revolver while on her way to him. A handful of Lower Falls residents, shift-workers and nursing mothers and the restless others who were awake at that early hour, had watched the mother drift with purpose down the street like a grim spectre lost in limbo, sickle at her side.

The millwright stared at the revolver, a cool detachment on his face, before looking up at the mother. "I know it was you," said the mother, but the millwright did not respond. "What's on yer sleeve there, then?" The mother gestured at the right cuff of his parka. He raised his cuff and saw the red stain and shrugged. "A donnybrook at the pub the other night," said the millwright. "Some yardie with a smart yapper." The mother narrowed her eyes and gripped the re-volver tighter. "You must take me for a fool. If that were blood, it would have dried black by now." She pointed at the graffiti at the end of the shallow drive. "Twas you!"

By now a small group of neighbors had started to coalesce, the gossip of the early-risers having spread like wildfire. The mother turned to the growing crowd. "Have any of yous seen this Proddy bastard get into any tussle at any pub of late?" No one answered. "Ask the man yerself, mum," said the millwright. "The dockworker. Why would I deface your boy's shrine?" The mother raised the revolver at him. "To rejoice! One less Catholic, the better. You've got the albatross hanging from yer bloody neck." The millwright glanced down at the wooden cross that hung out above his shirt. Unlike the ornamental golden crucifixes that Catholics wore, his was the simple and understated totem of the Protestant.

The priest and the kid from Greysteel arrived on the scene and watched from a spot in front of the grocery. The mother held the gun tight on the millwright. "We should have ran you down long ago. A fox upon the heath." The millwright took a step towards her, but stopped when the mother cocked the hammer of the revolver and held it upon him. The crowd held their breath, only the whistling of the dawn wind between them, as the kid from Greysteel struggled to see from behind the encumbrances of the bodies. The crowd began to launch parrying slurs at the mother, some egging her on, some pleading her to stop, and the kid grew outraged with the growing hysteria. He began shouting himself, begging the crowd to listen to him, and found the bullhorn resting on the milk crate in front of the shop. The priest saw him going for the bullhorn and he began yelling at the crowd as well, imploring them to listen, and one-by-one the rows of onlookers turned around and faced the front of the shop.

The kid got up onto a milk crate and raised his hand. A murmur went through the crowd and then it fell silent, except for a few people shouting words of encouragement at him. The kid acknowledged them with a nod and a shy smile. In the full light of day, he looked less angry and more beautiful. He waited until people stopped shouting. A siren could be heard, maybe five or ten blocks away. The kid raised the bullhorn, pressed the button, and began to speak.

"Stop! Please, all of you. Stop. Look around." The crowd became aware of themselves. The mother looked over at the kid as well, but continued holding the revolver upon the millwright. "This bloodshed, the chaos – we are all God's children," said the kid. "Catholics and Protestants alike. All paths to the same light."

The kid looked directly at the mother and lowered the bullhorn. In the hushed silence, the police siren receding, the morning light ashen, he raised his voice and spoke directly to her. "The utility, mum. Omega. Will killing this man or all the men on Shankill Road or all the Protestants in Belfast – will that bring your son back? Will it make you feel any better at all? If you cannot see the good, please, at least stop pushing the bad forward. Cut off the sins that pull ye down, mum, and you cannot but ascend."

The mother and the kid stared at one another, the crowd around them dissolving. Her face tightened like a clenched fist, contorting, hard and ugly. Simmering with hatred towards the millwright, the Proddy's, the world. And underneath that, at the basest level, towards the kid himself for cracking the onyx walls of her perfectly constructed mausoleum.

"I've seen you, mum. In the cathedral. Around the neighborhood." That same familiar expression fell across the kid's face and the mother finally realized that it was not distrust, not malevolence that so colored the light behind his eyes. It was disappointment. "This is not you."

"And what would ye know?" said the mother, defiant and raw, the revolver still tight upon the millwright. "I'm sorry to tell you, son, but all yer good intentions don't mean a thing. Not out here. Not in Belfast – that black spot upon the heart of God's country. Perhaps it's time ye went back home."

A low rumble simmered through the crowd. The mother looked around. "What? We've all suffered here, have we not? Every one of us in this city. Our sons, husbands, cousins, fathers. All cut down.

And this here kid starts on about peace? Trying to rob me of me retribution." The mother looked back at the kid from Greysteel. "What suffering could ye possibly have endured?"

A single gasp cut through the air and the crowd grew still. The millwright removed his cap. The mother looked around again, perplexed and irritated with her ostensible ignorance. The old shopkeeper broke away from the crowd and mercifully approached the mother and whispered in her ear. "Mum, that boy is the orphan from the Lough Foyle Massacre."

On the outskirts of Greysteel, upon a sloping hillside that overlooked the icy water of the Lough Foyle estuary, a small farmhouse sat black against a moonless sky. A dark Volvo sped along the empty waterside road, turned up the muddy access that led onto the farm, and shut off its headlights as it continued towards the house. The three Provisional IRA in the Volvo pulled balaclavas over their heads as the car stopped in front of the farmhouse. The two passengers got out of the car and the driver turned a full arc to face where he had come in and left the motor running. The two masked passengers separated and flanked the farmhouse on opposite sides and paused to light the Molotov cocktails in their hands.

The family slept soundly inside, totaling ten: a Protestant husband, his Catholic wife, and their eight children. Persecuted by the townspeople for marrying a Catholic, the husband had learned to isolate himself from village affairs. But when one of his sons was badly beaten up at school for who his mother was, the husband sought an unorthodox remedy. Instead of retaliation, the husband made the strategic decision to allow the loyalist Ulster Volunteer Association to train on his sprawling hillside property and just like that, inside of a week, as he had hoped, his family and him began to feel increasingly more welcomed by the small Greysteel community.

The youngest son awoke in the middle of the night and tip-toed to the washroom. He relieved himself and flushed and as he made his way back down the short hall to his bedroom, he heard a window shatter in his parents' room. Startled, he turned around and began towards their door but heard an identical crash inside his sisters' room. Within moments, the boy heard family members on both sides of the house begin to panic and scream and heard the knocking over of furniture and kerosene lamps and the roar of accelerating fire and saw silver smoke begin to escape from the cracks beneath the doors. Three of his brothers emerged from their shared room and saw the burning doors and grabbed quilts and pillows and tried to extinguish the fire while screaming for the youngest to get out of the house.

The two masked IRA outside ran to the waiting Volvo and jumped inside and the car sped down the muddy access and onto the roadway where it turned on its headlights and drove off into the night. Behind the farmhouse, the boy fell hard onto the cold ground beneath the bathroom window and quickly ran around to the front of the house. Flames devoured the facade, exploding out of the front windows, black smoke merging into the void beyond the light above the house. The kid cried out for his mother and father and brothers and sisters and watched as the roof of the farmhouse collapsed in on itself. When the fire brigade did finally arrive, they found the kid catatonic, his small body silhouetted against the flames, his gaze vacantly pitched down the hillside towards the sprawling abyss of the icy black lough.

The kid from Greysteel stood stoic atop the milk crate, the bullhorn at his side. The mother became overwhelmed with embarrassment and felt the ground shift beneath her. She looked over at the mill-wright, cap in his hand, and back at the kid, finally lowering the revolver in her hand. Staring deep into misty cherrywood, the kid spoke. "I wrote 'Rejoice,' mum."

The crowd swallowed their breath. The kid stepped off the milk crate and set the bullhorn down and walked towards the mother. She stared with incredulity as he drifted to her and took her free hand and fearlessly disregarded the revolver in her other. He closed his eyes and read a selection of Romans he had committed to memory.

"We rejoice in hope of the glory of God. Not only that, but we rejoice in our sufferings, knowing that suffering produces endurance, and endurance produces character, and character produces hope, and hope does not put us to shame, because God's love has been poured into our hearts through the Holy Spirit who has been given to us."

The kid smiled bright, his eyes still closed. "Do not despair, mum. You will see your boy again." He opened his eyes and looked up into the searching confusion and vulnerability of the young mother in front of him. "You remind me of my own mother, ye know."

The mother pulled her hand away from the kid and stepped back, her face sinking and grey, becoming acutely aware of the embarrassed crowd around her. She looked down at the revolver in her hand and delicately uncocked the hammer and slid the gun into her coat pocket. And without another word, the mother turned back to where she had come from and walked home.

❋

Over the following days, the Lower Falls returned to normalcy and the ghosts of suspicion and distrust evaporated. The concrete wall continued to blaze 'Rejoice,' but in light of the revelation made by the kid from Greysteel, the graffiti had become a source of pride.

The mother still visited the shrine daily, still lit a candle for her boy, but she allowed her heart to soften when she did and very slowly, she shifted her focus away from the death of her youngest and onto the life of her three eldest. The days turned into weeks and the weeks into months and the mother found hope and wonder in the eyes of her sons and in the kid from Greysteel, and that boney fist that had so tightly held her heart gradually relinquished its grip. Thereafter, whenever she thought of her youngest, though the pain lingered, she was warmed by the memory of his sweet face and his mellifluous voice and at times, even allowed herself to rejoice.

Buds sat pregnant at the tips of the trees that hung over the atrium of the cathedral as faint sunrays cut through the overcast sky. The devout residents of the Lower Falls poured out of the front of the church into the warming spring air, black crosses on their foreheads, the day's first recipients of that year's Ash Wednesday blessings. The mother stayed behind after the ceremony to say a prayer and light a candle and emerged outside as the priest was saying goodbye to the last of the retreating parishioners on the steps of the cathedral.

"It's nice to see you back on the path, mum," smiled the priest. The mother smiled back and, looking around, inquired where the kid from Greysteel was, as he typically was never far from the priest's side. "He'll be back for the mid-morning blessings. A man from the neighborhood – the millwright, actually, that you... he takes the boy up to the pitch to play football on his days off. Been spending time with him ever since I brought the boy back from Greysteel. The man lost a child himself, ya know." The mother stared off, looking out towards the river that cut through the city, and felt ashamed. She had not known.

Walking home from the cathedral, the mother ran into the dock-worker and, having not addressed it since, she apologized for her outburst in the shop back in October. The dockworker was gracious and receptive and told the mother that she need not apologize for her grief. "Yer a good man," she said. "I find most things be settled with a pint and a chat, mum," said the dockworker, smiling, and he took her hand and patted it in reassurance. The mother was relieved and smiled in return. "Suppose someone should have told that to the millwright back then, huh?"

The dockworker looked at the mother with confusion and asked her what she was talking about. "'Twas only a joke," she said. "Yer split lip and black eye back in the fall. The millwright struck you in the pub." The dockworker pulled back and his expression soured. "I was never hit by no millwright in no pub." His eyes shone fragile and delicate like razor thin glass. "My wife... the booze gets on her bones and sometimes she... for Christ's sake, mum, don't you ever let dogs lie?" The dockworker turned on his heels and stormed off down the street.

The mother knew the dockworker's wife. A large and fiery wom-an who had been captain of the Falls rugby team. The mother stood for some time, replaying the events of October in her mind, uncer-tainty flooding into the hull. Someone was lying to her. Was it the dockworker or the millwright? She once again became frustrated by her own ignorance. By the fact that she had been made a fool of. She thought a moment more before she turned around and headed back to the cathedral.

The priest had retired to the anteroom at the back of the church to prepare for the mid-morning ceremony and the parishioners who had missed the early service had begun to congregate on the cathe-dral steps. The mother entered the church and searched for the kid from Greysteel. She told herself that if the kid could promise her that it was indeed him that had vandalized the concrete wall all three nights, then she would disregard the anomaly the dockworker had presented and put the vendetta behind her once and for all. Unable to find him inside, the mother returned to the front of the cathedral and there found the kid from Greysteel ushering the parishioners into the church. She approached him and told him that she had something urgent to discuss, but the kid insisted on finishing his seminary obligations and said he would join her on the bench in the courtyard beside the cathedral as soon as he had finished.

The final parishioners entered the cathedral and the bell tower struck the hour, causing a swath of pigeons to frantically disperse from the belfry. The mother glanced up as the escaping pigeons threw shadows over her eyes and she was hit with a twinge of melancholy and all at once became aware of the emptiness of the courtyard around her. She rose quickly and returned to the front of the church.

At the bottom of the steps of the cathedral, a white Volkswagen van screeched to a halt and a man in a balaclava jumped out of the side door. The mother watched in numb disbelief as the man galloped up the steps, pulled the large door of the cathedral open, and tossed a small package inside. He pulled the heavy door closed and the mother glimpsed the red stain on the sleeve of his olive-green parka and watched in horror as the kid from Greysteel raced down the steps with the man and climbed into the waiting van. The last thing the mother saw before the pipe bomb ripped open the bowels of the cathedral was the kid from Greysteel staring back at her from inside the Volkswagen, his eyes unmistakably malevolent, a wooden Protestant cross swinging below his neck.

Paper Ocean, Paper Forest, Paper Sun

BY TRAVIS DAHLKE

·❦·

Beyond the cracked sidewalk, and the telephone pole with layers of
flyers in a rainbow of colors, and the patch of dry brown grass there
stood a ten-foot high concrete block wall, caked with dozens of coats
of paint. There was a small shrine at the foot of it, with burnt out
candles and dead flowers and a few soggy teddy bears. One word of
graffiti filled the wall, red letters on a gold background: Rejoice!

"We did it Nan. It's ours again," Barbara said, gesturing at murky
gift shop windows and a marsh now visible beyond the public lot,
cleared of its cars. "It's truly ours," though I could tell she was still
numbing her worry by yanking off a dolphin pendant. A gift from
her husband. It reigned over the freckled triangle of her chest, still
brown from the summer. But the summer was over now. Canned up,
sealed and labeled to stow away with the rest of the summers in the
factory. We could cross the street without worrying about colliding
with drunk tourists unsteady on their rentals. These accidents happened enough where eels started making nests in the the blanched
memorial vespas that were tossed over the bridge. Without tourists,
the canal's brackish slime reeked more, or it could've been I only
took notice of this in their absence. Barbara looked exactly like a
woman who had and would infinitely be a Barbara, with her gingivi-
tis and keyhole turtleneck that had become flaccid from our shitty
laundromat. She was once an infant named Barbara and would be
one if reincarnated. I told her we should bail to nab frosé and scallop
fritters one last time, but before we could leave we were interrupted
by another local who seemed to be on his way to manage some kind

of quarry or unload timber. Taking off his gloves and quadrupling his hands, the man got to talking with Barbara. I didn't listen but I watched his chin, which was familiar. It jumped up and down like a perfectly round speckled stone you'd find in a riverbank. They say the harder the jawline, the more distant the husband. I thought of carving that into a plank of driftwood. He asked us if we had seen the 'you-know-what' and asked about our favorite parts of summer as if we were kids returning to grade school. I gave him nothing until he left us alone to rejoin the group now congealing for our main event. They were flooding the base of the wall to get a better view of a fifty foot tall papier-mâché man wearing giant cargo shorts with pockets made from used fishing nets. He had on crudely made sandals with velcro large enough to snare a bird and socks that stayed stiff in the breeze. Beneath a shirt for a basketball team I think I heard of once they had given him the rounded mounds of man-boobs. The mayor, a Kennedyesque young man who tucked his necktie into his windbreaker, was having difficulty adjusting the volume of his bullhorn. Though flanked by chaperones, they offered no help.

'You-know-what' was how we politely indicated there was a witch in our presence. It lived in whispers that had been kindling over the past couple weeks. The rumor germinated quickly with some claiming they had actually seen her and that she stood three feet tall, sweating acid from a boiled nose like some diseased gourd in a cloak. She had traveled across dimensions to derive potion from our dreams. To bite us in our sleep. Others conceived she was not actually visible and was only a scarecrow of our own excitement and fears. I imagined her as a shadow in fabric with claws and a sheet over her head like a widowed beekeeper. Ultimately, the scandal was what we needed now that we were without the drama visitors brought. Their sad marriages, their constant photography of us in front of sunsets.

Their obsessions with gelato and lobster rolls. With the effigy looking down at the crowd, desperate for someone to help, I felt sad for it. Part of me wanted to cut him down and set him free so he could find a giant papier-mâché wife and settle down somewhere away from us, terrible us. Who could blame him for wanting a break. To sample our lifestyle. Someone threw a glass Frappuccino bottle at him that shattered on the brick, to which someone yelled, no glass allowed! The entire shore is glass, really, if you think about, a lady next to Barbara said. I had chosen to be perceived as a quiet, mysterious type at the burning. Last year, I was a debutante, having my knuckles kissed, laughing and bucking in wild gestures. This year, rather than gabbing with our fellow locals, I stayed inside my own head, licking the 5 o'clock shadow on the back of my teeth. My clothes reeked of bakeries and children, from living off of fudge for three months. I needed new clothes anyway, but the fall Penny's catalogue had not arrived in my mailbox yet and the telephone number had been disconnected on last years. But they're all wondering, I can tell. Why is Nan so quiet, so mysterious? Look at her. Imagine what secrets she must have, how bored she must be of this place and its rituals. Part of me was fearful, convinced in the witch's plan to start slaughtering us the moment the effigy was lit. "I miss them Nan, I know they're awful and bring so much badness, but I miss them."

The Barbara had a point, seeing as how they'd gift us with houseplants and stories that took place in glass buildings or that were aabout cousins who couldn't stop blowing their thumbs off with M80s. Barbara caressed her dolphin even harder, polishing its rainbow oil surface. It was appraised at well over a thousand dollars on account of the eyes being real diamond. On my wrist was an ornate D. A letter drawn in permanent ink. I don't remember getting this, because when I got it I was very young or drunk, which are the same thing as I'm told. Years of direct sun blurred the marking as if I had tried to wipe it off and it got stuck that way. There are procedures, I've heard, to have these things zapped off. A shrieking came from the parking lot and at once we thought it was the witch unveiling herself to us. I wasn't the only one in crowd to turn away from the effigy, however the source of the interruption was only town trucks. They were already removing speed bumps for the plows, like dentists digging out overripe molars. We turned our attention to the snapping noises above us, to the cables hoisting up The Albert's shoulders and saw Miss Cape Cod 2011 touch the beacon to his gas soaked clothes. The mayor watched her hungrily. Some of the sparks rained down and briefly ignited the candles. All expensive, hand dipped wax jars from _conch., our town's flagship boutique, which I could only dream of being able to afford. The effigy's bald crown became alright with pointed flames. Its paleness turned to charcoal. There was a great rousing gasp which weakened to hissing as the flames receded to reveal a wiry skeleton, forced by heat to wave to us as he died. We all clapped at once. Something brushed my leg and thinking it was the witch I shouted out, not being able to cover my mouth in time. Barbara shot me a look and a cat scampered away from beneath us, its fur like the bristles from an old dish brush.

"Rejoice, rejoice," the Mayor led a chant, though I only lip-synched along. "The sightseers are gone from us." They would be remembered as those who had come to imagine they lived here too. Fair weather friends with important jobs who came to drink our chowder, take photos before our mural backdrops and fuck on our beaches. Barbara was the only person I knew who fucked on the beach, but she was also the only person I knew. She was not watching Albert's torched corpse anymore, but rather something by the docks. She asked me if I recognized him. Him? I followed my friend because I didn't want to be left alone and the ashes were reminding me of how much I was dreading slush leaching in through my shoes.

Unrefreshed iced coffee cauldrons and scrapes that seared in frozen air. The jellyfish were said to be extremely volatile this time of year when the cove was the warmest and the air was just beginning to chill. In the library there were all kinds of books about the 1989 Jelly-fish Massacre, where a spawning nest of Portuguese man o' wars killed three people and injured countless others. We remembered by graffiti above urinals and a mural that hung in the Town Hall depict-ing bathers fleeing from the waves with their tongues puffed out like pink broccoli. If that wasn't enough, the strong currents spelled cer-tain death for anyone dumb enough to wade out into them. This was just common knowledge. But we were safe now. The lifeguards did-n't screw around. Posted in towers, chained to floats, their eyes were binoculars.

It was a clever tradition from our tourism council to hold a funer-al for the season as an annual gift to the people who actually lived here year round. The ones who contend with storms in fall and pro-tect the precious views from eroding. We kept boutiques stocked in local crafts. Without our found object poaching, the gift shops would be nothing but mass produced 'wine-o-clock' dish towel shops. Later on, there would be a great hootenanny in the old Smithsonian barn where we'd stomp and rip all the tourism council's brochures apart. Former love letters to our community, resolved to shreds. Barbara yelled at heaven like she was addressing her dead husband. Her hus-band was not really dead, or at least I don't think he was. Our phones however had been dead since the hurricane in August, which suppos-edly took out some kind of tower. Barbara was extra horny and hop-ing that Ned from the market would be at the hootenanny. She had plucked her chin for the occasion and put on a cowboy hat she said was from back home - from where we originated before crossing the Bourne to the Cape, over oil tankers and lobster divers, to live in the constant feeling of vacation. We didn't talk about the jobs we had or whether we were old or new money. It was rude to do so. Barbara gave me a kidney from her clementine and said she felt like a new person and couldn't wait to peel off her own skin. Sometimes she'd apply Elmer's glue to her fingers just so she could do it. In my mouth, the fruit felt like a a bitter sack of nothing and so I forced it down whole. We left, both with the same tastes in our mouths.

"Don't forget to feed Boomhauer," she said to the coin operated telescope which only stared us down, unreplying with its gut full of quarters. Barbara would often get carried away with stories of her dog, Boomhauer, when she got nervous. "He was named after his father and his father's father." In the parking lot, we saw the town trucks had left behind fast food bags. Those jerks, we said, and found the beach sitting where we left it. The metal detectors doted along, obeying their masters isolated in headphones. Sometimes one would crouch down and unearth something, the others racing over like seagulls to see what was found. Barbara mumbled about how it was a waste of good shoes - digging around for stolen treasure and when I looked to her it was apparent she had something much more important she was waiting to tell me. "Someone has been watching me Nan, at night." She was talking as if reciting cereal ingredients in very small print. I asked her if it was the witch, but she didn't know. She said someone was stealing her things too. Moving them around. Items she swore she left in certain places one moment would be gone the next. But it was the time of the afternoon when one's mind baked itself if worked too hard. Grill juice was in the air, mixing with salt, causing a million things to rush toward me. Reese's peanut butter instead of Hershey bars. Forgetting a sweater in the car. Shooting myself with bug spray point blank until it foamed in the crease of my leg. The man handing me s'mores had black holes warping above his collar. I felt nervous, biting a marshmallow off a stick that had just been in the woods where our dog liked to pee or vomit up grass. Waking up inside a damp, dew infested sleeping bag. Then it was gone and I was dry. Recalling the campsite felt a lot like attempting to rejoin a dream. A woman was urging me toward a market and she acted as if we were friends. I decided to call her Marigold, because she reminded me of a perennial and her hair was obviously not naturally gold but who could care to think twice on such a morning. She was scared and trying to cover it up. "It's normal, I know, to feel as if you're being followed. You don't think someone's actually after me, do you? I mean, there are a lot of women here who might want me dead." She had spent the night at a suitors, and the night before she woke up behind the couch holding scissors. "Don't tell anyone, oh no, I don't want the whole town to think I'm losing it." I promised her I wouldn't, though I didn't even know who I would've told.

Marigold needed bread but put air quotations around bread, however I had no idea why was doing this or what real bread she needed. "Hurry up, hurry the fuck up Nan." My knee was bickering with my back which I could not convey to her but I knew I had to smile when we were in public. The more I tried to hide my limp the more it stung. The market was in between a laundromat and a shuttered boutique called boate shuze, that only sold things with sand dollars on them. Marigold said she was positive Ned was working. We were greeted by three different kids in aprons. I hated the market. The overhead lights stung my eyes and it was overly filled with doo-wop being played to bare tiles. Everyone was still catching up at the funeral. Shelves were lined by acres of laundry detergent that were being renewed by a girl grazing a feather duster. I tried not to step on the dark blue tiles, just in case the reflection was only a partially congealed eggshell surface of magma. Ned, she quietly pointed out, was on a cash register. Another kid with shaggy hair was trying to infiltrate a stack of boxes on a pallet. It was Randy. My son. I gave him a hug, but his back felt different. It twitched under my arm. You're not Randy. He shrugged and said he had one of those faces. A man who wore his shirt tucked in so far down his pants that it sucked into his naval came from out of nowhere and spoke sternly to the boy. I told him I wasn't sure where my head was, but the man gave me a warm smile and apologized. Both went off to whisper privately about whatever it is men whisper about in grocery stores. Marigold was already picking out a strategic array of items for Ned to ring out. Onion powder, condoms and short ribs, because she knew he loved barbecues and would quite possibly offer to cook for her on her tanning patio.

"You look nice Barbara," he said. Barbara, Barbara, that was her name. Not Marigold. She thanked him and turned her face how people turn their faces when they're drawn in pastel. He asked her about the cowboy hat and ignored the context of her groceries. "I simply have no idea what to do with this much meat." She acted like one of those women from the infomercials who live and die with their dish gloves on. Ned said he probably wasn't going to the hootenanny because he was tired and maybe had mono. He wasn't sure yet, but was definitely showing symptoms. This made Barbara or Marigold or whatever her name was, want to make out with him even more so, I could tell. The Hungry Shirt man appeared again and handed us gift cards for our trouble, though I assured him there had been no trouble and I was just tired from the day's festivities. "You know you shouldn't eat that stuff," Ned told her, pulling out a long scroll of receipt paper. "That meat, it's all packed with salt. I want to see you eating salmon, Barbara," and she blushed all the way out into their sidewalk display of mums.

Outside we drank free coffee which drew acid up from my stomach and tasted like a rotten Christmas decoration. When we left there was a group of geezers setting up their easels on a bluff. This was the best view of our lighthouse. A silo that reflected the sun's glare. "Look at those old farts," Barbara whispered loud enough for them to hear. One of them turned and bared his black gums at us. Good morning, we said. A man in a helmet of white hair told us we looked particularly lovely today and asked if we had attended the burning. "They really cooked him this time," he said. Another man who could've been his old balls cousin, held a thumb out, measuring the lighthouse. He had a set of paints contained in a wooden box, on which cursive was burned in. They were the old money, we agreed. "Who would want to paint that decrepit silo anyway," Barbara hissed and I pretended to agree, but unlike most Capers, I felt pride for our haunted silo. It gave this place character. In the 1950s it belonged to a dairy farm, and then a storm washed everything away except for the structure, a rocket frozen mid-flight, shooting out of a peninsula which could only be crossed if one had conquered the mathematics of tides and moons. Otherwise you'd end up like those cows that were delivered right to the bull sharks. There's a painting in the Saint Street Gallery of them, stupefied Oreos toppling in frothy green crests. Their faces totally serene as if the waves were just another pasture.

Everyone knew the story: Captain Jan Frances woke up in the morning to perfectly rare ham flesh pulled across the sky, under which his grandfather had built their family farm. The redder the sky the angrier the gale. He had his breakfast with his wife, Sara, and three children. He fed the chickens and opened the secondary gate so his livestock could escape if there was flooding. He said goodbye to Sara's honeybees, because she insisted their yield became sweeter if they were socialized with. Made sure the wood stove was stocked and exchanged a Folgers breathed kiss with his wife before leaving to wait out what was thought to be a mild storm in New Bernard's Tavern, now a boutique called Sailur on 720. According to the legend,

Captain Frances washed down a lobster and a half with thirteen beers and a pound of butter, in the exact future spot of an expired fire extinguisher fixed to a load-bearing beam. He spent the day there mulling about feed prices and throwing darts in the exact place where tourists would finger Square readers. Word got to the tavern that the storm surge had been absolutely devastating. The Captain rushed back to his farm but when he arrived he saw nothing but the sea and the silo protruding from it. The storm left no stone unturned. Its nails had left large gashes on the cement pillars of the docks. Its vomit riled the bay and turned it to acid. There was a painting of this in our public library. It did not show the part where Captain Frances took out his pistol, which he normally reserved for trespassers and rabid marlin and shot himself in the mouth. It did not indicate that Jan Frances had a predisposition for depression and was possibly allergic to shellfish, which would have put him in a poor, possibly even fevered headspace. It did not show his teeth in the soup of smoke and skull. The tavern, silo, his wife's washed out bee hives, and even that fire extinguisher were drenched in curses. Years of marshy water and air eroded what was once the tower's luminous exterior. You did not go near it and you especially didn't go past to the forest beyond. Everyone knows a forest bordering a cursed landmark acts as the grease trap for its maker's evil. A painting, Lighthouse of the Afternoon, depicted this haunted place with oil on canvas. Our Sunday farmers market sold a Sara Frances brand honey jam. Sometimes it was available from The Crown & Anchor, an adorable gift shop right across the street from Sailur on 720. Out of respect to the drowned cows, none of our restaurants served red meat. College kids did the thirteen beer & two and a half lobster challenge as a right of passage. You could get it for $50 with a student ID at the Beachcomber. If you really wanted the full glory, you'd eat the lobster's husk with it, antenna and all, just like Captain

Frances did on that red sky day.

Barbara and I did each other's makeup outside the hootenanny, where the face of the barn was waking up from its slumber as lanterns in the top most windows. Some men in heavy coats were making small talk around a meat smoker which burnt the air and made everything taste like winter. Pop music was thrumming out and washing over us, something like Prince or Madonna. It was inspiration for the purple rouge I used to recreate Barbara's jawline. "We're getting fucked tonight Nan, especially you. You need it. You've lost your luster. I hope you don't mind me saying it." Her brush was cold and wet against my eyelid. At the door we were greeted by chaperones in cowboy hats, which made me feel odd because I didn't even own one or know where people bought something like that. There was a punch bowl and a grinder that was longer than any sandwich I knew could have been born into the world. The thought of its creator unsettled me. Hay bails had been moved in, which Barbara said not to sit on because they were infested with pregnant ticks. Chaperones were dragging in a tiki statue that I was almost positive Lee Howardson created. Lee was famous for carving bears from logs, though I wouldn't be surprised if they had commissioned him for the tiki. His signature chainsaw marks were apparent even from where we stood, though the hard lifestyle as a former longshoremen made him sloppy.

"We sprayed them good," Ned said, swiping a hook into one of the hay bales. He had been hired for catering but couldn't stay. He told us they also hired him to clean the bails because last year several people were bitten by straw mites. Mites, not ticks. "Where's your hat Nan," and I felt him force one down on my head. When we weren't standing in line outside, we were standing in line inside, waiting to plop the pulled goose dinner on paper discs. There was also cornbread made with peppers and something that was either cold white macaroni and cheese or warm macaroni salad. Brian, who Barbara slept with sometimes was there. He had his own Swiss Army steak knife which he used to cut chunks away from the goose and eat with his fingers. They reminisced about how he loved chauffeuring her around in his Camaro but when she picked him up in her minivan he refused to sit in the front, choosing instead to hide in the backseat. "I can't be caught dead in a Ford, let alone a dang minivan," he said and laughed out pieces of fowl. I took off the hat and gently placed it in a waste basket, which made my scalp able to breathe again.

After we finished dinner, two-step country was forced harder from skyscrapers of speaker cabinets. The lap steel made a sound like sizzling wires under the singer's robotic commands. As we stomped, dust rained up from the beams and settled as a sneeze in my face. Our budget must have gotten bigger, because last year they had just hooked up an iHome to an old guitar amplifier. Ceiling rigged lights scanned those brave enough to dance. They kicked the air, and thrusted their belt buckles at one another. When the song ended, a new one with banjo in it made everybody erupt in applause. Even me. But the rum made everyone go off time, so the clapping was more like distant firecrackers. Someone flipped on a fog machine. Spider leg lasers turned pink against the flannel and tight fitting denim of the frontline dancers. The lights dimmed and darkness placed us all into obscurity, taking away our fingerprints, though the chaperones remained with their arms folded in the sawdusted smoke, cupping their hands over each others ears. They'd only stop to mock someone who was extra drunk. Pointing and snickering. What secrets would the chaperones have? How interesting could their lives really be? The tiki statues were the ultimate judge, glowering at us, their eyes fiery.

Mrs. DiStefano, who was one of the oldest people in town, stood alone with her back directly to the largest speaker. Every wrinkle stuck into a big grin, clapping along. That dumb old broad, I thought. But when I saw the chaperones pointing to her and laughing I felt awful and began making my way towards her, dodging the eye contact of cowboys whirling their invisible lassos at me. As the music roared, I gently pressed down on her shoulders to guide her away from the speaker's shaking grill. She was a wispy thing, and she felt as if I could've steered her anywhere, with her droopy earlobes pulled that much farther down by her giant earrings as the dice on our dashboard. When we were far enough from the music that I could park her, she asked if I'd seen her father. I figured her father must've been well over a hundred. She said the engine wasn't a quitter. Her father built it, and things DiStefano's made didn't quit. I gave her a ladle full from the punch bowl which had been moved to look like the tikis were urinating into it, and bid her goodnight.

Barbara found me and we went out to the beach where Brian was half stumbling, half shaping a teepee of driftwood. It was still breezy, and someone's cowgirl hat had blown into where the bonfire would be started. "Capers all taste the same," Brian said with his arms around Barbara. He was being inappropriate though tomorrow he would apologize and say he had gone too hard on the Captain & Pepsi. Brian was not Barbara's first choice but he would do. Thick wrists, sideburns, scar somewhere on his lip. Boyish face complete with some faint freckles on their way into becoming liver spots. Smelled like toothpaste. Totally her type, though she was trying to repurpose herself into more of a cougar. I didn't have the heart to tell her that the younger ones were not interested like how they were in the programs we watched. Ned was just one in a long line of twenty-something's who were not charmed by her orange skin and surgically enhanced bust. This didn't stop Barbara from insisting her makeup be mirrored against those women in the decade old reruns that we'd rely on to get us through winter. A woman who joined us bragged about incorporating sea glass into brooches, and how to effectively stitch an anchor onto a tote bag. Brian said it was best to start from the head, while another woman who I couldn't make out in the dark assured us it was best to begin threading at the crown. Her teeth and glasses were the only things I could see until after squirting turpentine on the smoldering teepee, we were all made orange. Barbara told me she would fix me up with Brian's drinking buddy, Joel, who had arrived with a fishing cooler full of beer in tow. When he offered me one I declined, however he had foreseen this and came prepared with wine.

It felt unsafe to be so close to the silo without being able to see it. This proximity was usually manageable in the daylight, maybe even comforting because we knew it was a nocturnal creature. Yet there was a sensation that it could sidle around in the dark to appear right beside you. A distant dog barking might be a warning. The witch could be lurking just beyond a dune or sleeping standing up in one of the tool sheds. I feared speaking too loud would attract the things lurking outside the safety of our halo. They could smell my apprehension, even in our blind joy, inflating more by the moment. "The hurricane happened in the day," Drinking Buddy said. "Don't look so happy to be here. You're too cute to worry about cursed barn-jarms and what have-you." This made Barbara scratch Brian's forearm in jealousy. Some subconscious marking of territory. Drinking Buddy announced that he had to bleed a lizard, before disappearing. I secretly hoped the dark deal made between the witch and silo would result in him being the first and only sacrifice.

"You'd think with how much I'm paying for taxes, we could live in maybe a little less, I don't know, fear," I said, forcing my mouth into a crescent shape. This put everyone at ease. Taxes comforted them. Those reliable obligations comforted me too. The zinfandel was getting the better of me, which the heat off the fire had turned into nothing but warm raisin juice. All of us clutched our Solo cups as if we were teenagers. If I blurred my eyes enough I'd swear we all were teenagers, maybe circling in a field, a forest or the backyard of somebody's mother's house. Brian kicked a hunk of driftwood and the fire licked the tip of his boot making it smoke a little. He shrugged back and quietly kissed his cup. "Oh I miss this," Barbara said. The men made howling noises, pretending to be the witch. They slurred ghost stories, now full blown drunk off tiki piss. I didn't like ghost stories after dark. They put a tightness around my throat and made shapes out of the night. Drinking Buddy came back with an armful of timber. Alive. "It's from one of the shacks. Pressure treated, I think, but it'll burn."

"You didn't wash your hands," but no one heard me. Smoke forged us in an aurora of purples and greens that could only be conjured by arsenic. Drinking Buddy gave up and went home with his cooler, bringing with him a pond scum smell I had been unable to place. In unison, we found quiet solace in embers. The support of the last intact log cracked, bringing the teepee down finally on the half burned up cowgirl hat to destroy it once and for all. It smoldered from within like a geodef. Then our cups turned to a dripping red wax. The smoke burned my throat, and everywhere I tried to move away, it chased me, until this became some sort of game. The must've caught the attention of the chaperones, because two of them came rushing over armed with super soakers. One grumbled that he knew letting us burn anything was a bad idea, and then fired directly at its core. "We're giving them too much freedom," he snapped and from the hands of a third chaperone manifested a bucket, and from the bucket came a great pillow of steam.

II.

In the morning, we sat on Barbara's porch and complained about Brian while breakfasting on Entenmann's and Snapple Tea warmed up in her best faux bone china. We watched the gulls bounce around, daring closer to the metal detectors, before being startled off by chirping whenever one hovered over a coin. In an attempt to ignore its staleness, Barbara tried baptizing her crumb cake, but it fell apart. She told me Brian was like a dog lapping up water from a dish. "He was all over the place. I kept saying, make an ampersand, make an ampersand for fuck's sake. It was okay though. Kind of weird. We let Joel watch." I imagined her growling, her yellow breasts like plastic googly eyes glued to a plain of cardboard where dolphins roamed, while Drinking Buddy sat in the corner. His breath heavy. Brian did not know what an ampersand was, because his knowledge fell only in how to create things. A partially restored whale-ship from a nearby living history maritime museum had banked on our jetty during the last blizzard, from which we salvaged for found art. From the timber, Brian made a seahorse shaped swing that was as breathtaking as it was structurally sound. Some New York fashion magazine editor spotted the swing in conch.'s Memorial Day sale and we later found it cloned on Etsy, selling for quadruple its initial cost. Brian was born too dumb to care about artistic rights. He had forgotten he even knurled the seahorse in the first place, just as he had forgotten how to make Barbara cum.

When anyone talked of the mainland like somewhere impossible to return to, I went especially silent. My reservations were well plotted personality points implemented to instill a sense of wonder. I had been laying the foundations for a great escape. No, a retirement in the Cape was not Nancy Ballister's final act. Not if rustic lighting continued to outsell everything in the craft marketplace. From the same wreckage others had scuttled, I found my ticket in the form of lanterns hidden in a compartment under a heap of rope. Our boutiques were already inflated with rope crafts, so no one had bothered to touch it. It wasn't until I inspected the lanterns at home, that I realized how valuable this treasure was. Copper and tin housing orbiting a handmade glass orb, perfectly blown without any air bubbles. The encased candle within was original, made from a paraffin and spermaceti blend. Even the hinge was intact. All I had to do was position it upside down and glue a basin of Dawn, vanilla extract and clementine skin in the burn pot. My masterpiece was to make its big debut in the summer, as a part of the first holiday displays. Deconstructed, aromatic lanterns from a time when men hunted beasts. They'd all ooh and aah, turning my genius in their hands and in their heads. Nan, I knew you were creative but not this creative. You were just hiding in there all this time, with your secret gift. Look at you. I would buy Barbara the botox she always talked about. I'd get Ned that bus ticket to see his girlfriends, so he wouldn't have to deal with us old biddies anymore. I'd free everyone here.

The crumb cake was trying to sneak back up my throat on a sluice of Snapple, now all a restless swamp within me. Stay down, stay down, I told it. It was the day when they cut down what was left of the effigy and the food trucks emptied what was left of their season's bounty. This year they had both extra oysters and bluefin, which was being served with plastic cups of pineapple salsa. I thought it tasted like crushed Advil, but no one believed me. Every autumn, high winds and cold temperatures trapped a bevy of marine life, keeping all kinds of stunned fish and crustaceans in our cove to be scooped up. There was a painting in the library of the original indigenous population taking advantage of this exact weather pattern, their nets busting with cod. Fried oysters, pickled oysters, double repacked oysters capped with mustard and raw on the half shell. Somebody in an ambiguous mollusk costume roved in the crowd. We watched it dance, chewing only on our ginger beers. Barbara said she had her fill of swallowing slimy things whole last night. The mollusk mascot stopped to pose with the mayor, who was wearing two windbreakers at once. There was no one photographing them.

Mrs. DiStefano was making me nervous. She had ventured far too close to the railing of the bridge and curled her toes around the first rung. I thought of the ghost bikes and mopeds all stuck in amber down there and then I recalled the pond behind my old house. How the geese made it seem like a farm, before turning our pool into a swamp. Off the springboard, pool water clapping at my naked ribs. Chlorine mixing with gin in my stomach. Something brushing against my feet and wondering how a sea monster made its way into a neighborhood pool. Being yelled at for tracking water on the new wooden kitchen floor and then sleeping in the guest room. Swallowing sushi hole like a tequila shot after work instead of going home. Going home to find a 'Nancy's Farm' sign, hand carved and displayed above our fireplace. Sorry, I'm sorry for the way I acted, that wasn't me and that wasn't us. The rest slipped away. A locked room that I could only wander from.

There was a stack of milk crates used to transport bags of chowder broth. The chaperones carried these like sleeping babies with the fat corners resting on their shoulders. Some of the sacks had been punctured and their trails had to be chased away with a hose. The mollusk mascot stood still, a fabric crescent with a basketball sized pearl for a heart, watching Mrs. DiStefano, inches from toppling over into the canal. He waved at me, but it was a slow wave as if it wasn't sure it recognized me from afar. Barbara was still talking about Brian's cunnilingus technique, letting the diluted chowder broth reach her open toed sandals. She always said she wasn't complaining, whenever she was complaining. Then I saw the cloak dragging through the alabaster torrent. A brushed trail. Our witch.

She swerved in between chained mopeds. Though her face was obscured, I could make out a scowl. The jagged chiclets in her mouth. Chaperones noticed her next. They took out their phones, but they were unlike any phones I had seen. They appeared to be made of steel and slid out from themselves. As the witch went by me I could hear her growling. A spell. Fruit snacks on her breath. She was clasping something and I knew when she revealed it that we would be in danger. Luggage I had bought my son for Christmas stacked on the tiny dorm room bed. A roommate with two dead parents. Embarrassed hugs. They hurried through the hallways of my thoughts and broke apart before I could clasp them. The witch approached where they had stored the chowder bags, becoming taller on the pallet. With tiny, white fists she pulled her hood down and that was when we saw what it was. Its face was not that of a hag, but a young boy. Barbara dropped her chowder spoon and one by one we turned our attention to the kid. All of us, intoxicated with fresh seafood, cheered him on. Helping with art or math homework at the kitchen table. A pit when my husband refinished it and cut away the crayon wax. Birthday present Saab split by a crater where it smacked the guy in the crosswalk. You shouldn't of spoiled him. Barbara's mini-van. "Barbara when's the last time you even drove a car?"

The kid got up onto a milk crate and raised his hand. A murmur went through the crowd and then it fell silent, except for a few people shouting words of encouragement at him. The kid acknowledged them with a nod and a shy smile. In the full light of day, he looked less angry and more beautiful. He waited until people stopped shouting. A siren could be heard, maybe five or ten blocks away. The kid raised the bullhorn, pressed the button, and began to speak.

"Look down at your hands, how veiny they've become," the kid said, trailed by the bullhorn's cough and feedback. His mullet chased the breeze, which gave him an air of the presidential. "Focus on them. They've let you invent your own lives and have trapped you here like fog. But you're free now. You've been free. Run. Go. Out of the gates. Run to the sea! Go!" He lisped through a space of bare gums. There were no gates. Just the cement and the chaperones now setting up a new crab tent. The mascot spinning in circles. Sirens were screaming from a distance, but they weren't like the sirens I was used to. He looked back down at us with the sadness I felt when I saw the pesticide signs by the farm, knowing my husband had killed the geese. It made my sinuses sting when I thought of this and Barbara started cackling like she had forced herself to understand a joke. From the intersection, a pack of black SUVs tore in, lights spitting from their muzzles. Out of each door came police except they weren't the chubby, whistle bearing police that normally patrolled our town. They had guns and radios on their shoulders that emitted ghostly signals of people from the past.

"Remember, try to remember under your-," but an old hand reached up and stole away the megaphone and the kid was then scooped off the milk crate where he disappeared into the clutch of a red haired woman with a puffy face who looked like she had been crying. "Your lighthouse, your lighthouse," he screamed, looking directly at me. "Your missing things are behind the lighthouse. You can go there. I've seen it." The megaphone was kicked to the ground where it lay inanimate again. The child witch was gone. Fried oysters, get your oysters and bluefin here. Get'em on the rocks.

Our initial shock devolved to laughter. The crab men shrugged and made jokes with their little cigarettes just barely balancing on their lips. Presented to us their crustaceans, their heavy and overfed claws drooping under their armored bellies. Regarding us with black bulbs that could either be dead or asleep. The ice under the bins was melting into larger tributaries that collected at the storm drain. "Well

I guess we found our sorceress," Barbara said, but her own laugh was metallic and afraid. We found our voices shook when we tried to use them. Everyone buried themselves back into the festival, sucking juices through the plastic limbs, and the familiarity was not a comfort this time. Get your fresh waffle cone crab meat sundaes.

In the morning, the sun had cooked death into fallen leaves. The front page of the Chatham Gazette read TIME TRAVELING SORCERESS FINALLY CAUGHT BEFORE NEARLY SPOILING 6TH ANNUAL OYSTER FESTIVAL. Barbara told me she was going to papier-mâché the article directly onto a globe for her newest idea – a line of 'kid-chic science projects.' She had stolen a cue ball from the Beachcomber Bar & Grille which was going to be Pluto. Its actual lightness as a celestial body would be ironic in the heaviness of the resin. A long awaited sequel to her yarn river systems and baking soda volcano that erupted onto an unsuspecting town. She pined for dwarf starfish to wash up so she could super glue them into her milky-way.

It would be the youthful thing to do. To follow the warning of a fake witch that probably had been living off ladybugs and moss in the woods. There was something very Nancy Drewian about all of it. We'd get close to the lighthouse, but just close enough where we could brag forever at parties. The afternoon had barely broken, so our excursion would have concluded long before dark while it was still safe. We'd make a day of it, pack a picnic and even stop at Brian's house to pick him up. He'd love nothing more than to guard two ladies on a dangerous voyage into the unknown. Into the world of accursed nautical landmarks. It would intensify the survival-sex that him and Barb would get into afterwards. We had both received Vineyard Vines sweatshirts as gifts from tourists last year, which we had fixed around our waists in case it got cold. I sharpened a letter opener on some bricks outside Barbara's house, and snuck the weapon into a fanny pack.

We found Brian in his driveway, swirling turtle wax on his Camaro. It was one of the few remaining rows of homes which resembled the ranches of our former neighborhoods. Here I could usually see him watching sports on TV at night. Sometimes Barbara would be on the couch beside him, presented in blue light and knitting things that would never be finished. We told him about the child witch and how it had stolen the mayor's bullhorn. He did not seem to care or trouble himself enough to make anything of it. We told Brian we were going to to the lighthouse. "You can come, but it's going to be dangerous," Barbara said, which was Barbara english for something else. His brows joined together like a sorrowful and unrealistic figure in a painting. I had never noticed Brian had so many threads of white in his beard or how he swam in his denim jacket, which had bloated in the shoulders. At the announcement of our mission, Brian did not seem scared, but rather surrendered. "You go," he told us. "You go." I thought then Barbara was going to kneel and kiss his mouth, but instead she patted him on the head like a dog. "I'll need some lunch," he said and left to hide in his house. We could see then under where his rag had been, the silver under the Camaro's paint showed and its tires were flecked by rot.

Neither Barbara or I had ever been close enough to the silo, where it wasn't a blur. The cove it presided over had lost its drawl. In a receded tide, it had collected its daily kelp around the base. We could see the wounds. Its metal skin. Up close, where lush green plants climbed its skirt of seaweed, the missing squares made it human. Getting close enough to touch it, I could swear I heard a faint buzzing. Like a hum of bees. We forged on, down the coast. No human footprints were present this far. I found a bag of oyster crackers in my pocket which the humidity had gotten to, somehow through the plastic. Perhaps it would've been my last chance of eating, before having to forage for yams. We saw one abandoned sandal next to a volcanic looking rock. Its thong was torn. Barbara was starting to doubt the point of our adventure. "I don't know if this is the time to tell you, but that feeling I've been getting, of someone watching me," Barbara said. "It's happening right now."

"You're imagining things. Let's just keep pushing forward. I mean, we're already this far." Retracing back toward the silo would mean giving up. Ahead there was a swatch of forest, just how I'd seen hanging in galleries. To reach it we trampled up to our shins in a ceramic mud that sucked at our boots. Horse flies hopped across its surface, picking at shells and the remains of whatever animals had been unlucky in their own crossing. "Don't get pulled in, I'm not strong enough to get you out." Barbara nervously carved at her fingernails, spitting the slivers out like sunflower seed hulls. We made it through, and when we turned to mark our distance, the silo was once again only a familiar smudge on a slab of sand. Here we found ourselves, at long last, reaching the forest. A palace constructed of the same vines that suffocated the silo. Except these vines were angry and tangled into themselves, giving an appearance of unkempt fur.

Guarding its borders were signs that screamed PRIVATE PROPERTY at us, forcing both Barbara and I to question once more if we should turn around. A final warning. It must've been about noon, which meant the daily tapestry weaving class would begin. Our mud imprints would've been intact and retraceable. We could surrender. Nancy Drew surrendered sometimes. She had homework. But we didn't. We kept on into a forest that only grew denser. Its sandy floor became dirt and then leaves, until we were in a thick with birds and shade and things I had not seen in a very long time. It smelled of spatula left on a burner and the apartment of a very lonely person who made forts of poorly cleaned jars of Ragu next to their garbage can. The property markers dissipated too, putting us truly in the wilds, a place without plastic or the invention of written language. I could feel seeds and briars latching themselves to me, desperate to get anywhere else. We had to be careful not to step in the many droppings that littered the forest floor. "Did you notice how weird Brian was acting. I don't understand men," and then Barbara stopped speaking to scream and it was in that moment I knew our inevitable murders were finally upon us. "Oh my god, oh my god, is that what I think it is?" Some accent was resurfacing where god sounded more like gawd. She turned to me to measure my reaction. Behind her was the shape of a body, blackened to its skeleton, except its arms were protracted, leading up to a mouth capable of eating car tires. More bodies were piled nearby into a mass grave. I told her to calm down because I recognized them immediately as effigies. Getting closer, they were perfectly entwined. A classic form of space saving - one that I employed when I packed luggage. The freshest one, Albert, was on top and the only body not crept on by the wild grapes and beach rose. An art show at the community center. Candid black and white film photography of our family not speaking at the dinner table. My husband drinking from the hose. Some childish statement about desperation in suburbia. My son would've loved to photograph this. Should we turn back? No. Only more turds on the ground. A path of them winding somewhere. Paw prints, like the padded pattern I would wash away with windshield wiper fluid on my way to work each morning. The coyotes must've gotten her. They love the pond. We'll get a new one and make her an indoor pet. Being murdered wouldn't be so bad I guess. I could spill my secret to Barbara. Telling someone about the lanterns instead of finishing them could actually be easier.

Olive moons hung in the trees. A cat approached us carefully, ragged and sulking off from a branch drowned in moss. It was joined by two more, and then a half dozen before I realized the entire canopy was populated by them, their tails dangling below them or trailing as their own pets. Some of their collars were rusted, while others were naked in their mange. "Have you ever seen anything like this ever? In your life?" I told her they must be feral. All living together out here. There was a smoke haired one whose belly was low and feathery that seemed to be leading us, or it could've been we were chasing him. Whether it was toward an escape or into a trap we didn't know and I half expected to be greeted by some neolithic feline queen.

Then through the trees there was a comfort of manmade things again. Of pollution and mechanical bearings. No queen cat waited for us on a throne of yarn. We bathed our eyeballs in the cement gray of buildings and embraced our being possessed by electrical spirits again. But the sanctuary of this place was short lived. Written in spray paint, on the broadest wall facing the forest it said: BEWARE THE DRUMS. The cat seemed to know it had showed us something important and chirped expectantly. There was a sensation of wildlife recoiling under the oculus of surveillance lenses. Familiar scents. Urine, stale sweat on cheap hotel blankets that would never not be itchy. Old grill grease spilled on the grass your son carved paths into with the lawnmower. Clover breath cut in the massacre. Another oily cat was wrapping itself around my leg like a python. Barbara shooed it away. "What is this place? Maybe we should leave it alone."

"I've never seen this part of town," I said, stepping over a border of dead sidewalk. Every building appeared to have been painted by depression. Wandering the streets were elderly either in wheelchairs or grazing with the help of walkers. Those confined to chairs had the air of something being left out to dry. They hid their faces, cracked from the chin to their infinite foreheads. They sat complacent in scarf gauze, staring at a place we didn't know about yet. "Maybe they're speaking to people we can't see," Barbara said. In this vacuum bag stuffed in lint, hair and dust, the constant static of crashing waves must've been deadened by the forest. Breathing it made me feel as if I'd become infected with a terrible illness that would be delayed in showing its warning signs. I imagined for a moment a room of all the eggs these people were laying, but shuddered it off.

We paused to check on the well being of a woman who had taken delight in our presence, lifting her claw out from layers of shawl. Barbara crouched down beside her. "Steven? Steven?" She said, scanning Barbara with gray eyes. Her scalp reflected the overcast above. We asked where we were. "No one tells me anything. Who has time these days?" I brushed off a hunting party of ants from her arm, and saw she had on a plastic bracelet. None of the businesses looked like they had been open in a number of years. A sign for Sal's Ice cream had faded into its own paint. Another for Dunver's Pizza & Surf Shop seemed to have been almost entirely eaten by time. "They're not open yet, dear." The doors of the ice cream parlor were glossed in a filmy yellow, and inside we saw trash strewn on old root beer float machines and the like. "Are we leaving? I'll get Harlan. Have you seen Steven? I can't find that boy anywhere." A second woman sang to us from far away and the two began chattering to each other in their own language.

From the town's heart there came a chorus. One that was youthful and without gravel. It summoned us to something of a common square, presided over by a statue - a man whose chest was crossed in ropes, with a mermaid prowling at his legs. His head was missing. Above them in the clearing was a diamond shaped sign that said 'Sal's Pre-Owned Volvo and European Cars.' In this lot they had gathered a circle of maybe a dozen wheelers. They sang through oxygen tubes a song about American highways. They were gathered around a girl, reading from a paperback novel painted with a shirtless firefighter on the cover. Something you'd find at a grocery store. Another twirled a tongue of bubblegum while speaking to a man in a reclining beach chair. The old listened intently. Several of the men could've passed for dead or sleeping, concealed under oversized baseball caps proudly displaying patches for submarines and naval ships.

"Can I help you?" Our presence must have caused the girl severe alarm because she had placed her book down on the ground. She wore nursing scrubs, and her hair was fixed up into a massive bun with an array of neck strands that fanned out to make her appear as if she were on fire. "Are you supposed to be here?" She looked to the man lounging on his beach chair. He had a goatee that bore the offspring of three necks. All three wore sneakers so white they burned my eyes. He asked if we were from Hyannis and if we had any ID. One of the geezers cackled at this. Goatee explained to us that we were confused and most certainly lost. He spoke slowly, as if we were children. I felt his fist open on my shoulder. From my fanny pack, he found a license which I didn't remember having. "You all have come a long way haven't you? Shan, you watch them. We'll be back," he said to the second girl. She snapped her gum. Claimed his chair. The six o'clock news promoting a snow storm from the living room while I fixed dinner. Melting the glaze. Cracked an egg with blood in the yolk. Screaming smoke detectors from a duck left in the oven. Black, black, black. "We'll help you. We're here to help you."

Where the sneakers took us was warm. The belly of a tavern, or what had once been. I asked who all those people were. "They see in black and white," the Goatee said. "Not like you two. You still see things in full color, isn't that right?" There were faces of fishermen watching us from photos on the walls. Each draft tap was coated in dust - the flesh and beard hair of these men, given to protect their sacred drink. Surely in its time, Barbara and I would've caused quite a stir amongst such a crowd. Next to the photographs was a crudely composed painting, finished by someone with a grotesque sense of color. It depicted a herd of ship cats leaving docked galleys. Their faces were humanlike with a determination for new land, though this was most likely not the artist's intention. Some kind of protest, a refusal to hunt mice, I presumed.

"Barb, look at this," I said. Bun Fire complained it was getting too dark and there wasn't enough electricity in this part of town. She lead us back up to the curb. When the two sneakers wandered off to share a cigarette, Barbara turned to me with a plan in her face. Counted to three in head nods and we were gone. Their lazily plodding footsteps and shouting wore out quickly. They stopped calling after us, as the escape caused an uproar amongst the wheelers, and the sneakers had stopped to nurse their cattle.

We were safe only in the forest, free as needles in a hay bail of jungle. My knee burned, furious at my sudden demand of it. Our sweatshirts reeked with death. With plaque. Branches were dull knives, whipping any flesh that was exposed. The cats had grown wary of us and retreated back to the underbrush. Neither of us stopped running until we could hear the beach again. Until we ended up on the other side of civilization, in the place of bright signs. On the reverse of them, in three different languages, there were longer warnings. Do you have these symptoms? Do NOT psychically engage with patients. Please wear mouth protection. Do not introduce. Foreign germs can KILL. We ignored them and carried onward so our backs were to PRIVATE PROPERTY again. Caught our breath and swallowed what insects had gotten trapped in the chambers of our throats. In falling temperatures, the mud had frozen. Silo, sound asleep. Over the hill it was just starting to get dark. Bullfrogs mooed from some unseen marsh. The painters had left behind their work, which didn't surprise me as the glowing meadows of summer had grayed considerably. Who would want to paint something so sad? When I saw their abandoned canvases, I saw only a violence of slathered markings. Handprints. Their easels were anchored by bricks, so we kicked them over. We destroyed them.

III.

It was exactly one week later when the boat came. There was no alert to warn of its arrival. Any remaining lifeguards were on their break, as their ranks had been thinned out from the ease that shared whistles and germs filled them with snot. He was a fisherman. A gunner from a far off war. Tattoos of scripture tangling with strange desert beasts reached all the way to his knuckles. Barbara confessed her love for him almost immediately. She had moved on from the strange place beyond the silo, so I ignored it too. This was how secrets were best kept. The gunner had found something in the sea. Pulled it up with a haul of bluefin. The body of Mrs. DiStefano. Spat out by the canal and trapped in the cove by the same weather that gave us our bountiful seafood. The chaperones carried her, still wrapped in a net, and they would say she looked like she was just sleeping but I saw her and she did not. The police came back. The one's with flashlights instead of whistles. They stood in a circle with the gunner and laughed and tugged up their pants by the belts.

"They went to school," Ned said. To college. The two of us were playing rummy in the booth of a fancy tapas place, shuttered up for the winter. "Me? I'm not going back. I'm going to actually make some money laying tile with my uncle." He had thrown his apron over the bridge. "It's for the eels now." Ned had told me how fond he was of Mrs. DiStefano, only when I asked him if he missed all the girls who left. I never imagined he would give so much credence to a foolish fossil of a woman like her. "Don't worry, I left some scones in the apron pocket." I didn't know if he meant they were for the eels or Mrs. DiStefano. I told him he could get another job. There were jobs everywhere. America, a giving sow, bred opportunity in boundless quantities. It was what she was born to do, I said adding to the discard pile. But Ned didn't care about pigs or advice from someone who we both knew was not there. "I saw her too Nan. No one should have to see their own grandmother like that." I wasn't sure what he meant by grandmother. I didn't follow how young people spoke anymore. "She was see-through. The cove is merciless on a body. All those crabs the restaurants have been harvesting and doping up. They got her good. They'll go for anything that's cartilage. Nose, eyes, ears," and then Ned put his head down and whimpered. I think it was Ned. He could've been anyone. I rubbed circles onto his back and told him things from the cougar show reruns, but whispered them in a way that was gentler. Then he wasn't crying, I was. He pushed some kind of pamphlet towards me and said: "Think of it as a new version of yourself, everyday. You don't have to pay for heat or worry about who's going to take care of you. You're here because someone out there wants to take care of you. That's a good thing. Not everyone has that," and I saw then he had given me a brochure.

We slowed in and out of hibernation. The chill made my knee act up. It was a blank winter of forty-one degrees days. Snow melted just as soon as it streaked the dune grass. Some of the winter tourists came for discounted rates, sitting to dinner with new transfers. People I had never seen before. Probably from the city. They avoided the constant wind and sleet by sheltering inside a Hibachi restaurant that served grouper sour enough to conjure almost immediate nausea. They loved the silo. Our monument would come back as black and white portraits in every gallery. Locals left. Some forever. Lee Howardson, our resident woodcarver, had accidentally cut himself in half. The rumor was suicide, though Lee loved tortilla chips and had most likely finished off nuking his brain with GMO's. Something Ned would've said.

On Labor Day weekend, I had visitors. They were looking for directions to the Atwood Gallery and we 'just got to talking,' as Capers called it. They were two tourists, an older man and a younger one. Randy senior and junior. They had the same faces too. The old one said there was a third who couldn't make it because she had gotten trapped somewhere out in the midwest, but she sent her best. I asked them if she was Randy too and they laughed. They worried about my limp. We sat in rocking chairs in an enclosed porch, enjoying the heat from propane lamps. We sat down to breakfast at Sandy's Diner, where the eggs tasted like trout on account of our farm chickens living off fish feed for the winter. They took care of the bill, though we purposely forgot our doggy bags. We washed our mouths out with coffee and we saw in the parking lot, a seagull kill another seagull. "Let's go to the beach. You people like the beach," I told them.

At the shore, wind was chopping up the waves, battering any surviving sand castles the young tourists had built. Their royal subjects long buried or consumed by fleas. In their remains was a calcified starfish. Randy Jr. picked it up. "I'll bet you could make something real nice out of this. Isn't this like gold to you people if it's got all five limbs?" When the afternoon got too chilly we walked back to town. They had already painted the effigy wall with another coat of golden primer. On another building, they were touching up a mural of a whale. Its smell was sticky and narcotic in my brain. In the window front of our newest boutique, citrine&SALT, teddy bears waited in a perfect, miniature forest made from cones of rich green construction paper. A card indicated they were hand sewn with found sea glass eyes and stuffed with mallard down. Their whiskers made from real fisher cat pelts. A remedy for the homesick young tourist. Something about the display made me want to set fire to the forest. Free the bears before they were sold for their $80 listing price, only to be left behind. More familiar, tried and true bears waited at home for the summering children. The two Randys brought me to their hotel, to a chilly room on the fourth floor. They turned up the thermostat and I fell asleep watching reruns.

"Hey, they've got Ray Liotta as Colonel Sanders now," the younger Randy said, when I woke up. I had slept until dark. His chin was like my chin. We shared a long goodbye, which are my favorite kind of goodbyes. Old Randy still had his sleeves rolled up and I saw on his wrist a drawing of a long arrow. The kind a hunter would fire. When he saw what I had noticed, he gave a brief nod to my wrist with its letter D. We hugged. The smell off his nape brought with it spilled nail polish on a computer keyboard. Typing about forgetfulness and finding early onset dementia. Asking Jeeves to diagnose the signs. Reading forums late into the night and then sneaking into bed, him totally oblivious to the expiration date now given to his wife. I wondered how many of those posting in the forums had since died. The Randys promised they'd be seeing more of me now that it was going to be getting warm again.

It was a good day to settle into the cafeteria. Here I found a woman whose hair bloomed like a marigold with silver roots. I liked that about her, though she hated the cold and made everyone suffer for it. Seated next to her was a man with work gloves, trying to push tea across the table. He had a small white dog on his lap. The woman was chatty. "Do you remember when we visited the colony of leopards? Did you see the stillborn Camaro?" She asked me this and the man took back the tea, taking his gloves off. Putting them back on. "This is my husband," she said. "Have you met him?" The man gave a warm smile, though his chin was too bristly to read. I dreamed of this back in my room. Here I kept my brochure that I reviewed each night before bed. It showed me paintings of people, walking an outdoor mall, where weeds did not grow from the gaps in the sidewalk. Dignified care for your loved ones. Only in the crown crest of Arbors: New England, can you escape together. I felt sorry for these faceless watercolor figures that no one had bothered to erase the pencil outlines of. How awful it could be. I cut pictures out of this place to tack them to my wall. I saw in the streets someone I thought I recognized. Tourists came and went, came and went.

Turn, Friend, Turn

HELEN DENT

⬥

Beyond the cracked sidewalk, and the telephone pole with layers of flyers in a rainbow of colors, and the patch of dry brown grass there stood a ten-foot high concrete block wall, caked with dozens of coats of paint. There was a small shrine at the foot of it, with burnt out candles and dead flowers and a few soggy teddy bears. One word of graffiti filled the wall, red letters on a gold background: Rejoice!

The kid walked by, made the block and walked by again. This time he scuffed at one of the teddy bears, knocked it over, caught the picture of the Preacher with his toe and slid it around so the face wouldn't be staring out, the simple face in the stupid fake gold frame. Bet you didn't figure this, huh? Didn't figure they'd bring little bears and sing kumbayah with their stupid candles lit. Not exactly a golden chariot taking you home, was it? "WAS IT?" He yelled the last words without meaning to, and Shoshanah Lennox from two doors down stopped dragging her dolly through the puddles and stared at him with wide black-lashed eyes.

"Beat it home," he yelled, but she just stood there, staring. "This isn't any place to play. Beat it." He picked up one of the milk crates stacked by the wall and flung it hard, not to hit her, just to emphasize his point. She didn't flinch, her hair a mess of golden ringlets all down her shoulders.

"I saw him," she said, sticking her thumb in her mouth and taking it out again. "He fell down. I saw him." "Then you know you should scram. You hear me? Get out of here!" Her face crumpled and she ran forward to fling the doll on the shrine.

"Oh, for the love . . ." said the kid, reaching to pick it up, but Shoshanah shoved him away. "I want her to stay there." He grabbed the bullhorn that had rolled to the fence when the Preacher dropped it a few days back and shook it in her face till something came loose inside, rattled all around. "All he did was shout and point the finger. Why'd you give up your dolly for someone like that?" "He shouldn't of had to fall," she whispered. That made the kid so mad he had to set the bullhorn down to keep from throwing it, too. "Something had to stop him, didn't they? Make him shut up. He just would not shut up."

Shoshanah fixed him with a deep brown-eyed stare. "He gave her to me. I want to give her back." Wasn't that just like the old man, throwing a trick even from beyond the grave. Where did he get off, standing up above them like that, yelling about heaven and hell and then giving presents to the kiddies.

First time he'd seen the Preacher was so far back the outlines had gone hazy, but he could still feel the clap on the shoulder and he could still hear the voice, smooth as a peppermint drop. "Morning, son." He'd looked up into a sun of a face, shining with sweat and vigor. "You stick around here and I'll learn you a thing or two."

He didn't have anything else to do, never really did, so he stayed that day. Then he'd stuck around for years. Got the milk crate arranged just so every Saturday, listening for the backfiring of the Preacher's pickup that meant he was about to baptize their street with sermonizing. "Hell's mouth's a-waiting, folks, and we're just dancing on its teeth." "Turn back! Turn back to the blood that saves!" "Being good's the angel's game. Ain't no man, woman, or child getting to heaven on that ticket." The kid loved the rhythm of the old man's voice, loved the flame that snapped from his eyes to the passersby.

Some would nod, raise an arm to the sky with a loud "Amen.

Amen, brother." Some crossed to the other side of the street, kept their heads low, but the preacher never let them get away with that. He'd sweep his shock of rough white hair from a tall forehead and yell through the bullhorn, "Neighbor, hear me now afore it's too late. The curse can be turned to a blessing if you turn from your ways. Just turn, my friend, turn."

The kid practiced at night, trying to get his eyes to burn, shaking his hair back and pointing an impressive finger at his reflection. "Just turn, my friend, turn. Hear me now afore it's too late." Even in the bathroom, his voice played thin and high, but if the Preacher ever turned to him, handed over the bullhorn, he'd be ready. Sometimes when he shut his eyes, he could see them, the angels going up and down the ladder, the cross on the hill, just like the old man said.

One Saturday the Preacher turned up one Saturday wearing overalls instead of his shiny black suit, lugging two cans of paint. The kid helped jimmy the lids up and they washed the wall together. "Red for the blood," the Preacher had said, painting a rectangle on the concrete they both filled in with thick brushes. They were just starting on gold for glory when a patrol car pulled to the curb next to them. "You got permission to do that?" the cop asked. "Yes, sir," the Preacher said, "on the highest authority." When the car pulled off, he'd winked down at the kid. "The earth is the Lord's and the fullness thereof. That makes this his territory, too. Don't you ever forget that."

Then they painted "REJOICE" in bold golden strokes. "Why not REPENT?" asked the kid, who'd been sure after the R and E that's what the word would be. He cleared his throat, tried to pitch his voice low, "You know - Turn, my friend, turn." The old man had chuckled and patted him on the shoulder, his second time to do that, and his last. "Because, boy, rejoice is what the angels said. I figure I can't do better than that. And people got to know what they're repenting to, ain't they? Hell's poured in all the gloom and doom this world can take. We're on the rejoicing side." That very day the Preacher added a new phrase to his repertoire, "Love each other, folks. Is your name written in the Lamb's Book of Life? Then love each other and rejoice."

The kid's voice had just begun to crack into the deeper registers on an occasional midnight "Turn, neighbor, turn," when the world went slantwise, everything slipping to the edge. First his father lost his job and couldn't find another one, no matter how many flyers he peeled from telephone poles. He'd sit on the couch with them piled up on either side, just drinking up all the empty angry hours. Then he let it all loose on whoever was around when they couldn't duck out fast enough. Mostly the kid's mom couldn't. Sometimes it didn't seem like she even tried. But every so often he caught it too.

First time the preacher saw the shiner on the kid's face, light blazed from his eyes. "You been fighting, son? Only fighting you and I should be doing is against the world, the flesh, and the devil. That what happened to you?" The kid thought the devil was the closest explanation, but he shook his head. "Well, I don't want to see that again, you hear? That's the broad path. You got to keep to the narrow. Only safe place, the narrow way."

It was then the idea had come to him. The Preacher could talk to his father, clap him on the shoulder, beam down on him and put everything right the way it had been before. Early the next Saturday morning, before his father had poured his first drink, the kid coaxed him down the steps of their tenement building with vague promises and pleadings. And for a wonder, between the hangover and the temporary lack of liquid determination, he came, holding up a hand against the light when they came out to the sidewalk.

The Preacher stepped off the milkcrate when he saw them, stuck out his hand. His father did not reciprocate. "What is this? What is this?" he'd yelled, stumbling in place. "You think I need saving, is that it?" He spit on the ground. "That what you think?" "We all need saving," said the Preacher, setting the bullhorn down and speaking as quiet as the kid had ever heard. "Being good's the angel's game."

His father spit again and turned away, dragging the kid with him, his grip surprisingly strong with everything else about him so uncertain. The kid looked back to the Preacher, waiting for him to run after them, to say the words that would turn his father around. But the Preacher was climbing onto the crate again, bullhorn back in hand. When they got upstairs, his father grabbed the kid by the collar, pulling him so close that beard stubble scratched his face and he couldn't turn away from the sour stench of the man's breath. "You ever pull a stunt like that again, your mother'll answer for it. You understand?"

He understood all right. And he sure didn't need the threat. When he thought of the Preacher getting back up on that crate, his face burned hot. Even after a knock came on the door and the Preacher's voice boomed through, asking after him, he wouldn't come out of his room. His father started in to screaming, "Get off my property! Go on, get!," and the words followed the Preacher out the door and down the stairs till they stopped like someone had switched off a radio. Next thing the kid knew his mother was coming in, her face crumpled and wet. "He fell, baby," she said. "Your father fell. He's gone."

For weeks, a roaring in his ears drowned everything out, especially the man by the rejoicing wall, and it was all just a dream till the Preacher found him at his father's service, pressed something into his hand. "I'm so sorry," he said, his peppermint voice barely coming through over the roar. "I know what it is to lose someone. I lost someone, too." Back at home, when the kid opened his hand, a Swiss Army pocket knife lay there. A knife. As if a trinket like that could make up for any of it. He shoved it down deep in his pocket where he'd never have to see it, and when at last the roaring went away, he found a different voice, his own voice, strong enough to shut out the preacher in his head.

The first Saturday after the Preacher had slumped off the crate with a hand clutching his heart, the first Saturday he wouldn't be coming, a clamor on the street woke the kid before dawn. Curious, he pulled on pants and a shirt that didn't have holes in it yet and joined the jostling crowd. They gathered at the Preacher's wall, those in front squatting down by the overturned milk crate under the circle of the street lamp, those at the back swaying together. The bullhorn lay where he'd thrown it the day before, but someone had turned the picture back around to face him.

"You fake," the kid whispered. "What?" asked Mrs. Edna Noles, cupping a hand around her ear. "I said he was a FAKE." This time the words came out full volume, and all eyes turned toward him in the dark. He stepped into the circle of light and turned to face them. "You know it as well as I do. He got up here every Saturday shouting his stupid words. Where did he get off coming here? Should have left us all alone."

"I guess you don't know," said Elton Adams, who ran the grocery where he stocked shelves after school. "You were probably too little when it happened." The kid wanted to ask the obvious question, but the roaring had come back, worse than before, and he couldn't get the breath for it. "Had a son shot down here. Where was it now?" "Corner of Spruce and Main," someone called. "That's right, down by the halfway house. Next Saturday the Preacher showed up, started telling us all to rejoice."

The roaring rang in his ears like crazy now and he pushed his way through the crowd, out to the darkness, the Swiss Army knife thudding in his pocket. At the line of trees on the edge of the neighborhood, he collapsed against a trunk and pulled out the knife, felt the weight of it, ran his finger across the nicks and scars he hadn't put there. "I know what it is to lose someone," the Preacher had said. Then he'd given a furious, ignorant boy something from his lost son.

But what difference had it made, that gift, all those Saturdays coming to the neighborhood? Nothing on the street had changed. Not one blessed thing. A splatter of tears speckled the leaves around him, drained the roaring from his head, leaving only Love each other and rejoice. He drew a long breath and got to his feet. That was one thing, at least. For better or worse he couldn't get the Preacher's words out of his head. He brushed the leaves from his pants and ran toward the rising of the sun, retracing his steps to where everyone huddled together by the shrine. Relief pulsed from his temples to his fingertips. He could still set it right.

The kid got up onto a milk crate and raised his hand. A murmur went through the crowd and then it fell silent, except for a few people shouting words of encouragement at him. The kid acknowledged them with a nod and a shy smile. In the full light of day, he looked less angry and more beautiful. He waited until people stopped shouting. A siren could be heard, maybe five or ten blocks away. He raised the bullhorn, pressed the button, and began to speak.

"I'd like to try again, to . . . to say a few words. You all knew the Preacher. And I guess you knew more about him than I did. But I stuck around with him every Saturday for years. So I . . . maybe I can say something too." His own voice rang strange in his ears, mechanical and canned. Maybe it had sounded that way to the Preacher, too. Or he'd damaged the horn with all that shaking the day before. No time to fix anything now with sirens just around the corner. Someone had seen the crowd and called it in.

Patrol cars, two of them, pulled to the curb, but no one jumped out and the sirens died away with a chirp. They were watching him, he knew it, blank faces through the windows. He shifted and the crate wobbled under him, but even if was disturbing the peace, he couldn't stop now. He hadn't said it all yet.

He opened his mouth to tell them all about the angels when a shadow drifted around the back of the crowd. No, not a shadow, exactly, someone in a hoodie and sneakers. And whoever it was held himself like his father had at the end. Shoulders, stance, all the same. The figure bent, spit on the ground, just like his father had done. The kid reached for his knife, bullhorn shaking in his other hand till he had to drop his arm to steady it.

People glanced at each other, heads turning this way and that, as the figure spit again. The kid's fingers tightened around the blades. Whoever that was, he didn't deserve REJOICE looking down on him. None of them did, with their uneven greasy parts, grey lines of roots behind the bleach, the beginning of a bald spot on Elton Adam's head.

Shoshanah wandered up with her thumb in her stupid mouth, holding a dirty green plastic pony, so putting her dolly on the pile sure hadn't been much of a sacrifice. And Mrs. Edna Noles next to her, nodding her head like a saint, everyone knew she was the one who called the cops when a shantytown of sorts sprang up under the Rejoice wall.

That had been around the same time the kid's father lost his job, and he hadn't been the only one. Some of the folks huddling there had been neighbors. A few souls went out with soup and an extra blanket or two, but not Mrs. Noles. No, she couldn't wait even a night to dial that number for people control, get the lot of them swept out like cockroaches.

Anywhere he poked a finger it'd be the same. Every one of them - Elton Adams who put recalled food back on the shelves to pinch his pennies and Mrs. Otis Norfolk who ran a prescription drugs scam out of her pink kitchen and the cops sitting across the road who were probably on the take – every one of them stood like a blight by this wall where the Preacher had called to them.

The kid remembered the bullhorn in his hand just as his words rushed out like bile. "So let me share a phrase or two from what he used to say." He cleared his throat. "You're all dancing on the teeth of HELLLL." He drew the last word out, the reverberations throbbing through his hand like voltage. "Of HELL," he cried again, savoring the vicious joy that came with the words, with the perspective of a few feet of altitude. And this time the voice that came out sounded like his own, though he'd never practiced that phrase.

The figure in the hoodie had stopped, half-turned toward him, face still in shadow. "Turn back," he should say now, "Turn back," but he couldn't, even though the words rang in his head clear as if the Preacher had been standing right beside him like before, like always. Being good's the angel's game. The angel's game. Who'm I to do better than the message they brought.

All he'd just yelled about hell hung in the air. And his words had found their mark. Shoshanah crossed her arms around her pony like she was trying to keep it safe, nailing him with the look from the day before. Whoever it was in the hoodie had disappeared. Everyone else stood apart from each other, worry lines deepening on their foreheads, separate islands on the ocean of the sidewalk.

The kid licked his cold lips. This was no way to honor a memory. He had to do better by the milk crate. "Turn, friends, turn." The words, thin and wavering, came out nothing like he'd practiced all those years. "Hear me now."

"Amen!" someone called from the crowd. "Amen." It sounded

like Mrs. Noles, but he couldn't be sure and he forced himself to go on anyhow. "Being good's the angel's game. Isn't any man, woman, or child getting to heaven on that ticket." That's as far as he'd go. No way was he going to hand out love and rejoicing to this bunch of hypocrites.

Elton Adams shrugged at Mrs. Otis. The others just stared off into space. No, this was nothing like what he'd pictured, and heat rose up his neck, set his face to burning as they began to drift off in twos and threes, whispering together, stealing looks back, while his strained voice repeated the old phrases.

By the time the patrol cars pulled off, only Shoshanah was left. "You the new preacher?" she asked he stepped down from the crate and leaned the bullhorn against the wall. "No." His voice came out hoarse, cracking from the yelling and the crying before that. "Never was, never will be." To keep her from saying anything else, he turned his back. "I got to clean up."

A plastic bag fluttered under one of the crates and he grabbed it. Flowers, candles, matted teddy bears with dirty satin hearts, he just stuffed it all in. But when he got to Shoshanah's dolly, a little worse for wear from a night outside, he held it out. "Here. He'd want you to have it. Really."

"I said it's his now. I gave it back to him. And you're the Preacher." She turned on her heel and stalked down the sidewalk. The kid threw the doll in with the rest of the junk and knotted the handles. That was the end of it. When he had time and a few extra bucks, he'd paint over the wall and everything would be back to normal.

On his way home, he threw the bag in a dumpster. Then he stowed the knife in a shoebox at the back of his closet. To keep any stray preacher words from running through his mind, he hummed anything that came to mind. "Jingle Bells" came most often, and for days he caught his mother staring, eyebrows raised. "You're in a festive mood," she finally said, twisting her lower lip in the way she had when she wasn't sure about something.

He couldn't hum in class, so first and second period he took in Lila Beth's slim shoulders, the curve of her back. Third and fourth she sat across the row, all lashes and legs, and he learned them hour by hour. "Stop it," she whispered, but he couldn't.

At the grocery after school, he stocked shelves at breakneck speed till all he could think of was the flash of cans. Mr. Adams scolded him for putting rows of sweet potatoes where the fruit cocktail should have gone, and all the time in the back of his head the earth is the Lord's and the fullness thereof. When the mixups didn't stop, Mr. Adams sent him out on deliveries. "The only good thing is, they can tell you if you get it wrong. Don't know what's gotten into you this week." But the way he looked down, something sharp in his glance, he suspected.

For his first stop, the kid carried a bag from the pharmacy to Mrs. Otis. Of course she'd call for pills, fodder for her fixes. "Just a minute," she yelled when he rang the bell, and slippers shuffled around on the other side, stashing evidence, probably. Then the door opened and she motioned him in, a soiled pink bathrobe wrapped around her massive form. "I really can't thank you enough for coming. Ma's been so bad today I didn't want to leave her." Sure she has, thought the kid. How stupid do you think I am.

But for once someone lay on the bed in the back room and the whole place stank of ointment and urine. While Mrs. Otis ran the tap for a glass of water, the old woman's groans made his stomach twist. "Here you are," Mrs. Otis said, fumbling with a sequined change purse and stuffing money in his hand. She smiled at him with panic behind it, back deep in her eyes. He knew that look. She was bracing for the blow.

He bolted back down her stairs, away from that suffocating room, but panic flashed out everywhere now, even from the eyes of strangers. When he got back to the store, Mr. Adams looked up with the sorrow so plain the kid had to look away. He kept his eyes down all the way home for fear of seeing anything else because he hadn't saved his father and he'd let down the Preacher and he couldn't lay another matchstick to that blaze. At the old wall, REJOICE pursued him like the rest, all the way to the apartment where his mother looked up, bruised to the core though the blotches had long since faded from her face. Hear me now afore it's too late. Hear me now.

He couldn't go on like this. There was only one thing to be done. That night, he reached in the back of the closet for the shoe box and pulled out the Swiss Army knife. Then he ran to the pawn shop, swallowing down a choking all the way, and stumbled back with two cans of paint banging against his knees.

That night he stayed up staring into the bathroom mirror, his reflection twisted by the one working bulb. He'd done it. The words in his head were gone, leaving him alone with the world. "Turn, friend, turn," he whispered as he switched off the light at dawn.

It was Saturday, so he carried the cans and two brushes to the preacher's wall. He dipped one brush in yellow and touched up the bend of the "R," the chips in the "O" and the broken prongs of "E." Then he dipped the other in red and sharpened the edges of the rectangle. With each stroke of the brush, the words came flooding back until when Mrs. Otis opened her front door, the Preacher kicked a crate into position and picked up the bullhorn.

Holy Mess of Accidents

Katherine Doar

◆

Beyond the cracked sidewalk, and the telephone pole with layers of flyers in a rainbow of colors, and the patch of dry brown grass there stood a ten-foot high concrete block wall, caked with dozens of coats of paint. There was a small shrine at the foot of it, with burnt out candles and dead flowers and a few soggy teddy bears. One word of graffiti filled the wall, red letters on a gold background: Rejoice!

Over time, the shrine reaches a level of public invisibility. It is like the body of a deer carcass flattening into the side of the road: slowly disintegrating, and yet, for what it has been through, remarkably intact. Its skull lies there with pleading eyes. Meanwhile, life rushes by.

Women in pantsuits, an old man with a cane, a teenager with large headphones on and toothless man in tattered coat: they all pass by without a second glance. There are groups of middle-schoolers, squirming in blue uniforms, with their lanky teachers stationed in the front and back, shepherding them. There are men with newspapers and wireless earsets, holding to-go coffee cups in meaty palms. On their way to the trains the people pass by and see nothing. They ignore the new interpretations that surround the word, "Rejoice!" Some one has written: Rejoice! –in zombies! Rejoice! –In sea monsters! A squid has been scrawled across the curve of the J, and seems to be wrestling with it.

On their way to the trains some children, not yet attuned to the mandate of invisibility, crane their necks over their parents' shoulders, or twist their bodies backwards like ballerinas, still holding tight to their parents' hands. One little girl, loose from her mother, goes running up to the block wall with her arms outstretched and a budding smile on her lips, like she can't believe her luck.

The girl doesn't stare but immediately gets down on her knees before the shrine and digs her hands into the pile of abandoned objects. She takes up several grimy candles and then, one by one, drops them into her coat pockets, like stones in a well. She plucks a rusty locket from around a bear's neck and then places it around her own. And lastly, she arranges all of the teddy bears in a circle—picking them up again as they fall on their backs—so that they are propped up-right, and facing each other.

"Now then," Martha tells them, putting her hands on her hips, "Stay put." She walks around the bears and with two fingers taps the heads of each. It looks like she is beginning a game of duck-duck goose, but instead of calling them ducks, she christens them something else: mother, father, sister, brother. Martha is a six-year-old girl. She is smart and bossy.

Filthy!" Martha turns as a voice comes rolling down the alley toward the block wall. It is coming from her mother, a slim, pale woman with a black stroller and a tight ponytail. The woman is in a state of emergency: her daughter is touching something untouchable, something dying. Martha starts to cry before her mother arrives, and the little dog encased in the stroller starts to bark.

As Penny (Martha's mother) approaches, so does a toothless man in tattered clothes. He totters toward them, shifting unsteadily in his damp sneakers. Penny looks down, and instinctively tries to both grab Martha's hand, and close her large purse, the mouth of which is drooping open to show an expensive wallet. But she's too slow. The man addresses them, laughs a honking laugh, and points to the circle of bears. He smells foul. "A tea party," he laughs, looking at Martha. His bloated finger trembles in the air as it stretches toward the bears. When he laughs again his eyes become slits, surrounded by a sea of dark wrinkles. Martha notices that Penny is impatient; she taps an enormous rectangular cell phone into the palm of her hand.

"No, not a tea party" Martha explains, to him, flustered. "It's a meeting." She gestures to the bears again, as if a closer look would explain everything. Dutiful, the old man crosses his arms and considers this. "Is that so?" he says. But Penny pulls Martha away before she can answer.

Once they arrive at the platform, Penny folds up the black stroller while Martha fits Silby, the little dog, into her travelling shirt. Her mother corrects her. "It's a harness," she says, snatching the leash away. "You're irri-ta-ble," Martha quips. But in her mind she already forgives Penny. She knows how her mother loves Silby, which is to say desperately—she is always afraid for her. "We won't let Daddy take Silby," Penny is always saying, "no matter how hard he tries."

On the train, Martha watches the landscape rush by like so many fishbowls. Everything looks slick from the rain, even the people, who disappear and reappear as if by magic, taking their lives with them into their holes, their secrets folded in the crooks of their arms, in the graceful deflation of their umbrellas. "Who's that?" Martha keeps asking. But for most of the train ride, Penny is asleep. Martha doesn't dream of telling her about the candles in her coat—and the locket—and the note that she had found behind the door of it, curled up in the center like a bug.

Back at the train station, the old man paces around the circle of bears. Ben has been coming here everyday for years, and yet he can't for the life of him remember how the bears appeared. Like the little girl, he touches the tops of their heads and tries to summon up their names, to find some hidden order. He notices that the one called Molly is missing something: perhaps a ribbon around her neck. Ben is still lingering among the animals an hour later, when Martha and Penny arrive at their train stop.

Once they have left the train station, Penny and Martha quickly come upon a large park. Penny gets in line for a hot dog, and Martha, idling near her mother, notices a teenage boy asleep on a park bench. Martha inches discreetly toward him, and comes to stand behind his head. She leans forward and whispers in his ear. "Dreams," she says, and he, nodding his head twice in his sleep, snorts in response.

Soon, Penny is standing behind him too, munching on her hot dog. "What, is he homeless?" asks crassly, with her mouth full. "He doesn't look like it." And he doesn't: the boy looks freshly showered and clean, lying flat on his back with his arms crossed, his legs dangling off the side of the bench. He wears dark jeans and a sweatshirt with a scarf tied around his neck. His hair is disheveled and dirty blonde, and his glasses lay across his stomach, rising and falling with his chest. "He's going to get mugged." Penny says. "Mugged," Martha repeats. As he turns and slings his arm off the bench, Silby sniffs it.

They find Penny's friend in the park. Jasmine has an angular face, glossy brown hair and light brown skin. She tips her body sideways as they approach, like a tea pot, to stare at Penny's stomach. "Pretty far along, aren't you?" she calls. Penny is pregnant in a way that defies pregnancy: her limbs are so bendy and thin that the bump of her stomach looks amiss, protruding unexpectedly under a tight black shirt. Whenever her arms brush her stomach, she looks surprised, like she's forgotten about the whole thing. Penny's friend wears a puffy black jacket. It teems with static as she leans over to kiss Martha on the cheek.

"I guess I am," Penny says to her, looking around the park. "Three? Four months?" Jasmine closes her eyes and shakes her head from side to side in deep sympathy, but then, realizing that it is too late, exclaims: "how exciting!" opening her eyes wide. But every one knows about the unwanted baby, the nasty divorce. Penny just says: "Thanks for watching her." After she leaves Jasmine takes a long look at Martha, whose pockets are positively drooping with the contraband. "And you," Jasmine says, "What do you have there?"

In a little while Jasmine and Martha are lounging on a blanket with the candles laid out before them. Jasmine makes a yellow and a blue candle kiss (saying, "mmuah! mmuah!") while Martha arranges the remaining candles in a circle and names them, over and over. "Mother, Father, Sister, Brother, Mother, Father, Sister, Brother."

Jasmine pauses with her candles in mid-kiss, "Martha," she asks, "What are you doing?" For awhile Martha just stares at her, slobbering in concentration. But then she abruptly swipes her mouth and clasps her hands together. "I'm making a family," she explains. Her words make a large crease in the middle of Jasmine's eye brows. "A family," Jasmine repeats. "Let's make a zoo instead, or a village, or an office, or maybe a theme park."

Martha extends one arm forward, and with her palm up like a dancer, knocks all of the candles down. Jasmine exhales. "That's better," she says, and they start their game over. Just a few feet away from them, the sleeping teenager sits up. Henry has had trouble sleeping lately, especially in solitude. Now, he finds that he needs a very specific set of circumstances to sleep: he needs a lot of people around, or the TV on way up—neither of which his parents will tolerate in their home. Lately, he has slept on park benches or in movie theaters and sometimes on the floor of his parents' bedroom. And yet no place summons such consistent sleep for him as this one: Henry needs this particular park, and this particular bench, in this particular kind of mid-morning sunlight.

Sitting upright, Henry extracts the bible from his backpack, but the smell of his own foul breath keeps him from concentrating, setting off a string of strange thoughts and associations. And though he can hear the recitation of the words in his head, the meaning floats free—he crawls slowly after it. Instead of concentrating, he thinks about the insides of human beings; he imagines blood, and its gritty smell; he considers its texture, and color—which is so like paint, something industrial rather than natural. He closes the book and begins to walk. Then he feels hungry, and thinks about eating; he smells a falafel cart, somewhere south; he sees the blood oozing around his sister's head, and he tastes it in his mouth.

A shriek, a cry. He looks down to see that he has stepped through something—a bunch of toys. "Our village!" a little girl in a pink coat shouts at him. An older woman laughs, covers her mouth and then whispers to him behind the curtain of her hand, "It's okay." As Henry bends down to help them, the woman speaks slowly and loudly. "We were building a village," she says, looking intently at the girl for confirmation. But the girl shakes her head. "A zoo," she says, "I decided it's a zoo." Henry then realizes the toys are candles, and, turning them over, sees that they are filthy. "It could be Noah's Ark," he suggests, raising a pink candle to the sky. The woman frowns. "That's enough," she says, and then, looking at the girl with raised eyebrows: "Say thank you." And then he is done for. Henry cannot help but think about it.

In the weeks following his sister's death, family friends and distant relations alike brought lavish wicker baskets, full of fruit and bread and cheese. They did not stay to talk, and their gifts remained in their harsh, crinkly plastic, sitting tall, proudly as peacocks, on their kitchen counter. But their sympathy soon faded into awe, and the family's physical presence could not contend with the tendrils of neighborhood legend. Bundled up dog-walkers would pause before their house, wrapping their leashes twice around their wrists, to behold the cite of the tragic accident: they gazed at the shut-up curtains, and behind them, what they knew to be shells of people—victims of the holy mess of accidents.

For the remainder of his childhood Henry stayed alone in his room, burning through innumerable movies and clutching a village of stuffed animals around him. Late at night, he would try to make out the sporadic hush of his parents voices, which came from the kitchen downstairs. He imagined them at their opposing stations: his father at the head of the table, as if waiting for a meal, and his mother leaning against the refrigerator, her eyes cast down. They hardly conversed as they tried to find a place for the tragedy. Even then, Henry knew the truth: that he had killed his little sister. But other people, even his parents, would try to take his guilt away from him. He's just a kid, they'd say, until he was long past that. In his own mind, Henry has always been two people: a kid and a criminal. Sometimes he sees himself as that kid, without recognition, as he is walking through the park.

The kid finds himself in the middle of a scene, the performers in the middle, and the crowd around them. It has just ended, and once the performers have packed up their instruments, they are gone. Moving as quick as thieves—with their large bags slung over their shoulders—they made vibrant blobs of color for the grey landscape. They've left behind a few milk crates.

The kid got up onto a milk crate and raised his hand. A murmur went through the crowd and then it fell silent, except for a few people shouting words of encouragement at him. The kid acknowledged them with a nod and a shy smile. In the full light of day, he looked less angry and more beautiful. He waited until people stopped shouting. A siren could be heard, maybe five or ten blocks away. The kid raised the bullhorn, pressed the button, and began to speak.

And now that he must speak he is himself: repentant, and criminal. "Rejoice!" he yells. And he feels every action. As he extracts his bible from his backpack, a chunk of people leave: this is not the type of entertainment that they were looking for. Henry, though, is used to the exodus, to the dirty looks—he has done this before.

He reads from the bible at random: "So He said to him, 'Bring me a three-year old heifer, a three-year-old female goat…a turtle dove..'" Someone from the crowd throws a half-eaten falafel sandwich at him, and Henry will not dodge it. The sandwich hits his middle, splattering hot sauce onto the frames of his glasses; it flops limply to the floor, like a dead fish.

"…Know, certainly, that your descendants will be strangers in a land that is not theirs…" Two college-age women in denim jackets walk by, murmuring something like "bigot." A Midwestern tourist tries to reason with the boys who heckle him, but to no avail. Henry, though, is satisfied to be the pilloried criminal in the town square. He reads the words though doesn't get the meaning—and behind the recitation—he prays that the meaning will come.

As a young boy, Henry liked family therapy TV shows. His favorite part was the end of the show, where Dr. Phil would suggest a few far-fetched ways to make it even again. Henry thought it was nice to have the ledger created, to know who was wrong and how. People may or may not change, but just you wait. Punishment is forthcoming—Dr. Phil's flat look seemed to imply it—punishment indeed! It came naturally enough to such people. They did not need to be told.

Henry remembers Dr. Phil's voice in the background of his sister's death. His voice is the start of the memory: six-year-old Henry finds Dr. Phil on the small television that sits on top of his parent's dresser. The dresser is old and as tall and heavy as an ogre—as tall as the start of his father's neck. The bottom drawer hangs open, showing a nest of white sheets packed into it. Henry wipes his hand over the sheets, bends down to smells their warmth, and then steps gingerly into the drawer, with bare feet, clutching the top of the dresser to steady himself.

After awhile his sister walks in. She's tiny—just three at the time, and she likes to chase Henry around everywhere. On the television, a group of three sisters are squabbling over their dead father's estate. The youngest sister, Dora, who is the executor of the will, must to defend herself from the manipulations of her older sisters on a daily basis. They insist on receiving larger installments of money, more than they are due. Dora begins to cry as she thinks on the degradation of their sister-relationships, especially considering the love and trust that had previously characterized their idyllic childhood. Plus, she adds, the drama between them has interfered with her ability to grieve.

Dr. Phil arranges to have a photo of their dead father on appear on the screen behind them. But hysteria ensues (as he knows it will) and Dr. Phil seems unsure if a reconciliation is possible. As their emotions are being unsuccessfully corralled by Dr. Phil's questions ("doesn't that photo remind you of what's really at stake here?") Henry helps his little sister step into drawer beside him.

They watch for a minute or two before the drawer begins to fall. As Henry jumps to the side, there is enough time for him to turn and see Eliza still standing there. She doesn't even put up her hands, she hardly moves at all. Her neck is still curved to see the screen; her doughy hands still cling to the side of the dresser. The drawer pins her to the ground and the TV, as large as an old computer monitor, thumps onto her head. Underneath the rubble a pool of blood begins to form. Her body is so straight underneath that she looks like she's already been laid out for the coffin.

As Henry sees the blood gather around his sister's head he feels own mouth fill up with it. He puts a hand across his lips and then leans forward to vomit but nothing comes out. Now, standing on the milk crate, Henry feels that rust stuck along the sockets of his teeth. It has congealed there; he can smell it.

After a few pages of reading, nearly everyone has dispersed. Just a few people walk hurriedly past, permitting themselves a quick backward glace at him. They know that they should not see him, because is dangerous—his bible is aggressive, and his reading might try to suck them out of the narratives of their lives—which they must constantly hold steady, even as they move, like a train on fragile tracks that they have laid themselves. We tell ourselves stories, Henry thought. What was the full quote? We tell ourselves stories in order to live.

On the train back, Henry watches the sun go down until it is just a thin coin of something, its last burst of light defiantly streaking the sky. He shares a ride with the little girl from the park. She sleeps for most of the way, Henry notices, but once they arrive she springs out of her seat and goes running down the isle. The skinny pregnant woman starts at this, and then rushes down the isle after her—her eye mask still plastered to her forehead, and her little dog trailing behind.

From his seat Henry can see the girl's pink coat bouncing toward the alley where he used to read the bible. He sees that his graffiti has faded somewhat, and that his old stuffed animals have been moved—they are now arranged in a circle. The old man, Ben, who haunts the train station, is there with the bears, sitting down in the circle with them like a chief.

The little girl touches Ben on the shoulder, and when he peeks out from among the abandoned things, it is with great surprise, like he's just discovered an expansive river amid the usual slabs of concrete. The girl starts rearranging the bears while the old man stays sitting down, watching with his hand on his chin. As he says something to her she crosses the bears' legs and pushes their backs forward, making them sit up straight.

Henry remembers Ben; he used to be in the habit of buying him a cup of coffee every time he came to the train station. Ben's post is just outside the entrance, and still, he paces in front of it and shakes a cup of change at passerbys. For some time, Henry would offer to buy Ben coffee, and they would stand in line together at the dunkin' donuts. At the last minute Ben would always lean in close and put his chapped lips up to Henry's ear. "Something to eat, too," he asked. Henry could not refuse.

After awhile Henry started preparing to meet Ben. They would stand in line and talk a little, and he'd bring random things: his old ipod, a few of his mother's knick-knacks—glass animals from small nativity set. All of those things were eventually lost or stolen or sold, but the old stuffed animals Ben kept. He displayed them against the gold block wall as if it were his private bookshelf.

Once Henry had tired of this routine, it was easy to recede back into anonymity—to pretend that Ben was invisible even after they had seen each other every day for months. Ben had a weak memory. So, from a distance, Henry watched Ben's museum of lost things shrink and expand. He saw the candles and the locket appear, he saw passerbys throw their old coffee cups and fast-food wrappers into the shrine, their shopping receipts and tattered pamphlets, their gum wrappers and crumpled water bottles.

Now, getting off the train, Henry sees the girl returning the dirty candles to the shrine. Ben watches as she sets them down, one by one, inside the circle of bears. Eventually the pregnant woman reaches them, her shaggy little dog getting loose from her in the process. The mother yanks the little girl's pink sleeve away from the scene while the dog rushes past them, the girl yelling: "Silby—Silby—Silby—Bad girl," with tired, monotonous urgency. Both mother and daughter waddle after the leash, which drags on the concrete before them, through puddles laden with floating trash and dead leaves.

This little girl must remind him of Eliza. As a young girl, she was full of wonder, she was especially in awe of churches—their stained glass windows and robed priests. She would always point to the church spire, and then the crowds of people, who clomped out of the two, grand doors that were thrown open after the service. She had never actually been to church, and their parents were not religious, but she was enthralled by the mystery of such gatherings.

Henry started going after she died, trying to make himself believe. The order was attractive, and he wanted to have someone else decide things for him. As he thinks about all of this—the toothless man's museum of accidents, his little sister and her religion, his own wish to have it—he steps out of the train just in time to see the little dog, Silby, getting squashed by a car.

He runs toward the scene, though he's not sure why. The pregnant woman doubled over in agony, she clutches her stomach as she screams. Henry can't take his eyes away from the small body of the dog, its short tail that, moments ago, he had watched twitching from side to side. Now the dog is reduced to a series of colors, grey and red and pink.

The little girl still yells for Silby, ("Bad girl!") even as she kneels down and tries to hold her corpse and rock it like a baby. The pregnant woman, in her agony, still can't help but try to shield her daughter from the filthiness of it all, the contamination of the accident. "Martha!" she yells.

But the girl ignores her mother's urgent summons—she is unabashed. She holds the dog's bloody head in her lap and looks queasy, her plump face becoming dimpled and puffy and her mouth forming a crinkly circle as she begins to cry. She pets Silby furiously. The driver has exited his car, and he stands to the side, rotating slightly now and then, with his hand over his mouth. He wonders if he should speak at all.

Henry needs to leave. But first he stops by Ben's museum. The toothless man seems to have been undisturbed by the dead dog and the commotion resulting from it—he stays amongst his bears. "Excuse me," Ben says. "Can you please help?"

Henry reaches into his back pocket for his wallet and extracts a few dollars. He tries to hand it to him. But Ben is lost in thought, and waves the money away. "Can you tell me the names of these bears?" he asks quietly, sweeping his arm over the scene like a game show host displaying a prize. Henry puts the money back in his wallet. He says that he can.

Unveiled Redemption

Kelsey Dunn

Beyond the cracked sidewalk, and the telephone pole with layers of flyers in a rainbow of colors, and the patch of dry brown grass there stood a ten-foot high concrete block wall, caked with dozens of coats of paint. There was a small shrine at the foot of it, with burnt out candles and dead flowers and a few soggy teddy bears. One word of graffiti filled the wall, red letters on a gold background: Rejoice!

Marcus leaned against the door frame of the small shop across the street, tattooed arms crossed over his plain white t-shirt, and watched the little girl in the Halloween costume that she wore year-round approach the wall. She knelt carefully, hiking up the tunic of her nun's habit and smoothing the veil that framed her face. That she used the wet, filthy teddy bears as kneepads against the cement seemed borderline sacrilegious to Marcus, not to mention gross, but then again it wasn't like he gave a damn. He didn't know the kid personally and they were just crappy Made-in-Taiwan toys, not baby Jesus himself.

He ought to be tending to the tasks that Sal had left for him to do, but the list wasn't long and there'd be plenty of time to see to that before the old crank returned. The weather was good enough to keep the door propped open and the miniature Sister was worth watching if for no other reason than to pass the time. This part of the day, after lunch but well before evening, was the quietest time in the neighborhood. Kids were in school. Adults were at work. Old people were reliably either napping or sometimes attending funerals, as Sal was today. Marcus and the fruity kid whom some called Hannah-Banana were the only souls on the block.

The costume was by traditional necessity black, and by financial necessity polyester. Cheaply and crudely fashioned, the costume was less convincing than the girl herself. While most costumes transform the wearer, in this case it was the girl within the garment that made it believable. With her grimy hands pressed precisely together, fingers aligned meticulously and palms so lightly touching as to allow the Holy Spirit itself to pass through as needed, Hannah prayed. Or at least that's what Marcus assumed she was doing.

She was not praying. Not exactly. Hannah knew a few prayers, of course she did. Who doesn't know The Lord's Prayer and Psalm 23? It wasn't for lack of material that the girl forewent these favorites, the problem was that she was just flat-out too hungry to be reminded about daily bread, or a banquet prepared for her in the presence of her enemies when her stomach was growling louder than Daniel's lions! Hannah bowed her head closer to her hands and with her nose nearly touching her fingertips she inhaled slowly, savoring the lingering scent of glaze from the single magnificent donut-hole Mrs. Botham had given the child at the back door of the bakery about an hour ago. Likely, it was one that had rolled to the floor by accident, but Hannah, assuredly, had not minded at all.

Mrs. Botham had not become wealthy by way of honesty. She herself had probably accidentally mishandled the treat, snatched it up quickly, and dropped it deftly into her apron pocket, never pausing in her sales pitch that was reliably a repeated loop of forceful suggestions such as insisting someone would also be needing some bread for their supper, or that some other customer simply must have two of something because it was too wonderful to enjoy only one! She would have fully intended to put the donut-hole back on the tray with the others later, but instead had forgotten about it.

When the morning rush of customers was over, and as she removed the empty tray from the case, Mrs. Botham would only then have recalled the fallen treat and been predictably loathe to throw it in the trash. She did have a favorite stray cat referred to locally *as Sir Somebody* on account of his regal yet secretive nature, and he would have enjoyed the treat himself had the grubby little nun not chosen that exact moment to peer through the back door and witness the woman pulling the fried dough ball from her apron pocket, picking at some lint stuck to it.

Marcus pushed off from the door frame and slid his hands into the pockets of his jeans, standing straight, his body now effectively blocking the door entirely. The girl, bowing her head, her veil falling forward to shield her vision like blinders on a harness horse, did not notice. The gold cross on the chain around Marcus's neck winked at the girl. Hannah's tongue emerged from between her somber lips and licked her finger.

Sir Somebody appeared atop the wall abruptly, as if a genie from a bottle just rubbed. He sat. While the concrete block wall was ten-feet tall at the street it was not an independent edifice but rather the back of a short, squat, flat-roofed building that faced out onto the street parallel to this one. An abandoned building that had once been a shop of some kind but few could remember what and even fewer cared. From the ground, to the dumpsters, to the roof, to the top of the wall, the cat regularly ascended as part of his daily ritual, particularly on cooler mornings when this was the best perch from which to gather some morning sun. And to watch the nun.

Staring down at the donut thief, he too licked at a paw. Stopping then, and with his tongue sticking out from between his lips, his foreleg frozen in mid-air, he actively pretended not to notice Marcus watching him, as cats are wont to do.

Hannah also stopped in mid-lick. Her face burned with a flare of guilt and she drew her tongue in slowly, swallowing before parting her hands to cross herself and greet this Brother properly. But Sir Somebody turned away from the child and instead gazed far down the street, his tail tip twitching. Both child and cat startled when they heard the telephone of the shop across the street.

Marcus jumped too. Sal was so hard of hearing that the bells on the wall attached to the phone clanged loud enough to wake the dead. The boy reached the telephone in three long strides, before the bells could take another shot at resurrecting someone, and spent the next five minutes firmly insisting to Mrs. Johnson that no, Sal did not do sandals, only shoes and boots. Yes, he was certain. No, never sandals. Never. No, not even for Jesus.

Sir Somebody leapt down to a branch of the dead Elm tree that hugged the wall and descended to the street. Hannah's eyes brightened and she held out her arms to welcome him as he ran to her, and then beyond her, to the open door of the shop. The girl, hands outstretched, drew them back to straighten her veil and wimple before letting her hands fall to her sides, her voluminous black sleeves following her arms as feathers on the wings of a pigeon, spreading up, then tucking back down into place. She gave a tug on the knot of the rope around her waist, and serenely traced the cat's tracks.

The cat crossed the threshold and strolled directly down the long aisle toward the back of the building, glancing briefly this way and that as if browsing but certainly not shopping. The girl stopped in the doorway, waiting for her eyes to adjust to the darkness, identifying immediately only a white t-shirt moving behind the counter. She blinked, and clasped her hands together at her waist.

Marcus was still on the phone and knew no urgency to end the call as he would have had a real customer entered. Not only was this nutty girl always barefoot and therefore not in need of shoe accessories or repair, she had no money. That much was clear. It was also said that she was mute. Not born mute, but initiated mute. He stared at the girl's lips as if to challenge them otherwise.

Mrs. Johnson, the exact opposite of mute, was still enjoying her weekly plea over the telephone line, that Sal certainly ought to at least have a *look* at her sandals for Heaven's sake, and Marcus, accommodating the woman in her relentlessly futile quest, continued to steadfastly refuse her.

Hannah, eyes adjusted somewhat now, looked at all of Marcus not just his shirt. One hand held the phone, one hand rubbed at the back of his neck as if to release a tension built there. His mouth was moving but she looked not at his lips or wispy moustache, she read only his eyes. He wasn't talking to her, but he was speaking to her. His eyes squinted. Hannah blinked again.

Sir Somebody marched back up the aisle to the front of the store, ears cocked sideways in the attitude of an aggravated man who has hastily crammed his hat upon his head in a declarative manner. Disappointed by the lack of customer service, perhaps, or finding the offerings to be beneath his requirements. There was not a single trace of mice in Sal's shop. He paused not a moment in his mission to depart from here to revisit the bakery and see if Mrs. Botham had perhaps left her back screen door unlatched.

The cat brushed the tattered hem of the girl's tunic as he passed. Marcus glanced down, his dark eyelashes pointing at the cat before lifting again to settle at half-mast and meet the eyes of the child. The silent Sister's pewter stare held for only a few seconds before being shuttered completely as she bowed her head, her slight shoulders arching inward as she took three paces backwards before pivoting to return to her wall. She picked up the fattest, tallest candle she found there, crossed herself again, and slipped out of sight behind the block wall.

The telephone cord was not long enough to reach the doorway and by the time Marcus extricated himself from Mrs. Johnson's diatribe the street was once again deserted. Several blocks away, the bells at St. Michael's began to toll. Eight times, and then eight more. Sal would be returning with whatever handout had been offered by the ushers to staple it to the wall behind the counter as he had in memoriam of all of his customers over the years, but for the immediate moment Marcus now knew that Old Lady Haggis (or "The Hag" as decades of youth had called her) had made it to 88. Probably true that only the good die young.

Marcus resumed his position within the door frame, arms folded across his chest, necklace winking at the empty street and wondered where the little fruit had gone. Today was the first time he had seen her face so clearly and closely and he now wondered how old she really was. Not as much of a kid after all, he had thought. Taller than he had previously considered her to be also. He wondered what color her hair was. He tried to recall if he had ever seen her in regular clothes and had only a vague memory of a woman with a child on her hip when he himself was still tearing around Sal's shop in rompers. Same eyes.

A breeze began to whoosh down the sidewalk, threading itself between lamp posts and teasing at the awnings. Better to shut the door than to have even more sweeping and dusting to do, so the boy did just that and, remembering that cat's visit, hurried to the back room to get the cleaning supplies and make sure the old tomcat hadn't engaged in any unsolicited business.

Hannah climbed in through the window of the squat building that belonged to the painted wall and moved easily in the dark of this familiar place. The electricity had been shut off years ago, but the girl got free matchbooks at the gas station on the corner and she kept them carefully preserved in a zip-lock baggie. They also let her fill her water jug in the service station bathroom and she poured some into her single cooking pot and placed it on the wire plant stand she had found next to a garbage can one day. The fat candle's wick was damp and it took two tries before it crackled to life. Today, Hannah had nothing to put into her water to make anything at all in the way of soup or tea, but she had discovered early on that drinking warm water is more filling and satisfying than cold. Sometimes, the pot held a faint flavor of a previous effort and with some imagination the girl could feel very blessed indeed.

As she waited for the candle to warm the water, Hannah removed her hair coverings and began to brush her hair. She studied the calendar on the wall that was thirteen years old (not as old as her, but close) and guessed at what day today was. If her guess was lucky, and she hadn't been unlucky yet, she needed to get out of here before tomorrow. She braided her hair carefully, and her brush was the first thing she hid. The way the wind was gathering itself, she'd better leave soon if she wanted to outrun the rain. Tomorrow, they'd be here looking for her. Again.

Three days later an automobile pulled up and parked beside the concrete wall. The driver opened the door, but did not get out of the car. Although her face was in shadow, it was easy to tell she was sad. There was something about how she turned away from the sun and rested the weight of her hands on the steering wheel, something about her silent composure, that caused Hannah to sigh. The young girl watched the driver lean out of the car and stretch her hand out towards one of the burned out candles.

The rains had not come behind the winds after all and the teddy bears were finally dry, as was the woman's face. The tears had stopped, eventually, and left in their wake nothing but weary, dry lines of exhaustion. A shame to see on a countenance so youthful otherwise. She couldn't have been more than twenty.

Hannah's free hand fumbled at the homemade Rosary beads hanging from her belt and Sir Somebody struggled to be released from the grip in which she clutched him with her other arm. Not that his efforts were entirely sincere. He was curious about this car and this woman whom he had never seen in his neighborhood before, but everybody knows what curiosity can do to a cat. As Hannah squeezed him tighter, he stilled.

The girl and the cat peered from behind a dumpster in the alley, the one belonging to the creaky hardware store that regularly held some interesting and useful items for resourceful individuals. On Fridays there were even little baggies of popcorn discarded at the end of the day that were free for the taking ever since The Hag had become too frail to come for them and scatter the treats in the park for the ducks. Hannah ate the popcorn. Sir Somebody ate the sparrows he caught when Hannah tossed a few kernels on the rooftop behind the wall to aide him in his efforts.

The woman in the car swung her legs out the open door to lean her elbows on her legs and press her face into her hands. It was a beautiful day and that is why she was here. The temperature was ideal and the breeze was still. She was thankful for that, and for many things, really, but oh, she felt so disgusted by the whole ordeal. Thank God no one she knew would see her. She'd better just get started so that she could get it all over with and get out of this crappy place. She lifted her face and touched the button to pop the trunk.

At this development, Sir Somebody could stand it no longer and he launched himself free of Hannah's embrace to race behind the wall and silently traverse his climbing obstacle-course to the roof, where he then peered down over the edge. Hannah looked up at him, then at her arm, pulling up her sleeve to examine the scratches left there. They were barely bleeding and they itched more than they hurt. Hannah hesitated not at all to lick them clean. The pharmacy's dumpster, unlike that of the hardware store, never had anything helpful in it, just trash bags of paperwork and used Kleenex, and sometimes soiled bandages or adult diapers.

From the car the woman removed a short step ladder which she carried to the wall first. Next, she pulled out a brand new paint tray, a roller with an extending pole and a stiff-bristled brush. The paint cans came last, five of them in total, all containing the same exterior, white, matte latex. They had just been shaken at the big box store on the other side of town and the woman felt in her pockets to find the tool the man had sold her to open the cans. Hannah's eyes grew wide and her hands covered her heart. A low moan rose from deep within her. She turned and scurried silently through the heavy shadows of the alley.

Marcus turned the corner, his arms loaded with groceries for Sal's sister. Sal had never married and neither had Rosa, the two of them preferring the less dramatic union of siblings over that of romantic bonds. His step faltered almost imperceptibly when he saw the car and a head of cabbage in the bottom of one paper bag bumped at his hip. He strode on, and resettled the fussy bag more securely to his side. The scent of fresh fennel was drawn up from one bag as Marcus drew in a sharp breath.

Using his elbow to ring the buzzer to the door next to that of Sal's shop, Marcus waited for Rosa to answer and turned to stare across the street. The woman was on a stepladder that was too short for her to reach the highest portion of the wall and as she stretched to scrub at it with the stiff brush, glittering gold paint flakes sprinkled down on her and her clothes and the ground. Her shirt had become untucked and Marcus saw that her skin looked golden too. Tan from a vacation, or a tanning bed, or maybe even a pool at her parents' house by which she regularly lounged. The woman wobbled a bit, recovered, swore, and continued her efforts.

Rosa's voice crackled over the intercom. Marcus answered and ascended the steps to the familiar flat and the tiny kitchen where Rosa greeted him by patting at his cheeks and telling him he was a good boy. He put the bags down on the tiny kitchen table, but instead of sitting down in Sal's chair as he normally did to visit and listen to Rosa praise her vegetables, he crossed the sitting room and drew back the curtain. Across the street, Sir Somebody noticed the movement in the window and stared at Marcus for an instant before returning his watchful eyes to the woman who was assaulting his wall.

Marcus had seen plenty of people come and paint that dumb wall, but usually they were nervous, jerky black youth, holding their pants up with one hand and slapping a paintbrush half-heartedly at the wall with the other. Or, sometimes, loud young white men with their brash sneers and gym bodies, the kind of guys who would pick up the teddy bears and make them do lewd things to one another and laugh. Community service, they called it. Eliminating the graffiti in this unfortunate part of town. Discouraging gang activities, the leaders and elected officials declared proudly. As if there were any gangs. Not in this old neighborhood.

The most recent painters had actually been a church youth group who had adopted the wall as a project for the Glory of God, or some bullshit like that. Marcus had seen the Sunday School teacher yapping away with a television reporter that day, but had heard very little of the actual interview, rather he had followed the flapping arms of the animated mentor as she gestured about these things. Pointing to Heaven is always a dead giveaway.

The gold paint had probably been expensive, but Catholics always have a lot of money. The red paint they had bought far too much of and the can was still three-quarters full after they had completed their message. The lady teacher and her pupils had disposed of the empty cans and used supplies in the dumpster behind the hardware store, but you cannot throw real paint away like that and for about five minutes it was a real dilemma on which the lady paced and fretted, picking up the can and carrying it to the dumpster, then back to the van, then back to the wall. The kids by then had all piled in and were getting loud and kicking at seat -backs and needed very much to be hauled out of there.

In the end, the woman had glanced around and set the can down on the ground near the passenger-side front tire of the van before quickly skirting the grill of the Chevy, climbing in, turning the key, and departing. The paint can stood there alone for a while, like a person stranded at a bus stop with no fare, but it hadn't taken long at all before the little nun darted out to snatch it.

Rosa had finished putting away her groceries and was asking Marcus wouldn't he like some nice hot tea? Marcus didn't, but with a few cubes of sugar added it was tolerable and he knew she didn't want him to leave just yet. He left the window and returned to the kitchen to sit in Sal's chair. He admired the teacup and saucer with the yellow roses on them which he knew represented friendship because Rosa had told him so once before, and the old woman and the young man gestured toward one another with their cups before drinking.

Hannah had gone the long way around, traversing several blocks before returning at a different angle down an empty alley, stopping only when she had reached the back door to the shoe shop. She had a small ache in her side from running and she paused to catch her breath before knocking lightly on the door.

Sal was in the back room, resoling Mr. Landon's loafers, and the radio was so loud that Hannah could hear the baseball game quite clearly through the closed door. She knocked again, a little harder, then clasped her hands tightly in prayer. Sir Somebody walked lightly across the girl's bare feet, taking care to keep his claws sheathed, and meowed so loudly that the effort of the emission elicited a brief, harsh coughing jag. Rosa, who always kept the back windows open but never the front ones, heard him.

Her tea cup clattered a clumsy landing in its saucer as she rose swiftly to hurry to the biscuit tin she kept on the kitchen counter. Calling out to her "*peppino*" three times as was her habit she then leaned out the window and dropped the cookie. Her fingers abruptly clawed at the air a second after they had released and an exclamation fell from her mouth at the unexpected sight of not one but two sets of hungry eyes looking heavenward. The biscuit's fall was broken by the costumed shoulder of the waif, and it bounced lightly before continuing its descent. Sir Somebody made a grab for it and trotted away with his treasure in his mouth as Hannah continued to gaze up at the open window from which both old woman and boy now looked down.

Marcus was on the fire escape in an instant and scrambled under the railing to hang and drop to the asphalt beside the little nun whose hands remained frozen together. He held up both hands, imploring her to be still and not run away, only belatedly remembering that she was mute, not deaf. But the sign-language was all that had come to him on short notice and Marcus yanked open the door to Sal's back room and rushed through.

Sal glanced up in time to see the back of the boy who strode quickly to the shelves underneath the counter in the shop and returned just as quickly with an ancient but well-cared for paintbrush that he used every Fall to touch up the building's exterior window and door trim. He slapped the old man on the back which brought forth a grunt of indeterminate nature, slammed the door shut behind him, and stopped in front of Hannah who had, to Marcus's relief, obeyed his command. He held the brush out to her and their eyes met. She smiled at this answered prayer.

It was over an hour later when the car finally drove away. The golden girl's clothes were greatly speckled with white splatter, and swaths of paint were smeared across her forehead and cheeks as if to mark her publicly as the offender she was. Marcus had gone into the hardware store alone earlier to get a free paint stir-stick and Mr. Asleson had also given him two bags of fresh popcorn. He and Hannah had sat on a bench down the street to slowly eat their snacks and pretend not to be watching the wall being defaced in the name of redemption. Marcus watched Hannah when they saw the girl gather up the candles and the stuffed toys and throw them all into the dumpster with the used painting supplies, concerned for her reaction, but Hannah did not even flinch.

It was harder than either of them had thought it would be. Unlike writing with a crayon or marker on a regular sheet of paper, a spatial relationship so familiar and practiced, they found they had to frequently stop during the course of this effort so that one or the other could jog across the street for the necessary perspective with which to make adjustments so that their message would indeed fall within both the physical and aesthetic definitions set by the huge wall. Sal perched on a wooden stool on the sidewalk, stitching some leather pieces by hand and glancing up periodically to watch the kids. Sir Somebody sat beside him without any obvious occupation at all. From the now-open front windows of the upstairs flat, the smells of ham and cabbage began to waft.

As difficult as the task technically was, the most difficult part had come before they'd even begun. Convincing Hannah to remove her costume had required some great effort. Marcus had done enough painting in his years that he predicted that even this gentle water-based latex would not be easily washed from her cherished garments and there was a real risk of ruining them. Besides, the paint was as red as blood which assuredly could raise alarm in anyone seeing it upon her clothing in the future. She knew he was right, and she folded each item carefully as she removed it, placing the small pile in the crotch of the dead Elm tree. In her torn jeans and snug t-shirt Hannah hugged herself as if naked. Marcus reached both hands behind his neck and unclasped his necklace, refastening it around Hannah's neck to cover her. The cross winked and beamed at the boy.

They had just finished and were standing beside Sal and the cat, the entire group feeling pleased and admiring the new wall. Hannah was shaking her hair free from its braid and Marcus was wiping the cleaned paintbrush on a damp rag when the big black sedan turned the corner and purred down the street. Marcus felt rather than saw Hannah stiffen and prepare to bolt. He quickly grabbed at her wrist and waved the paint brush at her face, loudly threatening to give her some fresh rouge for her cheeks and in a lower voice he quickly instructed her what to do.

Sal yelled something about damn kids had better knock it off. Sir

Somebody darted across the street immediately in front of the car making the driver jam on the brakes and watch to make sure the cat appeared again on the other side of the street. Marcus continued his horseplay act and poked at Hannah's face so that she doubled over and hid behind her hair and her hands. The squeal that came out of her was a foreign sound to her, and when Marcus pulled her closer and grabbed at her waist to tickle her, the real laugh that escaped her sounded like something familiar that she used to know.

Behind the dark windows of the car, the people looking for the little nun child paid no attention to these rowdy neighborhood teenagers and their deaf uncle or whatever he was. The car rolled on and turned the next corner out of sight. From the window above, Rosa announced that everything was done and to come on up. Sal handed Hannah's new shoes to her and went into the shop to pull a pair of new socks from the display in the corner. Marcus put the paintbrush back where it belonged. Sir Somebody, waiting at the door, was the first up the stairs when Rosa buzzed them all in.

Rejoice

DANIEL EARL

-❧-

 Beyond the cracked sidewalk, and the telephone pole with layers of flyers in a rainbow of colors, and the patch of dry brown grass there stood a ten -foot high concrete block wall, caked with dozens of coats of paint. There was a small shrine at the foot of it, with burnt out candles and dead flowers and a few soggy teddy bears. One word of graffiti filled the wall, red letters on a gold background: Rejoice!

 I passed that wall every day on my way to work. Shame what happened to that girl, thirteen years old is all, way too young. I was there when it happened. Not when she died of course, only her mom and her sister were there. And the gunman, I suppose. But I was there when she, well, you know. I wasn't the only one either, that saw her come back.

 She'd been dead three days. Open and shut, bullet right to the heart, no need for an autopsy. Unsurvivable. And she sure as hell looked dead when she got to my funeral home. The family wanted an open casket, so I had Frank start to work on her, to get her looking nice. Frank's one of the best.

 I was upstairs working in the office, meeting with a family to get the particulars sorted out for another burial when it happened. Frank said he had already set the features and was about to make the cut to the femoral artery. Then she took a breath.

 Dead bodies make all kinds of noises, Heaven knows. They fart and squeak and sometimes even will give off a moan if the chest collapses and the neck's at just the right angle. Scares the hell out of many first-year mortuary students. But Frank was no fresh-outta-mortuary school embalmer, he'd been at it nearly as long as me.

I heard the crash from the embalming room. Frank started screaming something terrible, like he was on fire. I excused myself from the family, not knowing what was going on. When I got back there, Frank was still on the floor, next to the overturned pump, in a pool of formaldehyde, just staring up at the girl, who was sitting up and giving off a muted scream of her own.

The glue had already set on her eyelids and lips, which is what we do for a kid her age. Must've scared that girl half out of her mind to wake up from being dead only to have her eyes and mouth sealed up like that. Thank Heavens Frank didn't plug her nose when he set her features, or she'd have suffocated right there on the slab. How'd that've been for irony?

In hindsight, I'm a little shocked she didn't tear her lips open. I got some hot water and started working at it. Eventually it worked free. I had Frank call 9-1-1, and she could talk by the time the paramedics got there, but her eyes were still glued shut. Her temp was 68 degrees, same as the embalming room. They managed to work her eyes open, so she could see. They were the first ones to notice that her heart wasn't beating.

One of the paramedics, the darker-skinned one, crossed himself. The other one, the heavy-set woman, she checked every place you can take a pulse on a human at least twice before she started to cry. She shot off a text to someone. Who knows who she texted, but that opened a damned hornet's nest, I can tell you.

Some folks, and not just the religious ones, said what happened was a miracle straight from God in Heaven. Some people, and more religious ones than you might think, thought she was possessed by the devil himself. A few idiots called her a zombie, a real-life walking dead. You could see plain as day she wasn't. At least not like the kind in the zombie movies the kids watch. All I know is that there wasn't any blood pumping through her to keep her alive, so who's to say what was. Maybe her brain just decided it didn't want to be dead anymore and dragged her body along with it.

The paramedics didn't know what to do. Other than not having a heart beat and being room temperature she seemed fine. And they certainly don't cover anything like this in mortuary school, so I called her mom to come get her. Strangest damn phone call I ever had to make, I can tell you that. She threatened to sue me if this was some sort of sick joke. When she saw her daughter, she just fell to the ground and started to kiss the girl's feet.

Like I said, her whatever you want to call it– rebirth, ignited one hell of a media storm. Some pastor down in Georgia picked up on her name being Joice and started calling her Re-Joice. Which was kinda clever if you ask me, except people started saying it like it was a bad word. It never ceases to amaze me how people can take something amazing, something unique and wonderful and turn it into something bad so fast it'd make your head snap.

Every damn news outfit set up shop in town too. Which was a hell of a boost to the economy, every hotel room was booked solid for near a month. But after they cycled through interviewing anyone and everyone who wanted to see their face on TV, they started pestering the people who didn't want to be, just for something new. Eventually the sheriff had to step in to get them gone, but he couldn't stop it. Like the Dutch boy with his finger in the dam.

Frank thought it would be great for business, that people would want to send their loved ones to us, just to see if lightning would strike twice. He figured that people would start offing themselves because they'd 'be right back' as the kids say. But that never panned out, at least the people coming to us part. The whole industry took a hit for a while, no one wanted to bury anybody, just in case they came back. But no one else came back.

Weeks went by, then two months, and half-a-year came and went and that's about when the people who had hope started to lose it. Hope has a remarkably short shelf life. And when it expires, it rots into hate and anger and meanness.

Rejoice - by this time even she was calling herself Rejoice - hit the talk-show circuit. All those Hollywood types were just pawing at her, throwing all kinds of money her way. She was everywhere, you couldn't escape her face on the TV or her voice on the radio. Talking about what it was like to be dead, what it was like to come back. She'd make the same jokes for them late night guys, and those ladies that are on during the day, and they'd laugh like it was brand new. You'd think something like that would burn out quick, but she was a bona-fide celebrity. And rightly so, I suppose, people coming back from the dead is certainly a better case for fame than the good-looks-and-luck needed to make it in Hollywood.

One of those celebrity doctors had her on his show. Did a live ultrasound of what was left of her heart to show everyone on live TV that it wasn't beating. That she was truly and honestly dead. The world stopped for that like the aliens had landed, even the Stock Exchange in New York City stopped. Half the planet thought it was a trick, and not just the tin-foil-hat wearing conspiracy theorists neither, nurses and cops and doctors- folks with real jobs- lots of people couldn't believe what they saw.

And why should they? Flies in the face of reason and science, a person coming back like that. That's why someone, really a group of someones I suppose, sued her. Well, they sued her mom anyway. And the production company of the show. Then Frank and me. Said we were all a part of the scam.

But by this time Frank had quit. He wrote a book, it was one of those rush-to-publish hack jobs that some nameless ghost writer did all the work and got none of the money, and boy did it sell. Would've been nice if Frank asked me to help. People wanted a piece of Rejoice, and Frank started making money hand-over-fist. First thing he did was buy some place on a tropical island, didn't even leave a forwarding address, the bastard. So that just left me, alone, to deal with the fallout of all of this.

The big shot lawyer the production company had on retainer told me that I should come to New York just in case he couldn't get the case thrown out. Well of course he couldn't get it thrown out, and I had to be there at three in the afternoon on Tuesday. So I hired some guy fresh out of mortuary school to run the business while I was gone. I'd never been to the Big Apple before, so I figured that it would be like a vacation, I'd get to see the sights.

Some vacation. I was in some lousy hotel, no upscale Midtown hotel suite for me. A street light kept the room illuminated like it was day, even with the shade drawn. The room next to me must have been rented by the hour judging by the rhythmic knocking on the wall. Between the light and the lovers, I wasn't going to get any sleep.

Who knows what time it was, some terrible time of the morning when no one is up, except in New York, it's true what they say- New York never sleeps. I must have been wandering the city for a couple of hours, the sun was starting to peek through the spaces between buildings, elongated fingers of light jabbing into what was left of the night.

I was standing in a park. Not Central Park, but one of the smaller ones that are like small green pimples on New York's concrete and steel face. There was a small crowd gathering for something. And some street-urchin looking boy, probably the same age as Rejoice, was handing out flyers. He looked angry, and not just the regular teen-angst crap they all go through. Real honest anger. He thrust a flyer at me, nearly smashing his hand into mine.

The headline was in big blocky letters and colored in with a magic marker, that color now lost to the xerox process. "Rejoice and be Exceedingly MAD". The marker strokes on the last word were violent and lashed out into the open space around the letters. The rest of the flyer was written in large squarish paragraphs, all in different handwriting. Each one a virulent testimony of how the hope that Rejoice had brought into the world destroyed their family, ruined their lives. Across the bottom, written in all caps, "THE ONLY WAY TO END THIS IS TO END HER".

The kid got up onto a milk crate and raised his hand. A murmur went through the crowd and then it fell silent, except for a few people shouting words of encouragement at him. The kid acknowledged them with a nod and a shy smile. In the full light of day, he looked less angry and more beautiful. He waited until people stopped shouting. A siren could be heard, maybe five or ten blocks away. The kid raised the bullhorn, pressed the button, and began to speak.

"Thank you. Thank you all for coming." An approving murmur rustled like fall leaves through the crowd. "Rejoice has torn our world apart. We've all lost loved ones, good people that aren't here anymore because of her. Because she came back. Some of us have lost our businesses." The boy looked right at me, like he knew what was going on. "I lost my mother. When she saw Rejoice on the TV, she was so happy. She thought that God was going to usher in a new order, that there was gonna be no more death or sorrow, like the Bible talks about. She stayed up late, watching cable news shows, televangelists, any station that had that, that *thing* on." The crowd nodded in agreement. "She bought posters online and had them up all over the apartment, she even bought ten copies of that book the funeral guy wrote. She was so very happy. And I was happy for her. All that happiness, all that misplaced hope, it changed her. It changed all of us. Once she'd decided she'd had enough of living and just wanted to return, like that girl. She slashed my sister's throat, then stabbed me in the back as I ran away, then killed herself."

The boy's shoulders heaved in heavy sobs. An older man came and wrapped his arms around the boy. He whispered something in the boy's ear. The man reached for the bullhorn. The boy offered no resistance as the man took it from him.

"I'm so very sorry," the man said, "but he just can't continue. But do you see what this has done to him. What *she* has done to him? He was such a happy boy once, full of smiles and happiness. Full of life. But now." He clicked off the bullhorn for a moment. These guys certainly knew how to play to the emotions.

"But now, my son, he doesn't smile anymore. Not like before *she* came." The man spoke for another twenty minutes with a rambling and twisting story. "I wish he could tell you more of my ex-wife's story. But everything is there, on the website. Don't believe what the media tells you, they won't tell the truth, let us tell our own story."

I flipped the flyer over, looking for the website, it would at least give me something to laugh at later at the hotel, I thought. But it was just a blank page of anachronistically sunshine yellow staring back at me. The crowd started to disperse, perhaps they had hoped for more theatrics.

I approached the man and his boy, who was sitting on the milk crate now. No longer sobbing. The man had his back to me, and mustn't have heard me coming, though I wasn't making any attempt to hide my approach.

"Excuse me," I said, "excuse me sir. That was one hell of a speech you gave. I was hoping to get the address for the website you mentioned, I can't seem to find it on the flyer that your son gave me earlier. Again, hell of a speech, I have to say."

"Thank you," he said as he turned. He reached for the flyer, pulled out a pen, and began to scrawl the address on the back. His eyes locked onto mine. "So, what was it that attracted you to our humble little gathering, if you don't mind me asking?"

"Well, I know her family. Rejoice, er, Joice's I mean." His eyes glared at me. "I own the funeral home where it happened, where she came back." He kept staring, I couldn't tell if he was angry, or sad, his face was a shifting sea of emotion.

The man sighed and extended a hand. "Well, it's nice to meet you. My son and I appreciate your willingness to even entertain what we are saying. Since you've probably made quite a bit of money off of her, haven't you?"

"Well, no, actually. That was my partner Frank. He's the one who wrote the book, you see, the one your ex, your mother, bought so many copies of. I guess some people bought that book." I chuckled, like there was some inside joke only I knew, "Lots of people."

"More people than you realize, my friend. That's why we do what we do, because too many people got hurt, and more people are getting hurt every day. I heard she's in town, some big lawsuit. We're going to be protesting outside the courthouse. Would you want to join us?"

"Oh, I'll be there alright." The man's face broke into a smile. "But not for the reason you're hoping. I'm a part of that damn lawsuit, pardon my French. There's a whole group of us that got pulled in as a part of it."

"See, son. More lives being ruined because of her." He shook his head. "When is it going to stop? When will someone stand up and do something? I'm sorry you're a part of this, friend, I hate lawsuits but if that lawsuit helps to stop her, then I hope you win, brother, and win big."

I smiled as though he had made a joke, we shook hands and then I started my walk back to the hotel. I glanced on the back of the flyer and written in all caps was the address, www.rebelagainstrejoice.org, I immediately pulled it up on my phone.

The main page has a picture of Rejoice on it, with a big red x across her face. Surrounding it were dozens of names all followed by 'story'. Steve's story, Diana's story, Brendan's story, Aidan's story. I flicked the screen down, and there were hundreds of names.

I stopped at a coffee shop somewhere, I couldn't even say where, and started reading. I started with Steve's story. His wife had died a few years earlier and he had feared that if she'd come back like Rejoice, that she'd suffocate in her casket. So, he dug her up and brought her home, like *that* was a sensible thing, you see. Had her sitting on the couch, propped up and watching her soaps when the cops showed up. Got a good laugh out of that one.

I tapped the home button then opened Diana's story. Her little sister had a treatable infection of some sort, I can't remember, but her parents refused to take her to the doctor, they were confident that if she died she'd come back, just like Rejoice. She didn't, of course. And now Diana's living with an aunt in Detroit while her parents wait for their trial date.

I read story after story. Not sure how many, a couple of dozen maybe. At first, I thought some of them were funny, like Steve's, just examples of humans being idiots and making bad decisions, which as a species we have been known to do from time to time. But after so many stories, so many people hurt like Diana was, I began to wonder if maybe the boy and his dad from that park were right.

I looked at my watch and realized five hours had gone by. Five hours reading those damn stories. I'd have to take a cab straight to the courthouse to make it on time. No way to get back to my hotel and change into my suit. Oh well, I guess. I saw a guy in a t-shirt on the People's Court once, the judge raked him over the coals for being underdressed, but he still won.

I got there with ten minutes to spare. I waded through the protesters. I couldn't help wonder if Steve was there in the crowd, or Diana, or Aidan, or the rest of them, from the stories. I looked around but didn't see the boy, or his dad. I showed my license to one of the officers out front and he let me in.

I crumpled up the flyer and threw it in the trash before I walked up to the security station. I put my wallet, phones, and room key into the plastic bowl, passed through the metal detector, and retrieved my things on the other side. The guard pointed out the elevator to me with a curt nod.

It took me a while to find room 9-23A, but when I did, they'd already started, the lawyers that is, getting everyone prepped for the judge. She was in the room, Rejoice. First time I'd seen her in person since she was in my embalming room, confused and scared. She was smiling now though, like she didn't have a care in the whole world, like she didn't even know what she had done to all those people. To Steve, and that boy, and Diana. What she had done to me.

She was just as young, and pretty, and dead as she was before. Oh, they had make-up on her for sure, to make her look natural, to look alive, and they did a damn fine job, but you can't fool me, can't fool someone who makes the dead look life-like for a living. She laughed at a joke one of the lawyers had made, and that's when it happened. Hate and anger and meanness flashed bright and hot in my head. The room swirled in shades of maroon and red. That's when I killed her.

But, is it really killing? Because, you see, I don't think you can kill something that's already dead. And that's what I told myself as I stood there with a chair in my hand standing over her body. What I still tell myself. I made sure to hit her in the back of her head, much easier to reconstruct that way, especially for that new kid running my funeral home. Her family will finally get the open casket funeral they wanted.

The Therapy Session

Lila Evans

.♣.

Beyond the cracked sidewalk, and the telephone pole with layers of flyers in a rainbow of colors, and the patch of dry brown grass there stood a ten-foot high concrete block wall, caked with dozens of coats of paint. There was a small shrine at the foot of it, with burnt out candles and dead flowers and a few soggy teddy bears. One word of graffiti filled the wall, red letters on a gold background: Rejoice!

It wasn't my fault, of course. But sometimes if you repeat a lie enough to yourself, it becomes your ultimate truth. It becomes real. I would pass a lie detector test with flying colours if asked about it. That's how good I was at lying to myself. I had not actually 'pulled the trigger', metaphorically speaking. But I was a moving gear. Or at the very least a lowly cog. I had to be something or I would be nothing. To be nothing was to be boring, and to be boring was my greatest fear. After eels, naturally.

My first memory was of my mom throwing a huge pan of hot French fries at my dad. That's what I longed to share with Dr. Monroe, but unfortunately, she didn't ask what my first memory was, so I never got the chance to share this juicy tidbit. Instead she gestured for me to sit and looked over her glasses at me with a neutral face. I knew right then that she would be tough to crack. But I was up for a challenge.

"Why have you come to see me, Melissa?" There it was. I'd Googled frequently asked therapy questions and this was always one of the first. They asked this question as if it was a conscious decision. As if I had a say in this and wasn't being dragged here screaming and kicking. But I was prepared.

I tented my hands solemnly under my chin. "Mostly it's because my friends don't find me as funny as I find myself." Dr. Monroe's head jerked up in an unprofessional double take. "You're getting therapy because your friends don't think you're funny?"

Oh God. She doesn't think I'm funny either. "Sometimes I'll send my friends text messages and let's just say the LOLs are lacking. Like for example, I'll ask them where they are and what they're doing and they'll say something like *'Just grabbing dinner at my dad's'*. Then, to mess with them I'll send a message back to them saying *'She's eating dinner at her dad's'*, to make it look like I'm informing someone about their whereabouts."

Dr. Monroe's brow crinkled and I had a fleeting concern that she thought I was actually a head case after all. Or maybe she was just trying to contain her delight. Yes, that was probably it. She scribbled something down in her plain brown notebook. "Do you do any more of these 'texting pranks'?" Dr. Monroe enunciated 'texting pranks' as if they weren't quite real. *Do these voices in your head ever tell you to do bad things? Are they the ones forcing you to make bad jokes?*

"Sometimes I text people pretending that I think they're someone else. I'll–" As I said this, my phone buzzed on the table and I flipped it open. I realized then that this was exactly the behaviour I'd been schooled on by my parents and teachers, ever since I answered a phone call during a job interview, but old habits die hard.

"Anything of value, Melissa?" Dr. Monroe peered at me, her knuckles turning white from gripping her notebook. She was clearly irked, but unwilling to let me get the best of her. I really did admire her patience, but I knew it was only a matter of time before she unravelled like the rest of my test subjects.

"Just a message from my friend Jodi," I explained. "She accused me of being too drunk last night and when I denied it she claimed that I was pawing at a man with a beard screaming 'Gandalf! You're alive!'" I gave Dr. Monroe a conspiratorial wink. "You know how it is. Though I don't consider myself drunk until I'm orc-hugging drunk.'

Dr. Monroe watched me with masked annoyance as I typed back a reply, making sure to speak each word out loud so that she didn't miss out on any of my wit. *'Sometimes I get Dumbledore and Gandalf confused. The beards, the magic, the sex appeal. You know? Anyways, I g2g, my therapist is watching me like my grandma the first time she saw me dance to Baby Got Back.'*

Dr. Monroe frowned at this last statement and looked pointedly at the clock on the wall. "You should turn that off if you want to get the most out of this session. You aren't paying me to watch you text your friends, right? Now tell me again why you are here? How can I help you?"

I put down my phone and sank farther into the plush couch. "Don't you guys usually have those lie down couches so you can sit beside me and write notes on a clipboard? That's what therapists have in cartoons. Cartoons are usually pretty spot on in my experience, like how Tasmanian devils make little tornados wherever they go. Actually, I don't know if that's true, but it would be pretty cool. On second thought, I think they might be extinct..."

"I think that this couch will do just fine." Dr. Monroe's mask was beginning to slip. *Rejoice! A new record!* "Why am I here? Why am I here?" I picked up one of Dr. Monroe's pens and tapped it against the coffee table, trying to decide how to keep her going. "I guess it goes back to breakfast a few weeks ago."

Dr. Monroe leaned forward waiting for the big reveal. She was just a morbid pervert like every other therapist. I would bet good money that she took this job because she was just plain nosy. Or maybe she was an ambulance chaser who couldn't stand to have a tragedy unfurl without her to bear witness. "What happened at breakfast, Melissa?"

"You see, I cracked two eggs into the frying pan and I put one of the shells into the garbage, and the other one I put into the compost. Two different disposals. I looked at what I'd done and thought to myself; oh great, this is how it all starts."

"How what starts?" Dr. Monroe had taken several more notes since I started speaking. I felt that she deserved something interesting to write about and I wanted to be the one to do that for her. Maybe then she would throw away that plain brown notebook and pick out something with a little pizzazz. Maybe one of those Lisa Frank ones with bright pink kittens sitting on the rings of Saturn. "I could explain to you like a tired old preacher, using these boring words. Or I could sing you the answer through a Broadway-style song." I gave Dr. Monroe a sneak peak at my jazz hands, waving them enthusiastically in the air. "Please don't sing," She pleaded. "Now, you were saying that this was how it all starts. How what starts?"

"Fine," I conceded to Dr. Killjoy. She would never get that rainbow kitten notebook with an attitude like that. "What I thought was, oh great, this is how the insanity starts. First, I put the eggshells in two different places by accident, then it becomes habit, and then it becomes a burning need that I can't control. Soon everything in my life will be separated into two bins. It will be total chaos."

A pigeon landed outside on the window sill with a thump and began a series of guttural coos that piqued my interest. Pigeons led such mysterious lives. Tucked away in ledges and hovering over pizza shops. One eye on the sky, one on the crumbs scattered about by humankind on the paved streets. I wondered if Dr. Monroe had ever thought about what life as a pigeon was like. Probably not. She looked like someone who lacked any imagination. The trials and tribulations of a feathered rat were of no consequence to her. She was the type of person who would get reincarnated into a pigeon and then immediately get crushed by a streetcar. Coooooo–SPLAT!

"Melissa. You've been staring out the window for two minutes. Now, is there any specific reason why you've come to me? It's important that I know if we're to continue. You understand that in order to help you, I need you to open up. To trust me."

"Well..." I searched my mind for an interesting story. "I think about suicide. "Dr. Monroe's eyes widened very slightly and she made a note on the margin of her page. "Tell me more about this please. Remember that this is a safe space. I'm here to support you." I had to admit that I was a bit envious of her ability to relinquish annoyance, though now that I had the idea of her as an ambulance chasing weirdo in my mind, it was hard to take her seriously.

"Sometimes I think about how great it would be if all the people I didn't like would just kill themselves," I laughed, but quickly stopped myself when I saw the barely contained wrath simmering beneath the surface of Dr. Monroe's face. I wanted to avoid my head accidentally exploding through her use of Jedi force, so I stared down at her blazer instead of her narrowed eyes. I found her blazer to be a particularly heinous article of clothing. It was a sad mothy grey with shiny irregular black buttons that were not all of a matching size, as if they had been sewn on as they were collected on street corners and friends' button jars. Aha! She was like the pigeon after all. A scavenger, not of crumbs, but of buttons.

"You're not married?" I asked when I noticed her fingers were bereft of rings, suddenly interested in the woman behind the blazer. She shook her head. "No, I'm not. Do you not see that you're deflecting? By making the conversation about me, you're purposefully avoiding sharing anything meaningful." If meaningful was what she wanted, meaningful was what she'd get. "I had a boyfriend," I offered, wondering again why my parents had sent me here to waste their money. Maybe they were tired of my voice so they had hired a friend for me. Yes, that was probably it. It would've been thoughtful if they'd chosen someone a little livelier. "Did the two of you break up?" Dr. Monroe asked through gritted teeth.

"He didn't know we were dating, so no, not technically. But I did end it when he started seeing someone else." Dr. Monroe put down her notepad. "That seems to be all the time we have for today, Melissa. Hopefully next time you come prepared to share." I gave a non-committal shrug, both of us fully aware that there was little chance of me returning. It had been an utter waste of both of our time. But in the end, quite cathartic for me to have an audience. I thought that was the last time I would see Dr. Monroe, but situations, like my moods, rapidly change.

Three days later an automobile pulled up and parked beside the concrete wall. The driver opened the door, but did not get out of the car. Although her face was in shadow, it was easy to tell she was sad. There was something about how she turned away from the sun and rested the weight of her hands on the steering wheel, something about her silent composure, that caused Hannah to sigh. The young girl watched the driver lean out of the car and stretch her hand out towards one of the burned-out candles.

Hannah was the younger sister of one of the victims and I was fairly positive that the woman in the car had been one of their mothers. An overpowering surge of guilt washed over me and I had to pick myself off of the park bench and keep moving away from the small crowd of mourners. But I hadn't done this, right? I was a harmless troll. I toyed with people's anger and baited them into fights in the YouTube comments. That was all. But once again I had bought into my own lies and now I was just confused.

I knew what I should have told Dr. Monroe, but my stellar personality had prevented me from giving her even a shred of helpful information. What I really wanted was to talk to a death row inmate who was never getting out and would therefore never have the opportunity to share my insanity with the world, but a quick internet search revealed that not only was this extremely difficult for a minor to arrange, but the death penalty no longer existed here. Go figure!

Then what to do with all the fog of culpability the shrouded me? I'd seen a painting in a museum once that was called 'Guilt.' It was a rendering of a man sitting on a bench looking ragged and despairing, all in different shades of grey-blue. Over him like a cloud, was a dark shape that enveloped him, as if trying to overtake him. I felt that now. That cloud of suffocating onus. Sarcasm and revelling in weirdness were coping mechanisms for me, but I'd reached a turning point where no matter what I did, the feeling of blame remained.

But there was more. I was beginning to seriously question myself. The story about putting the eggshells in two different bins hadn't been conjured out of thin air for the sole purpose of annoying Dr. Monroe, that was just a perk. My facade was starting to crumble and I felt that I could no longer be relied on. My own truths could no longer be relied on. And so, the following week, against my better judgement, I returned to see Dr. Monroe.

She looked less than thrilled to see me, but I couldn't blame her. I was no longer in a manic upswing though, so at least there was that. She might even appreciate me as a downtrodden youth instead of the gremlin that came in like a wrecking ball last time. I didn't have the energy to toy with her the same way. Maybe in a different way.

From the moment I sat down, I could see that the dynamic between us had shifted. Dr. Monroe held the power now because I'd come in with a need. My skin crawled. I hated that feeling. I hated being at her mercy. But I decided to play along. She stared me down with those sharp, grey eyes. "Why have you come to see me again, Melissa?"

My mind flashed with an image of the shrine. Of the soggy teddy bears and cards. The candles and photographs. Of the woman with her arm reaching out of the car and the sighing girl watching from the sidelines. "Because I think I've done something unforgiveable."

Yes, she was still scribbling in her notepad, and yes it still annoyed me. But a true, deep panic was taking hold and I felt that I had to purge myself or risk being devoured. I had to tell her my truth. I started at the beginning, reminding her of my tendency to troll chat groups and YouTube comments which all seemed innocent enough. And then I told her about Dan.

Dan was a reclusive kid at my high school and in one of my manic upswings, I began to zero in on him. From his Facebook I somehow traced him through an internet rabbit hole to an online forum where he was an active member. The forum was basically all about being too ugly or weird to be loved. I could sense his seething hatred through his posts, lamenting about how life was unfair, he'd drawn the short straw, good-looking kids were cruel to him, blah blah blah. His list of complaints was long and drawn out.

Dr. Monroe cocked her head to one side and it took every ounce of effort not to mirror her actions. Today wasn't the day to mess around. Not yet. So, I continued. I told her about the first time I struck up a conversation with Dan on the online forum. I asked him one simple question: *What are you going to do about it?*

He'd been hesitant to give away much at first, but I wore him down. I created an echo chamber of his own ideas, bouncing them back to him so that they began to build. He wanted someone to blame, and I practically hand fed him names. *Show them that you're no one to mess with*, I told him. *Put an end to it once and for all.*

Dr. Monroe asked me what I'd meant by that, but the truth was, I really didn't know. I was just being me in one of my euphoric blitzes. I wrote screenplays, I signed up for teams, I started new hobbies. But then there was this. My dark side. What had I wanted Dan to do? Did I know what he was capable of? Did I subconsciously want this?

Tears began to well in my eyes when I remembered the shrine by the concrete wall. But like always, they were selfish tears. I wasn't sad for those people, I was scared for myself and what this would all mean for me. I wanted to live a normal, guilt-free existence. The shrine was crowding in on me, threatening to suffocate me. *Rejoice!*

"Do you need to take a break?" Dr. Monroe asked. I shook my head. If I took a break now, I'd close off forever. I swallowed hard and vowed to bulldoze my way through the rest. I told her how Dan and I had come up with a plan. I helped to reassure him when he had doubts and I was always there, the devil on his shoulder whispering into his ear. *Put a stop to it. Put a stop to it forever.*

I guess there was a part of me that thought he wouldn't actually do it, but there was a larger part that hoped he would. And after weeks of coaching, late night chats, and reassurance, Dan was finally ready. He suddenly stopped talking to me one night, and then two days later he posted on the forum: I'm going to do it. North Side High better watch out!

He sent me one final message telling me not to go to school the next day. I faked being sick and stayed in. I remember my mom calling from work when she heard the news. She just kept repeating Thank God you were sick. You see? The Universe was protecting you. She wouldn't have been so thankful if she'd know just how twisted I was.

"So, you knew what he was going to do?" Dr. Monroe had stopped writing in her notebook and was now watching me with furrowed brow. "Why didn't you tell anyone?" I hated that question. It was hard to worm my way out of it and so I had no choice but to face it head on. In a rare move, I told her the truth. Well, my current truth anyway; That I wanted to see how far I could push Dan. That I wanted to see if he would actually pull through.

At this point Dr. Monroe wasn't doing very well in hiding her disgust and grimace lines appeared on eithers side of her mouth. The pigeon was back on the windowsill calling out in muffled coos, but it did not interest me today. Today only the flickering emotions on Dr. Monroe's face interested me. She was my new fascination. "Why did you want to see if Dan would do what you wanted him to do?" She had finally hit on the money question. Points to her for finally getting there, but also points deducted for taking such a painstakingly slow route. She was averaging zero.

I leaned back in the chair, stretching my hands overhead and hearing faint pops from my joints. I was really starting to enjoy this. I had something Dr. Monroe needed and her impatience for me to spit it out was clear. I took a long, slow drink from my glass of water, then wiped my mouth. "It's actually really simple," I began. "I wanted to see how far I could push Dan, because I wanted to have power over him. By the end of our exchanges, I was in almost complete control of him without him even realizing it."

Of course, this was the point that Dr. Monroe reopened her notebook. Scribble, scribble. Probably writing about what a sociopath I was. But she was probably wrong. I was just the world's greatest troll. I just wanted to waste a little bit more of her time and I was succeeding. I was the master of my own truths. I believed every word of what I was telling her. I almost had tears in my eyes from the poignancy of my saga.

"You know," I began. "My earliest memory is of my mom throwing a steaming hot pan full of French fries at my dad." I finally got to say my piece, and now Dr. Monroe was writing down everything with care, most likely imagining interviews with the press about how she'd been the first to see inside the psychopath mind of the girl who'd been the underlying cause of the tragedy. But she wouldn't get any interviews, because I was almost finished with her. It was a new year, new me, and when I said I was finished, it meant we were finished. Because I held the power. I would always hold the power when I made the rules.

"And how did it make you feel when your mom threw the French fries at your dad?" Dr. Monroe asked earnestly. She sounded ridiculous. I almost gave up my charade and started to laugh. But I was nothing if not an excellent actor. Ask anyone who witnessed me in the Grade eleven production of Macbeth. No one had portrayed Lady Macbeth's death like that before. In fact, the teachers had asked me several times to tone it down, until they finally decided that like the play, her death would occur off stage. Buzz kills, all of them!

Suddenly the pigeon on the windowsill seemed highly interesting to me. Maybe it was because I was now bored of Dr. Monroe, but it seemed to glow with an abrupt feathery charm. I wondered if people still sent messages by pigeon. It couldn't possibly be too hard to reach out and capture one of those bobble-headed sky rats. But what message would I send? Who would I send it to?

I stood up to leave, deciding I was going to spend the afternoon researching carrier pigeons. No more text messages for me! My friends would now be getting bird mail. Dr. Monroe's eyebrows shot up in alarm and she stood, dropping her book of useless notes to the coffee table. "Where are you going, Melissa? I feel like we're finally starting to make some progress here?" I grinned back at her as I moved toward the door. I'd already moved on to greener, more interesting pastures in my mind. So much, that I barely felt like explaining anything to her. But she had put up with me all this time, so I supposed I owed her. Now that I was ready to confess, I could feel the lie unearthing itself. The cloud of guilt dissipated all at once. Poof! As if it was never there. I was too good at this. I scared myself.

"I feel much better after talking to you," I said, pausing with one hand on the door knob. "You did end up helping me, you know? Now I can say with certainty that I never once talked to Dan, I never did any of that stuff. I'm not that far off the rails. I mean, sure, I have my own set of problems and believing my own lies is one of them. But at least I'll never be an ambulance-chasing, brown notebook writing looky-loo." I left Dr. Monroe behind in her office as I made my way back home. I longed to glance back to see the expression on her face, but I didn't want to give her even a shred of control. I passed the shrine on the street, taking in the wilted flowers and photos. A terrible tragedy, but it had nothing to do with me. Which is why I had to make it about me and why I had to get someone to believe it was about me. I was nothing if not a master of my own truth.

A Summer of Rare Tolerances

Scott Adam Gordon

.♣.

Beyond the cracked sidewalk, and the telephone pole with layers of flyers in a rainbow of colors, and the patch of dry brown grass there stood a ten -foot high concrete block wall, caked with dozens of coats of paint. There was a small shrine at the foot of it, with burnt out candles and dead flowers and a few soggy teddy bears. One word of graffiti filled the wall, red letters on a gold background: Rejoice!

Sydney stood with a cigarette in her hand, the streetlights casting her shadow long against the stone, the wind teasing the tails of her overcoat. She rested the cigarette between her lips and reached inside her coat for a crinkled photograph, a lake scene in summer. A rabble of kids crowded the foreground, some with bands tied around their heads and sticks for swords, some with tongues tickling ice cream. One child drifted on the left of the picture – close enough to pretend she was one with the children, far enough for an old photograph to expose she was not. This girl didn't look at the camera like the other kids; instead, her eyes were pointed at something over her shoulder. Sydney took another draw on her cigarette and followed the gaze of her younger self into the fading background.

The lake stood South-East of Ashland City, Oregon, where Sydney had grown up. She was the only child of a single parent – her father, who blamed Sydney for his wife's absence. Sydney would never manage to reconcile this, and would stop trying before her teens. In her adolescent years, she tagged along with friends as a stray hair might to dark clothing, and there was only one time when she didn't feel so alone and unwanted. But it was brief, like all the best times.

Nothing ever happens in a tiny city like Ashland until the day something does; so-called sleepy towns are only towns still to wake from slumber. Ashland was awoken on June 16, 1963, when Sydney was 12 years old. Its alarm clock was deafening.

Sydney had been in her bedroom, widening a hole in her sock when the sirens screamed past her house – several of them in as many minutes. She climbed to her window to take a peek outside and saw some folks scrambling across gardens, pointing and chasing after the sounds. Sensing action she may not see again for years, Sydney hauled on her boots and dashed out of her house.

She followed an ever-growing crowd to a crossroads on the edge of town. The police and fire service were already there and had set up a perimeter to keep people at her side of the street, though Sydney still hadn't learned why. On a patch of grass diagonally across from the group, she saw a figure silhouetted in the evening light. It was an imposing structure – perhaps a statue, thought Sydney – facing the mountains. She climbed a dumpster to get a better view above the bustling crowd and to try and stifle her runaway imagination. She listened a moment for scraps of information, tried to lip-read police officers, when there was a collective gasp. Sydney returned her attention to the something on the outskirts of town and decided, if it was a statue, it was an uncommon breed. This statue could move.

As the figure stepped into stronger light, Sydney saw it looked just like a teddy bear – only one would've needed a fireman's ladder to reach its head and a lasso fit for a water tower to wrap its waste. The bear had a round, slightly squashed head with a snout in the lower half – shape of an upturned heart symbol. Two globes rested on its muzzle at ten and two o'clock – mammoth, ceramic-like eyes, black and almost buried in golden fur, fur that remained similarly thick and shiny across most of the bear's 20-feet-tall form. Its nose, meanwhile, was a glistening, many-dimpled black triangle with shallow nostrils; a dark line ran down from it and split upwards into an arc – a smile that couldn't part. The bear's arms and legs grew wider towards where one might expect hands and feet to be, but they ended in flat pads of the same, thin material as its snout. It was naked but for a red and gold striped bow tie around its neck.

The teddy bear turned to the growing crowd and shrieks erupted; Sydney held her breath. Its motions were soft and slow, producing no creaking or clanking, as a fairground automaton might (it was the only place Sydney had seen anything similar). The police chief, chief Clemmons, remained outwardly composed, coordinating his team to push the crowd back. The bear undulated across the empty road, swaying its head as if taking in its surroundings, before pausing beside the gathering. Clemmons pointed a shaking pistol, two-handed, at the monstrosity as it towered over them. The bear took a beat, rotated its head a fraction, and made its first strides into the city.

At this point, the forces lost crowd control. The people chased after the bear and within an hour more than half of Ashland's 10,000 residents (including Sydney) were tiptoeing behind it as it walked through the city. It was puppy-like in the unpredictable way it studied and fixated, yet calmer; every movement looked like an intense act of learning. It prodded the sign above Vinnie's Roller Rink, seemingly amazed as it sprung back into position. It spent minutes bopping the sign – red and blue neon fizzling out, reanimating, fizzling – occasionally turning to the crowd, as if gauging their reaction to the wonder. Sydney crept with the citizens as the bear fumbled its way through the lamp-lit plaza, startling and startled by a homeless man waking to it from beneath newspaper. She laughed with them as the bear caught itself on the wires hanging between The Newserry and Hickler Shoes, happy to change course rather than maneuver under them. All the while, Sydney heard rumor upon rumor as to the nature of the bear's origin and, of course, its animation.

The crowd trailed the bear into the woods neighboring Ashland Creek around midnight when it was seemingly satisfied with its city stroll. It sat in a clearing – legs spread, the only way a teddy bear would sit – and bowed its head as if falling asleep. All the while, its marble eyes never changed.

Immediately afterward, Mayor Hobson and Chief Clemmons lead talks, just outside the forest, on what the next course of action should be (several officers remained with the bear to keep an eye on its movements, should there be any). The pair had spent more than 30 years in Ashland but had seen little in the way of trouble, though the Mayor hadn't been afraid to hide trouble from the police, sometimes, if he saw a benefit. Hobson leaned back on the discussions and Clemmons passed bullhorns around freely; they listened to what the city had to say, as they always had.

The suggestions were numerous. They should report the bear to the FBI for investigation, seeing as they couldn't rule out it being an international security risk. It was alien and therefore posed a global security risk. It belonged to the nearest zoo, so some people thought – a notion which Sydney found particularly upsetting and which sparked greater debate into whether it even qualified as an animal. During this battle, Joan Hockeridge shouted something that silenced the warring factions. Hockeridge, a recluse and former elementary school teacher, sat on a log, turned away from the largest part of the crowd. Many hadn't realized she was even there, drawn from her home at midnight, until she yelled. Yet her presence alone was enough to stifle the arguments. The bullhorn was passed her way, and she refused it before it landed on somebody nearby. The young man clicked it on and sighed. "Joan said, 'when did y'all forget how to be civilized?'"

So it was decided, then and there and by a narrow majority, that the bear would be treated as a new neighbor, so long as it was in town. It would be referred to as a neighbor, should an out-of-towner ask about it. And if the teddy bear – which the town would name 'Rejoice' in an ensuing vote – would proceed to act unneighborly, then it would feel the full force of the law. Clemmons vouched for that last part himself.

It was an absurd proposal to many, yet Rejoice made the transition from new neighbor to, simply, neighbor – an expected and incidental part of the city – with unforeseen ease. Rejoice would stroll into town around morning to make its daily inspections – it remained a curious thing – before returning to the woods each night. People would wave to it from cars, bicycles, and bus stops as it wandered. Postmen would tip their hats as it crossed the sidewalk with them and window cleaners might give it a thumbs-up. The patrons of The Mudd Bar would be drinking and smoking when their afternoon sunlight would go out and Rejoice's fur would creep across the glass, followed by an eye of obsidian. The patrons would raise a drink to it as the frantic barmaid tried to shoo it away.

Children enjoyed having Rejoice around especially and would spend entire days trailing it. Sometimes they'd climb it in an effort to reach its ears – what whispers had were its softest, snuggest patches. They'd be clung to a leg or hanging from elbow fur as the teddy bear marched down the street. The kids often returned home, themselves sore-eared, having been caught by their parents attempting the risky feat.

Rejoice routinely caused a minor fuss, might trample a backyard fence to regard clothesline unmentionables. Occasionally it would sit at a junction, beguiled by the changing lights, forcing traffic to circle it like toy trains around a department store plushie. To most, it was all the more endearing for it. For this was a simple time – a summer of rare tolerances – where a life-like teddy bear giant could attend a picnic by the lake as something approaching an equal. As had precisely been the case, the day Sydney's photograph was taken.

Hundreds traveled to enjoy the summer sunshine on that Sunday and Rejoice's presence made it all the more exciting. The bear had veered off its typical inner-city path, perhaps drawn by the crowd's commotion. It was early afternoon and Rejoice was lost in a scene of fishing and grilling and partying, one may have had to look twice to even notice it on the water's edge. Children were trying to show it skipping stones, but at that moment its glare couldn't be persuaded from the grassy area off the beach. Among those there, was Sydney, who'd been invited by a kind neighbor. Sydney had been lying on her front making a daisy chain when she rolled over with a start; Rejoice stood above her, its head cocked. Sydney stood up and sympathetically asked what it wanted. As Rejoice studied her, Sydney held her daisy chain aloft to show the bear before placing it on her head. Rejoice twitched and it gave Sydney an idea.

Sydney spent the next hour piecing together larger flowers and vines before returning to Rejoice with her rope of greenery. She offered it to the bear, urged Rejoice to hold out a paw to accept it, but it wouldn't be swayed. Defeated, Sydney left the twine in a pile on the beach and sulked for the rest of the day. Just before it was time to leave, Sydney's well-meaning neighbor ushered her to join in for one last photograph – she said she'd make sure Sydney received a copy. Sydney rolled her eyes and reluctantly stood alongside the other kids. In her tedium, she turned – just as the camera clicked – to Rejoice; it gazed across the lake, wearing an ill-fitting headdress Sydney had made especially for it.

Sydney couldn't be certain Rejoice had put the flowers there itself, but no other possibility ever entered her mind. She observed the bear more closely over the next weeks, and made greater attempts to get it to mimic her and interact with her. And if ever it did – through accident or not – fireworks exploded in Sydney. She had found a companion, she felt special, and she would become quickly jealous when other kids tried to play with it. Rejoice was no longer just the neighborhood puppy – it was Sydney's.

As Sydney's affection for Rejoice grew, troublesome stories about the bear grew in parallel. Children claiming Rejoice had almost trodden on them while they rode their bicycles – with the scars to prove it. A young girl said she'd nearly suffocated when Rejoice flattened her against a barbershop window having been dazzled by a fire hydrant. There were tales of late-night spying through curtain gaps and Rejoice was even blamed for a power cut one Thursday. Where seeing the bear once drew a smile, it slowly began to draw ire.

Chief Clemmons, having resolved to protect children and limit damage to property without interfering with Rejoice's whims, made several attempts to improve the situation. The first was an earnest move to train Rejoice like a household pet. However, this initiative failed, seeing as it could not be bribed with treats (it did not, to the best of anybody's knowledge, eat). Nor could it be beaten, lacking, as it did, physical sensation. In fact, every sustained effort to dictate the bear's actions ended in failure, and even when a crew managed to keep it away from the city for a day, it just returned to Ashland the next morning.

Quiet talk of "solutions to the bear problem" became louder. Sydney witnessed first-hand the heads turning away as Rejoice approached and the overblown frustrations for any perceived offense. Even the children, once enamored with their toy, had grown bored of its ceaseless meandering and repeated routines.

Until one day in Autumn, less than four months after Rejoice arrived, Sydney received a note on the schoolyard; a boy she didn't know had shoved it in her hand. The note referenced a meeting on the forest's edge taking place the next morning and it concerned 'a better life for Rejoice.' She asked the boy for an explanation, but he only scowled before speeding out of the school gates, pushing more papers on children as he ran.

And so the second town meeting to discuss Rejoice occurred, this time without Mayor Hobson or the police to mediate (though they weren't far behind) and with fewer – yet still significant – numbers. Sydney shuffled into the masses waiting at the back of the old picture house and waited ten or fifteen minutes before she saw him, the kid from the previous day who'd handed her the note. He was making his way towards the front of the crowd, carrying a bullhorn with him.

The kid got up onto a milk crate and raised his hand. A murmur went through the crowd and then it fell silent, except for a few people shouting words of encouragement at him. The kid acknowledged them with a nod and a shy smile. In the full light of day, he looked less angry and more beautiful. He waited until people stopped shouting. A siren could be heard, maybe five or ten blocks away. The kid raised the bullhorn, pressed the button, and began to speak.

"Thank you, thank you all for coming here this morning. Now, some of you already know me, but for those who don't, my name is Michael Chase and I moved here with my family a little while back. And… I've noticed I'm not the only newcomer, right?" The kid smiled and chuckles sifted through the crowd.

"We all love Rejoice. Even those who don't love it, do – don't they? I mean, come on, just look at the thing." Michael gestured towards the bear's head which could be seen bobbing between houses some blocks away. "This town has been blessed, though I know it's come with its share of problems. So… I bring you here today because I want to ask: does this blessing mean we all must pay a price?" Another ripple of agreement spread among the people and Sydney's reticence began to transform into fear. "I believe there is a way we can achieve peace for us and a better life for Rejoice."

Michael proposed the elegant solution that had crossed almost everybody's mind. They had been holding out only for a young boy with a pretty face to shortcut their ethical reservations. Who was to say what Rejoice itself wanted, anyway. If it even wanted at all.

The kid left his milk carton to high-fives from his pa and uncle, only moments before the police arrived. They tried to restart the dialog but the people there had heard enough – were already convinced of Michael's plan. Rejoice – clumsy, innocent, majestic, whatever it was – was no longer something they wanted to put up with.

Mayor Hobson agreed with the proposals too. It seemed the Chase family had a wealth of previous experience that could help the city carry off the feat, notably: construction, accounting, and fraud. This last asset was yet another discovery the Mayor would shield from the police, finding, as he had, a way to benefit from it.

The following Monday, the Chase family began building a wall on the plot of grass at the city's edge where Rejoice was first discovered – tall enough to cover the bear from top to bottom. The family erected three of the wall's faces there, as well as a human-sized front door, before assembling some oversized objects inside. These included a hastily-built chair; a wooden bed with patchwork quilt; a non-opening chest of drawers; a picture frame without a picture; a section of green carpet for a rug; and several other furnishings resembling what one might find in a person's bedroom.

Sydney had watched, and protested against, these developments but received only toothless arguments in return. "Rejoice will be happy as rabbits in a hutch, here," people would tell her. "It's to protect Rejoice as much as anyone else, sweety," folks would say.

Once the room's roof was almost finished and its windows installed – just before building the last section of wall – the Chases began their most important task. That evening, with the aid of a swarm of citizens, Rejoice was urged towards its new home. The bear put up no protest – it moved where it was able to move within the circle of people and cars. They marched it into its new dwelling and the Chases sealed it shut.

On opening day, Sydney watched with disgust as Michael cut the ribbon and shook Mayor Hobson's hand, grinning. The Mayor's wife handed Michael a gift, which he hung on the door; "Welcome to the Teddy Bear Playhouse," read the sign. As the crowd applauded, Sydney saw Rejoice had lain down to put an eye against one of its little windows. She clenched her teeth, shook her head, and left.

Now that Ashland's great teddy bear was an attraction, marketed as such and lodged in a sensible setting, out-of-towners flocked to see it.

They were permitted to look through the room's windows or even stand inside with Rejoice, for a fee. Through this, the Teddy Bear Playhouse made fortunes for the city, though the money would only end up in the pockets of the Mayor and the Chases.

Sydney continued to visit Rejoice during this period, but she grew increasingly upset. When school was over, she'd walk to its pen and peer inside; Rejoice would often be stood facing the wall, mere inches from it, which wounded Sydney further.

Occasionally, she'd argue her way to some free minutes beside Rejoice – typically accompanied by open-mouthed, goggle-eyed spectators from another town – and would touch it to see if it touched her back. To see if the contact kindled a memory of something once shared between them. And sometimes, sometimes, Sydney really believed Rejoice understood, and smiled not because the lining on its face dictated that it must, but because its old friend was there alongside. And other times, Sydney only told herself it had recognized her, though she suspected that it hadn't really at all.

Sydney couldn't understand how it had all happened. Rejoice was a miracle, the thought that it had been detained made her sick. As the days passed, Sydney became more aggressive. She would yell at Playhouse visitors as they lined up for entry, and get into fights at school. Once, she was even caught trying to hot-wire a bulldozer. But even if she could find a way to crumble the walls of Rejoice's room, she had no next moves; the bear was somehow attached to Ashland and it's not like she could keep it a secret.

Sydney also sought out Joan Hockeridge around this time, begged her to speak up like she first had and help free Rejoice. Hockeridge shared Sydney's concern, but told her there was nothing she could do now that money was involved, as was and had always been the case, with anything.

One cold morning, Sydney left her bed in the early hours to see Rejoice alone; she carried her backpack with her. The Teddy Bear

Playhouse was closed for business at that hour, so nobody should have been there, but Sydney briefly scouted around in the darkness to make sure. Satisfied, she removed a hammer from her bag and smashed one of the windows, then climbed inside the room and took a box of matches from her pocket. She lit one, revealing Rejoice, stood alone.

Sydney approached the bear and sat on its carpet rug as she shook out her match. She rested her hand on Rejoice, as she herself now shook, and asked how it was. Sydney apologized for not having managed to get it a new home – one without walls – and the bear was motionless as she talked. She lit another match and marveled again at how small the bear made her. And then, with the match halfway burned, Rejoice moved its head.

It was slight, and not in Sydney's direction, but it was enough to give her a start; she jolted and her match went out. Sydney held her hand to her breast and slowly began to laugh. She laughed hysterically, standing to laugh against the bear's leg, pushing her face into its fur, running her hands through it, smothering herself. But her laughter soon turned to tears. With a lump in her throat so big she almost couldn't swallow, Sydney entered her backpack, removed a can of lighter fluid from it, and opened it.

Tears and fuel splashed against the dirty rug as Sydney doused the bear. She struck another match, whispered an apology, and tossed it onto Rejoice. The fire sped up its legs and across the floor – almost scolding her as it did – only slowing down when it reached its stomach. The bear patted the luminous flames, softly, spreading them further across its body. Globs of smoke rose and ran around the room as Rejoice accepted the blaze, shifting its arms to see the effect the fire had on its fur. Sydney watched from outside until Rejoice's head was all that was left, smiling, crackling on the pyre.

Sydney was still at the room when the fire service arrived; she had no intention of dodging responsibility. It began to rain and steam rose from the building, but Sydney's tears had dried up by then. The police appeared shortly after and Chief Clemmons stepped out of his car, giving Sydney a look of disappointment, but not disbelief. Sydney would never apologize.

Mayor Hobson held a funeral service for Rejoice three days later and thousands showed up to mourn the great loss. Many people shared rose-tinted memories of happy days they'd shared with the bear, and decried the heinous act that had seen its passing. Sydney wasn't present, though she would have expected as much from the event.

Rejoice's former home became a hangout for others struggling to find their role in society. They turned it into a sacred place, dedicated to the bear God. It stayed like this for some years before being abandoned. The Chase family, meanwhile, tried (and failed) to sue the city for compensation – and that was the end of their close relations with the Mayor.

Sydney had to attend a juvenile behavior program for her offenses, but it was in another town and she was happy to get away. She left Ashland for good when she was 16 and moved to the South West. Sydney surprised herself, eventually, finding friends who cared about her. But she'd never care for them the way she had for Rejoice the bear.

More than twenty years later, Sydney would make a habit of returning to Ashland, to the spot where Rejoice used to live, on the anniversary of its appearance all those years ago. The area was still much as it was before she'd left – flyers advertising The Teddy Bear Playhouse still clinging to telephone poles. But only one piece of its room remained standing – a section of wall, which Sydney would tend to, like a grave.

Sydney picked up last year's teddy bear toys and candles and put them in her plastic bag before replacing them with a new set. She looked again at the graffiti sprayed on the wall. "Happy birthday, Rejoice," she said, wiping a tear away from her eye. "Happy birthday, my best friend."

Sydney lit a cigarette and then pulled a photograph from her pocket –

a lake scene in summer. Rejoice was fading into the background, had been fading more each passing year. Did it stand on the water's edge, staring at far-off mountains, pondering on the strange place it existed, as others had pondered on it? Had Rejoice known it was ever there or that it meant something to somebody else? Sydney would never be able to answer those questions, though she would believe forever they were important.

Mrs. Castalto's Garden

KELLY GRIFFITHS

♣

Beyond the cracked sidewalk, and the telephone pole with layers of flyers in a rainbow of colors, and the patch of dry brown grass there stood a ten-foot high concrete block wall, caked with dozens of coats of paint. There was a small shrine at the foot of it, with burnt out candles and dead flowers and a few soggy teddy bears. One word of graffiti filled the wall, red letters on a gold background: Rejoice!

A man wearing flannel and lace-less boots, emitting the stench of months, sallied up to the golden wall and began to piss on it, at first limply, then with gusto. He sprayed in arcs, trying to hit the *Rejoice*, but it was too high. Stepping back, he surveyed the dark and wild lines of his art, then shook his head.

One of the candles was a tall glass bearing the image of Jesus. Ignoring that, the man's grimy fingers fondled the fuzzy ears of a bear and the breast-like arcs of a stuffed heart. He plucked a votive and poured out rainwater, sniffed it, and dropped it in one of his many deep pockets. He looked around to see if anyone cared.

On the other side of the wall, Mrs. Castalto's espresso cup froze, mid-lift. Her ears quickened at the sound of urine. She pressed her lips together and willed *dead* the one who would do such a thing. By the familiar, uneven gait, she knew who that someone might be, that he had finished his vile business and was messing with the shrine.

"Don't you dare touch that." Mrs. Castalto tilted her coiffed head skyward and threw her frail voice with force. She was rewarded with a slurred curse and shuffling steps that got farther and farther away. "That's right, mister, you keep right on going…and don't you pee on my wall no more, neither."

The Italianized Castalto bungalow sat right next to the drunk's lucky traffic light. Lucky, because once a driver gave him a hundred-dollar bill. Ever after, the drunk sat cross-legged on his flattened cardboard box and worked the morning rush hour from Mrs. Castalto's tree lawn. He knew, no matter how much his presence annoyed her, Mrs. Castalto wouldn't say a word. For until today, she had spoken to exactly no one on Sackett Avenue. The drunk was so astounded by her phlegmy voice, he couldn't help but obey.

In spite of her grief, Mrs. Castalto chuckled at the thought of surprising the drunk with nothing but her voice. And finally telling him off. Why had she waited so long? *Hope you never come back. Hope, if you pee on my wall again, it shrivels and falls off.*

Today was the first day Mrs. Castalto felt up to having her espresso outside, among the hydrangea bushes and asters that framed her wrought -iron table and claimed the sweet shade provided by the hawthorn tree. For most of the week it had rained on and off, as if the Blessed Mother was crying right along with her, with everyone who heard about the awful thing that happened. For a week afterward, Mrs. Castalto refused to enter the patio. She neglected to sweep the cobblestones or wipe the table, and a layer of nature's lint had settled on everything. As she fluffed the cushions, tears blurred her vision.

She blamed herself. She defended herself. Inside her head was an entire jury trial, during which the espresso got cold. She dumped it into the asters and had a quiet cry. She closed her eyes, remembering. That day had been just like this one: mildly cool and tranquil, her tree lawn blissfully absent of one inebriated panhandler. She'd just found a new recipe for quiche and was poring over the ingredients, when she was interrupted by a thud and a clipped cry. Had a bird flown into the wall? She frowned and read on.

The thing chirped more, then came the sound of ripping fabric. Then, snarling. The snarling pushed Mrs. Castalto upright, ears cocked and straining to hear. If she wanted to see, she'd have to go through the house. By then the commotion would be over. And surely the bird—was that what it was?—was a goner anyway. Mrs. Castalto was beginning to doubt because, though it chirped like a bird, it made heavy scrapes along the sidewalk. And something tinkled like metal. Mrs. Castalto would later find out those were earrings.

"Hey. Old Woman." The drunk was back. There was no mistaking that scuffling gait and the box dragging along behind him. "What happened?" He waited for a response that wasn't coming. "I know you c'n talk. You just did…What happened here?"

The drunk didn't know. How could he not know? Everyone within a hundred miles knew what happened here. In her mind Mrs. Castalto went back to that morning, to the shaken voices on the other side of her wall. "Oh my God! My God! Oh…" Then footsteps and another gruff voice swore in a way Mrs. Castalto had never, in all her life, not *that* word—said over and over again. There was the wet sound of something poured onto the street, a voice spitting and choking out they'd better call 9-1-1. Another saying, "I am!" Breaks squealed, a car door opened. "Oh God Almighty!" And over and over Jesus was asked to help. Help them, please. *Please.* All this Mrs. Castalto took in grudgingly, the way one takes in a malodorous gust, her back straightening, her magazine pressing into her lap as if its pages would turn to wings and fly over the cement wall.

That morning, Mrs. Castalto called for her husband, who was in the john with his own magazines. He never answered from the john because it was his sacred place, from which he dished back to Mrs. Castalto her own perfected, tactical muteness. A flash of anger shot through her. The *nerve.* Though her auditory eavesdropping had the effect of sowing an electric, nerve-choking weed in her body, accelerating her heartbeat and popping her eyes wide, and should have rooted her to the spot, and though she feared acquaintance with the macabre incident beyond her wall, the magnet of curiosity won out. The wrought-iron chair legs screamed in protest along the cobblestones as she pushed herself standing. She took the turns of her cramped and ostentatious dining room at a sprint, banging into a chair. As the first police car showed up, siren and lights blaring, she cracked open the front door. Just a small crack but enough to let it in. How she wished she would've waited for her husband! She'd never be able to scrub the image from her mind as long as she lived.

"—I know you're there, Old Woman. I can hear you breathing…you all right? You don't sound so good." The clinking sound of glass against glass said the drunk was messing with the shrine again. "Hey. A kid bite it here? That what happened?"

At first, people thought the little girl had been murdered, but Mrs. Castalto came forward and told the police what she'd heard. The officers couldn't possibly know what thaumaturgy it was for her to speak to strangers, let alone *make a statement*. Though she lived three doors down, she didn't recognize the picture of a girl with honey-colored braids and a mouth full of braces. Did it matter? She didn't *see* a single thing until it was all over. What she saw were looping sausage-like things, rib bones, and chunks of bloody meat so roast-like, Mrs. Castalto vowed never to eat another. She didn't bother telling all that, but took the officers to the garden and pointed out the cement wall had no ornamental holes, no door. The officers poked around and were complimenting her paradise when a scream pierced the air. Then it collapsed, then erupted again like automatic weaponry. The girl's mother.

The police left. Someone took the mother away, and Mr. Castalto went outside to tell what he knew, which was more than anyone else, thanks to his wife. From an upstairs window she watched him flit from person to person, telling her tale. She liked it that way. Only, just for today she wished she could read lips. Her husband was gathering information as well as giving it. His next stop was the two men scrubbing a white flaky compound into the spot, the yellow crime tape still framing the area. The men stepped over or under the tape and mopped up what would come, until only a dark stain roughly the shape of Africa remained. Mr. Castalto and the city workers all wagged their heads. *Tragic.* That's what they were saying. Or something like that. Once the sidewalk was no longer sticky, people came with offerings: flowers and toys and prayers. When the sun set, they brought candles. Many people loitered—waiting for a revelation from a silent and frightening altar.

Because of the sordid nature of the content and because he secretly enjoyed making her squirm, Mr. Castalto made his wife wait for the details until after dinner. He poured himself a Sambuca with the intensity of a sloth while she sat at attention. "If you'd just come out with me, you'd know everything." He winked and took another eternal sip, swishing…swishing. "Apparently the dog belongs to some mechanic over on Chester. Idiot fell asleep while his pit-bull was in the yard. It dug under the fence—big surprise—and there you have it. You're just lucky there was a cement wall between you and that beast." Mr. Castalto's grisly imaginings gripped him for a moment. He shook them off and declared, "Horrible, what happened."

The ever-dry Mrs. Castalto groped for the crystal decanter and, ignoring her husband's frown, poured lavishly. "I'm a big girl, you know." She answered his wordless rebuke, then tossed the contents down her throat and stifled a gag. She broke, sobs wracking her slight frame.

The mister, not normally an affectionate man, wrenched himself out of his recliner and snuggled his wife, ruffling her silver curls. "No one blames you in the least, luv. You said so yourself, the girl didn't even scream. How could you know the dog tore her—well, you couldn't possibly know…"

He got up and went to the window. "There he is…the father. Look at him. He's lost his mind." Mr. Castalto held open the curtain and gestured. The father had scrambled a posse and was giving orders. Every upturned face reflected their leader's mask of fury, made grotesque by the flickering, hellish candles held in itching hands. One kid in particular looked bent on destruction. He moved with savage grace, raising arms of war, a butcher knife in one hand and the other curled into a fist mallet. But for the murderous expression on his face, it could've been Mrs. Castalto's own son Joey, now grown and living in California. She furrowed her painted-on brows and shook her head. *It won't bring the girl back.* Eventually, the congregation dispersed, and feeling the effects of her drink, Mrs. Castalto climbed into bed and slept the sleep of the anesthetized.

The minty gusts of Mr. Castalto's breath and his low whisper gently pulled her from sleep. They'd found the dog. And the mechanic. And she might want to wake up. He was going back out there because the sun was up and News Channel Five had arrived. He kissed her head and dashed out. Mrs. Castalto loped from her bed to the window seat, where a cup of steaming espresso and a plate of banana bread had been set out. Her mister was a prince.

The last time the street clogged like this was for the summer parade. A leashed dog licked at the stain on the concrete until its owner yanked it away. Kids did cartwheels on the yellow lines, oblivious. Moms leaned into one another, and in the low, respectful chords of atrocity, shared their mutual relief. Thank God, *thank God* it wasn't *x*. It could've been my little *y*. A beeping riveted everyone's attention to the white truck worming its way through the crowd. It was dented and rusty as if a giant had squeezed it and rust grew from the accordioned places. And the bed was the worst: completely rusted out or slathered with mud. Mud, right? Mrs. Castalto tried to remember where she'd set her glasses, but the fog of hangover prevented her. The kid, the one who looked like her Joey, killed the engine, stepped out, and flipped the shank of bangs off his eyes. Long Italian curls settled on either side of his face.

With help from the kid, a man emerged from the passenger seat. His shirt was torn and bloody, his face cut in several places. The father. Everyone gathered around him and the kid. Pushing, waiting to hear what they had to say. But the father's legs buckled, and he made the curb his seat, head between his knees. The kid whispered something and pointed to the crowds, but the father shook his head and continued being a turtle.

One of the cameramen made his way over to the truck and peered into the bed. He reeled back and clutched his head, then grabbed a bullhorn and thrust it at the father, who put up a limp hand to resist. The cameraman pointed to the truck and then to the audience and did a lot of what Mrs. Castalto recognized as Italian arm-flapping. Another man peered in the bed, then stumbled away, waving off others with the same idea. But it was too late. A tide of interest flowed toward the truck. Though the kid put up his hands to stop it, he was overwhelmed. He motioned for the bullhorn as the crowd flung questions at the father, the kid, and at each other.

The kid got up onto a milk crate and raised his hand. A murmur went through the crowd, and it fell silent, except for a few people shouting words of encouragement at him. The kid acknowledged them with a nod and a shy smile. In the full light of day, he looked less angry and more beautiful. He waited until people stopped shouting. A siren wailed, maybe five or ten blocks away. The kid raised the bullhorn, pressed the button, and began to speak.

"I'm going to say a few words on behalf of my friend Rex. He's too… he's not able to…" The kid looked at the sea of faces and froze. He shifted his weight and swore under his breath. He spotted something that galvanized him and found his mettle. "You know what? We *can* rejoice. Because in the back of my truck is one asshole mechanic who couldn't keep a leash on his mutt, and…it was worth it. For her." He pointed to the blood stain. "Nobody deserves that."

The crowd's approving shouts were shots of confidence to the kid, who seemed to grow taller as he got comfortable with the spotlight. He shot a fist into the air and shouted, "In this truck is justice. Sometimes it ain't pretty, but there it is. Rex and me, we got justice for his little girl." The kid flipped his bangs out of his face, just like her Joey, then jumped off the crate and landed in the middle of the Africa stain. As his feet hit the pavement, he cried out, "Damn straight, we can rejoice!"

From behind the kid, the father sprang up, lunged, and snatched the bullhorn out of his hand. He glared at Joey Lookalike for a long moment then sighed into the bullhorn. To the crowd he said, "I just wanted my baby back." He kept the bullhorn close to his mouth, so his sobs were amplified. No one moved. The father curled in on himself like a crashing wave and shook his head fiercely. Sirens and flashing lights washed the truck and crowd in penal splendor as police swarmed the scene. The father, still shaking his head in denial, put his hands up, one hand holding the bullhorn. The kid—he reached inside his pocket. Brazen. Eyes challenging. A black something in his hand. The officers shouted for him to stop, to put his hands up now. NOW. PUT YOUR HANDS UP N—

"—Old Woman. Somebody wrote on your wall, know that? It says here, *rejoice*. Not exactly your style." The drunk slapped his hand against the concrete like he was knocking on her door. "What happened? WHAT (smack) THEE (smack) FUCK (smack) HAPPENED (smack) HERE (smack, smack, smack)?" The drunk sighed and leaned against the wall.

Mrs. Castalto could just imagine his cheek against her gold paint. A six-inch concrete wall was not enough to keep out the panhandling drunk who blighted her view and peed on her wall—and who should've bit it instead of the little girl. The kid said nobody deserved that, but Mrs. Castalto disagreed. Some deserved it more than others. Though she felt a keen desire to confess what she heard and saw that dreadful day, to purge the anathema from her memory, she wanted even less to give the drunk what he craved. Information.

The memories allowed her no peace. She tried to focus on the recipes, but her mind kept drifting back to the day the father—Rex? —was cuffed and put in a squad car, how Rex leaned out to watch the EMT's work on the kid. Rex got his head bashed by the slamming door. The officer opened it again to check on him and, satisfied, drove away. One by one the EMT's gave up on Joey Lookalike, and he was put in a silent ambulance, gone the way of the girl.

As the ambulance pulled away, Mrs. Castalto found her glasses. Putting them on was a mistake. It wasn't rust all over the truck bed. The bodies lay side by side, a man and his dog. The man's arm was flung across his dog's body, and the dog's nose touched his master's cheek. Blood pooled in the straight, corrugated lines of the truck bed. Mrs. Castalto startled back and crushed her banana bread under her palm.

"—What the hell's the stink out here? Smells like rotten fish." The drunk sniffed and blew air between his teeth. "Was it a fish truck? That it? A fish truck run over somebody?" Smack, smack, smack. "The candles ain't helping, Old Woman."

What was he talking about? With the mantle of reek the drunk wore, how could *ff* smell anything? Besides, the incident happened nearly a week ago, and the blood had been scrubbed with what Mrs. Castalto assumed was baking soda. She lay a hand over her espresso demitasse and sniffed. Nothing but the perfume of hydrangeas and roasted coffee.

Then she remembered. The clam juice. They fought that night, Mrs. Castalto and her mister. She had burned the Ritz-clam casserole, and Mr. Castalto had one too many Sambucas and was in a mood to tease—a comment about oven timers coming standard for a reason. Mrs. Castalto offered him a substitute meal of room temperature clam juice. He parried with an offer to booby trap the cement wall with it. That got a laugh. Mrs. Castalto imagined clam juice falling on the drunk's greasy head as he did his dirtiness against her wall. But fearful some innocent would get doused, she dismantled the trap and poured the juice on the drunk's lucky spot. *Let him rot in it*, she had thought. What night was that? She tried to remember.

The drunk found someone willing to tell him about the shrine. Mrs. Castalto's eyes narrowed. *Son-of-a-bitch. Jesus-H-Chr*—No matter how mad she got, Mrs. Castalto stopped herself at the Lord's name. She squeezed both fists into tight little balls. If all she could do was keep the drunk ignorant, at least she had that. But no longer, thanks to this traitor. A youngish woman, probably the foreign student who took the bus. Mrs. Castalto tried to eavesdrop, but all she caught was a phrase or two. Didn't that woman know he peed on Mrs. Castalto's wall? The drunk's overtures of gratitude made her grimace. Did that foreigner just gave him money, too? And Mrs. Castalto had thought her a decent young lady. *Thought.*

"—A dog? Kilt a little girl, huh? That sucks unlucky socks," marveled the drunk. "You hear it, Old Woman? Cuz you hear everything. What, if you can hear me take a leak." The drunk set his cardboard down. Mrs. Castalto recognized the sound of his rubber soles against it as he settled himself. Then came more sniffs. Sniff, sniff, sniff. "Well I'll be dipped in shit if that dog wasn't rolling in this fishy grass." Sniff. "That what happened? The kid walks by, messes with the dog and gets herself dead? Kids. Can't put no sense in 'em. I had a cousin, scared a dog when it was eating. Thing turned on him and put holes right through his bottom lip. Bam!

"…So let me see…the kid walked by and scairt the dog while it had a nose-full of fish, freaked it right out, and it lost its shit on her. Pits, they lose their shit on a dime. Why didn't you just tell me, Old Woman? What, I gotta be a detective?"

Mrs. Castalto froze. The sounds of that morning played over and over. The possibilities. Getting up on hearing that first thud. Not pouring the clam juice. Getting up when the scrapings got heavy. Not pouring. Getting up. Getting up. Not pouring. Getting up. Not pouring. Not. Getting. Up. Why had she sat stapled to her seat? Why, WHY had she poured the clam juice on the tree lawn? Some part of her knew it wasn't a bird, but it was so preposterous and the asters were pretty, and the recipe, and the paradise. Mrs. Castalto had long ago decided not to participate. Her decision not to talk was her tallest wall. No matter what went on outside, she had her garden paradise, hedged by cement and brick walls and floored with cobblestones and the whimsical art of plush mold growing up in the cracks.

"Wait!" she called over the wall, then rushed through the house in a frenzy, throwing a shawl over her blouse and grabbing a jar of biscotti. The screen door swung open, just as it had a week ago, and there was the drunk, sitting cross-legged on his box, wearing his crooked nose and a tattered Carhart jacket several sizes too large. "Come inside." She said, and shook the jar in offering, noting how the finger-like cookies rattled unappetizingly.

The drunk's curiosity to see the what lay behind the wall on which he'd so often urinated overruled his suspicion. He stood, removed his snow cap and clutched it to his breast as if it were a Fedora. "Ma'am," he saluted.

She jolted. "*Now* it's ma'am. Whatever happened to *Old Woman?*" And with that, she led him to her paradise and let him sit on her plush pillows. She set down a steaming mug of espresso, black, as he asked. He ate several biscotti, and she told him he could have the lot. He poured them in a pocket and patted it lovingly. They talked. A Bible verse from Mrs. Castalto's youth kept coming to mind, but she didn't share it. *The wolf also shall dwell with the lamb, and the leopard shall lie down with the kid; and the calf and the young lion and the fatling together.* And she knew which one she was and which one he was, and she wondered what Mr. Castalto would think of this. That she'd lost her mind, that's what.

The drunk listened as Mrs. Castalto showed off her asters, her perennials, the hawthorn tree and how she'd pruned it mercilessly into the exact shape she desired. It wasn't easy to get a tree to do what you wanted. Easier to raise a kid. And she told him about her Joey and how the kid looked like him and how it was like watching Joey get shot by the police. That day, when things settled down, Mrs. Castalto grabbed her phone and dialed Joey and broke down when she heard his voice. Alive, thank the Blessed Mother.

The drunk nodded at that. He knew about that. The drunk's two children were dead. One got strangled by her umbilical cord and the other leaned into a ride at a carnival and got electrocuted. The drunk leaned into every carnival ride he could, hoping, but here he was. Alive. The drunk shook off his dead children and asked why she didn't run out when she heard the dog? Mrs. Castalto tried to explain: she didn't hear much, and without a throat, all that came out was the chirping sound she mistook for a bird.

"A bird, huh? It's probably just as well. You're lucky there was a cement wall or you would've been killed too." The drunk took a slurp of espresso, unaware he'd repeated Mr. Castalto almost word for word. The Sambuca was inside. Mrs. Castalto excused herself and came back with the whole decanter, dumping a generous slosh in each mug.

At the drunk's awed smile, she shrugged her shoulders. "I feel guilty, being alive. An old woman, when a beautiful young girl is dead. I must drink. Perhaps I can die for a little while this afternoon. That's how it goes, yes? As the Sambuca lit the coals of inner warmth and relaxed Mrs. Castalto deeper into her cushions, she considered confessing her sin: that she'd put the clam juice on the tree lawn. But there was *not enough Sambuca in the world*, she thought.

A hush settled on the garden. Mrs. Castalto cleared her throat. The drunk stood, and his chair legs released their usual complaint against the cobblestones. He thanked her and petted the cookie pocket once more. "That was kind of you…" The drunk trailed off and his eyes shone. He didn't want to call her *Old Woman*, but he didn't know her name. Mrs. Castalto wasn't telling. She offered her hand to shake. His skin was splintery, but warm.

That day, the day of the biscotti, was the last time the drunk came around. Bundled in her faux Sherpa pajamas and boots, Mrs. Castalto took her espresso in the lightly falling snow. The umbrella kept the table dry, and she brought a cushion from the sofa. She pictured the drunk sitting across from her as she sipped. She'd even bought the same brand of biscotti and tried eating one, but they were only good for dipping. She imagined him leaning into carnival rides, one after another. Almost, the drunk *almost* got his wish. Was that why she spilled the clam juice on his lucky spot? To answer his prayers?

After breakfast she would check the shrine, as always. All the original trinkets were stolen. Mrs. Castalto contributed the Jesus candles—four of them—and arranged pots of her own asters. She bought brightly colored vases and filled them with carnations and bouquets from the local grocery store. The flowers barely browned before she freshened them. An audience of stuffed animals piled against the wall and spilled onto the sidewalk so folks had to step over. She bade her mister paint over the sacrilegious *Rejoice!* and the midnight artist-thugs finally left the gilded wall alone. A more magnificent shrine did not exist, anywhere. People would pass by and tell her she was a saint for tending the shrine. She kept her mouth shut. People would say it was a stunning altar for a beautiful little girl, and she let them think that, too. The girl, the kid, the dog, and his hapless mechanic had turned a sacred knob and were on the other side of the tallest wall. She liked to think of them enjoying biscotti and espresso together, hot chocolate for the little girl. The dog curled at their feet.

Just as she opened her magazine, urine hit the wall in the familiar way it did. Her eyes brightened at the thought of her drunk, still alive. Then they narrowed. Still peeing on her shrine! Mrs. Castalto opened her mouth to curse him. No. He was already cursed. As was she, by the memories that breached her wall. The chirping sound she had mistaken for a bird threatened to send bile up her throat, and the faces of a jury stared hard at her. Gavels like gunshots ripped through her mind. Everything smelled of clams. The newest addition to her garden creaked as a breeze caught it: an empty bird cage. She sipped espresso and gulped hymns of imaginary birdsong. The undulating jet of urine would end. She had only to ride it out.

The Propheteer

KATHERINE KENDIG

◆

Beyond the cracked sidewalk, and the telephone pole with layers of flyers in a rainbow of colors, and the patch of dry brown grass there stood a ten -foot high concrete block wall, caked with dozens of coats of paint. There was a small shrine at the foot of it, with burnt out candles and dead flowers and a few soggy teddy bears. One word of graffiti filled the wall, red letters on a gold background: Rejoice!

Yevin was there early, but the man she'd come to meet was earlier still, and he leaned against the concrete wall with his arms crossed, wary, watching as she approached. She was wearing nice shoes. This wasn't the place for nice shoes, but it was the time. She needed armor, in whatever form she could find it.

Figaro was shabbier than he'd been, Yevin could see as she neared him; his coat was brown, of all things, and his own shoes looked like they'd been born in the patch of dirt they stood in. *Good*, Yevin thought. Good that he was shabby. Good that he was down. She stopped in front of him, the shrine a sad lump in the corner of her eye, and they stared at each other. Yevin was certainly not going to speak first.

"You look good," Figaro said, finally. "Or rich. One or the other." He shrugged, letting his arms fall and his hands find his pockets. His hair was too long, nipping at his collar, the same color as his coat. Yevin had never seen Figaro in any color less bright than blue. She hadn't seen him in ten years, though. Not in person, anyway.

Yevin pursed her lips, trying to hold back, but she couldn't. "Rich," she confirmed. "And happy, and safe, and successful." Her back had automatically straightened. Her cheeks felt hot: adrenaline. She'd waited for this. "They say the best revenge is living well."

Figaro smirked and then, seeing she was serious, he huffed into laughter. As a child, Yevin had learned to distinguish between fake laugh and genuine; it meant the difference between certain punishment and merely the possibility of it. But it had been ten years, and now she couldn't tell if this coughing bark was intentional. "Really?" Figaro asked her, shoulders bouncing against the wall. "Living well? You think?" He pushed off the wall and kicked lightly at one of the teddy bears at the edge of the shrine, a white one with a red jacket. "What the fuck do I care how you live?" he asked. "You're not one of mine anymore."

Yevin wanted to hit him. She wanted to kick his smug, indifferent face with her nice, new, pointy shoes. Instead she stood where she was, trying to breathe, waiting while his chuckles died away. "You could have shattered my kneecap," Figaro suggested. "Or burned my fucking house down. Or poked my eye out. That would have been revenge."

As if Yevin hadn't dreamed of doing those very things, a thousand times – but of course, he knew that. *Ignore him*, she told herself. *Ignore him*. She was grown up now. He didn't affect her. (Even if he did, still did, always would – even if there was no growing up, no living well, that could change that.) She took a deep breath, quietly.

He was staring at the shrine as if it were new, as if hadn't seen it before. As if he hadn't caused it. "There's a kid," Yevin said, changing the subject, keeping her voice level. "One of yours. He's making trouble downtown, and people are getting hurt. I need you to bring him in."

Figaro looked up at her with real surprise, like he'd thought this was a social visit, like he thought she'd asked him, after ten years, to meet him at the hellhole where her best friend had died so they could have a nice chat. Or – maybe he hadn't known she was with the government. Could he really not have known? He must keep tabs on her. He must.

"He's not one of mine," Figaro said, shaking his head. He took a few steps, aimless, but Yevin knew he just wanted to make her turn to keep him in view. He always wanted power, even a few tasteless drops of it, even when he wasn't thirsty. "He *is*," Yevin replied, moving only her head. "He's not," Figaro said again. Yevin felt as if she were being tied up; like Figaro's slow circle around her was a binding she might not escape again. "He is." Figaro kept moving, out of sight. "He's not."

"He *is*," Yevin insisted, giving up, turning to face him fully. "He talks like you, he dresses like you – or like you used to; he is yours, and you can help us with him, or you can watch us build another shrine, right here next to Lasinie, and start buying roses for the grave. He's playing with fire, and he doesn't understand that the one with the torch can still get burned. He's not going to last a week, the way he's going."

Figaro's face was flushed, and he scowled at her, and for the first time Yevin could remember, she knew she had gotten to him. Figaro ran children, used them, gave them a bed to sleep in and then chained them to it. But this kid – they were too alike for Figaro not to feel some pride, some kinship. All big words and loud colors and laughter in the face of anything, and neither of them cared one bloody heartbeat for what happened to anyone else.

Except that Figaro had cared, a little, what happened to Lasinie. She'd been willing to laugh at him to his face, as none of the other children would, and perversely, he loved her for it. Yevin thought it probably made him feel magnanimous, to love Lasinie; like a merciful king. Never mind that his mercy meant giving Lasinie all the toughest jobs, the kind he'd never trust to Yevin. Never mind that his love left Lasinie dead on the street, this street, with a bullet in her back. Yevin thanked God every day she'd never had to bear the burden of Figaro's love and mercy.

"Little Spit," Figaro said, grudgingly. Yevin blinked at him, lost – her heart was flipping through old emotions like a comic book, with an explosion on every page. "We call him Little Spit," Figaro clarified. "He might be a Christopher, though. Or an Aiden." All Figaro's boys had nicknames, Yevin remembered—never the girls. Figaro himself, of course, had a different name, a given name, buried under years of playacting. Yevin didn't know it. Her feet, she realized, were starting to hurt; she shifted her weight, and saw that the toes of her shoes were covered with dust.

"Is he following your instructions?" Yevin asked. "Are you part of this?" She hadn't known, when she agreed to meet with Figaro, agreed that their shared history might—*might*—influence him to help a government he'd be otherwise indifferent to, whether the kid (Little Spit, she supposed, although in the streets they called him the Propheteer, cheering at their own cleverness) was stirring up trouble because of or in spite of his involvement with Figaro. The Figaro Yevin knew wouldn't attract this much attention on purpose. But he might have changed, and just how much, Yevin couldn't know.

Figaro had circled back to the concrete wall and he leaned against it once more, jittery now, beating at the wall with his palm as he measured Yevin with a look, as if the cut of her clothing might tell him whether he should trust her. "Sometimes a boy has more initiative than I might like," he said. "Sometimes little spits think they're big. Nothing I can do to convince them otherwise. You should know that."

You should—Oh the nerve of this man, to tell her that. Who knew better than Figaro, in all the world, how to make a person feel small? Who knew better how to teach a child that they were, after all, despite everything they'd like to believe, well and truly powerless? "You're full of shit," Yevin began, starting towards him in anger, although she'd warned herself over and over not to get too close.

The danger didn't come from him this time, though. She stepped too fast; her heel twisted beneath her and she stumbled, went down on one knee into the gritty dirt, went down just like Lasinie had gone down ten years ago and it didn't matter that there was no blood and no bullet, Yevin could feel defeat in her bones, she could feel her heart stuttering with memories she wanted no part of. She closed her eyes for a moment, trying to suck in a breath past the closing of her throat, and was ashamed to find the heat of tears pushing through the seams of her eyelids. This wasn't what she'd planned. This wasn't how she'd wanted this to go.

And then, without warning, Figaro's hand on her arm. She jerked her eyes open; he had crouched down next to her. He was touching her with just the knuckles of his closed fist. "Look," he said. "You're fine." Telling her, not asking; but when Yevin blinked past her tears, she saw that his coat had fallen open, and the inner lining was a shiny satin blue. It made her feel, inexplicably, better.

"You never liked me," she said, surprising herself. Figaro dropped his hand from her shoulder but remained in his crouch. "Not in the least," he agreed. Yevin dropped her other knee – to hell with the dust – and sat back on her heels. "But you would have kept me," she said. "If I hadn't run that day, you would have kept me until I did. If you hadn't been so, so distracted by Lasinie, you would have caught me and brought me back."

"I almost did catch you," he said. "If you'd left an hour later, you wouldn't have made it." He couldn't know how gratified she was to hear that; to know that she had truly escaped, and not simply been let go. To know that she had been right to run when she did, when Lasinie's blood still stained the dust and red and blue lights still flickered against the concrete wall. To know that it wasn't simply cowardice.

Figaro stood, and Yevin followed suit, brushing at her knees. "You think I should have let you go," Figaro said. "If I let go of everything, everyone I didn't especially like – what would I have? Nothing. You get your hands on something, you keep it." Yevin cocked her head. "I would still have enough," she told him. "I could let go, and I would still have more than enough." But Figaro only looked at her, disappointed, like he didn't believe her – like he couldn't possibly believe her. "Let's see about Little Spit," was all he said in reply.

They walked. Perhaps Figaro didn't have the money for a cab; Yevin simply didn't want to close herself into a small space with him. The world was a small enough space for her. Figaro seemed to know where Little Spit would be, and Yevin kept her wits about her but let him lead. Her heels clacked loudly on the concrete; otherwise, the city streets were silent until they reached the streaming, seething edge of a crowd, and then finally the solid mass of it. There was chatter, excitement; some people held signs reading "Propheteer" (spelled wrong as often as not), or "Money for the mob!" or simply showing a photograph of Little Spit, taken at night with a reddish glow, his skinny little arm raised high and his face the picture of rage and revolution, with a thousand candles lofted behind him. Figaro elbowed them deeper into the mass until they were near enough to the front to see the reedy pip of a person that was the focus of all the fuss. Yevin thought he looked even younger than she'd expected.

The kid got up onto a milk crate and raised his hand. A murmur went through the crowd and then it fell silent, except for a few people shouting words of encouragement at him. The kid acknowledged them with a nod and a shy smile. In the full light of day, he looked less angry and more beautiful. He waited until people stopped shouting. A siren could be heard, maybe five or ten blocks away. The kid raised the bullhorn, pressed the button, and began to speak.

Yevin couldn't even distinguish the words, at first; she was too distracted by the tone, Figaro to the note; every dip and swell in pitch, every cheeky exclamation. It sounded wrong, coming from the kid; too big for him, like pants that bunched on the ground and shredded their seams with every step, or a pint glass he couldn't quite lift one-handed. Yevin had never heard him before, never seen him. Just the transcripts. Just the reports. It was different in person.

But the danger was the same. Here was a kid, she realized, as his words trickled in, who knew he'd found power but didn't yet realize how quickly it could get away from him. A kid who didn't realize that telling people what they deserved was as good as making a solemn oath to deliver it. Especially in this part of the city, where politicians made a careful effort to never tell them they deserved much of anything at all. Little Spit, little messiah, Propheteer. What happened when he didn't bring them sudden money and good fortune? What happened when they realized he was just a kid spouting dreams, and all the looting and violence committed in his name were still just petty crimes, with risks far greater than the rewards?

This wasn't Yevin's usual field of work. She handled financial crimes, but Little Spit hadn't committed any; he'd simply found a moderately large pile of money hidden away, and commandeered it. No one could prove whose money it was, and the kid had ridden his newfound legend to fame and spectacle. Somehow the story had twisted: it wasn't luck that suddenly filled his pockets but fate, it wasn't a modest sum but a fortune, and such fortune wasn't an unexpected windfall, but a human right finally fulfilled. They could have mugged him and taken the lot, these crowds that cheered him; but it wasn't such a huge sum of money, in the end, and they wanted to believe in the magic of sudden wealth more than they wanted to grab a tiny piece of it and dissolve the myth. Not everyone could be so lucky as to discover bundles of cash wrapped in plastic and buried at the base of an overpass, in the no man's land between jurisdictions where letting a child keep the money seemed less costly than fighting over it. But every person deserved a fortune and every person could have one, Little Spit declared. They were the masses. They were the mob. They had whatever power they were willing to take.

It was more rhetoric than riot, so far, but it scared Yevin; and it scared her more how much the kid seemed to enjoy it, how every speech seemed to demand more, even after people started committing assault and theft in his name. That was his upbringing, surely, product of a surrogate father who was never satisfied with anything. She looked at Figaro, intending to say something acid, but she was stopped by the sadness in his face as he gazed at his protégé. He looked almost – regretful.

Yevin shook her head slightly. She was projecting, surely. This was the kind of thing Figaro loved: big demands, empty words, dramatic gestures. The kid wore a red jacket and a yellow scarf and looked for all the world like the captain's boy on an old-fashioned pirate ship. He even sounded like one, waxing poetic on the promise of bounty. But no – Figaro was shaking his head, slowly, as if he were watching a train wreck in a movie, too late to stop it.

He looked at her, suddenly, a sharp turn of his head. "What's your plan?" he asked. "Jail him? For what? They'll riot." Yevin's eyebrows went up in surprise, and a woman in front of them turned slightly at the word "riot." "No," Yevin said, as quietly as she could under the bullhorn and the intermittent cheers. "Of course we won't jail him. He's what – eight?" "Twelve." "Do you really know that, or are you guessing?" Figaro didn't answer. Yevin shook her head. "We'll find him a home. Somewhere outside the city. He'll be safer, and so will everyone else."

"Such a little idiot," Figaro said, but without rancor, and Yevin realized he was talking about the boy rather than her. "Life's so much easier when people *aren't* watching. I told him that a thousand times. I told all of you." He sighed; Yevin saw it rather than heard it, because thunderous applause had erupted around them. She waited for it to die down; held her ground as the crowd started to shift around her, some surging forward to the Propheteer, some draining away, back to their lives. This wasn't the time, obviously, to try and reach him.

"That's why we need you," Yevin said eventually, when there was a little space. "We don't want riots. We don't want to grab him kicking and screaming from the streets. We need him to come to us. We need someone to bring him to us."

"So I gathered," Figaro said drily. He stared at the milk crate, which no longer boosted Little Spit almost to the height of his ravenous listeners;

they had moved on, sweeping him away. It stood empty, and Yevin realized she recognized it – or at least its type; it was the kind of crate she kept her things in when she was still with Figaro. This one was black and hers had been blue, and cracked, and covered with black marker where she and Lasinie had recorded their cravings, their crushes, their crackpot schemes for the future. But for all that, Yevin was almost sure this was Little Spit's crate; and her suspicions were confirmed when someone from Little Spit's entourage rushed back down the street and retrieved it.

"Why haven't you shut me down? Locked me up?" Figaro asked. He was staring down the street after the crate, as if afraid to let it out of his sight. "If you're so powerful now." Yevin opened her mouth to answer and found she couldn't. There were a million reasons – she wasn't that powerful, after all, and it wasn't her department; she'd moved on, she had left that behind, she had tried every damn day to become a woman with no resemblance to the child she had been, to live a life untouched by the past.

But why *hadn't* she shut him down? She had a million reasons, and no explanation. What had Figaro thought, when she asked to meet with him? What had he expected? Broken kneecaps? Tears? Nostalgia? "I've been biding my time," she said, but it sounded even weaker than she'd thought it would, and Figaro laughed. This laugh, though, she recognized as fake. "You thought I was a villain," Figaro said. "Some of you do. Funny though that it's always the ones I don't like, don't treat special, that think I'm rotten. Funny that for all my wicked ways, you haven't done a thing about it."

She should shut him down now. She should shut him down as punishment, not for her childhood, but for this moment: for forcing her to realize that all her excuses were no more than gibberish. Lorem ipsum. She was a coward after all. "You always wanted to be special, didn't you?" Figaro asked. "But you never were. That's all it is."

There was an answer to that. There was an answer to that, and it was sharp — Yevin pictured a knife, slicing through the air — Yevin was so angry she couldn't have spoken the right answer even if she'd had it on her tongue. "Lasinie is *dead*," she spat out, finally. And maybe that was all the answer that was needed, in the end, because the rotting shrine on the north side spoke volumes that Yevin didn't need to find the words for.

"Lasinie," Figaro repeated, low, like her name was almost too heavy a word to speak. "Lasinie is dead. True. Nothing I could have done there. No way I could have known what would happen. But I carry it with me anyway, for all the good that does. I light a candle every month, so she knows we remember."

Where the crowd had been just minutes before, now they were completely alone; but Yevin's skin prickled and her heart raced. She felt trapped, surrounded, outnumbered; she didn't want to hear Figaro's regrets, she didn't want to face the past again, she had only wanted to help one stupid kid escape a net of his own making. Payment, punishment, reparations; whatever she'd thought, she'd been misguided. "I don't want to talk to you anymore," she said, and her voice was so tight she could barely get the sound out. "Bring the kid to the Washfort Building as soon as you can. And don't ever say Lasinie's name again."

She didn't exactly run, but it felt like it; and by the time she was safely in a cab, with the buildings growing around her, newer and newer and then older and older, she was still trying to catch her breath. She didn't think Figaro was a villain; she *knew* it. She remembered his cruelty, she remembered his selfishness, she remembered how gaunt and anxious her life with him had been. She remembered Lasinie, god dammit, she *did*. But she had never lit a candle at her shrine, not once.

And she also remembered him crying, when he arrived at the scene where Lasinie had died. That was why she'd run away that day. That was how she'd known she could. She remembered Lasinie laughing at him, but she also remembered — did she? — Lasinie laughing with him. She remembered the way he looked at Lasinie, at some of the others — with something like pride. And he had never looked at Yevin that way. And he had suggested—as if she were merely holding a grudge, as if it were only her vanity he'd ever wounded.

She knew it was more. The heat had gone out, one winter, and he'd done nothing for months; his room had a fireplace. There was always, always, always the sense of debt, the reminder that she owed everything she had to him, the reminder that every day she worked to pay him back started with another night spent under his roof – a loan, not a gift. There were the risks he allowed them to take. There was the indifference to problems that didn't affect him.

There was this kid, Little Spit, the Propheteer – whatever his real name was. Figaro might lament it now, but he'd given the kid that hunger, the need that drove him to make bigger and bigger promises to capture louder and louder cheers. One day the kid had a milk crate; the next he had money; the next he had a following. One day he was a little nobody making wisecracks, and the next he was a leader. God, in his place – how could Yevin say she wouldn't be spinning speeches, too, in his place?

The cab let her out in front of her building; the Washfort, one of the most venerable workplaces in the city – smooth columns and marble arches, stone figures in the recesses like beneficent gods. She felt a rush every time she walked through the doors and no one stopped her. Maybe this was her version of a bullhorn. Maybe hers was the impossible dream.

Figaro brought the kid the next morning. Yevin hadn't expected it to happen so soon. They waited in the lobby; Yevin and two others came to meet them. Figaro had a hand on the boy's shoulder, still in a fist, just like when he'd touched Yevin the day before; she wondered if he even knew how one was supposed to touch another person in comfort. It happened so rarely that he even tried.

It was clear that Little Spit – Christopher, he admitted, when pressed – didn't know why he was here. He trusted Figaro. That was the problem.

That was the point. Yevin let her colleagues engage the boy in conversation, explain to him what was happening. They were trained to deal with children, as she was not. She and Figaro stood to one side. Figaro clenched and unclenched his fists, his mouth pursed into a thin line.

The two social workers stood up, and each put a hand on one of Christopher's shoulders. "I'm not coming with you!" Christopher yelled, finally seeming to understand the plan. He leapt up and tried to shake free, straining towards Figaro. "Figaro, stop them! They're trying to *take* me! They want me to—" He paused, and seemed to take in Figaro's stillness, his lack of surprise, his silence. "You—you knew? You're giving me away? Figaro, don't. Figaro, why? What did I do?"

Even the social workers seemed shaken when the boy started to cry; but with his realization, his resistance had gone, and they took the chance to lead him away. He walked between them automatically, his feet plodding, pleading with Figaro all the while, cursing him, asking him why. Figaro didn't answer. Figaro said nothing.

And the look on Figaro's face – Yevin wished she'd never gotten involved with this at all, so she would never have had to see it. "I'm sorry," she said, although about what she wasn't sure. Figaro looked at her without seeing. "That," he said. It came out as a whisper. He cleared his throat. "*That* was the revenge you wanted." He walked away as if he were old, or ill, or heartsick. For long minutes after he had gone, Yevin stood alone in the empty lobby, with its vaulted ceilings, with its perfect quiet and total security, and felt no satisfaction. She felt no relief, no triumph. She felt only – old. Or maybe ill. Or perhaps merely heartsick.

Seven Letter Words

AUTUMN MABRY

⁘

Beyond the cracked sidewalk, and the telephone pole with layers of flyers in a rainbow of colors, and the patch of dry brown grass there stood a ten-foot high concrete block wall, caked with dozens of coats of paint. There was a small shrine at the foot of it, with burnt out candles and dead flowers and a few soggy teddy bears. One word of graffiti filled the wall, red letters on a gold background: Rejoice!

I smiled at my creation, the burst of sweet acid from the spray can still clinging to the chilly autumn air. In a world as ugly as this one, I liked to imagine my seven letter words makes strangers feel something beautiful. *Seven*, I thought to myself. This number was said to be as close as one could reach towards perfection. This number has always found its place in my life, like a silent imaginary friend. My name has seven letters, the street where our shabby house once stood had seven letters, and I named my pup in kind, Phillip. With a whistle, I called to him and slung my backpack over my shoulder. The mutt came barreling from around the street corner, a string of drool dancing from his crooked snout.

Whimsey. Smiling. Winking. I counted the other seven letter words decorating nooks and crannies of the bustling street. I liked to think that others noticed them too. Unlike "Rejoice," singing out from the concrete wall for all eyes to see, my other messages whispered from the shadows and twisted around corners of the city. Only those in search of something more would benefit from reading them. A memory oozed from the back of my mind, smelling of cinnamon and apples, feeling like safety and love. My mother leaned over my shoulder, her golden-blonde hair floating down to tickle my neck. Her dainty hands squeezed my little shoulders as she examined the workbook in front of me. My pen hung in the air like a dagger about to sink into its mark. I was an intensely focused seven-year-old and hidden picture puzzles were my favorite pastime on cold fall mornings before school. I forced air into my lungs and back out, enjoying the icy prickles like needles sinking into soft flesh. My senses returned to the present. Pushing away the sad nostalgia of the past is harder to do around this time of year.

The sharp squeal of tires on asphalt interrupted my thoughts, peeling out then speeding past Phillip and I on the road. Phillip let out frantic howls and leapt at my feet protectively. I knelt to comfort him, my eyes following the automobile that was now slowing and gracefully parking parallel to the concrete wall. The woman who stepped out of the car wore a long black trench coat; her dark hair with silver streaks danced around her face. She was pale and her steady pace took a millisecond too long to accomplish each step, as if she had to contemplate each move carefully. A weight hung about her. Loss. She rounded the car, her hands clasped in front of her body. She observed the wall, from top to bottom and side to side. I imagined the edges of her mouth raising ever so slightly at the bold strength of "Rejoice." It would pain her at first, thinking about this word of excitement at a time of sorrow. However, there it would be, sealed in her mind's eye, to lift her when she would need it and to cling to when others words fall short. It would be a memory drifting in the air, reminding her that there is life to live and blessings to be had. *Rejoice. Embrace. Persist. Exclaim.*

Phillip left my side with an excited bark, his pace quickening to greet Hannah. "Nichole!" She called excitedly. I smiled in her direction and reached out my hand to welcome her into a tight hug. Hannah exuded warmth wherever she went, contrasting with the sharp chill of my world. I always felt more whole when she was around and at peace in her presence. "Are you headed to the gallery today? Can I come with you?" She looped her arm around to link it with mine and twisted me away from the woman standing at the wall. I hesitated in answering. *What day is it today?* My mind had been in a fog for about a week now, unable to shake free from the anniversary of the first day my mother forgot.

"I suppose so. The showing is tomorrow, right?" Hannah nodded with a grin, the heels of her boots tapping out a song as she walked in step with me. "And you are always welcome; you know that." I closed my eyes and breathed in the crisp air. Hannah asked me if I was prepared for the exhibition and I assured her I was. In theory this was true. My work was prepped and hung in its appropriate places amidst the other artists' work within the gallery. My husband William had meticulously been adjusting the lighting so as to optimize the focus surrounding each piece. But I hated the hectic preshow phase, weeks and months of planning and arranging, decisions and adjustments. In the end, however, when we get to enjoy the successful outcome of our hard work, it all becomes worthwhile.

Seeing someone's heart move at the sight of artwork is like watching two souls meet for the first time. Its as if an accidental glance is exchanged between them, followed by unexpected interest. Then the viewer is taken aback by the beauty, disgust, solemn sadness, or complexity of a what is displayed before them. The artist has succeeded when they beckon even one person to peer into their work for just a second longer than others would. One of the first times I noticed someone carefully examine one of my pieces, I felt completely and utterly naked. I fadjusted my shoulders and strove to stand taller as if it were my body they were scrutinizing… or admiring. A flicker of excitement started at my toes and crept upward little by little until they moved on and I could breathe again. My cheeks had flustered, my face had frozen, but I had felt a warmth bubbling. That was success to me. That's when my addiction to creating truly surfaced. The piece had been purchased after the show but that was just a perk. It strangely bothered me that is was gone; it felt like it had been taken. My only hope was that the person who had appreciated it was the buyer. *Connect. Dreamer. Artists.*

William, my wonderful husband afflicted with a fatal case of Peter Pan Syndrome, had been one such person. From the moment he first looked at me, I could see in his deep soulful eyes that he saw me- the real me. Even if he didn't fully understand, he accepted who I was as if I were a whimsical piece of art. What more could a woman ask for than to be admired for who she truly is? William was not an artist in the traditional sense but a creator of ideas. He could tinker and play with a thought, pull it from midair, and the next day it would be something tangible. As a team, being two very different people who had found a way to fit into each other, we created the Scarlet Stone Gallery. Named after my mother, this gallery had become a place of refuge for anyone who wished to truly be seen, anyone wanting to make a connection, anyone striving to feel something and become more inspired.

Hannah pushed the glass doors open, light spilling in from the skylight onto the hardwood floors before us. My footsteps were less hollow today now that the gallery had been filled. William had always described a showing as if it were a family reunion. "You've got the momma, the kids, the fat uncle and ugly cousin," he'd begin, pointing at pieces he deemed to fit those descriptions. "Then… there's always the few pervey grandpas you gotta hide in the back so as not to embarrass the family in front of the general public." William's purposefully sarcastic voice would be aimed directly at me, always referring to my work at that point. He loved my creations and claimed that evening the playing field with a smattering of snide remarks was only fair from time to time.

Phillip padded to his bed at the back of the room as William came around the corner. He welcomed me with a kiss and Hannah with a side hug. I watched Hannah as she excitedly asked William for a quick tour around the room. She was only about thirteen years old and had way too much freedom for a girl of her age. We had become like a second set of parents, or older siblings, to her in the few years following her family's move to our building. I would pass her in the hallway, noticing that she was always alone, quietly roaming the halls. At night, her parents would fight and we could hear it through the paper-thin walls of our old apartment. There wasn't any bumping or beating. I reluctantly listened for any signs of physical abuse. None ever came but crueler words could never have been spoken between two people who were supposed to love each other. William and I would look at each other sadly, battling with ourselves inwardly, trying to figure out what we could do. Eventually everything fell silent. I almost didn't notice the change until I realized that I had been getting better sleep and drinking less coffee. One morning, I noticed Hannah on the front stoop, the popsicle in her hand melting as she cried. She was only 10 when her father left. He left her very confused and conflicted. She told me that she didn't know how to feel; she had trouble feeling anything at all. Hannah was happy he was gone but empty in his absence. I had placed my hand on her shoulder and from that day forward, we would paint.

The way her father left her and the way my mother had begun to leave me were two very different ways of departing. The broken pieces left behind were similar though, so we spent long summers and holiday breaks together in my studio mending scars with paint. William's hot cocoa or sweet lemonade ran aplenty through these sweet memories, sugar highs fueling long nights and hot days. Hannah's talent flourished through her fingertips and she found some peace in expressing herself freely within the four walls of a canvas. Her mother would even come by to admire our creations after her graveyard shifts. Another memory surfaced; one from a more recent past. Just a few months prior, my mother sat at a window. Her golden-grey wiry strands tangled just above her shoulders as she slumped silently in her chair. I smelled disinfectant in the air as the nurse welcomed me solemnly into the room. Mother didn't turn her head, didn't shift from where she sat. William held my hand firmly during my then-weekly visits, each opening old wounds like scabs picked off flesh. My feet would ooze slowly forward as if walking through peanut butter. I would greet my mother and she would gaze my direction with a blank stare, never remembering who I was and much less trying to recall these days. I hadn't visited her in quite some time now. The guilt rests on my shoulders in a fitful slumber today.

"Nichole," William called, waking me from my hollow thoughts. "Where do you think Hannah's newest piece should go?" Awoken from my daydream, the anxiety that had built up in my chest released itself at the sound of his voice. I placed a finger to my chin, eyeing what had already been done. Hannah eagerly waited, her hands clasped together in front of her as I took my time thinking. I was teaching her more about patience lately and she quickly learned that I would make her wait longer for answers if she was impatient. It's a fun game for me and pure torture for her. I gave her a side glance and she whimpered, knowing I was teasing her today.

My face broke into a sly smile and I grabbed her piece from William, running to the right. She chased after me with a squeal of delight, our shoes squeaking on the ground as we twisted to run. I slowed near one of my favorite pieces, one that I had actually worked on while she had completed the one in my hands. "What if we sell these together?" I asked, "So they will always have each other?" Hannah eyed the canvas as I held them up next to each other, the light bouncing off the textured art. She nodded, pleased, and hugged me around the waist. Her piece was predominately green, it's texture like blades of thick carpet grass and golden light from a summer sun's rays. It complimented my piece perfectly, which was splashed with blue and turquoise.

That night, I absentmindedly stir-fried our dinner as William lazed on the sofa. He watched Youtube on his phone as the TV also played across the room. He swears that he can watch both at once but I know he just likes the constant noise and distraction. My mother used to say that too much screen time killed creative braincells so it wasn't until I had moved out that I had truly binged TV shows. The only thing we never watched was the news. You glean the most important things through other media, and, as William would say, "We don't need more rotten trash filling our heads." *I* muttered within myself. Come to think of it, the way the flickering television reflected across my mother's distant face in the home was one of the ways I knew she wasn't herself. She wasn't watching the screen but she wasn't really lost in thought either. She was just there, letting the lights of the screen pick at her cheekbones.

Before the early onset Alzheimer's, my mother was a vibrant woman of many talents. She would sing as she cooked, dance as she cleaned, tell stories as she taught life lessons; she was the most warm and wise woman I could have ever had the pleasure of being raised by. That's part of the reason why it is so hard to let her go. I had been fighting for so long to keep the old her, to force her to remember. Selfish... I thought. *Also, seven letters.* I plated the food and paced over to William, kissing his forehead. He thanked me, sitting up straighter. "Will you go out tonight?" He asked, "To write your seven letter stories?"

I smiled sweetly and nodded. At first, William didn't much like me going out to paint illegally on the walls of the dilapidated buildings. I had done it anyway, blaming the rebel artist inside of me and claiming that I couldn't control her even if I tried. I never truly tried. These were my only works in which I ever used words. It began when my mother was first showing signs of dementia, before William and I were married. It simplified the confusion and forced me to think of positive and uplifting things. Graffiti became a rebellious artform and a therapeutic practice all at once. After a few years, William had one of his grand ideas and approached the community board to commission a few artists to beautify parts of the city with artwork. It was approved and permits were given out. He made sure I was on the list. I was frustrated at first, part of the excitement stolen from me, but knew it was out of love and protection. I still refused to paint during the day. The anonymity was comfortable.

3 AM. My eyes opened slowly, adjusting to the darkness around me. William's breathing was steady as he slept, one leg dangling from the bed and pillows tossed around the room. *He's the most well-rested tornado I know*, I laughed to myself as I slipped out from under the covers. The night bit into my skin when I exited the building, like a dog's teeth clamping down on my body. I forced myself to run, knowing that movement would provide friction and friction would provide heat. During one of our harder financial years, my mother and I had used heat sparingly. I would complain loudly, frustrated and chilled. She would place her hands around my ears, the warmth of the gloves she wore inside heating them. "Let's do jumping jacks. Bet I can last longer than you!" Off we would go and just as she would get tired of jumping, she would begin a game of tag. My mother could turn any situation into a game; she was the master of distraction and I willingly fell for it every time. *Jumping. Playful. Delight.*

The sun peaked its head out with a wink, the night gone in what seemed like a flash. I hurriedly returned to our apartment and stripped off my clothes. Today was going to be a long day for us. William stepped out of the shower, rolling his towel into a twist and flicking it sharply in my direction. I threatened him with al fist in the air, playfully punching his shoulder before retreating to change my clothes. The smell of coffee was intoxicating, its scent hugging my tired body. The day that followed passed like a blur. There were so many people moving back and forth, in and out of the gallery. I allowed William to lead, handling details he overlooked in a calm and controlled silence.

The gallery filled quickly, more people attending tonight's showing than most others we'd had all year. I signed off on a few photographer's releases, allowing the local news to cover the work. The more exposure for our artists the better the gallery would do. My heart swelled at the smiling faces surrounding the artwork. Hannah and her mom glided from piece to piece as she passionately expressed her thoughts about either the work itself or the artist. We had introduced Hannah to many of the other contributors and she had quickly made connections with them all. Her mother was exhaustedly trying to keep up, the weariness sitting heavily on her eyelids. Her tired expression was very pleased though, proud of her daughter and the refuge she had built for herself here. She glanced at me with a small smile, a thank you lingering in the air. I responded in kind.

My heart swelled, watching Hannah and her mother together. In the past, I admittedly held something against her mother for staying with Hannah's father as long as she had. However, not a trace of that judgement is left in me. Her perseverance, love, and devoted efforts to raising her daughter alone quickly crowded out my outsider's perspective. You never know all the details to others situations and, as my mother always said, the kind and loving thing is always the right thing.

Scarlet. My mother. *Also, seven letters. Forgets. Silence. Disease.* These were not the seven letter words I wanted to creep into my head tonight. I paced across the room, weaving in and out of the warm bodies cascading shadows across the floor. I loved to watch the artwork people's shapes made, designs that others may not notice or appreciate, may not know they have been a part of making. *Kissing. Hugging. William.* I tried to recreate other seven letter words to ease the anxiety clinging my lungs. My eyes searched for him, for that dark hair and those deep eyes, the strong hands connected to the arms that supported broad shoulders. *My William.* From the outside looking in, I was a calm and collected statuesque woman, politely enjoying her evening. That's why I needed William. He glanced at me sideways as I approached, interlocking our fingers and melting my body into the side of his. He kissed me softly on the cheek, his eyes asking if I was okay. "I am now," I forced a smile. "I think I need to visit my mom soon."

"Okay," William nodded, giving me a reassuring smile before introducing me to the others around us. I nodded politely and laughed when others laughed but the fog in my head wouldn't lift. I have been missing her. I miss my mom. The last gallery night she attended, she was in a wheelchair. This was around the time she had begun to misplace simple words but she still had her bearings. Those days I tried to get her out of the home as often as possible. She was on a schedule. She was on her medication. Scarlet's personality had lost some of its spark but she could still hold conversations with specific people. My mother loved artwork, creative people and parties, so the buzz of the gallery had her on a high. She would gaze at a piece for what seemed like hours searching for hidden secrets beneath the layers of textures and color. My chest felt pained. She had faded so quickly this last year. My best friend was now a shell of the woman who had raised me. On a night like tonight, that thought hung above me like ropes from gallows, swaying back and forth in an eerie breeze. My eyes danced around the room, *she would have loved to be here.*

Suddenly, a beautiful woman caught my eye, slinking between people with the grace of a gorgeous black cat. Her eyes were striking and determined. She approached a piece and took a picture, passing others without so much as a glance. Two pictures were taken, three… and all of my work. I asked William if he had signed off on her photograph's releases and he said no. Something stopped me from approaching her, a faint memory tugging at my brain. She twisted to survey the room, her black hair streaked with silver falling from where it had been tucked behind her ear. Then, just as quickly as she had arrived, she left. I smiled, remembering where I had seen her last.

I didn't go to see my mother the next day or the one after that. I spent all my time in the gallery or painting late into the nighttime. The words were spilling out of me as I worked up the courage to visit her in that sad dreary place, in her sad dreary state. *Dazzles. Shining. Content. Purpose.* During the day, when I would need to get out of the gallery and studio, I took Phillip out for a walk. Sometimes Hannah would meet us and she would ramble on about her day, her friends, and her dreams. I would listen distractedly, especially when we passed "Rejoice!" I was always on the lookout for the woman who stared at my work for too long. I wanted to know why.

Three days later an automobile pulled up and parked beside the concrete wall. The driver opened the door, but did not get out of the car. Although her face was in shadow, it was easy to tell she was sad. There was something about how she turned away from the sun and rested the weight of her hands on the steering wheel, something about her silent composure, that caused Hannah to sigh. The young girl watched the driver lean out of the car and stretch her hand out towards one of the burned-out candles.

"She looks broken," Hannah simply stated, patting Phillip's head lovingly. I didn't respond but found myself quickly making my way over to the woman. Crossing my arms in the chill of the morning, I quietly approached her without thinking twice. She was kneeling next to the candles, her fingers delicately tracing what was left of the stubby wax foundations. She raised a camera to her face, focusing on the sad little details sprinkled before her. My shadow eclipsed her before I'd ever decided what to say, altering the light that had before illuminated her camera's capture.

"Good morning," I began. She peered up at me, standing abruptly. I had obviously startled her and apologized quickly. I shoved my hands in my pockets awkwardly and, against my better judgement, opened my mouth so words could come tumbling out. "I have seen you here a few times… and then at the gallery a few days ago." I hesitated, "Not like, not like I was watching you. Well, I was watching you in a way but… I just… I noticed that you were attracted to my work. I wanted to say thank you." *Ugh, this is hopeless. This is not what I wanted to say.* I peered at her hopefully, Hannah and Phillip trotting up behind me. A part of me was searching for answers within this woman. She had suddenly entered my life, gazed at my creations, and peered into my soul for a few brief seconds.

"Nichole, correct?" She smiled, laughing. Her voice was dazzlingly sweet like honey oozing off the comb. This was a reaction I had not expected and one that was in stark contrast to the state we had originally seen her. She held out her hand, "I am Annabel. I have visited your mother several times at the home." Her face flickers then instantly droops as if she remembers what brought her to the wall today. "My mother lived there for several years before she passed. They took very good care of her right down 'til the end." These words were meant to reassure me but instead hurt a little. I wasn't sure what I expected from this stranger, in this alleyway, but it definitely wasn't a conversation like this one.

Annabel continued, "I am a photographer. In the past, I've donated my work to the home as decoration, focusing on images that inspire hope and bliss. At least once a week I visit and show my latest photos to some of the residents. Your mother doesn't always remember me but she never refuses to participate. She especially loves the seven letter words around the city I had begun to stumbled across." Her eyes motioned toward "Rejoice!" and a small part of me leapt. "A few weeks ago, my curiosity got the better of me and I searched for the artist responsible by contacting the city. Imagine my surprise when I put two and two together."

"Her mom recognizes her paintings?" Hannah chirped almost too excitedly. Annabel sadly began to explain that in a way that could be the case but not exactly. My heart teeter tottered, part of it lifting in gladness that my mother hadn't completely lost all of herself. The other part was sinking, trying not to get too hopeful that she truly recognized my style, my hidden messages, my hopeful words to her. *I need to go visit.* Once Hannah and Annabel found a lull in their conversation, I asked when she planned to visit the home next.

"I would like to go with you, if you don't mind," I offered. She smiled, agreeing that that would be great. I was relieved at the thought of being supported by this stranger. There was someone here that knew what it was like to have lost a mother in more than one way but who hadn't allowed her kindness or her hope to follow suit. She hadn't hidden away, numbed, lost her sensitivity to the sadness. I wanted so much to be like her and to use my time in that way. I thanked her, exchanging phone numbers and she bid us good day. Hannah and I paced away, arm in arm, back toward the gallery. Phillip nipped at our heels, his jealous spirit begging for attention as any raggedy pup would.

After a few moments of silence, Hannah peered my direction, her flushed and freckled cheeks turned toward the sun. She was adorable. A beautiful young girl. "You know what you should do?" She began confidently, "You should paint at the home. Even if Scarlet doesn't remember you, I think she would still enjoy watching."

This thought had never occurred to me. I was almost embarrassed that it hadn't. "You know, you may have something there. You're a pretty smart girl when you aren't being dumb." I teased her and she crossed her eyes at me, sticking out her tongue playfully. For the first time in weeks I felt a little lighter. I was still afraid to be to hopeful, but the gloom had been somewhat washed away by the introduction of a new purpose. A memory crept into my heart, my mother and I both trying to get ready in the bathroom mirror. I was a teen and spent way too much time on my physical appearance, as most do during that stage of life. I remember her eyeing me curiously as I applied my last layer of mascara, scrutinizing every flaw of my face in the reflection of a foggy old vanity. She paced forward and placed her hands on my shoulders with a delicate firmness.

"Be sure to pay just as much attention to your beauty as you do your flaws, if not more. Not just the painted-on makeup. Not the canvas of your skin. To who you are, who you are within." She kissed me on the cheek as I jokingly asked what sappy poetry book she had pulled that out of. She shrugged, running her hands through her hair. "Eh, I made it up just now; that's a Scarlet original." She signed her name in the air with her finger as if autographing the invisible verses. At the time, I had rolled my eyes and blushed a little. Mom was always writing poetry in the air of our home. Sometimes I genuinely couldn't tell what was made up or what was memorized; so many beautiful words would fall from her lips and dangle in the air.

She would remind me of similar notions when I would criticize my artwork. My mother claimed that you could peer into the soul of not only other artists but yourself when you took the time to patiently peel back the layers of your work. "No judgement," she would say, "Don't judge yourself. Learn about yourself." Then she would step back, "Um… but yeah that may need some work." I would scoff and push her prying eyes away. She'd laughed and winked at me playfully. I could trust her not to sugarcoat her remarks of my work. She was the master of constructive criticism. I miss her detailed eye. She always made me better without making me feel worse first.

That tact and grace was one of the first things she had begun to lose. My mother became more selfish and inwardly focused which was not normal for her. Before I understood what was truly happening to her, I was so angry. Afterward, I was still bitter but not necessarily toward her. *Selfish.* That seven-letter word was one I had to continually fight against. I had to resist the urge to get lost in myself, focusing on how this made me feel instead of supporting the lost lonely woman it was happening to. Recently, I had been failing at this task.

The day Annabel had agreed to meet me at the home was a rainy autumn day, slowly showing hints of winter's bone-chilling nearness. William shifted under the weight of my supplies, hurriedly shuffling toward the gate. I gazed up at the eerily beautiful three-story home before me. There were only a handful of residents here to ensure personalized care. The nurses knew us by first-name basis and had been nothing but kind these last few years, especially this last one. Part of me accepted the biting cold and rain falling in that moment, the pain waking me up out of my groggy stupor. William beckoned from the door and I followed.

The house was warm, a fire crackling in the den as if it were the heartbeat of the house. I let my heavy coat shift off my shoulders, trying not to track water into the entryway. Margaret, the manager of the house welcomed us with a hug and the offer of coffee. William accepted, saying he would bring me back a cup. Annabel rounded the corner, her manner sweet and approachable. She had pulled her hair back into a tight bun, almost as tight as the hug she gave me in the next moment. "Everyone seems to be in a decent mood today. We have four residents in the den near the fire; your mother is one of them." I nodded and thanked her. "I told them that you were coming to visit Scarlett and had a special surprise for them."

Two to three simple things at a time, I thought, remembering what one nurse had long ago instructed. "That's all most can handle at one time," she had admitted. I smiled at Annabel as she motioned for me to follow her into the living room. I approached the comfy little group, wrapped in blankets and shawls. They seemed at ease, comfortable. I slowly paced to my mother, a small smile perched on her face that held no recognition of who I was. She said hello, her beautiful voice weighted with age.

"Hello mother," I said, leaning forward to kiss her cheek, "It's Nichole. How are you today?" She paused, her brain trying to gather information that had been misplaced. She politely smiled as anyone would to a stranger and responded in kind. "I have been well. We have a gallery," I continued, looking at the other residents so they could be included in the conversation, "And we had a show the other night. The art was beautiful and everyone had a great time."

"Oh!" She exclaimed, "I would love to see that one day. I believe I do love art." Annabel reassured her that she does. My mother looked very pleased with herself but said nothing more. Kate Brunes, sitting directly across, began to tell a familiar story about her grandchildren and how they would make stick people out of real sticks and leaves and twigs. Margaret had once mentioned to me that this story was almost as old as

Kate. Every time she told this tale it would change a little. Sometimes the children were neighbor kids, her own children, or her grandchildren when in reality she was remembering something from her own childhood. Some in the group would respond with niceties and begin stories of their own. It's in these moments that I want so badly to be happy for these people. There are days when they truly do have each other, my mother had friends. However, something inside me is always tethered to the sad reality that their words are skipping records, broken and repeating.

This is why I write my seven letter words full of hope. They help me lift my face to the sky, arms outstretched against the harsh winds of life. *Hopeful. Cherish. Scarlet.* I think of my mom as I begin to paint for them a half hour later. Annabel puts on some music, the kind you may hear in the background of a coffee house, and the room fills with warmth and calm. The group falls quiet, from time to time creating their own narrations of what could be filling the canvas. My mother sits on the edge of her chair, eagerly watching every brushstroke as it dances across the canvas. I don't have the heart to admit out loud that I have no idea what I'm painting. I'm unfocused and William can sense it in me as he watches from the doorway, his third cup of coffee poised at his lips. He winks playfully and I smile. Wings emerge from the shapes suddenly and I capture my direction. *Swallow. Seven letters. A bird carrying the message of hope. It's perfect.* My heart swelled within me, ignoring a grumpy old Mr. Martin who is complaining, "She's just blobbing paint on there. It's not even a picture!" William laughed and I continued to paint.

Upon completion, I allow the residents to gather closer to the piece. It features a barn swallow; a bright red silk ribbon is clutched tightly in its talons. This was the embodiment of the hope surrounding my mother, Scarlet. It was closure. It was freedom. It was the sincerest silent message I could have sent her. I am here for her, holding onto the good memories so she doesn't have to. One by one the residents shuffle off to lunch, leaving my mother behind with an unreadable expression on her face.

"Scarlet?" Margaret cooed, "Let's go eat now."

She hesitated. A slow smile spread across her face. She looked up at me from her chair, a hint of her old self in her eyes. "It's quite good," she complimented, "my daughter would like that I think. She would like you." I thanked her as Margaret wheeled her away, the bittersweet compliment dangling in the air. I tried to force away the part of it that had stabbed me, piercing my heart and reminding me of the loss. I clutched onto the fact that she knew her daughter loved art, that she would like me and my art. Somewhere inside herself she still loved me even if she didn't know who to direct the feeling towards.

I cried on the car ride home, more from exhaustion than sadness. Today had been a successful visit and I had surprised myself by accepting the invitation to make this a weekly practice. "You'd probably be painting anyway, why not paint here," William had encouraged. He was right of course. I loved this loyal man at my side, protecting and supporting me without hesitation.

The next week passed quickly, the fog having lifted from my heart for a moment. Hannah and I gathered my supplies in preparation of our painting appointment at the home. She had asked to come with me, to paint with me, and I was more than happy to oblige. I am continually impressed by how much goodness grows inside this little girl. The phone rings, Margaret's voice greeting me from the other end. "Good morning Nichole, are you still visiting us today?" I replied yes and that a friend would be coming with me. "How nice," she said almost too quickly. Margaret hesitated, "Nichole, your mother is completely lucid today."

My brow furrowed in confusion, "What does that mean, lucid?" Hannah stopped what she was doing, slowly crossing her arms and watching me with her bright eyes. I motioned for her not to worry but as Phillip padded over, concern stretched across his muzzle, I could tell they both sensed my tension.

"This means that your mother remembers, at least for now. She's confused but trying to fill blanks. Scarlet is asking for you. This state is very rare and may last a few hours or a few days…" She stops. "It is a gift Nichole. A gift not many receive and I wanted to make sure you were prepared to experience it before she leaves us again." I thanked her, not truly knowing what else to say or how to react. Upon hanging up the phone, I gave Hannah a synopsis and began throwing the rest of the supplies into our sacks. I practically drug her downstairs by her hair and toss her into the car. I called William on the way and sped to the home.

"You were in such a rush and now you're stopping?" Hannah was exasperated. "Just go already!" My feet felt glued to the walkway leading to the home. I had gathered all my belongings with such haste before becoming unreasonably paralyzed. Hannah bounced on her toes in the cold, her breath creating clouds of heat in the air. With a deep breath and a little prayer, I led her up the steps of the front porch and opened the door. The rooms inside were still decorated with dancing firelight. I hear a car park behind us, turning to see William running steadily up to follow us. He asked if I was okay, then asked if I was ready. I said I was with a shaking voice, his lips pressing against my forehead.

What does one do with an unknown amount of time to spend with their long-lost best friend? Will it be minutes? Hours? Days? Seconds? As I entered the room, remembrance glittering her face at my approach, I felt a warmth fill my body. In my mother's embrace, I found strength and comfort. She asked about William, she remembered traces of Hannah. The world was spinning much slower now, capturing the sudden youthful gaze of my mother's eyes. She took a single moment to be sad about her loss before deciding she would not waste time with it. "You better not be either, my love," she sweetly insisted. A thought occurred to me. The precarious bittersweet happiness of this moment wasn't much different than any other rare blissful second one could encounter. Day after day, we never know how much time we will truly have but we rarely remember its preciousness. In those few hours I had with her, I made a promise to myself that was filled purposely with my seven letter words. *I, Nichole, will wholeheartedly connect with others, embrace challenges, and cherish all moments past and present. They cannot be taken from me. I will somehow always have them, my mother, and my seven letter words. There is always a reason to rejoice.*

The Great Rise

R. Tim Morris

⚜

Beyond the cracked sidewalk, and the telephone pole with layers of flyers in a rainbow of colors, and the patch of dry brown grass there stood a ten -foot high concrete block wall, caked with dozens of coats of paint. There was a small shrine at the foot of it, with burnt out candles and dead flowers and a few soggy teddy bears. One word of graffiti filled the wall, red letters on a gold background: Rejoice!

The letters — as crimson as fresh blood from one angle, copper-brown like dried blood from another — had always been there, in one hue or another. The enormity of the single word was near-overwhelming, looming over the surrounding scraps and vestiges of heavy hearted human regard. The town of Buffleton was filled with them. Photos of lost loved ones. Crumpled notes of melancholic thoughts, stuffed into coffee cans meant for donations. And yet, if one looked closer, one would see that the tiny, complex details within the surface of the wall — written in red and scribbled in gold — belied the word's monolithic presence. Rejoice! The intricate details ranged from fine brush work to thick stabs of muted color. All of it added irony to the larger message: these were names of each and every citizen of Buffleton who had died. And how each one of them met their end.

From Alwyn EmberStone (natural causes) to Remi FrostBorne (lost at sea). From Tobias Brownbranch (eaten by goblins) to Her Highness Jaelynn Dew Rider (medical complications related to goblin bite). From the clumsy Bumper Marshburn (electrocution) to the brave Owl-Phoenix PhoenixBone (bee sting) to even the unfortunate Sir Ludwig FireScribe (bicycle accident).

On and on it went. Every moment that ended in tragedy was plastered to the surface of the wall; the what was known as The Great Rise. On and on. Were these meant as warning signs for the poor people of Buffleton? Lessons in the dangers that might present themselves to anyone at anytime? A statement on the fragility of living? The trouble with goblins? Well, it was all of that. And none of that. On and on and on.

In all the annals of history, folklore, and wisdom, the word "hero" is not a word to be tossed about lightly. But for the sake of this tale of The Great Rise, young Jonathon Morningmist, by default, might be considered as such. To Jonathon, the wall was an enemy. It was a thief, having stolen his father from him years before. As his father would explain it — and just as all of Buffleton would carefully explain to every curious child — on the other side of that painted concrete wall was a whole other land. To even the most hopeful, it seemed virtually unattainable, like another universe entirely. The official belief, as Jonathon's father first illustrated with his son on his knee, was that upon the grass on the other side there were no shrines. No candles or wilted flowers or stuffed bears. No names scribbled onto the surface of The Great Rise. Because there was one more thing that did not exist on the other side: death. There was no death by natural causes over there. No accidents. No goblins. There was only the possibility of ever more life and happiness. Ever more wonder and journeys of discovery. And always more love. A bottomless well overflowing with love. Jonathon Morningmist was both in awe of and afraid of this possibility.

But no one knew for certain what was over there. Over time, there had been a few who hopped the wall. Against town orders, they chose to leave everything in Buffleton behind in favor of the Forever-Life. They just wanted to know. They were so curious that they were willing to forget lovers, friends, and neighbors. Leaving vacant their blacksmith shops, janitorial supply stores, sushi bars, and generations old, family-run plumbing and heating businesses. Even young sons who once sat upon knees listening to fairy tales and legends of caution were abandoned with little more regard than day-old goldfish. All of the makings of these admittedly moderate lives were coldly, categorically dismissed in favor of what might be discovered beyond The Great Rise. For these were only ever temporary desires anyway, weren't they? The hope for something more, shrouded by the unknown — that was the more powerful siren call, wasn't it?

And yet, as the story goes, any and all who ever crossed over were never to be seen again. For whatever reason — whether it was the verisimilitude of the Forever-Life, or maybe something better, perhaps something worse — they never returned to the more hopeless and the less brave who continued to wait, and who continued to write ever more names on the wall.

Young Jonathon Morningmist did not know what to believe, only that his father chose hopping The Great Rise over the life he had in Buffleton. So Jonathon did not know much about heroes. He was just a kid — exactly as his father always called him: "a kid" — who wished for a day when the flames of hope might flicker. And one day they did, when a particularly curious wanderer found his way back to Buffleton again.

Jonathon had just finished his shift at *Ye Olde Espresso*, his aunt's coffee shop, where he'd spent the majority of his day serving mintberry tea and cleaning the washrooms. Jonathon was not a terribly happy kid; he hadn't felt much happiness since his father decided to make a spectacle of himself, catapulting over The Great Rise and disappearing forever. Unhappiness was not so uncommon a feeling around these parts, even for the majority of kids who hadn't watched their fathers launch themselves into the unknown via a creaky contraption they'd cobbled together in their sheds the night before.

Truthfully, most kids were like Jonathon Morningmist. For one, they disliked school, because there was nothing worth learning at school that could possibly ever get them out of, and as far away as possible from Buffleton. To add further layers to their melancholy, there were a few more factors at play: boys were in love with girls and girls were in love with boys and all sorts of children were in love with all sorts of other children, but every last one of them was unable to show it. Also, the weather was always terrible in Buffleton, and no one is happy in terrible weather. Not to mention: there really wasn't much in the way of hope for the children, since the grown-ups only ever seemed to care about what was or wasn't on the other side of The Great Rise. Grown-ups, it seemed, were weak and afraid of everything. All of them. And all kids would become them eventually. And what is there about being weak and afraid that might ever be appealing enough to make a kid wish to become one of them? Better to simply make coffee but pour tea and be lonely until your aunt's cafe is your cafe and you're left with nothing but fleeting ruminations regarding what could have been had you not been so weak and afraid to be something better. And on and on it went.

On his way home, Jonathon Morningmist walked upon the crumbling sidewalk which ran alongside The Great Rise. Jonathon brushed his smooth, youthful hand along the rough bumps of the wall's weathered concrete surface; generations of paint slapped on, layer after layer after layer. On and on and on.

Jonathon had just reached an aged, crooked telephone pole when he stopped. There was a new shrine that wasn't there that morning, painted rocks were still drying. It appeared as though Finnigan Hambone met his demise sometime that afternoon (cause of death still unreported). Jonathon had heard distant sirens earlier and wondered who they might have been for.

It was then, as Jonathon contemplated the details of what might have taken Finnigan Hambone away, that Jonathon looked up. And it was as he looked up, that he spotted a pair of hands at the top of the wall; fingers from the other side, clutching the rim of The Great Rise.

Jonathon gave his head a good hard shake, for no one had ever seen hands on the wall before. Never. It shouldn't have been possible.

But those hands were definitely there. "Hello up there!" Jonathon called. The fingers were more gray than his own, but they were definitely human so the fear of another goblin attack was probably out of the question. For now, at least. "Hello?" he called again, perhaps with more emphasis on self-concern this time. After all, one never could know when one could definitively rule out another goblin attack. The fingers quivered a little; enough to make Jonathon quiver himself, and he stepped backward onto the road without even noticing. Then the fingers disappeared, sliding slowly from sight like slugs and snails might travel over a hilltop. And with that Jonathon shrugged to himself, believing the vision had to have been brought on by still-lingering death fumes in the air, and he stepped back up onto the sidewalk and continued on his way.

To say something about his sheer indifference, Jonathon Morningmist had merely made it to the next twisted telephone pole by the time the whole occurrence was out of his mind; those gray fingers had slipped from his memory far swifter than they had from the wall. But Jonathon stopped immediately upon hearing a voice calling from behind him. He shook his head again, this time trying to recall what he'd seen mere moments before. "You, down there!" the voice called to the kid. It was a man's voice. "Might you give me a hand?"

Jonathon turned. "Me?" he asked, and pointed limply at his heart. As though there had been any creatures around besides himself, a few scuttling sluice-newts, and piles of crusty, mud-soaked stuffed bears. Then he saw the fingers again, up on the cusp of the wall. The best he could do was continue to stare blankly, and while he was already at his most incompetent, Jonathon went ahead and gave his slipping pants a bit of a tug.

"Nevermind," the man said, struggling to keep himself aloft. "I — I've got this." Then, with every bit of strength he could muster, the man heaved himself up and onto the top of the wall. He sat down and wiped his brow with a cloth he'd plucked magically from his pants pocket. "Boy, you really aren't very good help, are you? I'm not the man I used to be, but looks like I still got it. Don't I? Not that you would know what it was I had before what it is I've got now." This man, even from Jonathon Morningmist's point of view ten feet below, was slight. His bare arms were taut and sinewy, but overall he was certainly small, like a branch that had fallen months ago and begun withering. He wore a vest, torn pants, a belt with many pockets, and no shoes. Jonathon found it difficult to not stare at the man's gray feet and blackened toenails.

"Who are you?" the kid asked the man on The Great Rise. "And what brings you to Buffleton?" A good question, since not only has there never been a single soul who had ever crossed The Great Rise from the other side, but no soul had ever willingly come to Buffleton before now.

The stranger laughed an impish laugh. The kind of cackle that clattered unsatisfyingly off of everywhere and nowhere at once. "What you mean to ask is: What brings me *back* to Buffleton?" Jonathon wasn't sure if that *was* what he'd intended to ask, so he chose to say nothing more instead. The man stood back up, and stretched his wiry arms out wide. "I am Doyle Finncaster! Rejoice! I'm back!" Jonathon could not even be bothered to shake his head in transience. "You don't know the name Doyle Finncaster? I owned the auto shop on Blocker Street!"

The auto shop on Blocker Street had been vacant for years, before finally being razed and replaced by yet another paint store. But Jonathon didn't mention any of that. He asked, "So what brings you *back* to Buffleton? And is anyone else coming back with you? And also, why are you so gray?"

"Well, you see. As it turns out, I forgot my wrench. Did you know there's no such thing as wrenches over there?" With a traveler's thumb, Doyle Finncaster pointed behind him, back over to the other side of The Great Rise. "I don't know how I've gone so long without a wrench." The man scratched at his scalp for a few long seconds, then inspected his hands, first the fronts, then the backs, and then the fronts again. "And what do you mean I'm gray?"

"Your skin—" The grayness reminded Jonathon of the eldest mountain range or the freshest of ash. The shadow of a dark rain cloud or the brackish marshes in Buffleton Valley. "You appear to be...well. You look like an old tea bag. Are you certain no one else is coming back with you?"

Doyle just shrugged. He observed the ground below him, scanning the heaps of mementos and shrines. It was not long before his eyebrows jumped. "Well, what do you know. Boy, do you see that shiny object over there?" At the foot of the telephone pole and partially hidden beneath a cardboard poster with the picture of a woman who had recently been eaten by goblins, someone had left behind an open toolbox. Jonathon crouched to look, though he could not identify any of the tools within. "The contraption that looks like the anticipative claw of a hungry crab-bear. That's a wrench! Toss it up here, would you?" With an unsure arm, Jonathon miraculously launched the tool upwards and into the slight gray hands of Doyle Finncaster. "You may seem a bit angsty and angry, but you're not so unhelpful after all. Enjoy the rest of your walk, kid." And with that, Doyle Finncaster leapt off the wall, disappearing back into the waiting, curious land of the Forever-Life.

Angry? Jonathon Morningmist did not know he was angry, just as Doyle Finncaster did not seem to realize he was gray. Sure, he was unhappy that his father left him. And he was unhappy that he couldn't seem to admit his feelings toward Gisele Cloudskimmer, the most toothy girl in his class. And he was unhappy about the angle of the sun on most days. But angry? The kid thought about the whole peculiar exchange that had just transpired. He thought about it a bit harder than he usually thought about anything, for he knew the chances of its details fading from his mind were very good, and he did not wish to forget them. So he continued to think all night, and all the way into the next morning when he suddenly — and most surprisingly — had a plan: that he would be the next resident of Buffleton to cross over The Great Rise. If Jonathon's feelings were becoming muddled, then maybe there would be answers on the other side. And like his father did before him, he sounded the town gong in the middle of the Square the next morning, and made certain a crowd would be there to witness his bravery. And there was a crowd indeed.

The kid got up onto a milk crate and raised his hand. A murmur went through the crowd and then it fell silent, except for a few people shouting words of encouragement at him. The kid acknowledged them with a nod and a shy smile. In the full light of day, he looked less angry and more beautiful. He waited until people stopped shouting. A siren could be heard, maybe five or ten blocks away. The kid raised the bullhorn, pressed the button, and began to speak.

He started, "Yesterday—", and then realized the junky bullhorn he'd scavenged from the garage wasn't working. But he continued to speak into it nevertheless. "Yesterday, a gray man named Doyle Finncaster appeared over The Great Rise, like a neighbor might stick his head over the fence, and he asked me for a wrench." Some of the oldest amongst the crowd muttered and whispered, recalling the name immediately, for Finncaster's auto shop was not only reputable for great service, but also offered a complimentary mug of mintberry tea with every visit. "So I tossed him a wrench and then he simply disappeared again. Just like my father disappeared many years ago. And like people you've all loved have disappeared from your own lives. Even though the wall tells us to celebrate. Rejoice!"

"Rejoice!" the people repeated, as was Buffleton custom. Even Gisele

Cloudskimmer, the object of Jonathon's affections, was calling out amidst the crowd. And maybe it was just Jonathon's imagination, but Gisele appeared incredibly invested in what he had to say.

Jonathon bumbled a little, but he would not be deterred from delivering his somewhat awkward and poorly-planned out speech. "Rejoice? Why are we meant to take delight in their leaving? Living forever sounds like a terrible bit of burden, don't you think? What do you imagine they find when they get there? Do they ever get where they *think* they're going? Do they ever find what it was they hoped to find?" He thinks about the possibilities of what he could say next and how he might say it. What words would hit Gisele Cloudskimmer just right, so he might catch that wonderful, toothy smile of hers? "Do they ever think of the people of Buffleton? Do they miss us? Doyle Finncaster missed his wrench — enough to come back for it — and yet no one has ever come back for *us*. No one has ever really been a hero."

Jonathon paused; a hope in the front of his mind that someone in the crowd would ask if *he* might be that hero. If *he* would cross over the wall for the good folks of Buffleton, rather than escaping in the middle of the night like so many cowards, launching themselves from crudely constructed catapults. Aside from fear, what was stopping *him* from treading into the Forever-Life? But no one asked these questions. They were too afraid to ask. Maybe it wasn't heroism, but Gisele Cloudskimmer seemed impressed nevertheless. And to prove it, there was that smile of hers.

Then, someone did call out from the tense crowd. He said, "So what are you going to do, Ditch-Nut?" Hmph. *I am going to cross The Great Rise,* Jonathon thought to himself in his most bravest of inside voices. *I will be the hero you all need.* Another asked, "Will you bring them more wrenches?" Jonathon shook his head. Still another worried, "If you're not here, then there's one less person for the goblins to eat before they eat *me*. I don't like those odds!" Jonathon shrugged his shoulders.

The interim Mayor of Buffleton — who was only in power until next Tuesday, when the body of the late Queen Dew Rider would be ceremoniously sent down the slough into the waiting maw of ocean-wolves and her successor would then be plucked from a lottery system held at the bingo hall (the caste system in Buffleton was nightmarishly complicated) — was there with his royal entourage. He had a working bullhorn, and he himself asked, "Son of Morningmist, are you saying you spoke with Doyle Finncaster?" Jonathon nodded. "He just popped up over The Great Rise and asked for a wrench?" Jonathon nodded at this, too. "He didn't say anything about my car, did he? It's long due for a fuel injection cleaning, and once you find a mechanic you trust, it's terribly hard to change!" It seemed Jonathon was all out of nods. The town didn't care, or they were too scared to endorse or reinforce his decision. Even his aunt — who was initially at the forefront of the crowd — was silent at the very back. Did anyone in Buffleton have any encouragement at all for him? Did—

"When do you leave, Jonathon Morningmist?" It was Gisele. "When does your hero's journey commence?" More sirens clamoured off in the distance; nearly everyone scattered so they could do a head count in order to find who was missing this time. Jonathon and Gisele remained amid the chaos. The two of them locked eyes, as if each was just now noticing that the other had noticed all along.

Jonathon motioned behind him. "Just as soon as I cross this wall," he said. The Great Rise had felt so imposing before, now it seemed as though he could simply hop over it. Alas, even on the single milk crate, he still couldn't reach the top. "Looks like I may need a boost, however." Jonathon held out a hand for Gisele to take and she ambled closer. "I do have but one request of you, after I cross over." Gisele cocked her head a little in anticipation of his inquiry. Jonathon patted the wall and said, "When I'm gone, please do not add my name to The Great Rise. Because I plan on coming back."

From the milk crate to Gisele's surprisingly sturdy shoulders, the kid lifted himself to the top of the wall. He had some difficulty balancing, but managed to stand on his two awkward feet. Bisecting the two lands, Jonathon could see the town of Buffleton behind him — Gisele Cloudskimmer below him — but he could not see anything before him but thick vegetation on the other side. With a deep gulp and a big breath, Jonathon Morningmist leapt off, eventually landing into the plushy palm of some still-dewey, exotic shrub.

Planting his feet in the unknown dirt, Jonathon immediately saw the other side of wall, covered in thick fingers of ivy and other similar vines; some blooming flowers of fuschia, cerulean, and ivory; others full of prickly though harmless-looking spines. Every spine and thorn on every plant in Buffleton looked like it would kill someone instantly. And though everything on the other side was as green as the greenest of poster paints made from the freshest of harvested mountainside joonee fruits, Jonathon did stop for a moment and wondered if there might be any beaches over here. He'd always wanted to see a beach, feel the ocean breeze, and smell the surf. He may have even had dreams of taking Gisele Cloudskimmer there one day.

When considering if she might enjoy that dream too, he turned back to the wall and called out for her. "Gisele!" he called, but was answered by silence. "Gisele Cloudskimmer!" he yelled louder. But there was no answer. Already he was having misgivings about crossing over. Should he turn back now? He asked himself aloud: "Did I just make a grave mistake?"

This time he expected silence as an answer. But then, a woman's words startled him: "Of course ye made a mistake, ye bloated fool!" The words were spit from some knee-high bush. Its leaves rattled harshly, though none came dislodged. But Jonathon did not even step back. He actually leaned in and dipped his face of burgeoning courage even closer to the foliage.

The leaves parted in a kind of indescribable exoticism, like a magician might reveal some slight of hand, uncovering what Jonathon could only describe as: "A goblin!?" Indeed, this scraggly woman was merely knee-high; her skin a green-gray sort of worn leather; her mouth a toothless cavern of echoing, virulent hisses.

"Nay!" she yelped. "I'd have eaten ye whole t'were I a goblin!" Jonathon wasn't sure how that would have worked exactly—the *eating-him* *-whole* bit—considering how much bigger than her the kid was. "I crossed that wall, just like ye! Buffleton gave me the ol' scaly hoof too, be knowin' it." She scuttled closer, seemingly unafraid of this new traveler in her midst. Jonathon steeled himself, determined to remain fearless. One of her eyes twitched so fervently it almost appeared shut. "Name's Barbara. Barbo, I calls meself here. Use'ta teach kids like ye—smaller kids, mind ye—over in Buffleton." Barbo spit into the dirt so hard some grubs wriggled loose from the earth. "Teacher?! Shoulda owned the paint supply store on account fer all the coats there've been put on that blasted wall. Wouldst have made a killin'. And then...Well, then I go and find meself here." She seemed to transform from indignant to dispirited faster than Jonathon could process. "Well?"

"Well, indeed." Jonathon confirmed, though he was not certain what it was she was welling about. With hands in his pockets, the kid caught sight of a glint of something within a patch of long grass. It was a wrench. But this wasn't the same wrench that Doyle Finncaster had brought back over the wall with him the day before. No, his wrench was an adjustable wrench and this was most definitely of the socket variety. Jonathon wondered if this was the woman's home, here in the overgrown but wonderfully alive vegetation. He wondered if she realized that he was not a bloated giant, but she was likely just a shrunken, grayed version of her old self. He wondered many things. But instead, he asked Barbo: "You have wrenches here?"

Barbo tried to spot where the kid was eyeing, but she could not see anything of the sort. "Wrenches? Everyone perceives this cursed land differently. Be it the size of interlopers or the stink of a gringemeat sandwich. Some folks think they've come here to live, whilst others only remain for the hope of death. Some fools see wrenches, some don't. But surely ye have better questions than this?"

Jonathon Morningmist thought about the perceptions of others. And a little bit about his own. He did not know if the wrench even mattered or why Doyle Finncaster must have stuck his head over The Great Rise in the first place. He did not care to wonder why the denizens of this side of the wall were apparently shrinking, nor did he have a clue what gringemeat was. In fact, for the moment, he was not even concerned about Gisele Cloudskimmer. Instead he asked: "Have you seen my father?" And he took a moment to try to recall the man from memory. "He had one eye of green and another of a color I could never place. He had arms like the mountains in fables. He had a beard so virile and thick it took it him four days to shave and one day for it to grow back. He was a wonderful man but a terrible dad, and he hastily shot himself over The Great Rise from a catapult without even a word. His name was Morningmist."

"Doesn't sound familiar. But everyone perceives this cursed land differently," Barbo repeated. She plucked two grubs from the dirt and swallowed one whole, offering the other to the kid. "Would ye care? Methinks they taste like the pit of arm, but ye might find they taste like fancies."

Jonathon declined the grub, and Barbo gulped it down, too. Thoughts of what might be found on the other side kept firing through his mind; crissing and crossing like dozens of zapper bugs in a jar under the moon. How far could his father have gotten on his journey? Perhaps it's true: that those on this side don't know death. But are they shrinking and shriveling into crazed goblin-folk and discolored wrench-hunters instead? Do they regret their choices in coming here? Do they ever miss the good people of Buffleton? "I have one question for you, Barbo. Do people here live forever?"

"Tis true we know not of death. But that don't mean we don't ever hope to meet her." Barbo looked skyward; through the overlapping leaves and fronds and stalks and folioles, there remained a pinhole of sky above. She took it in, as though it were sustenance far, far more nourishing than a handful of grubs or gringemeat sandwiches. "Still, ye decided to come here too. But ye have yet to decide if ye be staying."

It was then that Jonathon Morningmist first concerned himself with what must be the truth. "Once I've decided to stay there is no return, is there? This is why no one has ever crossed The Great Rise and come back to Buffleton?"

"Some decisions are our own. Some are not. But rejoice in the decision ye shall make, son of Morningmist. And I will rejoice for ye. But make it soon." Barbo shuffled back into the vegetation, soon fully faded from both sight and memory. Perception of what is, what was, and what might have been, was indeed very much skewed in the land of the Forever-Life.

Jonathon stepped further into the foliage, though stopped himself before he felt it was too far, or far too late to turn back. Somehow he knew he would know when. There was a luring call from the vegetation; what it was saying, Jonathon could not tell.

Turning back to The Great Rise, he now realized the ivy for what it was. The distance from it proved to be important, for he could not have read the message from any closer: the ivy and vines grew together, forming the words "Never Is Forever." On and on and on.

Taking hold of the sturdy branch of a mossy and scaly-barked tree, the kid heaved himself upwards. He held tight; the branch seemed to pulse in his grip, like it had a heart of its own. Perhaps regrets of its own as well, if that was even a possibility. Likely it was. He carefully maneuvered along the trusty tree arm, before finally stepping off and returning to the top of The Great Rise. He could still see Buffleton there, but Gisele's whereabouts were cloudy. He sensed the worry and fear within the town, but also, he could simultaneously sense the misgivings and wantings within the green land of the Forever-Life. And just as a hero would do, Jonathon Morningmist made his decision.

Four Sons

Nancy Moir

⚜

Beyond the cracked sidewalk, and the telephone pole with layers of flyers in a rainbow of colors, and the patch of dry brown grass there stood a ten -foot high concrete block wall, caked with dozens of coats of paint. There was a small shrine at the foot of it, with burnt out candles and dead flowers and a few soggy teddy bears. One word of graffiti filled the wall, red letters on a gold background: Rejoice!

The war was over, or so they said. The wounded were returning home to walk amongst us, the left-behinds. We had pretended to be brave; we had lived their battles with our eyes covered, our hands tied, our ears shut, thousands of miles away. Around me, I did not perceive joy, but mostly relief. We were exhaling the fear that we'd all held in for so many years.

We collected at train stations and docks, waiting, our hearts pounding, still tuned to the cadence of the marches we heard on the radio. We received our loved ones carefully, afraid that they might shatter and skitter away. I guess we were all broken. My injuries just hadn't broken my skin.

During the war, the postman was the most wanted man in the village. We—the mothers, the wives, the elderly men, the others— stalked him like prey. Now he stood near me by the shrine at the dock. I hadn't realized that he too had been hoping for letters from his son. I imagined him rummaging around the bottom of his sack, clawing at paper chaff, pressing it into wads as though he could construct a message from nothing. I had done the same in my mind. I heard my sons calling for me, saw them showing up at my door.

During the previous winter, I received one letter from France. As ice girded our house, I imagined the boys in foxholes, subsisting on frosted breath for heat. I could waste a day in these kinds of thoughts. Only my younger children could snap me out of my reverie.

But it seemed like that had happened years ago. I heard some gulls squawking, the sluice of a ship's hull as it passed through the water. The shrine filled my eyes again. It offended me with its gaudiness and I blinked, flitted back to the day of the letter.

The children had carved a track between house and barn. The postman crossed it with his horse and sled; the runners cut its walls with a clean snap. I ran outside in a nightdress, pulled the letter from his hand, and nodded, tears in my eyes. I held it for some time before opening it. Its paper had worn into fabric and it smelled, I imagined, of foreign soil, grief, fear, love. It said, "Dear Mom... Love Adam." The words in-between were inconsequential.

He and his brother had left me the year previous. I could still feel the imprints of their chests as I hugged them tight, the two of them no longer boys but almost men, crisp in their uniforms, but soft and still malleable to my love. I had wiped my tears from their suits, and their tears from their cheeks. I kissed them hard while their siblings watched. The girls sat wide-eyed. Henry played with his toy airplanes and guns.

Now, my remaining children stood in front of the shrine. Certainly, there was no solace to be found amongst the anti-war propaganda, religious assurances, and the written pleas for news, for any sort of help. We were beyond that. My sons—my children's brothers—were gone.

There was a clear line in my mind between life before and after, as though a fault line in the ocean between them had opened up and simply swallowed them. Sometimes I imagined that I could see them in the water beyond the shrine, where the returning warships docked. They were splashing out for me, their pale arms beyond reach.

They had been such different boys, Adam and John, not just physically, but intellectually and emotionally. Placed side-by-side, one would not see much resemblance. Adam was tall and wiry, with straw-coloured hair and blue eyes. His younger brother was darker and shorter, with a compact musculature that made him seem larger than his physical truth. His quick temper was born of a sense of vulnerability that his older brother had never shared. Adam had been born carefree and easy, a baby who had never had colic, who smiled even as he shed tears.

John's crowd of boxing friends encouraged him to volunteer; it probably didn't take much convincing to get him to go. Adam followed, because he felt he had to protect his little brother. But it hadn't worked, and now they were both gone.

I blinked again, back to a present in which I had begun to convince myself that they were safe because they were already dead. They couldn't be hurt again. I stumbled, caught myself, fell onto my knees in front of the shrine, Isabella and Brigitte surrounding me, their dark braids falling over my shoulders. Henry remained standing, searching through the damp papers pinned to the stones for any sign of the brothers who I feared were fleeing his memory.

"How do you know they're gone?" he asked, gazing at me solemnly. Sometimes, when he looked at me, I could see the two of them—Adam and John—speaking through his face. He had idolized them, and he still did. He adopted their expressions, Adam's earnestness and John's quick smile. The pain was all mine.

I warmed their dog tags against my heart and shook my head. I didn't know the answer. At night, I watched the reflection of the clouds as they passed over the moon, this dark tempest, and could not imagine a world in which these two boys were not allowed to live. And yet, it would be the same for the mothers of those my sons had fought. How could I be so angry and sad and full of love at the same time?

"Irene?" It was the postman who called out for me. I felt a memory straining to emerge; his name did not come to me right away. Ah, Reid, and his young daughter, Hannah. They lived in a small house on the edge of downtown, and travelled to the outskirts to deliver mail.

I wondered where he had been since the letters stopped, and what had happened to his boy. Current events and other people had become inconsequential to me. I didn't want to lose the memories of my sons to things that were happening now when now didn't matter. I hung onto my recollections of them when they were young, Adam's dimpled cheeks, the cowlicks in John's hair, how they laughed when tickled. Their first words. Their last.

Reid was waiting for my answer; I shook my head in reply. "How are you?" I asked. It wasn't really a question so much as an acknowledgment of the answer he wouldn't give. He nodded, looked at me, then looked away. Cormorants skimmed the water; gulls screeched.

"There are seven of us," he said, solemnly. "Seven of us in this little village who have lost sons." He shook his head, loosed tears upon his cheeks. "They were so naïve and noble and young. Too young." He paused, tilted his cheek towards me but still refused to meet my gaze. "I sent letters to the regiments in which they served, hoping to hear from their friends. Two wrote me—a soldier and a refugee. I've been waiting here for weeks. I see you have been too. You're waiting for something."

I glared at him, but that quickly passed. This wasn't a moment for putting up walls. "I-I don't know what I'm waiting for. Maybe if I walked away it would mean I have given up on them, and accepted that they're gone. I'm not ready to do that," I said, pulling the girls together and embracing them as one.

He shook his head. "I stopped delivering letters. There's nothing more to say." Brigitte looked up at me, pleading with me to go. I nodded and walked us back to our vehicle. "Come back later," he said. He gestured to the water. "Someone has to talk to me." I nodded.

I dreamt of the other boys in their platoons. Were they idealistic like Adam, or brazen like John? Maybe it was unfair to characterize them so sharply. Already, my mind was summarizing my sons. Their faces, in memories, had been replaced by the still images that stared out at me from their photos, which hung on the wall within the dark staircase, limned by dust I could not press away. I should have been prepared for this, as this is what had happened when their father passed. The human mind is a terrible thing.

I took Reid up on his offer. I went during the day, when the children were at school. I rode my bicycle to town, leaned it up against a tree, and waited. But nothing happened. I watched the water lap against the concrete shore. I listened to the distant ships as they made their calls. The birds weren't singing. I wondered if they felt my grief.

I rode back home, the wind at my back. I fell asleep on one of the bunk beds, then woke abruptly when I heard the dogs barking, and pulled myself together to complete the chores. When the children got home, I was making supper. They knew my smile was false, but it was there. I would go back later, I told myself.

Three days later an automobile pulled up and parked beside the concrete wall. The driver opened the door, but did not get out of the car. Although her face was in shadow, it was easy to tell she was sad. There was something about how she turned away from the sun and rested the weight of her hands on the steering wheel, something about her silent composure, that caused Hannah to sigh. The young girl watched the driver lean out of the car and stretch her hand out towards one of the burned out candles.

Behind her, another motorist honked, and the driver reluctantly withdrew her hand. She glanced at Reid, at Hannah, at me, then away. Hannah ran up to her father. "Is it today?" she asked. His eyes skirted the horizon. He nodded curtly, ruffled her hair, and sent her off to play with my son and daughters.

"The refugee," he said, urgently, "He told me he would arrive this week. Travel is unpredictable. I've been waiting so long. But I think today is the day. I can hear the last ship in the distance." He jabbed his breastbone with the fingers of his right hand. "I can feel it here."

We sat down, slowly, on opposite ends of a stone bench. Fall was in the air; the maple leaves had begun to change, skipping the usual shades of gold, orange, and red, and progressing straight to brown. It was easy to imagine the world was grieving, even if it wasn't.

He began to speak, perhaps to the trees, to me, to the wind. "William wrote me letters every day. He had wanted to be a journalist when he grew up, if he grew up. So most days, I received a letter, sometimes two. I read them over and over as I traveled my route. They were so vivid that I could imagine being there." He paused. "Almost." He sucked air between his teeth. "And then they stopped. They stopped. I knew what that meant, even as I refused to believe."

"He trained with Adam and John, did you know that?" He glanced over just long enough to see me shake my head, then turned back to face the void. "And Jack's son Oliver, too. They weren't friends before, but knowing they were all from the same town brought them together. It broke his heart when John was moved to another regiment, because of course the brothers could not serve together." He shook his head again. "I'm sorry," he said, "I'm talking too much."

The ship was more than a speck in the distance. It was the size of an automobile; it cut the water, splashed waves, chased gulls. "No," I said, "I want to know. It's just that I only got one letter."

"Yes," he said, and rubbed his face in his hands. Sometimes I thought it would be easier to navigate if we wore badges that itemized our losses, but then we would have to deal with pity. I tried to smile at him to let him know that I was grateful for what he shared.

As the sun dropped from the sky, the ship began to empty out. I wondered, briefly, if the dock might give way beneath the urgency of those who had come to meet their loved ones, but then I remembered that joy was light, not weighty, that if anything the land might rise beneath their feet. I watched them from a safe distance—we all did. The children had settled between us like little ducklings, their feet kicking below, skirting the tops of the grass.

It was dark before the ship closed up. The children were cold. I wrapped them in my shawl. Finally, a voice called out for "Mr. Reid Doane?" In the shadows, I could not see the speaker's face, only his silhouette. He was tall and lanky, with a tanned face and a ragged beard. His clothes hung off him as though he were a doll donning the vestments of a child. As he reached to shake Reid's hand, I saw that he had young hands. Two children hid behind him, fingers looped through his belt, their eyes wide and glistening.

"Yes, Yes," Reid said. "Thank you, Jacob, for meeting with me." The man nodded; the children stared. "Let's get you warm and fed." He gestured to me. "This is Mrs. Irene Sampson." I shook his hand and he smiled painfully.

We followed Reid down a zigzag of streets. I could feel my children, sullen, at my sides. Their feet dragged along the heavy cobblestone but they said nothing to protest. They eyed Jacob's companions—a boy and a girl—but none of them made an effort to speak. I wondered how much English they spoke.

We entered a building and ascended three flights to a small loft. Reid rattled the door and it was opened from the other side. His wife wore a stained, bedraggled apron over her soft brown dress. The room smelled of soup. The children, all of them, suddenly perked up. "Come on in," she said. She took our coats and guided us to chairs, then placed bowls of soup in front of us.

Jacob and the two children were ravenous. They ate with restrained politeness, slowly lifting their spoons to their mouths but gulping down the liquid as fast as they could without burning their mouths. They paused to chew chunks of bread heavily laden with butter, to glance at us, their companions, and nod their thanks. I watched them through the path of my spoon, how as the amber light warmed them, it stripped years off their faces until I realized that all of them were children, Jacob and his sister and brother.

"Eli, Greta, run along and wash up now," he said, "It will be time for bed soon." The two children rose unsteadily, shyly, smiled their thanks and followed Ella to the back of the loft. Hannah, Henry, Brigitte, and Isabella followed. It was late for the children to be up.

Jacob turned his gaze to me. He removed his knit hat, which he had kept on for warmth, and brushed back his hair. "I understand you had two sons, John and Adam." I nodded slowly, unable to speak. "I knew Adam and William, Reid's son. They saved me and my siblings. It is because of them that I am here."

I gasped, and began to cry. Months after I had received the dog tags, tears were an automatic reaction to any discussion about my sons. There seemed to be a vast reservoir of them within me that could not dry up. I reached across the table, and took Jacob's hands in mine, not even considering if he wanted this, unable to stop this gesture any more than I could hold in my tears. He recoiled only slightly, then held my hands tightly. Ella returned to the kitchen and placed a hand on my shoulder.

Jacob's eyes lit up. "We were hiding in an old barn, in a pit dug hastily within a horse's stall. The walls were thin and the barn was empty save for us. It was cold and damp and it smelled of mould. All day I heard fighting—gunfire, shells, shouting, screams. Screams." He turned away, reclaimed his hands to briefly cover his eyes. "At night it was silent, but the anticipation was worse. We slept fitfully, only when our bodies took over and refused our desire to remain awake."

"I awoke to the sound of bootsteps on the slab of wood above my head. Then a creak as it was lifted, a crack of light—like a dagger— piercing our shelter. I could not see who stood above us. The light framed him and blinded us and I wasn't sure—was he our angel, or the devil? He pointed his rifle into our shelter; I heard the click and closed my eyes, wrapped them—" He looked to where his siblings had gone. "—in my embrace. There was a shot, but it was the soldier who fell."

"Someone extended a hand, then another stepped forward to help. It was William, and Adam, I would learn. They lifted us out onto the barn floor. They told us that the enemy soldier had been scouring barns, looking for families in hiding. They had come across him in the forest, and tracked him here. They'd been separated from their regiment, so they had been on the run, of sorts." He paused. "They sensed that their time was running out. It was just the two of them. I offered to let them hide but they said that would only make us more vulnerable."

He sighed, and looked up; I fell into his gaze back in the barn, how the dust billowed within columns of light, the smell of aged hay, the creak of leather. "They fed us their rations, tended to the children's wounds, and they sat with us until darkness fell, when they could continue to look for their regiment. John, he—"

He paused, and swallowed. "Adam told me that he'd received word that John had been killed. He wanted to get back to be with you. And William, he spoke of his sister and his parents. He had made copies of his letters, and Adam had too. They gave them to those they rescued, desperate for word to get back to you." He held our gazes. "Here," he said, "They gave me these."

He reached into his pocket and carefully removed two envelopes, and handed one to me, and one to Ella and Reid. They began to cry, and I turned away, burdened by a grief that I felt I could not share with anyone.

Jacob watched as the couple hungrily scrolled through William's writings. "They gave me your address, told me that you would accept me as family," he said, "When we needed to emigrate. I understand if that's no longer possible—" They shook their heads, took his hands in theirs, their tears flowing.

My envelope was soft, and discoloured. John had written my name upon it in his faint cursive. My photo fell from it as I opened it and unfurled several sheaves of paper. All started with "Dear Mom" and ended with "Love Adam. Love John." The words—I could not read them then. I hastily pulled them away from under me so that my tears would not stain them. "I need to know more," I said, "I need you to tell me everything. I can teach your siblings. I can give you land to tend, food—"

"You don't need to repay me," he said, "Your son gave me life. I will tell you all that they shared with me that night in the barn." I took his hand in mine, and realized that he had held my son's hand long after I had bid him goodbye. Suddenly, the fault line in the ocean began to close, and love rushed in.

The Crossing

Alissa Jones Nelson

⋅♣⋅

Beyond the cracked sidewalk, and the telephone pole with layers of flyers in a rainbow of colors, and the patch of dry brown grass there stood a ten-foot high concrete block wall, caked with dozens of coats of paint. There was a small shrine at the foot of it, with burnt out candles and dead flowers and a few soggy teddy bears. One word of graffiti filled the wall, red letters on a gold background: Rejoice!

Most people in town would have had a hard time following that advice. Bullhead was the kind of place where all the intersections had perfectly square corners. Night poured down over the streets like tar, and come morning it was still spiderwebbed between the leafless trees, dripping down from the telephone lines. It was enough to depress anybody.

Well, almost anybody. Hannah was an exception. A girl who sounded out every word she encountered, each one strange and beautiful. When she spun past Mrs. Grossman's makeshift shrine on her bike five mornings a week, she let go of her handlebars, muffleclapped her mittened hands and grinned like a chimpanzee. It never occurred to her that other people might find that strange. And they did, at first. When the smear on the train tracks was still fresh, people would linger in front of the flickering candles to bow heads and clasp hands, or fold arms and squint over the markered messages melting under the first flakes of snow. But days pooled into weeks, and pretty soon the candles snuffed themselves. Nobody paused anymore. So Hannah's smile stopped being strange. Most things do, if you wait long enough.

If you'd asked Hannah herself, and she'd felt like talking, she probably would have told you she was a rebel. That's mostly what everybody she knew wanted to be. Except she wasn't one of those bratwurst-legged girls who sniffed glue in the last stall of the yellowtile locker room, like Crystal and Addison did. And she wasn't the batwinged coffinsleeper kind with paperclips threaded through her earlobes and black eyeshadow plumping the pockets under her eyes, like Makayla was. And she wasn't even the kind who said fuck in class and then gave the principal that finger right in her own office, like Zelda, who was legend. Hannah was the kind of rebel who stole packs of Juicy Fruit from Mr. Bennett's Mercantile. The kind who swore under her breath whenever her mom told her she'd better scrub that toilet or else. The kind who swiped her mom's cigarettes one at a time from the skyblue packs fronted by the Indian chief saluting the redcircle sun with his ghostwhite pipe. The kind who kept her smoking a secret. Hannah was not a revolutionary.

Mrs. Grossman had been Hannah's teacher last year, when she was only ten. Hannah had loved Mrs. Grossman's bangle jangle and the way her long coral and amethyst skirts tuliped when she made a quick pivot to her chalkboard. She was never upset when you got the wrong answer, always disappointed when nobody put their hand up. So Hannah learned to raise her hand and guess, even when she didn't know. And in return she got honest answers and praise, which was way better than being right all the time. But now Mrs. Grossman was gone, and Hannah wasn't sure anybody else could heft her questions.

It was Vicky's mom who started the memory-L. Vicky was Hannah's nearest neighbor, eighteen minutes away on two feet and six on two wheels, not counting the time it took Hannah to lug up the steep gravel strip between her warped front steps and the buckled two-lane asphalt. Vicky's house had a finished basement and a refrigerator with cold water that came straight out of a fountain in the door. When Vicky's mom heard about Mrs. Grossman, she picked them up at school early, clutching a bunch of cottoncandy carnations and a couple of waxwhite tealights from Hobby Lobby. She spent a long time hugging Vicky and crying. Then she drove Vicky and Hannah over to the Rejoice! wall next to the train depot. The Rejoice! had been there as long as Hannah could remember, which was pretty much forever. Vicky's mom said it made a nice backstop. They stood there in the cheekblistering wind while Vicky's mom sniffed and wiped her eyes. Vicky played the zip on her lilac jacket like a kazoo until her mom grabbed one of her hands and held it so tight she winced. Hannah stood on her other side, reshaping the single word on the high wall with silent lips, hoping her mom would hug her and cry a little when she got home. But all she did when Hannah stationed herself in front of the sofa and asked about Mrs. Grossman's accident was press her lips into that starved line and turn up the TV.

Not that she wasn't a good mom. She just couldn't seem to stop herself rolling her eyes at Hannah's questions. She was still young, pointedly pretty. "What did Vicky's mom tell you?" She always spoke to or about Vicky's mom through gritted teeth. Hannah had to raise her voice over the canned laughter chirping from the TV. "She said it was a terrible trashidy. That it just goes to shows." She gestured at the TV behind her. "But I don't know which shows."

Her mom pogoed up to clatter the fishstick pan out of the drawer under the stove. Hannah dragged a chair up and crunched the cardboard box from the freezer. Her mom reached over her head for the rubber-banded bag of peas and carrots. Hannah knew better than to sigh. Once her mom'd slammed the padded door she circled back to Hannah's question, her skinnyjean legs backlit by the feeble ovendoor glow.

"Mrs. Grossman wasn't a good person. I know you thought she was, but she lied to us. She lied to you. You don't have to be sad about it. What happened." Hannah trapped her lip between her teeth. "But I thought it was sad when people died? Especially young people. Especially ladies." Her mom shook her head. "I'm going to tell you the truth." Hannah watched with horrified anticipation as the words bubbled up into her mom's cheeks. She held them there for a second, looking like a rainfull cloud, and then sent them all streaming out through her nose in a long unworded gust. "She was drunk as a skunk and no loss to anybody anyway." Hannah fled to her room, her mom's voice raised in pursuit. "Some people get what they deserve."

Hannah squeaked her window open and fished out a cigarette for company. Her door didn't have a lock, but she'd figured out that if she slipped four of the old coasters her mom had lifted from the casino where she worked under the uneven legs of her desk, she could slide it in front of her door pretty easily. She was resourceful. That was one of the words she'd learned from Mrs. Grossman. She liked to whisper it to herself, roll it around on her tongue. It sounded like a grown-up compliment.

Spelling had always been Hannah's best subject. She could spell most of the words the first time, before she'd even seen them written out. Mrs. Grossman said that was an outcome of all the time Hannah spent reading library books. Hannah'd had to ask what outcome meant. She only knew that combination of words the other way round, because Seth in the seventh grade had done it, before his parents sent him off to that camp over the border in Utah. So Mrs. Grossman had a bright idea. She offered Hannah extra credit for looking up the definitions herself.

That's how Hannah knew what resourceful meant. She was stretching her lips over the first syllable and wrapping them around the next two when the towhee appeared. He materialized through a wave of cigarette smoke like an old black-and-white I Dream of Jeannie. He wore rusty stripes like a cape on either side of his snowy chest. The garnet eyes in his executioner's hood caught the last of the sun winking off the river below Hannah's window. Hannah jumped, but she managed to bite down on both her cigarette and her yelp.

"Hello," she said softly. The bird fluttered and fixed her with one molten eye. "Who are you?" He gave her his standard answer, two mournful whistles followed by chattering laughter. At falling leaf speed, Hannah lowered her cigarette into the Folgers can where she hid the butts. The bird tipped his head but stayed balanced on the beam of her sill. Hannah giraffed her neck and peered at his mohawk crown, his earthworm legs. She remembered him from the poster in Mrs. Grossman's classroom, because his name was the echo of his song. It sounded like someone's first breath. Or their last. "Did you know Mrs. Grossman too?" The bird gave another giggle and disappeared in a bluster of wings, leaving Hannah shivering against the cut crystal evening.

Later that night, when news about the accident was still seeping through town, Hannah stood just outside the living room door, catching crumbs of conversation in her upturned ear. "Well, what do you expect?" Her mom's voice was slow and satisfied, like after she'd told you so. "If I was that way, living like that? And everybody found out? I might do the same thing." There was a pause, and Hannah heard shrill whimpers leaping out of the phone. "Well, even so. I'm just saying."

The day after the accident, there was a special assembly. Everybody sat on frigid folding chairs in the gym, and the principal blew her nose until it echoed. The noise made Hannah laugh, and snobby Katie Swift scrunched up her face like she'd smelled a fart and scooched away. So Hannah clamped her lips together, and she didn't even sing along when they all stood up to clutch their hearts for the national anthem. Hannah didn't really understand what the Star Spangled Banner had to do with Mrs. Grossman dying, but then Vicky's mom told her that you can't sing religious songs at school on account of the septicnation of church and state. So maybe it was just the only song everybody knew that didn't have God in it.

Hannah pictured Mrs. Grossman walking through the tardark Bullhead night. A pincushion of stars overhead and the grind of gravel underfoot. The branches reaching for her as she came to the crossing. Maybe the pines pinched her long swirly skirt. Maybe she got snagged, there in the arms of a hunchback ponderosa. Maybe she twisted her ankle in the iron gap, fell and hit her head. Maybe she never saw that myopic dragon coming. But Hannah's pretty sure she did.

After that, they decided to send a countslur around to all the classrooms. A baldie in tentcanvas khakis and a sweatervest the color of blood. He sat on Ms. Temple's desk in front of Hannah's class, rolled up his sleeves and stretched out his legs. Hannah waited for her teacher to tell him to sit down in his chair and put both feet on the floor or be held back at recess. But Ms. Temple just sniffled and corkscrewed the Kleenex in her hands until it fell in little snowy tufts all over the lemonbleach linoleum.

The countslur told them all it was okay to have feelings. To be sad or angry. And that it was okay to laugh, too. Relieved, Hannah mentally stuck her tongue out at Katie Swift. "If any of you would like to talk to me privately, you just come up and tell Ms. Temple after class. I'm here for you. Mrs. Temple is here for you. All the adults are here for you."

Hannah thought it might be nice to sit in the warm and talk to him instead of going out into the nose-dripping cold to get slammed with a dodgeball. But she couldn't conjure the right words. The recess bell punched the air, and all the other kids wriggled to their feet and ran for it. Hannah stood at the back of the classroom, balancing the toe of one sneaker on the laces of the other, waiting. But Ms. Temple was busy gulping down baldie's attention, and when he leaned forward and put a humpty hand on her arm, her cheeks bloomed. They got redder when she finally turned and saw Hannah dawdling.

"What is it, Hannah?" There was a sprinkling of salt in her voice. Hannah lost her balance and toppled. "Why don't you go on out and play with the others." The countslur smiled at her with all his teeth and didn't say anything. So she went.

She'd seen on the news last month where they brought puppies to a school in Texas after one of the boys packed his father's gun to class.

He'd shot his teacher and three other kids before the police screeched in and gunned him dead. She'd seen the afterimages on the screen through her splayed fingers when her mom told her to cover her eyes. But the puppies were wheaty wriggly golden retrievers, like shiny kids have in old movies. After the train ran over Mrs. Grossman, Hannah hoped they might bring those puppies to her school. But they never did. She guessed the puppies were only for kids who'd seen somebody get shot. Hannah'd never seen that. It seemed like a special kind of achievement.

But Hannah had accomplished other things. Mrs. Grossman had once driven her down to the spelling bee in Durango. Her mother had to work a shift at the casino and had told Hannah she couldn't go, but Mrs. Grossman showed up in her little ruby Honda and drove Hannah all the way, her knuckles white on the steering wheel. Hannah imagined bones knobbling under skin, fisted her own fingers until they flared white and smooth like pebbles sinking in a dark pond. She'd made it to the quarterfinals, but no one had given her any quarters. Just a piece of paper with her name in oldstyle letters. Mrs. Grossman sat on the drooping tongue of one of the crimson folddown chairs and smiled the whole time. Hannah'd never showed her mom that certificate.

Mrs. Grossman got flattened on a Thursday. Vicky's mom started the Rejoice! Mrs. Grossman memory-L on a Friday. By Sunday, the dry patch in front of the wall was littered with as many shades of dying flowers as there were layers of paint on the wall. There were more candles too, and a few teddy bears. One of the firemen walked by every day on his way home and blew out all the candles. Said it was a hazard. Hannah had to look up that word. She liked spending time at the wall. Unless it was snowing, she stopped on her way to school, leaned her bike up against the curve of the red j in Rejoice, and played a game where she tried to walk from one end of the memory-L to the other, tiptoeing between the flowers without crushing any. Mostly she won. And she thought about taking one of the teddy bears home. The big blond one with the red-and-green tartanbow around his thick squeezy neck. But she knew it would be wrong to steal him from Mrs. Grossman. So she went almost every day to visit.

One deadweight afternoon eighteen days after the accident, Vicky's mom dropped Vicky off at ballet and then drove Hannah to the Rejoice! Mrs. Grossman memory-L. She looked at Hannah in the rearview mirror with owl eyes and told her she needed closer. Hannah wasn't sure what she needed to get closer to, but she was glad not to have to ride her bike home in the cold. Vicky's mom's car had seatwarmers. When they got out at the wall, Vicky's mom started gathering up the musty flowers, and Hannah helped. When they'd collected all the muddy stems, Vicky's mom cradled them in her arms like a baby and then heaved them into the dumpster behind the telephone pole. That's when Hannah let out the scream. She hadn't known it was climbing up her throat, but once it was there, she couldn't hold it in. Vicky's mom gave her a steelwool hug and said it was time. Then they went and picked Vicky up, and they rode all the way to Hannah's house in silence, Vicky's soft pink leggings slouched down around her ankles, Hannah's soaked grey sneakers dripping slush on the black plastic floormat.

Three days later an automobile pulled up and parked beside the concrete wall. The driver opened the door, but did not get out of the car. Although her face was in shadow, it was easy to tell she was sad. There was something about how she turned away from the sun and rested the weight of her hands on the steering wheel, something about her silent composure, that caused Hannah to sigh. The young girl watched the driver lean out of the car and stretch her hand out towards one of the burned out candles.

Hannah wondered if maybe this was Mrs. Grossman's mom. She couldn't see her face clearly, but even so, she didn't look old enough. The skin on her bare arms was still tight, not butterflywinged like the other old ladies in Bullhead. And her hair wasn't grey, although Hannah had heard in church that you could pray the grey away. But then the woman leaned out of the car, and Hannah could see she wasn't praying. Her chin was a walnut, and her eyelids shuddered. Hanna sidled up to her back fender. Maybe she was Mrs. Grossman's sister? But probably not. Her skin was a whole other shade, and Hannah knew that people who belonged to each other mostly had to have the same skin color.

The license plate said California in curvy cherry letters. Hannah sounded them out, and her imagination swirled with slinky slitted sequined dresses, birthday candle flash bulbs, and palm trees black against unnaturally orange sunsets. Maybe this stranger was from there. Hannah liked the easy lean of the word. The license plates in her state were serious, with green letters that went straight up and down.

The woman wiped her cheeks with pink seashell nails and clambered out of the car like she was walking up out of the river. The way the water sucks you back and you have to airpunch your way out for balance. She wasn't wearing a jacket, but that didn't seem to bother her. She reached out to stroke the cheek of Hannah's favorite bedraggled bear, clamped his shoulder and lifted him up. She held him to her face and inhaled. Hannah already knew he smelled like ashy slush and almondy mold. That's when she had to intervene.

"You shouldn't touch him." She stepped away from the car as she spoke. "It's not…" she struggled for the word. "Respectful." The woman never took her eyes off the bear, but she murmured, "Respect," as if she'd never heard the word before. She put the bear down and reached for a candle instead. Hannah took another step back and studied her. She could be an emmagrin. Hannah'd learned that word from the tie guy on the news, and she knew it meant darkskin people who couldn't speak English. The stranger's skin was definitely dark, but it could be just a good tan. Hannah knew tanning was something people did in California. She looked for other clues. The woman wore little flashy square earrings that might be diamonds, and real Ugg boots. On her wedding finger was a fat, smooth gold ring, exactly the same as the one Mrs. Grossman used to wear. Hannah wondered whether the train had crushed that, too.

The ring flared, and Hannah noticed the flame. The candle the woman had been reaching for was lit. Hannah sniffed the air, but the acrid tang that holds hands with a struck match was absent. She leaned her left palm on the cold fender again, fished a contraband cigarette out of her coat pocket. "Got a light?"

The woman looked at the girl for the first time. Hannah pulled her shoulders up to her ears, ready for the inevitable how-old-are-you question, the does-your-mother-know-what-you're-doing question. But the woman just slithered her hand into her snakeskin purse and emerged with a lighter in her fanned fingers, like a cobra with a spread hood and a forked tongue.

Hannah held her breath and flicked the Bic to life on the first try, which gave her permission to unclench her jaw. She placed the cigarette right smack in the middle of her lips and held the lighter up to her nose. It was studded with hotpink flamingoes and applegreen palm trees. She stroked it with her thumb, side-eyed the stranger to judge how fast she might be, or whether she might be susceptible to pleading. The woman kept her eyes bolted to the candle flicker. So Hannah just slipped the lighter into her pocket.

"Did you know her?" Hannah took a heartbeat to feel who the woman was asking about. "You mean Mrs. Grossman? Yeah sure. She was my teacher." Hannah let out a puff, held in a cough. "Last year. When I was little."

"Mrs?" The woman wrung her face like a washcloth. Hannah thought she was about to say something, but then she bit her bottom lip until all the color bled out. She studied the writing on the wall. "Who's idea was that?" Hannah followed her gaze. Rejoice! She smiled without thinking. "Oh, that's always been there." The woman drew the back of her hand quickly under her chin. Hannah's eyes stroked the set of the stranger's jaw. She thought of the countslur and wondered whether this woman was more sad or more angry.

"Can you show me where it happened?" Hannah knew right away what she meant, but she asked anyway, "Where what happened?" The woman didn't explain. She slid back into the driver's seat, slammed the door, squeezed the wheel and stared straight ahead. Hannah waited for her to pull away. She counted to fifty, puffing as she went. When she got to fifty-one and the car hadn't moved, she shrugged, stomped her cigarette, and shuffled around to the passenger's side. The seatbelt buckle froze her fingers. As soon as that click sliced the air, the women stepped hard on the gas and they lurched away from the curb. Hannah pointed at the intersection up ahead. "You go left there."

The woman flicked the blinker and twirled the wheel. Suddenly Hannah's memory kicked her in the ear and her stomach tied itself in a knot. She was not supposed to get into cars with strangers. But in her mother's scary stories, the strangers were always men with candy. She'd never heard anything about women with flamingo lighters and Uggs.

Hannah considered the stranger's profile. "What's your name?" The woman sighed and answered without turning. "Ruth." Hannah thought that sounded like a grandma name, but she knew it would be rude to say. "I'm Hannah," said Hannah. She thought for a moment. "Are you from California?" The woman turned her eyes to Hannah but kept her chin pointed at the road. "I used to live there." Hannah stared until the weight of her eyes pressed out more words. "I moved here when Chris— when Mrs. Grossman got the job at your school."

Hannah nodded, although she didn't really understand. The woman pointed at the next intersection. "What do I do here?" Hannah waved like she was shooing a fly. "Keep going." They swished under the green light noosed on its wire, rushed between the candycane arms of the train crossing, raised up to heaven. As they bumped across the tracks, Ruth shuddered and sucked her breath. Hannah leaned forward to turn up the heat.

"There." Hannah pointed at the pocked parking lot behind the KFC. "We have to walk from here." They jostled to a stop, straddling one of the flaking white lines on the cracked blacktop. "You didn't park very good," Hannah told her. "Well," said Ruth. "I didn't park very well." She turned the key and the car went quiet. "You're right. But who really cares?"

"There are rules," Hannah told her, still belted in. "You have to care about the rules." Ruth yanked the emergency brake. "You mean like the rule that says little girls aren't supposed to smoke?" She threw open the door. The cold reared up from the wet asphalt and galloped into the car. Hannah grumbled, unclicked her seatbelt and got out, slamming the door behind her.

As they crunched over the brown grass towards the tracks, Ruth reached for the girl's hand. Hannah stiffened, held her fingers rigid. But as Ruth bent over and let her tears drip on the rustred rails, Hannah relented. She squeezed the woman's hand, gently and steadily. "My Sunday School teacher says Mrs. Grossman probably went to heaven." Ruth made a snotty noise that could have been a sob or a laugh. "Probably?" Hannah thought for a minute. "I mean, if she was a good Christian. A good person." Ruth wrapped her free hand around her narrow waist like she was trying to keep from splitting down the middle. "She was. The best."

Hannah was not naturally patient, but she did her best. Mrs. Grossman would have been proud, she thought. Pleased. Satisfied. Gratified. Impressed. Hannah'd learned something. She waited for Ruth's eyes to crinkle and dry. For her nose to stop dripping. Then she pulled her hand away and stuck it in her pocket to warm it up. That's when she saw the towhee. Balanced on one of the grappling branches, he fixed her with that blazing eye. She knew he was the same bird because he had to be. And she knew he felt it too, Mrs. Grossman's warmth still rising out of

Ruth like steam, fizzing in the frigid golden air. She reached up to point him out. "Look. Up there." The towhee offered up two short sobs and a heap of giggles. But Ruth didn't look. "I can give you a ride home." The bird billowed into the sky, and Hannah and Ruth trudged back to the car.

"Do you know what your name means?" Ruth asked as they pulled away. Hannah smeared her eyes across the windshield and shook her head. A name was a name. You couldn't just find it in the dictionary. "It means grace and favor." Two more words Hannah would have to look up later. She tried to hold them in her mind so she wouldn't forget. She pictured grace as a kind of lilac flower leaning into a soft spring breeze, favor as two smooth round stones dropped into still water, the ripples reaching out and out forever. "It's from the Bible. A woman named Hannah prayed for a son, and when God answered her prayer, she said, 'My heart rejoices in the Lord.'"

Hannah pictured the red letters on the gold wall watching over the stubby candles and the damp teddy bears and the dumpster of dead flowers. She turned to Ruth. "How come you know so much about the Bible?" The stranger smiled for the first time. "My father was a minister." Hannah silently ran her tongue over the peaks and valleys of grace and favor again. "We go to church too," she said. "Or I do. Sometimes my mom comes. Sometimes the neighbors take me."

"Do you like church?" Hannah sat up straighter. Church was something you just had to do, like school or the dentist. It hadn't occurred to her that it was something you could decide not to like. She frowned into the chalkdust heating vents in the dashboard. "I like the singing."

"Me too." Ruth smiled wider. "I used to play gospel music at home on Sunday mornings. She had the most beautiful voice." Hannah scrunched up her forehead. "Mrs. Grossman?" Ruth nodded. "You mean you lived with her?" Ruth looked over at Hannah again, hit her right in the eyes for three whole seconds before she nodded. "Yes. We lived together. Over in

Bayfield." She turned her eyes back to the road. "Yes we did." Hannah opened her mouth to ask another question, but the words slipped and slid through the gaps in her teeth. As they rumbled through the darkening evening, Ruth hummed a few notes under her breath. Her eyes flashed wet in the streetlight strobe.

"Now what?" They'd come to another intersection, this one marked with red lollipop stop signs. Hannah balked. She pictured the kind of house Ruth and Mrs. Grossman must have had. Small and neat, white with lacy green trim, a solid porch with a swing. Her house was a long, thin rectangle on wheels, with peeling grey lattices propped up around the bottom so no one would guess you could just tow it away anytime you wanted. It sat all alone on a bend in the river, too far from town for streetlights or trash trucks or any of that. An idea rose up in front of her, with a shadowy motive napping behind it. She decided not to poke the reason why she didn't want Ruth to see her house.

"Left," she said, making the L with her hand and pointing. The car lurched over the train tracks again where they flowed out of town and into the thickening forest. Hannah saw Ruth's knuckles go white on the wheel, the same way Mrs. Grossman's had. She clenched her own fists and felt her eyes prickle. She whispered the towhee's incantation to herself, over and over again. The comforting clench of the first syllable, then the deep stretch of the second.

When they pulled up in front of Vicky's house, Hannah bolted from the car without saying thank you. She ran up the flush bricks of Vicky's neatly shoveled steps. Suddenly fear filled her lungs. It was Thursday. Vicky's violin lesson day. What if they weren't home? How would she explain to Ruth why she had no key? She took a drag of dry air and reached for the curved brass handle just as Vicky's mom flung the door open. "My goodness! Hannah." She eyed Ruth's profile through the passenger window, sucked her teeth and reached for Hannah's bony shoulder. "What's wrong?"

For just a moment, Hannah felt her train grind to a halt. She tried to gather all the afternoon's good feelings in her arms and clutch them to her chest. The air hugging Vicky's mom trickled with the smell of ovenroasting. The light in the entry was honeysweet. She smiled and turned to wave to Ruth. Rejoice! She held her hand in the air as the car pulled away, eyes trained on the ruby taillights until they vanished around the blind corner at the end of the cul-de-sac. Vicky's mom squinted from Hannah to the car and back again. "Hannah. What is it? Why are you crying?"

Shadows on the Wall

Zackary Pierce

⸎

Beyond the cracked sidewalk, and the telephone pole with layers of flyers in a rainbow of colors, and the patch of dry brown grass there stood a ten -foot high concrete block wall, caked with dozens of coats of paint. There was a small shrine at the foot of it, with burnt out candles and dead flowers and a few soggy teddy bears. One word of graffiti filled the wall, red letters on a gold background: Rejoice!

The homeless teddy bears were huddled around the candle nubs at the shrine's base. Their fur was matted with rain. The shining highlights of their dark eyes had witnessed the dance of flames. The sputter and flicker that drowned itself, mourned by the shed of wax tears.

Twelve hydraulic pins, contracting in a steel and concrete blast door. Opening to reveal the tip of a white steel nosecone. Stage one begins after the missile leaves the silo. Approximately sixty feet long, leaving behind a cloud of white smoke that drifts over the quiet hillside. Dissipating slowly as the wind whispers, rustling in the leaves of nearby trees. The smoke is a memory after the blast doors close. Fading with the roar of first stage thrusters venting flame.

Droplets ambiently pattered around the bears, forming little impact rings in the puddles surrounding their congregation. The air smelled of the rain that sloshed beneath a girl's pink boots, bouncing off the canopy of a black umbrella. The girl held her mother's hand, stepping in those puddles. Splashing past the bears after her mother. She wore a white parka where her mother's coat was long and black and trailing, flapping wildly around a pair of pale slim ankles.

Tornado sirens are both electrical and pneumatic. A rotor spins inside, drawing in air, driven by centrifugal force. Revolving so fast that the chopped air produces that haunting sound, amplified through tubes and a cone-shaped structure within the horn. The frequency is determined by the rate at which the flow of air is interrupted. The rate at which the flow of that air is interrupted is determined by the amplitude of the current spinning the chopper.

When the girl opened her mouth whatever she said was lost in that slow but deafening howl. Eerily rising and falling, echoing for miles in the gray waves of that ocean in the sky. Flocks of starlings burst from the trees to wheel from cloud to cloud.

A missile is guided. A rocket is not. Both rely on solid or liquid propellant. Leveraging thrust and resistance to climb the atmosphere. Stage two begins beyond the troposphere and stratosphere, in the mesosphere sixty seconds after launch. At 100,000 feet the missile tilts at a forty-five-degree angle. The second stage motor ignites as the first stage falls away.

A distant flash bloomed in the pupils of the girl's eyes. Less than a fraction of a second later the thunder came. A thunder that drowned out even the sirens. The girl had her hands over her ears even after lines of blood trailed down the sides of her neck.

Solid propellant differs from its liquid counterpart in that, unlike liquid hydrogen, it does not need cryogenic treatment. Stage three begins in the thermosphere, one hundred twenty seconds after launch. At 300,000 feet the nosecone is jettisoned. Revealing clustered warhead reentry vehicles that taper to form cones, approximately eight hundred pounds apiece. Oceans and continents curve beneath the missile propelled into orbit at 27,000 miles an hour. The third stage engine ignites. The second stage falls back to Earth with the first.

A second sun flared on the horizon in the center of the street. The mother and the girl were bathed in blinding white. She dropped her umbrella and covered her daughter's eyes too late. After the flash took the girl's sight.

Solid propellant is pre-mixed. Once the fuel in the missile begins to burn, the missile cannot be stopped. Stage four also begins in the thermosphere, one hundred eighty seconds after launch. At 700,000 feet the third stage falls and the post boost control system is engaged. Its motor is the only bi-propellant component of the missile. It uses solid fuel for velocity and liquid fuel for course correction. Its only exhaust is a small blue flame on the bottom of the platform securing the reentry vehicles.

Advertisements stapled to the telephone pole flapped violently. Hurricane force winds carried the teddy bears and their shrine off. The mother and daughter were forced against the ten-foot tall concrete wall. Her hands were on either side of her daughter's face beneath the O of that word graffitied in red. The wall with all its layers of paint was painted orange and red like everything else. The cloud on the horizon was no sunset but literally set the air on fire, as sunsets appear to.

Stages five and six consist of the post boost control system's inertial guidance system, operating independent of commands from the surface. At their apogee the warhead reentry vehicles are deployed in sequence. Tongues of fire blaze around the cones, tracing their descent back through the atmosphere.

The mother pressed her forehead against her daughter's. Wrapping her arms around the girl. Burying her nose in the child's hair. Closing her eyes. Unable to hear the roar and collapse of buildings after her eardrums have burst. The sigh of so many trees bowing like waves of tall grass in the wind.

The line that separates night and day is obvious from orbit. But the man who stood at his kitchen sink had no idea where that shadow was until it overcomes him. His house and neighborhood and city lay in one of the browner patches between greener coasts and mountain ranges. A desert known as the Mojave. Whose name, in the language that word is formed, meant *by the water.*

The man who washed his hands at his kitchen sink had wild curly black hair. His widow's peak was growing thinner and sparser. His arms remain thick with that dark hair, no matter how much remains on his head. He wore a blue polo shirt banded silver. His frame was thin, yet his stomach was distended. His jeans were a faded gray. When he walked it was with an almost imperceptible limp.

He had a view of mountains through the panes between the curtains of the kitchen window. During the day, the peaks were a hazy periwinkle. But as the sky darkened their crags bruised so purple their features were lost in shadow. At twilight the silhouette of those ranges was a sharp unbroken line against the sky, tinged yellow where the sun last sank.

The closest mountain was the darkest. The antennae of radio towers at the summit blinked red intermittently. His neighborhood was built on a terrace cut into the foothills. His house was one of five at the end of a cul -de-sac. A basketball hoop stood at the end of his driveway where the sidewalk rounds out and the asphalt begins. The frayed net skirting the rim stirred when the backboard was struck. The ball bounced back into the hands of one of three boys while the other two jockeyed slap it from his hands.

The father of one of those children dried his hands on a rag he draped over the arch of the sink's faucet. The pendant lights over the kitchen island behind him had cast their bulbs onto mottled granite countertops. A second son younger than the one playing outside swiveled on a stool there, leaning over a tablet. Its speakers blared the obnoxiously nasal laugh of a sea sponge who lives in a pineapple beneath the Bikini Atoll.

The scream of the man's third and oldest son from the living room made his youngest son drop the tablet on the kitchen tile. The cartoon continued to play even with the screen fragmented into three segments. Webbed with translucent cracks.

The father stops before he can cross the kitchen archway. Only the toe of one shoe crossed the line between kitchen tile and living room carpet. He saw his adult son with a remote in his hand, eclipsing images displayed on a muted flat screen. The bottom of each picture was banded red. The words that scrolled beneath were white. But they were a blur in the father's eyes. The question his son turned to ask him was like speech heard through cotton in the father's ears.

From orbit the only light leaving earth is electric. Dotting the dark half in glowing swaths. Thermonuclear weapons are high-yield, two-stage chain reactions. Fission begins through implosion triggers. Plutonium or uranium cores surrounded by high-explosive lenses. Compressed like the cores of stars, burning to prevent collapse under their own gravity.

A cyclone's white arms spun somewhere in the northern hemisphere. Forming a spiral around the nexus of an eye in patchy masses of crystallized vapor. Bridging the distance between sea and land on earth's brighter half. Beneath the clouds was a city almost seven hundred years old. Its *altstadt* had cobbled streets and half-timbered houses. The ruins of a church were left for ivy to grow over, bombed in the second world war and never rebuilt.

A stone was thrown from somewhere below the trees on the sidewalk. Shattering one of the church's remaining stained-glass windows. Crowds thronged the street, surging without guidance around a single f in a reflective green vest. He stood shouting into a bullhorn over the noise, unable to stem the human tide. Knocked down and throwing up a hand with his eyes closed. Expecting to be trampled. Not for a boy with feathery blonde hair and blue eyes to free his hand from his wrinkled grandmother's. To snatch the bullhorn that had clattered to the ground. To scream one word. A word so full of rage and fear that the mass of heaving bodies actually stopped. A word that reverberated, echoing through the overgrown gray spires of the ruined church.

The kid got up onto a milk crate and raised his hand. A murmur went through the crowd and then it fell silent, except for a few people shouting words of encouragement at him. The kid acknowledged them with a nod and a shy smile. In the full light of day, he looked less angry and more beautiful. He waited until people stopped shouting. A siren could be heard, maybe five or ten blocks away. The kid raised the bullhorn, pressed the button, and began to speak.

Whatever he intended to say was trapped in his throat. No sound left his open mouth. More two-tone sirens joined the chorus in the distance. An urgent melody perpetuated by the doppler effect. Waves of mechanical energy vibrating the ear drum, transmitted through the bones of the inner ear to the cochlea. The snail-shell-like organ whose basilar membrane detects disturbances in the fluid contained within. Translating the movement of particulate matter into electrical signals the thalamus can interpret as sound.

The crowds that surrounded the boy grew restless. Shoving and shouting rolled through the masses in waves again. The boy brought his thumb over the bullhorn button again, but the first note was shaky leaving his lips. Almost lost in the uproar. But his voice grew steadier the longer and slower the rhythm became. Lingering on the syllables of words belonging to a language the men and women around him could not understand. The only thing they had to find meaning in was the vibration of his vocal cords. Air forced from his lungs through the trachea and larynx.

The shoving and shouting stopped all the same. Heads turned to find the source of that music. The mournful flutter in the last syllables of the first line. The kid on a milk crate singing, eyes fixed on something distant. The wetness that shined trailing his pale cheeks.

It was an old Icelandic ballad about two lovers, in a forest called Vaglaskógur. About dreams that come true sleeping in the woodland sky. The deep calm of quiet waters as evening comes on. The way your hair glows, counted by the wind.

Fusion takes place between small amounts of lithium and tritium gas in the fissile pit. Enabling more fission in the plutonium-239 or uranium-235 core. X-ray particle bombardment irradiates polystyrene foam around the uranium-235 tamper, creating plasma. Ablating the tamper to compress the sparkplug, producing high-energy neutrons through a deuterium-tritium reaction. The peanut-shaped uranium-238 case containing the chain reaction is normally not fissile but undergoes fission at thermonuclear temperatures.

From orbit the fireballs flare in silence. Clustered around places where electric light clusters on the half not facing the sun. Forming chains and waves of detonation, whether the warheads reach the ground or explode in the atmosphere above their targets.

The line between day and night has chased itself around Earth for over 4.6 billion years. Marking the passage of days and weeks and months. Years and eras and ice ages. Over ninety-nine percent of all species that have ever populated Earth are extinct. That of *homo sapiens* will likely share the fate of all its tool-using hominid ancestors. *Homo habilis* and *homo erectus*. *Homo heidelbergensis* and *homo neanderthalensis*.

A red glow crept into pale skies above the desert. A basketball's trajectory brought it through the orange rim of a hoop with a *swish* of the net. A boy's shout echoed strangely between the houses of a cul-de-sac. In the house behind the basketball hoop was the father of that boy. Staring through the television and its pictures of mushroom clouds. Staring through his oldest son as the young man repeated a question only to be ignored again.

The oceans will boil in 1.5 billion years. Forcing *homo sapiens* to colonize other planets of the solar system. Migrating as *homo erectus* left Africa to colonize Europe and Asia. In 5 billion years the sun will become a red giant. Burning helium once its hydrogen reserves have been depleted. Expanding to swallow Mercury, Venus, Earth, and Mars.

The father's gaze penetrated the walls of the house. Traveling miles and miles of highway through Joshua trees and cacti and sagebrush.

Flying over the cracked beds of dry lakes stretching under the dusky outlines of plateaus. Finding the irradiated craters of test sites. Military bases whose perimeters have motion sensors and signs that say trespassers will be shot.

The man's son threw down the TV remote and ran for the front door. Yanking it open to bound out onto the porch with its awning. Its garden hose coiled in a pot between the hedges. Its view of the light dying on the faces of mountains behind the boys dribbling a basketball in the street. Two empty rocking chairs rocked faintly together above the steps of the deck.

Before the young man could call out to his brother he gave a yelp. Yanked back by the collar of his shirt. Forced against the siding of the house and face to face with his father. Who had run down the hallway and out onto the porch with that slight yet persistent hitch in his step.

The father slapped his son across the face. But roughly pulled the younger man toward him immediately after. The son held his reddened cheek in a daze as his father hugged him. He was taller than the man who had sired him but could not consistently grow facial hair yet. His father's goatee was neat and full and flecked with gray where the son was clean shaven.

The elements in the cores of stars will eventually become too heavy to burn. The only remaining light will be shed from the dense remnants of their cores, cooling for trillions of years. Relics of nuclear fusion. White dwarfs and neutron stars.

The son pulled away from his father. Releasing his cheek to expose the red shadow the hand had left on his face. Drawing his brows together in a deep frown. Asking his father that question a third time: "What do we do?"

Twilight settled over the street. Lending a bluish tint to the remaining light. The father had turned to watch the boys play basketball in the street. In the reflection of his eyes one of them tucked the ball under one arm at the hip, waving in the direction of the porch.

The father waved back with a small smile. Speaking quietly with none of the panic that had shaken his oldest son's voice. "Nothing," he answered. Looking down when his youngest son tugged on the leg of jeans. Bending to pick the boy up, bouncing the toddler in his arms. "Let them play."

"*Play?*" the son echoed. Eyes widening, nostrils flaring. Clawing at his scalp to pull back his hair and pace back and forth. Gesturing toward the boys that had gone back to shooting hoops. "We have to get out of here!"

The father shook his head. A breeze picked up what remained of his hair. His youngest son took his arms from around his father's neck, playing with his father's nose. He allowed the toddler to squish his nostrils against the septum and said: "I'd rather spend the time I have left with my family."

The oldest son compulsively twisted a strand of hair between his thumb and index finger. "They're gonna—We're all gonna . . ." He groaned and ran a hand over his face, winding up to kick over one of the rocking chairs.

A wind made the dark leaves of their neighbor's plum tree whisper. Against a backdrop of purple mountains a hawk circled, landing on the wooden arm of a telephone pole. The father nodded. "That's why we should let them play."

He started down the steps with the youngest son in his arms still. Crossing the lawn with a nearly indiscernible bounce in his stride to compensate for the limp. Joining his son and the other boys in the street. Letting the child down to accept the ball that was passed to him. Getting his wrist underneath to send it ringing around the inside rim of the hoop before falling through. Kneeling once he had the ball again to show the toddler how to do the same, even though the child could only manage to throw it a few feet at a time.

The oldest son joined his father and brothers in front of the hoop with his arms crossed. Waiting for the flash and boom, eyes flicking down the street and up at the sky every few seconds. Shielding his eyes once the head of one of those clouds did appear in the distance, smaller than the thumb he squinted at down the length of his arm. His father knew that trick was a myth. That the size of the cloud compared to a thumb has no relation to one's safety from the fallout.

Only four percent of the known universe is visible light. The rest is some combination of dark matter and dark energy. Forces believed responsible for the expansion of the universe. Known only as black holes are known, for their gravitational effects on matter. Gravity will survive the death of light in trillions of years. Gravity made it possible for stars to burn in the first place.

The skies above the father who told his children he loved them had lost their light. Clouds over a place somewhere else on earth began to absorb it. But those clouds were a sickly mix of purple and green. Hanging over the last standing section of a cinderblock wall. Two shadows embraced on the face of it, burned into concrete.

Like Machines

JAMES POTTER

⚜

Beyond the cracked sidewalk, and the telephone pole with layers of flyers in a rainbow of colors, and the patch of dry brown grass there stood a ten-foot high concrete block wall, caked with dozens of coats of paint. There was a small shrine at the foot of it, with burnt out candles and dead flowers and a few soggy teddy bears. One word of graffiti filled the wall, red letters on a gold background: Rejoice!

I passed the spot almost daily—on the way to the music studio, out to drinks with my girlfriend Hannah. Sometimes at night, clearing my head of the day's session, I'd find myself walking towards the shrine as if my feet somehow knew I would get a charge from the mural. Though I could no longer see the original, it was there, hidden like some secret document beneath all the grime and salt erosion, the graffiti and stickers, the collective iconography of a diverse Baltimore community who felt compelled to say that Chavez was *their* hero, *their* native son.

Today as I drove past the shrine I was mad that some evangelical with a spray can got to make the latest revision. In the moments before the twenty-seven year-old songwriter, beatboxer, vert skater, and graphic novelist known as Chavez took his life, I doubt he was rejoicing over the kingdom of heaven. The letter he had written before hanging himself from the rafters of his green house and studio in Hampden had been addressed to his dog.

Of all the millions who knew and loved him—A-list movie stars, liberal politicians espousing some sort of campaign direction based on one of his many emotive lines—he had written his death letter to his dog, a half-blind beagle named Tupelo. I'll never forget the last lines of the letter leaked a week after his suicide via a Tumblr blog: *You were made by laughter, treats, the smell of chain-link parks where the sun hovers all afternoon warming the backs of drug dealers and saints. Same as me.*

I remember when I first heard the news. Hannah and our roommate Bugs and I were all sitting in a patch of sunlight outside the Hampden Coffee Collective, a former warehouse turned overpriced but delicious coffee emporium and deli. You get a real weird mix of people at the HCC. A new tech giant is putting their offices in down the street, so you see a lot of those Bluetooth earphone wiz kids walking around, brandishing their cold brew coffees and bags of avocado toast like mental ammunition. I can't tell you how many Teslas I've seen in one month. And it was from the lips of one of these tech wizards that I overhead the news.

Hannah had reached her weekly boiling point with Bugs' inability to clean *anything* in the apartment. Without any warning, she reached over and wiped a long smear of vegetable cream cheese across his beard. That was when the guy in the table next to us held up his phone to his friend's face and blurted out:

"Holy shit, man! Chavez is dead! No…not drugs. Dude *hung* himself. Can you believe that? He just did SNL like…what? A week ago? He and Aubrey Plaza were Russian tourists watching Trump and Putin bodysurf. *Craaaaazy.* I mean he was just on SNL…"

I turned to Hannah. Her finger still hovered in the air thick with cream cheese. But I knew she had heard. She ripped open her purse and dug around until she found her phone. A few seconds later her eyes went wide and wet like the time she told me about the things she had to endure in high school, all those mind games played by pathological Upper West side Catholic school girls. She dropped the phone and covered her face while Bugs—who had just returned from cleaning his beard using one of the deli's windows—assumed that Hannah was really losing her mind over his apartment hygiene. He started pouring out apologies. I cast him one silencing look then got up and went over to Hannah and threw my arms around her. I could feel her tears run warm down my back all the way to the base of my spine.

"What the hell, Eric," she sobbed, her voice muffled in a mesh of hair and t-shirt. "You just saw him last week...did he...I mean...why didn't he reach out to you? Did he say anything in the studio? What was so horrible that he had to *hang* himself?"

I didn't know what to say. All I could do was feel numb all over and hold her while she shook like a broken radiator. My mind felt dry. I kept staring at the tech guys across the table. The news was a blip, a footnote to their workday. Maybe they had heard a few songs off of Chavez's classic *Gutter Garden* on a HBO movie special. But neither one of them had spent the past month working on Chavez's return to the East Coast record, still unfinished and untitled. I had been there for every moment, every paroxysm of joy and outburst of dysfunction. And I can remember getting the call from him, the one that would take me to a cabin in the middle of nowhere where I would learn where songs really come from, all the backdoors and jagged holes in the chain-link fences you have to worm your way through in order to speak the truth and warmth of the sun that touches all things.

I grew up in a small rural town in southwestern Vermont called Pawlett. My graduating class had a total of thirteen students. There wasn't a lot you could hide from anyone. I had a band called PizzaSalad that sounded about as good as its name. But in all my fumblings to try to write songs like Tom Petty or Townes van Zandt I learned I had a hidden second talent, one for recording and arranging music—sometimes my own, but mostly area bands that needed high quality demos to send off to annoy the slush piles of already eroding indie labels.

There was a girl I fell in love with who I thought was in love with me. Her family was from Manchester. We met at a summer festival between our junior and senior years where we both did mushrooms for the first time. To this day she's the only girl I've ever met named Echo that's not just a handle or stage name. It was right there on the birth certificate. She slapped it down in front of me on the kitchen table at Thanksgiving later that year when I was invited to meet her hippie parents and her twin sister dubbed the equally unorthodox "Elwaina" from a character in a fantasy book they all assured me like cult followers was better than *Lord of the Rings*. I read it. It wasn't. But I never told Echo or Elwaina. I guess I really was that much in love.

That holiday Echo slipped me a burned copy of MP3s from a MySpace page called "Chavez Sings." That was my first brush with what would later get gathered together to form Chavez's debut record *Gutter Garden*, a low-fi masterpiece full of eerie harmonies layered like a Tim Burton love song and slightly out of tune upright piano melodies that jangled like wind chimes strung with silver dollars. The song that stuck with me the most was a half-sung, half-rapped hymn to non-violence. It was told from the perspective of a girlfriend's cheek that had just been punched by her coke-addled boyfriend. I had never heard anything like it before. Even though the production included layer upon layer of intricate beatboxing and raspy vocals, it was all presented with deceptive simplicity:

> *You dip your wick*
> *& let fly your fist*
> *Then shit a brick*
> *When you can't hit it*
> *Little boy in man*
> *Used to hold her hand*
> *Talkin' Promised Land*
> *Now you twist love*
> *Break love*
> *Baby just an egg*

Like Machines

She a bleeding dove
You crush cheeks
You used to make blush

He played and sang everything on the record—the guitars, the vocals and harmonies, piano, percussion, even something that sounded like a detuned cello—splicing the tape by hand in the old way like the Beatles in "Tomorrow Never Knows." It was raw, off the cuff, and totally bracing like getting hit with a spice you've never tasted before and now can't stop craving when consuming life's blander dishes. The descriptions of violence didn't really make me think about it then. *Was that his experience? Did he grow up in that world? How could he have detailed the scene so vividly?* It wasn't a red flag then. It should have been.

❖

Twelve years later I'm doing a live recording for a swing band at Mobtown Ballroom in Baltimore when I get a call from an unlisted number. I let it go to voicemail. At the end of the night, nursing a beer, I listen to the message. It's from someone named Sheila who claims she's Chavez's agent. She has this fast way of talking and getting down to business without sounding curt or all about the money, which is hard, especially on voicemail. "Why don't I just pass you to him?" she says at some point in the message. There's a slight pause. I hear birds screeching in the background and the sound of crashing and receding surf. After some fumbling a man's voice comes on, just a fraction above a whisper. "Hey, Eric…"A shiver runs the length of my spine. Even from those two words I know it. It's him. I know the voice because it lived in my car, blasting at epic decibels behind frost-rimmed windows on psychic vision quests across the country with *Gutter Garden* on repeat and its electrified follow-up *Friending the Fire*. It was Chavez.

"Eric, I'm standing on a really crappy beach…I think my toes are getting sunburned. They look like cocktail wieners. Someone just told me that Crosby, Stills, Nash and Young used to come down here in the 60's. There's a lot of reggaeton now…I hate reggaeton. Anyway, I'm coming back to Baltimore. I'd like to do some recording with you if you're down…I got a whole lot of ideas coming. I don't want to make this record like the last one. It's gonna be…well…it's gonna be a bit of a monster, I think. I really like what you did on Gabriella Vossi's record. It kind of made me start rethinking things. I wanted to track you down and see if you wanted to Batman and Robin some shit. Sheila can e-mail you everything if you're interested…Alright. Sheila's telling me I need to get off. We have to go meet some guy who wants to license some of my songs for a film about a guy who thinks his wife is food and tries to nibble pieces off her when she's asleep. Real weird. But I guess that's a lot of things out here. Well…thanks, man. Talk soon. Bye." *Click.*

What do you say to something like that? I checked the clock on my phone: *11:38. Not even nine o'clock on the West Coast. Still a completely reasonable hour of night to reply to a life-changing voicemail, right?* I hit the La Jolla area code number not thinking about what he said, about how it's "gonna be a bit of a monster." *Was the record a monster or was he?* I read somewhere in one of the few interviews he gave after *Friending the Fire* that the opening track "Tell Me You Can See the Dark Between Us" took over one hundred and eighty hours to record. *What the hell was I getting myself into?*

There are a few beeps and then, like a dream, Sheila picks up. I introduce myself. Sheila answers "Oh, hey, Eric," as if I was her neighbor remembering I'd left my jacket at her dinner party. I don't tell her about the two other projects I've got lined up—the first full length for the Baltimore goth metal collective Slaydoll Parade and Gabriella Vossi's sophomore project that apparently is supposed to sound like a Brazilian version of Queen's *A Night at the Opera*…whatever that means. Those projects won't be hard to delay. The mystique surrounding Chavez at the time was so strong that I'm sure Sheila spent most of her time turning down offers from all sorts of people. I tell her I'll do it. Yep, I'll do the record. When do we start? She says she'll e-mail over the label contracts and schedule. "One more thing," she says right before we hang up and I try to slow my pulse which is skyrocketing (BECAUSE I'M DOING A RECORD WITH FREAKIN' CHAVEZ!). "Not to sound like a Nazi or anything, but the sessions need to be super secret. If anything gets leaked, the label…" She pauses and sucks in a deep breath. "Let's just say they can be real…pricks. The single Rick Rubin did with Chavez got leaked and they hit him with all sorts of hellfire. Almost became a lawsuit. And with *that happy introduction…*" She laughs. "Can't wait to hear what you guys come up with! He's…well, he's Chavez. He'll be back in Baltimore on the 15th. Good luck!"

A little over a week later I'm standing at our kitchen window of our apartment overlooking Falls Road. I watch some crazy driver do a u-turn right in the middle of the road with three cars bearing down on him. It's a near collision, but surprisingly *par for the course* for that stretch of road. A few minutes later, after some more spirited honking, I watch a silver SUV pull up and a skinny character slink out the back seat.

He's wearing a crushed felt hat propped over shoulder-length dark hair and a jean jacket with all kinds of patches covering it. He holds a small parlor guitar case in one hand, a backpack with fraying sleeves in the other. No entourage, no hanger-oners, no agents. Just him. I yell to Bugs to leave the house and not come back for a while. Like for a *long* while. I know he's going to say something that will either spook Chavez or make him want to fight him. Bugs has that double gift. He starts to protest, but realizes he doesn't have a leg to stand on since he hasn't paid the last two month's rent. He mopes through the backdoor into the garden and is gone a few seconds later right as the doorbell rings. I open the door and find myself staring at an olive-skinned face with crow's feet way more pronounced than their years. All I can think of is some kind of saloon villain from a spaghetti western. *This town...she's too small, kid. You best saddle up. Go on. Git.*

"Hi, Eric!" a smoker's voice greets me. "Do you know there are seventy-two potholes between BWI and your house? What's happening to this city?" And with that introduction he drops his bag and takes out a small moleskin diary from his pocket. I try not to see them—the rows upon rows of furious ink marks. There are pages of them. They flap open in front of my face as he thumbs his way to the right spot. They make me think of Kevin Spacey's character in the movie *Seven. But at least those journals were filled with actual words,* I think. Chavez's pages are filled with some sort of insane cuneiform. They're not even straight lines, but all over the place like something scrawled on a public bathroom stall. Once he's finished he folds the diary back into his pocket like he's just done a site check for the Maryland DOT. He takes a look around the apartment. The door is still open. The pungent aromas from the Jamaican jerk chicken lady next-door waft through the doorway. I can tell he's absorbing *everything*: the smells, Hannah's oil and mixed media paintings drying on easels in the living room that doubles as her studio; my framed photos of my grandparents from pre-Nazi Germany; the fishbowl with no fish left alive in it (Bugs). A second later a pair of hazel-brown eyes revolves back towards me as if recognizing I'm still here, that I do indeed exist. Cracked lips widen into a fiendish grin. He nods his chin a couple of times in approval. "I like that it's blue—your living room. That's great. Hey, you want to catch a buzz?"

A few days into the sessions I realize we're not going to be able to make this record. Not at this studio at least. While no sonic material has been leaked—I limited the day to day staff to myself and an assistant engineer, put new padlocks on everything, and made sure the Wi-Fi had C.I.A. level encryption thanks to Bugs' friend Malcolm who graduated M.I.T. at fourteen—the buzz surrounding Chavez's return to Baltimore to record at Audible Slices Studio has led to a full-on circus every day. In the afternoon of the second day of demos a girl outside threatens to slit her wrists if Chavez doesn't take her cat. According to the girl, the cat knows the secret meaning behind Chavez's song "Amelia," which despite its clear lyrics being about a seamstress who sows and repairs her musician husband's stage clothes, is *really* about how our government is "fashioning us all into wage slaves." Like a cursed version of the "The Twelve Days of Christmas," the third day brings us two pet adoption agencies who proceed to get in a fight over the same hashtag for what they call their Baltimore "pet adopt-in" in honor of Chavez, a known SPCA supporter. On the fourth day the police show up because a man has been spotted selling two coolers worth of edibles along with unpermitted, slow-cooked beef brisket. Every night we have to create a diversion, a foil to sneak Chavez out the back that leads through a winding alley few cars bother to traverse because the potholes are the size of kiddie pools. On one of these nights I enlist Bugs and eight of his friends who come up with the idea of running to the studio completely painted head to toe as zombie runners. They announce to the crowd that it's the finish line of the 2018 Hampden Zombie Stalk 5k! *Does it matter that Halloween is over two months away?* Nope, not according to Bugs. The trick miraculously works. Chavez escapes in the silver SUV commanded by his Senegalese driver Kenny as the first hailstorm of "zombie guts"— water balloons filled with red food coloring—rain down on an already incensed crowd. *Merry Chavez-mas, everybody!*

As for the man himself, things have already started to take a weird turn. The day I know we need to switch locations or else lose all hope of getting anything worth saving Chavez presents me with what he believes to be the first ever "dope chime" constructed entirely of empty bottles of antidepressants filled with water to exact levels to offer a dynamic range of pitches when struck. A willing acolyte to any mysterious process of creation, I place individual mics around each of the prescription bottles. At his feet he's setup a bass pedal organ. Behind the smudged glass of the control room I watch as he erupts with child-like glee every time the intestine-rattling bass notes of the organ collide mysteriously with the pitches of his dope chime. "You hear that?" he shouts with his headphones cranked all the way, spoiling any exploratory recording in progress. But that's not the only thing spoiling the recording: something is blaring outside the studio, breaking through the soundproofing. I get up from my chair at the board and walk out into the hallway, pulling the door behind me. I look out the second story window into the street. A young African-American boy is jumping up and down waving a bullhorn in his hand. It's about four o'clock in the afternoon. A dozen hardy souls are already camped outside, many of them I recognize as the real core of Chavez followers, the true believers. Sure enough, cat girl is there. She has her prophetic feline who knows the real messages behind Chavez's songs attached to a leash at her feet. A pair of feathery wings sprouts up from a leather bustier attached to the poor animal's back. There are simply no words.

The kid got up onto a milk crate and raised his hand. A murmur went through the crowd and then it fell silent, except for a few people shouting words of encouragement at him. The kid acknowledged them with a nod and a shy smile. In the full light of day, he looked less angry and more beautiful. He waited until people stopped shouting. A siren could be heard, maybe five or ten blocks away. The kid raised the bullhorn, pressed the button, and began to speak:

"Ladies and gentlemen…WE ARE DIRECT N' EFFECT!" At this announcement spinning out from behind a parked car appeared another kid about his same age dressed in a heavy Rocca Wear sweatshirt holding pieces of cardboard and a small speaker in his hands. He positions the cardboard carefully on the ground then clicks on the speaker to full blast. Distorted bass and dirty South ride cymbal fill the airways. The kid on the milk crate starts rapping with the bullhorn over the beat while his partner performs backflips, one hand twists and stalls, a barrage of impressive break-dancing moves while the crowd watches completely entranced. I hear the door behind me unlatch and Chavez come to stand at my shoulder. "Man, we should get those kids in here," he says. I turn and flash him a look like somebody's mother watching her kid about to put his pinky into an electric socket. "Grab your guitar," I say. "We're getting out of here. I know a place we can go where we won't be bothered." He looks at me despondently then glances back down at the street just as Direct n' Effect alternate positions between rapper and break-dancer. "Really?" he says. Then he sees the cat girl. He sighs. "Fine. But I'm bringing my dope chime."

After a quick pit stop at Chavez's condo for clothes and his faithful dog Tupelo, we are speeding along 83 North in Kenny's SUV that smells like vanilla, sex, and weed all rolled together. Kenny is the happiest person I've ever met. But as Chavez's driver and bodyguard I'm also terrified of him—almost as terrified as I am of Tupelo who never lets his one good eye off me from the front seat, raising his lip periodically in my direction while panting beneath one of Chavez's arms. As the sun dissolves in a crimson wash behind us Kenny tells me about how his ancestors in Senegal were some of the first African musicians, the first rappers, in fact. Their bodies were buried in *baobab* trees instead of village ground because they were basically the ancient equivalent of stoners never wanting to contribute to the rigors of village life, just laze about all day and play music.

"There are these guys called *griots*. They don't work. They just like to sing. All the time they are singing. They are lazy these guys. But the women, the women all want them. You know the Genesis Peter Gabriel? He sings with Youssou N'Dour. This guy Youssou is like a *griot* who comes back from dead. I don't think he likes women. He just likes to sing. I think Mr. Chavez is *griot*, too. Very lazy. Like his dog." He bursts into laughter so strong it shakes the car. Or maybe that's just the wind. I really can't tell.

Chavez comes in and out of the conversation. He turns around and grins at me after hearing the part about Kenny's *griot* ancestors being buried inside trees. Then he goes back to making notches in his diary, perhaps noting the amount of telephone poles along the road or the seams in the concrete. I look at the bag of mics at my feet and the suitcase. It's a surprise. I don't know how he'll react. We've got nothing usable from the two weeks of demos—the first week at my apartment before the jerk chicken lady had a noise ordinance citation sent our way; and the second week at the studio exploring the dope chime and being mobbed by cat girl, amateur beatboxers, and skate fans who still remember Chavez fighting Tony Hawk and most of the Bones Brigade in a bootlegged skate video from the 1980's. Inside a latched suitcase on the seat next to me is an Akai GX-77 reel-to-reel recorder, the same machine Chavez used to record *Gutter Garden* all those many years ago. *It's a long shot...* but frankly a better starting point than prescription bottle and foot organ duets.

We're headed to Hannah's parents' cabin. It sits on the world's greatest sledding hill overlooking a long-defunct 120 acre cattle farm some twenty miles outside York, PA. Ever since we started dating it's been a mental retreat for us. Hannah commutes four days a week to an art college in Lancaster where she teaches graphic design. There was a time when the spark and court went out of our relationship and we would retreat to the cabin to patch things up without any roommates or distractions getting in the way. There is no place like Baltimore. Only New Orleans tops the city in sheer amount of cultural mojo. But the city kind of nibbles at you even when you're asleep, just like that weird movie about the cannibalistic husband Chavez almost had his songs included in. You have to get out now and then and see trees that don't have plastic bags all stuck to them. You have to see stars.

We reach the cabin after dark and I jump out to unlock the gate. We rumble over the old grates installed long ago to keep the cattle from getting out. Tupelo casts me a final look. I see it now clear as day: *the path to his master and the record we need to make comes through him and him alone.* That's why there's a second bag at my feet stocked to the gills with dog treats. We pass the one light installed in the driveway to keep people like Bugs and his drunken friends from rolling their cars over the side of the fifty foot drop to the valley below. In the passing glow of the orange lamplight Tupelo's eyes lock with mine. *You're in my house now,* I tell him. *Actually, it's not my house…it's my girlfriend's. Actually, it's not even hers. But you get the idea.* I hold up the bag and make some seductive crinkles. I feed him a pretzel dog treat that looks exactly like his lipstick he proudly waves at the world every other second. *House = not yours,* I tell him with my eyes. *Treats = endless if you just let me get one song out of him this weekend. Just one song. That's all I want.* One song. His snarling upper lip relaxes like a Cold War *detente*. *Okay,* I tell myself. ƒ

Sometime in the middle of the first night at the cabin a scream goes through the house. I wake up completely disoriented. Instinctively, I fumble for the light on the side table…but it's not there, because we're not in Baltimore. I zombie walk for a few seconds through the dark towards the doorway framed by a faint rectangle of light coming from the Glade plug-in in the hallway Hannah's mom loves but smells like old lady perfume. The screaming gets louder. Tupelo is barking batshit crazy. I start thinking about whether or not the cabin has an emergency medical kit. Or more importantly: *do we have any cell reception.* A vision of my summer camp CPR class flashes across my mind's eye. I make it up the stairs, tripping on the fourth step and banging my knee so hard that pain knocks the wind out of me. I pull myself up and make it to the landing and run to Chavez's door. The screaming and barking finally stops. I fly into the room to find a scene like something out of a David Lynch movie.

Tupelo sits in the middle of the room completely still, lipstick out as usual. I can see Chavez, but he's all but disappeared like a baby inside Kenny's massive black arms. Kenny's rocking him...*rocking the icon of millions like a toddler who has just had a night terror.* I don't even think Chavez knows I'm there. In the light of the room's single lamp Kenny stares up at me. He smiles a big gummy smile like everything is perfectly normal, like it's just part of his job. I hover in the doorway for a few moments looking at the bizarre scene—the pill bottles on the table and the various other vials filled with weed tinctures. Feeling out of place, like a voyeur in a peephole of someone else's intimate experience, I retreat and head back down the stairs to my room. I fall back into bed and clutch my bruised knee. *What the hell did I just see?* I drift back into the folds of sleep as a deep cooing sound—Kenny's voice—ushers the genius upstairs back into some semblance of peace.

The next morning I wake up late and groggy. I find Kenny on the porch speaking loudly in another language. He's perched on the porch railing waving his arms and laughing heartily with an earpiece poking out of one ear. He points to the field out front. I descend the steps gingerly like an old man. The pain in my knee has receded from a 10 to a 7 thanks to some Aleve recovered from Hannah's mother's bathroom. I hobble across the thick, unmowed grass until I find Chavez. He's setup a small card table from the porch and placed it directly on the hillside overlooking the epic sledding drop. Tupelo sits at his feet and raises his lip unsurprisingly at me as I walk up. I see a flurry of pages on the table weighed down with rocks. I'm half expecting to see another OCD tapestry of ink scratches. But instead as I come to stand at his shoulder I see a different scene on the page. Gorgeous pen and ink drawings of all sorts of faces and animals wrap around the edges of the paper. In the center of the open page there are words. My heart speeds up a few beats. *Lyrics. Oh God, please be lyrics.*

"Hey, Eric," Chavez says turning to greet me. His hair is tied back and he looks smaller in his seat at the table. *And older*, I think. *He looks terrible.* He reminds me of the drawings in my European History book from high school of the surviving members of Napoleon's army limping home after the failed invasion of Russia. I ask him what he's working on. I can see the guitar case open at his feet and the small parlor guitar—the same one he used to play two songs on SNL last month—wedged out of the case with the capo still on. He's been playing.

He stops drawing for a second. It's a beautiful, detailed face, more detailed than the others. A woman with coal-black hair and full lips stares up from the page with inquiring eyes that hold me in my place for a few seconds. Chavez laughs a little and looks down at his work like a child examining the world he or she has just created out of thin air. "I got a message yesterday on my fake Facebook account," he says. I almost spit out my coffee. *Chavez has a fake Facebook account?* "Yeah," he continues, picking up the pen again. "Don't you think it's weird that people feel the need to share everything? I mean *everything*. Last week I got a friend request from some guy in Atlanta who just posts pictures of assault rifles. Oh and the Atlanta Falcons. He's a big Falcons fan." He pauses. He looks up at me with glassy eyes. The smile slips a little. "I'm sorry we haven't come up with anything you can use yet. I'm going to work on some songs today. Tupelo told me to get my ass in gear. He's a real slave driver." *That's one word for him*, I think. I tell Chavez about the upright piano in the living room. He nods with muted interest then goes back to drawing. Then I mention the Akai reel-to-reel recorder and he stops what he's doing like he's just heard aliens have landed at the U.S. Capitol. His entire body language changes. For the next ten minutes he flies through everything there is to know about reel-to-reel recorders. When he's done I want to kick myself for not recording his impromptu TED Talk. I ask him if he wants me to go setup the machine. He says not yet. I start to worry if "Not Yet" is going to be the name of this record. Maybe it's my youthful idolizing kicking back in, but I don't push him. I have to trust that some kind of magic will find him out here parked on the edge of this hill looking down at the bent and storm-wracked barns. I'm hoping it's enough space to swallow up whatever monster makes him wake screaming in the middle of the night.

I leave him and Tupelo to the process. By nightfall I realize that I'm dealing with a different Chavez. We sit in the middle of the dusty living room with the mics all around us. He's requested a change in vibe. Kenny moves the furniture to the sides while I do my best to assemble Hannah's mother's least noxious candles from the bottom drawers of every bathroom cupboard. We are reaching that unplanned, indescribable zone. I can feel it. No full songs yet, just snippets. But it's coming. Chavez sits with his back to me at the keyboard. I play enough guitar to be useful—major seventh and weird minor shapes to augment the melody lines he's pulling from the piano. Every now and then I hit something that works and he smiles back at me and the prematurely old person from earlier that morning on the hillside disappears. In the light of the candles he looks thirteen. I watch in awe at the process. He takes a melody then backs it up, twisting and bending it until it's sweeter, like a clearer, more direct language between new lovers. He still doesn't want anything recorded on the Akai, but he's allowed me to use my laptop to document the session. From the time I left him on the hillside to sundown he's assembled pages of lyrics. An old banker's lamp sits on the Knabe upright illuminating his scrawled testimonies. The world's most precarious joint hangs on top of the piano, but just when I think it's going to fall Chavez reaches out and snatches it and puts it in the corner of his mouth. The air is thick. I can see Kenny's white teeth gleaming in a corner of the room untouched by the candlelight. Music fills the wooden walls as Chavez's voice rises and falls from some smoky bellows in his stomach. The words change the architecture of every passing moment. He's singing about a girl with forgiving eyes. *A lover? A girlfriend?* I realize I know nothing about the man seated at the piano other than the little I've read in interviews. But I know if I close my eyes I can feel the crunch of gravel spilling under me, a moonlit stretch of pines through the Green Mountains rustling past too fast to be substantial, and that voice guiding me like a compass towards some manifest destination, a vague Valhalla that only the hopeful and the insane rush to with fire in their bellies and absolutely no fear of turning back.

Sit back in your chair, Juliet
I'll tell you the lies I've spun
The filament and the net
To keep me warm when you're gone
The red-eyed women
& the lamplighters
Beneath the bridge's bend
To keep me warm when you're gone...

Around 1 a.m. he rakes his hand through his sweaty hair and swivels around. The session is over. The elastic bending of magic time straightens. The only sound now is Kenny snoring from the couch. I wonder how he can sleep through it all. But I have a feeling this is not the first five-hour musical *séance* he's been privy to in Chavez's company. For a few moments I can't muster words. I reach over and click stop on the session on the laptop. Chavez gathers up the lyrics then walks over and hands them to me. He smiles and the sadness that wells in his eyes seems to dissipate a little. "That was pretty rad," he says. "I haven't…well…" He smiles and the thirteen year-old from before resurfaces. "Thanks." I make some stupid remark to cover the emotion garbling up my throat. My hands are shaking. Thankfully, Tupelo farts and cuts the awkward silence in the room. "We'll hit it again tomorrow," Chavez says. "Good guitar playing, by the way. I never knew." Tupelo gets up from under the piano and follows his master to the staircase. Chavez smiles again then disappears up the steps. I sit for a moment in the candlelight holding the lyrics. The page on top has the drawing of the woman's face with the coal-black hair and searching eyes. He's written under her face in swooping cursive. *My Forever Darling. Forgive Me.*

It's Sunday morning after the epic creative session and I'm cooking breakfast for everyone. As I pull the bacon out of the oven my phone starts to ring. It's Hannah. She's blown a tire halfway between Baltimore and the cabin. Apparently she was on her way to surprise us with some "home baked recording fuel" when she hit the pothole. "Surprise!" she says and lets out a forced laugh. I look at the bacon that's blackening and disintegrating before my eyes like it's been placed under a rocket at Cape Canaveral. Man, I suck at cooking. I tell Hannah to stay put. I leave the charred remains of the bacon on the stove to smoke out. I pull the smoke alarm off the wall as I walk through the mud room to the garage. I can't take Kenny's car in case another emergency happens while I'm gone. So I turn on the garage light, brush a few cobwebs from my mouth, and pull back the tarp on Hannah's grandmother's ancient Mercury. I say a little prayer as I turn the cold key in the ignition. Fortunately, the automotive gods are on my side. The engine sputters and coughs then settles to a throaty hum. I let the car warm up and head out to the hillside. I find Chavez sitting on the edge of the hill without his guitar. Tupelo lies spread-eagle on his back, Chavez rubbing his belly while staring blankly out at the drop below. He doesn't even turn at the sound of my feet.

"Hey, man! Good morning!" I say as I walk up. "Hannah was coming up to surprise us and blew out a tire. I gotta go help her get it sorted out. I screwed up the bacon. But there's eggs and toast on the stove if you and Kenny are hungry. I don't think I'll be gone too long. A couple hours, maybe." He nods a little. I ask him if he's okay. He nods again then goes back to scratching Tupelo's belly. I stand there with the wind sweeping up through the valley, the sound of a crow up in one of the pine trees doing its dismissive *aat-aat* call. I feel brave enough since our musical bonding session to ask him if he's really okay, if he needs me or Kenny to get him something. He summons a smile that looks like he's fighting back tears. It's one of those moments you don't get back, when you never say the right definitive line from the handbook of universal human communication. There are so many pages torn out of that book. You can recover some of them with time, but they get blown out of reach. All you can do is scramble on your hands and knees and reach your hardest, hoping you recover the simplest, most direct line to the heart of the matter *when* it matters most. He had Kenny as an anchor. And of course he had Tupelo. I wasn't a *familiar* to his world. I don't believe in sin—not in some kind of impassive equalizer of preceding and semi-permanent doom. But what I do believe is that we *should* all be familiars to each other when it comes to mental illness. If sin exists it must exist in silence, multiplied and fed like a virus in the spaces between what we are not willing to say. I didn't know then it would be the last time I'd see Chavez. Even if I could have had some clairvoyant window into his future plans there was still no timing for what I would have wanted to say. I would have told him that he was surrounded by love on all sides. And, above all, I would have said thank you.

By the time I get back to the cabin it's dusk. Few tire shops along 83 stay open Sundays, so we put the dummy tire on Hannah's car and drive it back to Baltimore to be worked on in the morning. She hands me two packages of chocolate-oatmeal cookies and kisses me at the foot of the steps that lead up to our apartment. She asks me how everything is going. I tell her about last night—about the amazing session and how I could see the beginnings of something really special. "Beginnings?" she says, cracking a smile. But she knows better than to drive home the obvious point: *we are way behind schedule.* She kisses me again, and I climb back into her grandmother's car. It nearly gives up the ghost when I turn the ignition. Hannah stares down at me from the curb with the expression of someone watching an amateur bomb diffuser vacillate between the red or blue wire. But the car hacks its way into a steady hum and I'm off again. When I'm about a half hour from the cabin I get a call from Sheila. She wants to know how things are going. *Is a Christmas release still feasible?* I lie through my teeth and assure her it is. Then she lets me know that Chavez has left the cabin and is en route to a benefit in Chicago, but that he'll be back on Tuesday in Baltimore to resume recording. I don't know which is harder to process—the fact that I've been left out of the loop of these plans, or the fact that we are supposed to "resume" recording on Tuesday in a place that seems impossible to get any work done. We end the conversation on a note of false promise that does not correspond at all with the image I have in my mind of the semi-catatonic man from earlier that morning sitting on a hillside rubbing his dog's belly.

I reach the cabin and open the front door. The smell of burnt bacon still hangs in the air. I hold the two bags of cookies in my hand like someone arriving for an abandoned housewarming party. Behind me the last auburn and orange rays of the sun filter in through a crack in one of the lace curtains. It's then that I notice that the Akai reel-to-reel has been moved across the room.

※

A few days before Chavez's funeral Sheila calls me. For the first minute of the conversation we do a broken dance around our mutual confusion and sadness. I've never met Sheila, but she's started to feel *familiar*, like a cousin you knew growing up but rarely see since they moved to the opposite coast. After we share our respective ways of getting by since the news broke, she drops the bombshell. "He has a will," she says, getting choked up. "It looks… well, it looks like he made it before the sessions started." I feel my heart sink to the pit of my stomach. "Eric…I'm sorry. I had no idea he was…well, I had no idea. Everything goes to his wife and son in Oakland." Some viral video I've seen that week flashes across my mind's eye: *a woman with coal-black hair and searching eyes standing outside a chain-link fence with a teenage boy wearing a Golden State Warriors jersey slunk behind her in the shadows. His wife and son.* "The label is going to put out some kind of tribute record," she continues, sadness now changing to bitterness. "They need everything you have from the sessions." I tell her all I have is the ambient recording of the session in the cabin full of starts and stops, tweaks, not to mention intermittent farts by Tupelo. "They still need it," she presses. "I can't believe they are capitalizing on all this. It's gross. Really gross. Anyway…are you sure that's all there is?" As she says this the fine hairs on my neck start to tingle. "I need to call you back," I say. I hang up the phone. It's a little after three in the morning on the east coast. I'm sitting in our living room in the darkness broken only by the moon or the light pollution—I can't tell which. I'm the only one in the apartment who can admit their insomnia by not trying to toss and turn in bed. I look at the Akai reel-to-reel on the floor next to a canvas bag full of Hannah's paints. It's been untouched since the return from the cabin. *He moved it at the cabin. It was under the chair and he moved it.*

I get up and cross the room. I setup the machine and wire it for playback through a speaker on the floor. Hannah's at my shoulder a few moments after the first words echo through the apartment. We stand there holding each other in the artificial light while we listen to a ghost. "This is called 'Like Machines,'" a throaty, smoker's voice says. And then the parlor guitar comes in. It rings out, fingerpicked with delicate intonation and natural reverb, bass and melody in the same hand in the Piedmont style. When he starts to sing I can feel Hannah's heart beating against the sides of my ribs.

> *Got a Book of Faces*
> *A thousand friends who say they know me well*
> *Got wires in all the places*
> *Says I'm connected but it's hard to tell*
> *I'll update them sometime, say I'm feeling fine*
> *But you know that that's a lie*
> *'Cause over and over*
> *The surface it covers*
> *But Sisters and Brothers*
> *There's a deeper well*
> *Don't give me a picture of your toes*
> *I wanna feel your hand on my Soul*
> *Tell me where do we go*
> *When we don't need to tell*
> *Don't need to tell it to machines?*

I turn back to find Bugs' bearded face looking at me abstracted like some ghoul in the weird pink light. "Holy shit," he says. We listen to the whole track…and then again. *And again…*It's a five minute testimony of dissatisfaction with where we've come as a people, having infinite access to sharing information but not necessarily any increase in vital human connection. When it's over there's a long pause. Then Tupelo barks. There's nothing else on the reel. Just the one last song. We stand there for a while like loiterers at an unplanned wake. Hannah comes up with the idea. She and Bugs gather up all the materials while I box up the tape from the recording. I tell them I'll meet them at the spot after I head to the studio for a bit. It's almost four in the morning now. Outside the city is oddly peaceful—no one honking, no one shouting expletives from their car window. We head our separate ways with our separate tasks that feel as important as prepping a bomb shelter for an imminent blast. I get to the underpass on Falls Road an hour and a half later to find Hannah on a ladder beneath a large mural half obscured by the shadows of the underpass. Bugs stands at attention at Hannah's side, flashlight in one hand, a can of paint in the other. Hannah gets down from the ladder and holds a paint-caked hand to her forehead surveying her work. The light from Bug's flashlight and the soft blue light that comes right before dawn faintly illuminate the mural. Bugs tells me that no cops or night creepers pass them the whole time. It's like an unspoken pact has been reached with the city to let them get their job done in peace.

We stand there until the sun comes up. Hannah's painted an incredible likeness of him: the crow's feet and the cracked smile, the black hair with the faint blue you sometimes get in the coats of wild animals. Paint is splattered all over her—her clothes, her cheeks, along the fine bird-like collarbones that peek up from her t-shirt. We collapse back against the hood of Hannah's car gazing up at the mural while Bugs finally sets down the brushes and paint cans like a man who has been released from artillery duty. At the base of the mural I've stacked burned copies of Chavez's last song "Like

Machines." They're there for anyone to take and listen—in the old way. That's what I'm hoping at least. I want it to feel like a mixtape someone handed you long ago with the ink still not dry, full of songs from someone else's experience that somehow reflected the light of your own. I'm sure the label is going to crucify me for it. I don't care. We stand there letting ourselves be gutted by the scene, the stamp of it being real, final. Who knew how long the mural would stay up? It didn't matter. Before we leave, Hannah paints some of the lyrics from the song next to the mural. I hold her hand when it's over. I can feel the hollow places left by his passing starting to fill with something. The beginnings of peace, maybe.

> *Got my sights on Sunday*
> *But Tuesday cuts me right at the knees*
> *Try to rest on Mondays*
> *But there's someone in my brain that just don't sleep*
> *All the beer and all the wine*
> *Can taste like turpentine*
> *When that pick-me-up is just a letdown in time*
> *'Cause over and over*
> *The surface it covers*
> *But Sisters and Brothers*
> *There's a deeper well*
> *Don't want to numb down my Soul*
> *Want to feel the rock and the roll*
> *Hear your voice on my phone*
> *Before you text it*
> *Before you text it like a machine*

Some nights when I feel this city nibbling at me I take out my phone and find the voicemail. I walk to the shrine looking up at the telephone lines painted in the moonlight, the way they crisscross the potholed boulevards spreading human connection, or at least they used to—before the satellites took over, bouncing our voices up into the dark invisible ether. *Hear your voice on my phone before you text it like a machine*…I hold the speaker up to my ear. I hear Sheila pass the phone while the gulls screech in the background and the surf crashes and recedes. Then he's there, that wavering smoker's voice and frail laugh on the other line between past and present, life and death. "Hey, Eric," he says. "I'm standing on a really crappy beach. I think my toes are getting sunburned. They look like cocktail wieners…"

Coloboma

ROB ROWNTREE

◆

Beyond the cracked sidewalk, and the telephone pole with layers of flyers in a rainbow of colours, and the patch of dry brown grass there stood a ten-foot high concrete block wall, caked with dozens of coats of paint. There was a small shrine at the foot of it, with burnt out candles and dead flowers and a few soggy teddy bears. One word of graffiti filled the wall, red letters on a gold background: Rejoice!

Daniel reached forward, depressed a window switch and as the vehicle's smoked glass rose, he took one more look at the wall. Surely this pathetic shrine, this damp excuse for a meeting place, held little interest for the Azua. Just a cold, dank remnant, a wish born of wastrels and misfits. Sound interrupted: the distant noise of Azua surface vehicles mixed with city police sirens toyed with Daniel's hearing and as the ground effect vehicle's window shut with a snick, his gaze settled on the scrawled graffiti. He felt heat caress his cheek. No, he fought against the emotion, he'd done his best, worked hard to carve out a life after the change. Survival had no use of shame, and Daniel knew that if he let it in, he'd never be rid of it. He waved a hand to signal his driver and as the vehicle glided away from the sodden flowers and teddy bears, the red paint of the graffiti tugged at his mind. He'd look elsewhere and find the boy that had his masters rattled. He'd do his duty.

Acceleration pushed Daniel back in to the vehicle's plush seats. He caressed the faux leather seating, a perk most people would now never know and wondered at his good fortune. No accident had brought him to this point, no hand of fate. Just hard work and acceptance of the new reality. Glancing at his driver he caught the man's face in the rear-view mirror. Did he detect reproach? Daniel shook his head. The driver said, "What?" Daniel ignored him, the man had no right to criticise. Aware that some called him traitor, Daniel had come to a comfortable mental arrangement with the facts of his new existence. He called it, expedience. They could go to hell.

As the car moved out of the urban decay once known as Detroit, he reached into his pocket and fetched out his decorative pillbox. One tab forced a chemical calm upon him. His qualms receding, he absently gazed from the car. Below, queues of workers; grey clothing against dower concrete jostled listlessly ready to begin their production shifts. The Azua needed Quar; we made it. Since the Azua's arrival, humanity had done little else.

In a bizarre twist of ironic fate, the Azua allowed an underworld of sorts to flourished. A wise decision on their part? Perhaps? The illusion of some normality at least paved the way for less intervention. Petty disputes, some measure of order. Illusions all, yet this quasi-substratum had its uses. Daniel decided he'd look there after he'd reported in. He'd soon find the boy's location.

The expressway took his vehicle higher, leaving public roads and greyness behind. His vehicle slipped smoothly in amongst elite traffic on Gov-tier and from his seat he saw the so-called Enablers sliding by in their sleek pods, the odd warbling sound they made just discernible within Daniel's vehicle. A smile parted his lips; Enablers, just flunkies, survivors finding a way to make a space, to live. *The Azua required no assistance.* In their presence your very soul is open to them. A mere wish or though could cease existence. But some of these fools, these remnants of the rich and powerful persisted in their elitist delusions and unfortunately, Daniel's position as Arbiter liaison forced the same status upon him. He'd gladly shake it off. Ahead, the huge twisted spires of Azua compound reached heavenward, the shade and darkness of old Detroit vanishing as sunlight caressed the golden towers' surfaces. He'd have to report, yet he had nothing. *Where and how?* A young boy, ten or some said twelve years-old, street smart, places to hide and now, after his blizzard of Rejoice tagging, people to hide him. *Where and how?* He might not know the answer to that, but he realised he knew people that might.   Reaching up and forward, Daniel tapped the glass partition.   The driver, Cort or Caul, switched the vehicle to driverless and spun his seat around. The glass slid down. "Yes?"

"Take me to the Souq, to Jamal's place." He'd have to press, but he'd get something, anything. The Azua required results. He'd provide some. Cort just sat staring. "Something wrong Cort?" Cort shrugged and turned back to the control panel. Moments later the vehicle pulled off Gov-tier and head down and east, towards old Detroit.   Daniel heard the driver mutter, "Caul", and the car sped on.

Unconsciously, Daniel pushed back into his seating. The vehicle he travelled in drew attention, especially here amongst the workers and drifters. As the car manoeuvred through the narrow streets Daniel allowed a small mantra to calm his mind; he'd been trained and coached, most situation management required only two things, the ability to analyse and to communicate. Graffiti drifted by, gold on red, Rejoice! On street, corner, and wall, Rejoice! Surely just misplaced rebellion, a mental crutch for the masses. No doubt worrisome for his masters, but a trifling matter, all the same.

Jamal's club, Perpetual Change, shone like an ocean liner on a dark sea. Brash light blasted out from its gawdy facia illuminating a small square. A rough patch of ground held sway in the square's centre, rusted metalwork testament to an earlier era as a kid's playground. Daniel turned his gaze away, looked up, past the vertigo inducing buildings to spy a thin sliver of blue sky. Down here in the Souq, one could be forgiven for thinking the world remained in constant darkness. He exited the car and made his way inside. Jamal always held court at a reserved booth on a mezzanine overlooking the club's dance floor. Daniel hated having to compete with the noise. As the heavy-set bouncer escorted him through sweet smelling smoke towards Jamal, Daniel decided to take the high ground.

Jamal appeared relaxed, slumped backward lounging on the plush, expensive velvet of his private booth's seating. Daniel always thought he looked ill, thin and pale, scrawny, but behind the thin face sharp observant eyes soaked up their surroundings. Drugs no doubt lent an air of deathliness to the man's appearance, but those eyes added intent.

Make it official. Daniel reached into his pocket and before the bouncer reacted brought out his badge. Jamal gave the employee a quick nod and then brought his attention back to Daniel. He looked hard at the badge, too hard. "You bring that out, here. No curtesy."

Daniel hoped the flicker in Jamal's eyes was an indication of humour. "Not here. In back, your rooms." Daniel hoped his instruction held gravitas, he needed Jamal to move and not start a scene. For a moment hesitation held sway, a questioning look ghosting across the club owner's face. Daniel said, "Now. I don't want to drag a squad down here. And nor do you." Jamal looked about his club, glanced at the young and carefree, the drugged and the drunk, then he stood, straightened a lapel and finally extended a hand indicating that Daniel lead the way.

Jamal's rooms consisted of a large sitting room, an open plan bar/kitchen and a small hallway leading to bathroom and bedrooms.

The sitting room had a squat occasional table in the centre of a sunken sofa-nest, on the far wall a real log fire dominated as it burned in an ornate fireplace. A scent of burnt pine and citrus pervaded the air and gentle orchestral music filled the air.

A sudden rush of movement from Jamal brought the thin man's hand up and in, grasping for Daniel's neck. Daniel batted it away, took a step left and angled his body to present less of a target. Jamal darted in, threw an awkward punch, wobbled (*drugs?*), Daniel bent a knee, stepped forward reached up and hauled on the flailing arm, breathed in, expanded his chest and watched as Jamal flew over his shoulder onto one of the sofas. His thin body lay there, panting, a glazed expression on his face. Daniel said, "Stow the aggression Jay, I needed you somewhere quiet."

"My place. Mine. You come in and order me like some gutter grubber, me. Face man, I lost face." Daniel shook his head and moved over to the bar. There he threw ice into two glasses and poured vodkas. Back at the sofa, Jamal accepted the offered drink.

"Jay, I don't have a lot of time. That rat-shit boy is stirring up a heap of trouble. Not just for himself, but for everyone down here in the Souq. Azua are pissed. I don't find him, and they'll be exercising their own investigation. Now that's not good for business, not here, not out there," Daniel pointed for emphasis, "not anywhere. I know you know something, and I want it. You and I have our differences, sure enough, but this here thing is important. That kid has got them rattled. Worried."

Jamal rubbed at his shoulder, then said, "Always knew you were a hard-ass. How come you never came to work for me? I offered plenty of times." Daniel remained silent. Jamal then added, "Thinking you made the wrong decision? Can't be easy bowing and scraping to those yellow bastards. Must mess with your mind. What do they call it? Oh, yeah, a conflict of interest."

Daniel took a seat opposite Jamal. He thought the club owner had a point. After the change, security, money and a certain anonymity would have been his had chosen to work here in the Souq. But it felt like running away. *Had he wanted to?* "Better to try and work from the inside, change what little I could. Futile now. Yet at the time . . ."

Jamal smiled. Then said, "Futile?" Daniel watched as the club owner took a long sip of his drink. Like every other person in regular contact with the Azua, Daniel now understood the true meaning of the word 'futile'. His naïve aspirations to affect decisions from within, were driven by a pathetic misunderstanding. At the time he'd been sure there'd be opportunities. The Azua though saw everything, saw the very essence of person, could reach right in and examine a person's thoughts. No one escaped that. Daniel saw Jamal place his glass on the table, and then shake his head. "Daniel, you are so wrapped up in your guilt that you can't see unfolding events. I'd no sooner give up the boy than I would give up myself. Can't you see what's happening here? It's hope, it's a swell of public pride, longing, there's a sense of change in the air and writing on the wall." Jamal wagged a finger in Daniels direction. "And before you say it's futile and foolish just think on. Your masters are worried. Why is that?"

"They just want to stop unnecessary disruption. Why raise the hopes of a downtrodden workforce when it only makes their lives worse when reality bites back?" Daniel stood. "Last chance." Jamal remained stoic. "Right, fine, but when the Azua arrive don't come whinging to me about reduced takings." Daniel spun and slammed his way through the doors and on, out to the sidewalk. Finally outside, he stretched his arms back and took in a he lung-full of air. High above, full daylighted blue sky limned the upper reaches of tall buildings. A sudden shudder ran through his body. He reached into his pocket and retrieved his pill-box. One tab, just one to calm his nerves. As he swallowed, he glimpsed his driver waiting across the street.

Engine running and seated once more in the comfort of his vehicle, he decided to head back to the towers, however, before he could tell his driver, Cort turned in his seat and said, "He didn't provide the information, did he?" A lick of rain pattered across the vehicle's roof. *Had there been clouds a moment ago?*

"The whole town seems obsessed with this kid. Now, also you it would seem. All I want is to find him, to prevent any more rallies, any unwarranted political divergence. It's a kid with a spray can, a tag, and a hook into society's underclass. It's trouble brewing. Just want to stop it before it begins."

"My name is Caul. For the past two years you've known that, but always called me Cort. I tolerated that for hope, for the promises of a very unusual boy, and now, today that boy is going to change the world. There's a little part of you, Daniel, a small corner of your mind that wonders why the Azua are concerned. Don't deny it, it's a broad as the guilt you ware. So, if you'll allow me, I'll show you why. I may be a man without a memorable name, but I do possess information. Later today, I'll be with that boy, with a crowd of attentive followers and you could be there too. . ."

He hadn't wanted to agree, but he had his mission. Arrival at the distressed remains of an old sports stadium came on like a historical vid, all noise, crowds and clamouring people pressed up against the car. Hundreds, if not thousands threaded their way inside. Caul parked and ushered Daniel out. As he exited the car the stench of unwashed flesh assaulted his nose. He gaged, and managed to hold down his lunch, before easing into the moving crowd behind Caul. Daniel drifted with the flow, he had no choice, and presently he filed into the dusty arena. Over the heads of those around him Daniel saw a stage erected some thirty metres away: candles, teddy bears, flowers. People milled about the platform and then he spied the boy. Shirt hanging outside his pants, ruffled blond hair, his head at an angle, a scowl pinched his face. He might have been called angelic in another age, but a rough edge drew the comparison away. Possibly some aspect of the growing crowd displeased him. Daniel wanted to be closer. Dangling from the boy's left hand a bullhorn swung back and forth. Presently, an anticipation settled on the crowd. The teddy bears drew his gaze and for a moment he thought about roadside memorials and lost loved ones.

The kid got up onto a milk crate and raised his hand. A murmur went through the crowd and then it fell silent, except for a few people shouting words of encouragement at him. The kid acknowledged them with a nod and a shy smile. In the full light of day, he looked less angry and more beautiful. He waited until people stopped shouting. A siren could be heard, maybe five or ten blocks away. The kid raised the bullhorn, pressed the button, and began to speak.

"Rejoice. Our time is come. Rejoice as our re-education of those that would oppress us begins. Rejoice." Around Daniel all hell broke loose. People cheered, shouted out, and on the far side of the sports ground a chant of "rejoice, rejoice" spontaneously filled the air. How could a small kid be so calm, so stage crafted? It didn't ring true. Grasping Caul's arm Daniel pointed and edged closer to the stage. He needed more information and there wouldn't be much time. Azua technology woven into his skin had already provided the location of the meeting. But the information he sought now was of a more personal nature. The boy held a fascination that tantalised and toyed with Daniel's curiosity. *Could there be something here?*

As they edged closer to the stage, Daniel notice Caul receive curt nods as if in recognition, the occasional mouthed hello. The platform's edge blocked further movement. Caul waved at a security guard who rapidly forced a path between the front of the crowd and the distressed wood panelling of the stage. Daniel gasped as strong arms dragged him along.

On the stage the boy looked in his direction. Suddenly Daniel felt elated, over joyed and a longing settled upon him. The familiar sensation caused him to spin and look for the Azua, there mental massaging a sure sign of their presence. A crowd of humans, a dirty dusty arena, but no floating craft, no tall yellow aliens.

Again the sensation flooded in, forced its pressured calm. Stronger now. He turned once more and saw the boy. Nearer, the youth's face radiated a serene smile, while his pale blue eyes fixed Daniel with a deep, penetrating stare. No. It couldn't, but…

He saw that the boy's left eye held a defect, a Coloboma, the dark patch a hole extending the pupil into a distorted star. *Guilt is darkness.* A genetic distortion. *Was it possible that the boy's DNA held more secrets, more surprises?* On the stage edge, the boy knelt and raised his bull horn. "Here he is, my Judas." He indicated Daniel with an out-stretched hand and an accusing finger, the crowd surged, and then the boy quickly said, "No, please remain calm, it is no more or less than I wanted. This man searched for me and knowing that allowed me to organise my first meeting with our masters. He played his part and he too will see redemption. Rejoice. Rejoice."

Daniel shook his head. Having one set of masters with mind controlling *gifts* was more than most people could bare, having two would be intolerable. Perhaps this rebellion had potential, but he'd be damned if he'd let his hard work over the past few years vanish in a rush of hysterical group madness. He mounted the stage, approached the boy.

The boy ignored him and instead pointed off into the sky. Daniel followed the indicating arm and saw several float plates approaching over the distressed grey buildings. There were three, each carrying four upright Azua, their yellow, unclothed bodies held a subtle internal radiance that made them at once mesmerizingly beautiful and utterly alien. Their approach remained steady, statesmanlike. *Sorrow has a dark heart.*

How had it come to this? Years of careful, steady, quiet planning, undone. He remembered cool nights on a veranda, the afternoon's warmth held tight in the newly painted woodwork, early firebugs dancing with porch lights. He'd been so proud, so smug. His neighbour, a Quar collection regulator had, Daniel recalled, accepted Daniel's self-bolstering diatribe with good humour and now he saw his reasoning as nothing more than internal justification. He'd sold out. First to the new invading masters and now, worst of all he'd sold out a small boy on some suicidal crusade. It couldn't really be like this. Surely a puppet master lay behind the boy's message. Some deranged fool.

The crowd thinned, parted and as the Azua landed their floats Daniel saw some people flee. The boy came up beside him, reached out a hand to grasp his in role reversed comfort. *Fear has a dark heart*, but here a spark shone.

Azua are tall. Propelled on a multitude of stubby legs they sway as they move, thin saplings in some uncontrolled resonance. Of course, no one knew much about them. Their tall slim bodies held parallel, upright rows of small tentacles, that ran upward towards a rounded domed organ. The head? A scent pervaded the air, honeysuckle and spice. Was it real or some mind trick? Did it matter?

Four Azua now stood at the foot of the stage, their immense height forced Daniel to lean backward and gaze upward. He hesitated, looked down and around the stage at the teddy bears, flowers and candles and once again he saw the similarities with accident shrines. A memory kept alive, a place of remembrance. So simple and yet so poignant. Had the boy selected this iconography on purpose to elicit a deep-rooted sense of the familiar? Of loss? But to what end? A large yellow domed head lowered into Daniel's eye line. Pushed in close.

Music, glorious and uplifting echoed loud in Daniel's mind, closely followed by pastoral images of Azua and their happy client race, humans, walking in unity through unbroken fields of green. The image held such power that for a moment Daniel wondered if it was real. But then a small boy appeared, holding a red balloon. He smiled at Daniel, waved a hand washing away the beauty, replacing green fields with grey block buildings, blood streaked streets and cold howling wind.

Struggling to free his mind, Daniel shook his head as if it would free him somehow from the mental battle taking place there. Two masters were worse than one. It needed to end. Opening his eyes, he saw the boy head to head with two of the Azua.

As he watched his mind filtered out the fireworks dancing there. The boy dropped the bullhorn, as it clattered to the floor Daniel knew that the Azua had control, they were in the boy's mind, probing, twisting, destroying. *The mind is Darkness.*

The boy's hand slipped free from Daniel's sweaty palm and for a moment, sorrow nestled in Daniel's mind. The boy surely meant no harm, he just wanted things the way they were, the way they should have been. The boy's shoulders slumped. Should he be punished so severely? Daniel, Judas. A witness to a new sacrifice.

One of the Azua quivered. A wave raced the length of its body generating shimmer in its internal light. Daniel had never seen that before and beautiful as it was, he found the development odd. As he watched the two remaining Azua bend and drifted their large domed heads down and towards the young boy's face. A smile lay there, small but strong.

Daniel felt a release, a slippage in his mind and found that he could move freely. He backed away but found he wanted to remain, to bear witness. The boy shrugged and slowly raised his right hand. Daniel saw what he was about to do and reacted. "Don't."

The few people that had remained, gasped as the boy reached out and gently caressed the nearest Azua. Almost a supplication, as if the boy wanted to offer a chance. There appeared to be pity in the boy's eyes, a simple act of forgiveness.

The Azua shivered. Its body began to shake racked by some internal physical conflict it writhed, shuddered and wobbled. As it did so a dull grey patch began to spread from the spot where the boy had touched it. Daniel stepped closer and observed that the other Azua also showed the rapid onset of whatever the boy had unleashed. *How is the boy any different?*

How is the boy different? Had he heard that? But even as Daniel questioned his own thoughts, he knew that it came from the Azua. He saw the truth of it. The boy had the potential to be just as oppressive as the Azua. How could anyone resist?

Calm descended. And as he watched his masters die and farther afield their craft and buildings begin to crumble a new resolve took hold. He found a new purpose in that resolve and knew that the course of action had a logical ring to it. There could be no other way.

The Azua before them now lay in curled heaps at the foot of the stage. The remains of their bodies shed material like dry leaves to blow away in the breeze. In the distance, the golden towers of his masters shook and fell in a torrent of dust and metal.

His masters? Yes, a true slave to the end, but he would use his freedom for one last act, one selfless moment to truly free mankind. The edge of the stage sported a rusted metal band, the oxidation a bloody scab. *Teddy bears, flowers and candles.*

His mind somehow free of clutter, Daniel grabbed the boy and crashed to the floor, smashing the boy's head against the rusted metal. Blood spurted. He smashed it again and as he did, he saw that the boy smiled still, had this been his plan all along. To die a martyr, to drag Daniel in to some awful end-game.

The crowd fell on him. And here in this pathetic damp shrine of wet teddy bears, limp flower and spluttering candles, hope was born anew. Daniel felt the blows but felt no pain. Some called him traitor, some still would, but in his deepening darkness Daniel finally realised that his careful planning had always been leading to this moment. The boy's smile engulfed his mind.

Jubilation

Erin Ruble

⚜

Beyond the cracked sidewalk, and the telephone pole with layers of flyers in a rainbow of colors, and the patch of dry brown grass there stood a ten-foot high concrete block wall, caked with dozens of coats of paint. There was a small shrine at the foot of it, with burnt out candles and dead flowers and a few soggy teddy bears. One word of graffiti filled the wall, red letters on a gold background: Rejoice!

I didn't look at it anymore. Shrines sprouted everywhere after the Rust hit, even in Montana, which never grew much corn. Then about a year ago, the jubilations came on in a rush, sweeping the Midwest, the waterlogged cities of the Atlantic seaboard, the Denver -Boulder metropolis. At first it was just a word scrawled across a wall. Then we heard rumors of prayer meetings in Elks' lodges and veterans' halls, where they praised the Rust and sang hymns to blasphemy. Now national news streams had seized on what they called the "fungus messiah." I tried to ignore it all.

I kept my head down, playing it safe, though no one apart from drunks and the police was likely to be downtown at six a.m. With my hair dyed blond, I looked more like my Scandinavian father than my Chinese mother, but my eyes tended to give me away. I'd learned to keep my face averted in public.

As I submitted to the retinal scan at the entrance to my office, a man came up behind me. I flinched, but he dipped a hand into his breast pocket and withdrew a badge, not a weapon. "Autumn Larson? I'm Agent Anderson, with the FBI. I'd like a word." When I just stood there, contemplating what the FBI could want with me (*not WWII-style internment camps, surely the anti-Chinese rhetoric hasn't progressed to that*), he gestured at the door. "Perhaps we could speak in private?"

I turned and led the way into my office. He must have been watching me, if he knew to find me here so early. As we passed the kitchenette, I thought maybe I should offer him something. Would he be insulted if I gave him barley coffee? No one liked that stuff, but surely he wouldn't expect hand-pollinated java.

As we entered my cubicle, the workstation whirred to life, displaying my notes on eighth grade biology. We were halfway through a contract with the Montana state educational board to update the public school curriculum. About time, too; the last edition was 23 years old. When it was written, the effects of the bee die-off were just starting to be felt, and Denison Corn Rust hadn't even appeared. I'd spent the bulk of the prior week trying to condense the collapse of our agricultural sector—and therefore our economy—into a two-page insert at the end of the chapter. The cursor blinked below a list of things that changed radically or vanished with the demise of corn. No one missed ethanol, but we did care about the texture of toothpaste and ice cream. Corn had been in car parts, wallpaper, glue, antibiotics, candy. Fireworks and soap, insulation and aluminum and crayons. Dairy took a dive, and the cost of eggs and meat sky-rocked. Half the country, priced out, sullenly turned vegan.

The agent pulled over a chair and seated himself by my desk. "Ms. Larson, the FBI is interested in what you might be able to tell us about an old friend of yours, Maud Jorgensen." I closed my eyes, seeing the jubilation graffiti again. I'd wanted to believe it wasn't *my* Maud. We'd been what, twelve when she moved away? I didn't even remember much of her face, just that she was blond and skinny and full of freckled energy, none of which might have outlasted puberty. The Maud Jorgensen in the news was still freckled and slight, though her hair had darkened over the years since I'd last seen her. The energy she'd piled into dance-a-thons and mock rodeos and whispered evaluations of boys had changed too. Now she stood on improvised stages from North Carolina to Colorado, describing the end of the world with a rapturous intensity. In the empty lots of old equipment dealers, from the loading docks of decaying grain depots, and sidings off silenced railroad yards, crowds gathered by the thousands to hear her speak of God and His plan.

"I don't know what to tell you," I said. "It's not like she was into any of that stuff when we were kids." I knew her family was Mormon, sure, and she must've known my family weren't religious, but neither of us cared. "We mostly just played, normal stuff. Same as everybody else."

He wanted to know if we'd been close (yes), if we'd kept in touch (no). I answered his questions, then crossed my arms, ready for him to leave. Instead, Anderson reached into his briefcase and pulled out a slightly dented plastic bottle, its middle swathed with a faded version of Coca-Cola's trademark white wave. I couldn't help reaching a finger toward it. "I haven't seen one of those old Cokes in years," I breathed. He cracked open the seal and handed it to me. I hesitated, then took a sip, letting the carbonation fizz into my nostrils as I savored the taste. I ran my thumb over the nutritional information. Second ingredient, after water: high fructose corn syrup.

"Ms. Larson, I'll be straight with you. Your government needs your help, and we're prepared to make it worth your while. You know Maud's pitch to her followers?" I did, in fact. People had been discussing it around the office. The couple Mormons on our staff were the most indignant, no big surprise. "She's riffing on normal

Mormon doctrine," I said, obliging him. "All that purity 'your body is a temple' thing, except she takes it beyond just drugs and caffeine. She says all of us have violated the spirit of the rule, so God is taking things away from us one at a time. Bees were the beginning, then corn. Wheat'll be next, then rice. Pretty soon there'll be nothing but air. She says it's a blessing though, a path back to righteousness. Air's pure and close to God."

"That's part of it," he agreed. "But she's just announced a new way to get close to Him. You familiar with Mormons' take on family units?" When I shook my head, he explained, "They believe that families blessed by the Temple spend eternity together in heaven. She's enlarging that to communities of interest. She says if her followers band together, they will create their own family in the celestial heaven. But to do that, they have to renounce the world together." I frowned. "Like some sort of monastic community?" He shook his head, face grim. "Like mass suicide. She's proposing to lead them out into the cornfields."

I felt sick. The Corn Rust toxin permeated the soil. Its effect on the human body varied but even a brief exposure could kill some people, which is why America was forced to accept handouts from India. One third of our arable land was now permanently offline. You couldn't replant it, couldn't treat it, couldn't neutralize it. I'd never heard of anybody going in. "Won't Maud die, too, then?"

He hooked an arm over the back of the chair. "Apparently not. Not everyone knows this part of the story—the media's kept it quiet to discourage copycats—but she's gone in a few times. Had her first revelation in there, which kicked off this whole thing. Still seems right as rain." Immune, then. Some people were. And some just took longer for the toxin to kick in.

"So why don't you go arrest her?" He scowled and rubbed at an invisible spot on his knee. "We have jurisdiction over *federal* crimes, which suicide isn't, and none of the states is eager to go after her. In fact, her people have just pushed legislation through in Iowa to legalize what they're doing—if each participant pays a hefty fee, of course. You know what it's like there." I did; the same old litany of Midwestern misery led the news each night. Riots in Omaha, soup kitchen robberies in Cedar Rapids, breadlines and bankrupt hospitals and refugees shunned when they tried to leave. I wasn't surprised the state wanted to make a buck off fields that were otherwise a liability. Plus whatever hotels and restaurants were left would get a boost from a one-way pilgrimage to corn country. Anderson continued, "We need evidence of a federal crime. Then we can arrest her. For that, we need someone on the inside." He leaned forward, and I had to stop myself from edging back. "Maud's divorced, no kids. She's been cut off by her family, her community, everyone close to her. The Mormon church is calling her a heretic and a false prophet, and anybody who follows her has to got to be bat-shit crazy from the get-go. So she's isolated. We think that this last doctrinal shift shows that she wants to reach out, subconsciously at least. If she was fond of you, she might take you in. Talk to you. Let you travel with her! If you can get enough evidence of wrongdoing for us to show probable cause, then we'll nab her."

"Why would I want to do that?" The question seemed to surprise him. "They're estimating three thousand people are headed to Iowa, maybe more. She's killing people, Autumn. Just as dead as if she'd thrown a grenade into a crowd. Don't you want to stop her?"

I looked down at my lap. "Not particularly." He lifted an eyebrow, and I raised my hands. "Obviously it's terrible. But all the children starving in Iowa is terrible too and there's nothing I can do about it. I'm just trying to survive."

He pulled out a screen and called up a still shot of a house surrounded by gardens. "You know, there are places far enough out from farm fields and neighbors that you can still get some non-honeybee pollination, enough to grow your own garden. Melons, squash, berries, maybe an apple or a pear tree. Nobody around to bother you. Solitude." He looked at the walls of the hallway, as if their beige uniformity held some kind of information for him. "Places like that are hard to find these days. Expensive. But it's possible, if you pleased the right people, that you could find a little house in its own valley. Your name on the title. Plus cash enough to keep you for a few years if you lived modestly."

I took a long pull of Coke as he watched. I could feel the bubbles scratching at my throat. "Is that an offer?" When he nodded, I looked down again. I hadn't thought much about what I wanted from life. Mom got sick not long before the Rust began, and the next few years were all about trying to make things easier for her. After she died and I felt like I could look around again, the whole world was off-kilter. Since then, I'd made myself a hole to burrow into, keeping to myself as much as possible. It wasn't just that it had gotten harder to meet people; there also didn't seem to be much point in it. We were all waiting for the other shoe to drop. Anderson was dangling the prospect of a more comfortable hole from which to wait. And I kind of wanted to see Maud again, if only to understand how the blazing star of my childhood had turned homicidal. I swallowed. "Ok."

I sent Maud a message through her organization, RePure, leaving my number. I thought it unlikely she'd call back, if the message even reached her, but two days later, my phone rang. "Autumn! I can't tell you how often I've thought of you. How are you?" She sounded too friendly for a mystical cult leader, but what did I know? Maybe they were all like that. We talked for nearly an hour. It was oddly comfortable, like trying on a pair of gloves you'd discarded long ago and discovering they retained the curl of your fingers. We still laughed at the same things. I hadn't had someone to laugh with in ages.

After the third urgent-sounding interruption from someone on her end, she admitted she had to go. "I'm planning a Gathering next month, and there are an incredible number of logistics to see to. Paperwork and registrations to be sent to the state government, money held in trust for relatives, bus charters and airport shuttles. Then of course all the public appearances have their own logistics, and speeches to write." She might've been a mother coordinating children's schedules: harried and vicariously proud. "Listen," she said, as I prepared to hang up. "How about a visit? You can see the operation, meet the crew, and I'll make sure we get some time to talk. I'll be in Denver most of the next month, but I'm going to be giving a speech in Billings soon." Anderson would be doing a little jig if he knew, but I bit my lip, wondering if I could really spy on Maud. "Think about it," she urged, and it was the same Maudie urging me higher up the tree, daring me to put on eye shadow, sneaking out on sleepovers to roam the neighborhood at midnight. Half the time the escapades ended badly, but it was never about the thing itself. I was a sucker for the frisson of a shared glance. I suppose that's what drew everyone to her. It wasn't hope, and it wasn't the things she promised. It was the promise itself.

We met at the Montana state fairgrounds the day before her speech. The auditorium held 12,000 people and Maud was projected to fill it. The back office was a snarl of screens, processors, recording equipment. I spotted Maud standing with her back to me, gesturing as she spoke to one of her security team. When his eyes shifted toward me, she turned, and her old smile crested her face like a sunrise.

She crossed the room and pulled me into a hug. I could feel the knobs of her backbone through her sweater. "You're too thin," I said, before I could stop myself. She laughed. "You sound like your mom. Remember how she fed us cookies?" I laughed too, surprising myself. It had been a long time since I could even smile at a memory of my mother. Maud continued, "She thought they'd fatten me up, but it never worked. Though my metabolism's slowed enough that now it's more a matter of forgetting to eat." Her eyes lit up. "Hey, let's go downtown and get a bite. I haven't been to Billings in ages." The suggestion appeared to appall her security detail, and I started stammering excuses too. It was six o'clock, and the streets would be full. There'd been some ugly rallies lately. One of them had dredged up a Rust orphan, a blond boy of about twelve who would have looked angelic if hatred hadn't twisted his features. I'd seen him on the news in a poorly lit rock venue, shouting at a crowd whose answering cheers nearly drowned him out.

But Maud was unstoppable. "It'll be great!" she said, drawing me and her security along through the hallways. Before I could register an opinion we were in a van with black-tinted windows, pulling out of the parking lot. *It'll be ok*, I told myself, trying not to clench my hands. But the wide avenue was filled with cars, and traffic slowed, then stopped, well before we reached downtown. Maud opened the door and stepped outside, squinting at a line of people blocking the road. I followed her, needing to see how bad it was.

It was the boy from the news. He stood in the center of a circle of white protestors carrying signs and banners. Half of them were wearing clothes emblazoned with American flags. I reached for my sunglasses and put them on, though clouds veiled the sun.

The kid got up onto a milk crate and raised his hand. A murmur went through the crowd and then it fell silent, except for a few people shouting words of encouragement at him. The kid acknowledged them with a nod and a shy smile. In the full light of day, he looked less angry and more beautiful. He waited until people stopped shouting. A siren could be heard, maybe five or ten blocks away. The kid raised the bullhorn, pressed the button, and began to speak.

"My name is Eli, and my parents died of Rust," he began. The crowd cried out in support. "I don't even remember them. My big sister died, too, and my grandparents. But I'm no different from each of you. We've all lost something. We've all had something *taken* from us. And we know by who." I got back inside the car and tried to draw Maud with me. His voice followed me inside. "We know the Rust came from China. We know our nukes still work. But the government is dragging its feet. Why? Because the Chinese control it, through their puppets, the globalizers and sympathizers. It's time for those of us who care about this country, who made this country powerful, to *take it back*. China tried to destroy us, and they almost did! We can't wait for their next attack. We need to act *now*!" His audience roared.

"Maud, get in!" I hissed. The driver managed to turn the car around, and we retreated in silence. We finally found a restaurant off a deserted side street, and commandeered a table. After picking at the corner of the menu, I looked up into Maud's beautiful face. Even as a child, I'd never warmed to people easily, but I had loved her. I needed to know that she was different from the boy leading the rally. "So how'd you get into this?"

She asked her bodyguard to order for us, then clasped her hands like a schoolgirl reciting a poem. "There was this cornfield I used to drive by. I was going through a crisis, I guess you'd call it, and one day I just stopped the car and got out. It was so quiet out there— transcendent, really. I kept walking until I was right in the center. You could actually feel God's love there. I thought, everyone should have this." She leaned forward, expression intent. "You should come, Autumn. Not tomorrow—I mean, yes, tomorrow if you want, you can sit right up front—but to the Event. Out in the cornfields. You can feel the spirit move through you. It's like that moment on the Ferris wheel when you're almost at the top and the view's spreading out in front of you and you're just about to be at the highest point for miles around." Her face transformed with the glory of her vision. I'd never seen her like this. Charged, yes, but this was something else.

She took my hand. "I want this for you. For us. To let you bask in God's purity. In the fields, there's nothing in between you and Him. The rest of the world just falls away and things are suddenly clear." She frowned. "The media gets it all wrong, of course. It's not about *dying*. There is no death in God. Life and death are beside the point. It's that feeling of oneness I want for people. That openness. How could I have felt it and *not* brought it to others?" Her eyes widened and there was the girl again, puzzled by my thanks when she shared her candy. "I couldn't *keep* it," she'd said then. "That would be selfish." As if selfishness were a thing beyond contemplation.

"But I don't want to die, Maud." Certainly not for a God I didn't believe in. She nodded, sitting back. "You could watch from beyond the perimeter. Not the same as being inside, but you'd be close. That's where my staff will be. You could watch with them." I raised an eyebrow, wondering why she thought I'd want to watch thousands of people die. Maud squeezed my hand. "I did it before, you know. Not with so many, just about fifteen of us. This was on my third trip into the fields. Everyone just got quieter, more peaceful, and then they started seeing Him. They were radiant. They touched God *together*. Everyone says you're alone when you die, alone in life, but Autumn, it's not true! They were together then and they ascended together and they are together now. A family." There was longing in her voice.

"And you were left behind." She shook her head at my words, though she looked wistful. "I was given the task of spreading the message more widely. I am honored to be God's vessel on earth." She didn't look honored, though. She looked sad. I tightened my fingers around hers. "Ok, I'll come."

Maud's caravan to southeast Iowa filled three tour buses, and that was just her staff. By the time we neared Lincoln, cars of all descriptions jammed the interstate: 30-year-old Priuses, broken-down pick-ups, convertibles, motorcycles heavy with chrome. A few tractors putted along the shoulder, keeping company with bikes and at least one riding lawn mower. One guy trotted across soybean fields on a pinto horse. Everyone was laughing and waving, hanging heads and hands and legs out the windows.

The familiar slate-gray smudge of tainted earth marked the cornfields. In places the government had planted windbreaks of Dutch elm and juniper along the perimeters to contain any drift, but they still closed the roads during high winds. The towns that lay too close to the fields were abandoned, and the rest had decayed, with peeling paint, chipped siding, potholed streets. There were plenty of people, though. They'd lined the overgrown yards with lawn chairs, as if we'd become a parade. Kids zoomed around in circles. Adults blew kisses or clapped, or shouted, or stood silently, frowning.

I watched through the windshield, not eager to get close to the window. I regretted having let Maud and Anderson beguile me into this. Everyone had heard about the lynchings and burnings in the Midwest. As we turned a corner, a man caught sight of me through the glass, and snarled something to his neighbors. One lifted a chair. The first guy grabbed a brick and hurled it against the side of the bus, screaming, "Die for your sins, you Chink bitch!" After that, I kept my sunglasses on.

It was dark by the time we climbed a concrete bridge that spanned the slow current of the Des Moines river. The water shone under the lights from the usual flotilla of houseboats. Just past the parking lots and shuttered brick buildings that made up the downtown lay a once-grand residential street, its yards now full of bits of paper and shredded plastic bags. We pulled up beside a faded blue Queen Anne, where a middle aged couple had offered to host us for the last couple days of organizing before the big event. They opened the door and ran to greet us, looking like they didn't know whether to bow before Maud or hug her. They settled on a kind of sideways shuffle, ushering her in. I'm not sure what they were expecting—spiritual revelations over barley coffee in their linoleum-tiled kitchen, probably—but what they got, within the first hour of our arrival, was a command center. I stood in a corner and watched in astonishment as Maud's staff set up equipment, hauled out lists and forms, and began cranking through the business of dying. The state required all "participants" to wear portable combustion units to incinerate their bodies after 48 hours, to prevent rotting corpses from contaminating the water table. There were all the transportation logistics, and then there were the financials. In addition to the state-imposed fees for entry, Maud had insisted that anyone with dependents establish a fund for their care. Staff had been verifying the funds for months now, but there were hundreds of new registrants and very little time for records-checking. Maud sat calmly in the center of it all, fielding calls, approving or correcting things people brought to her, and occasionally moving her lips as if practicing a speech, or speaking to God, or singing under her breath.

Our hosts had set up pallets in a few rooms upstairs. I used the restroom, then stepped inside what looked like a sewing room. Rectangles of fabric lay in little stacks along shelves on the wall, next to spools of bright thread and a bundle of cotton batting. They'd shoved a big table to one side to leave room for four thin mattresses. I sat and sent a quick message to Anderson, letting him know we'd arrived, though he'd about given up on me. He was distinctly displeased with my continued failure to turn up evidence of crimes. He kept suggesting new issues to investigate, but I knew they wouldn't pan out. Maud wasn't a con artist. She was a believer.

I lay down and drew the blanket over me, wondering what Maud saw beyond the ceiling, beyond the sky. Sunsets and dawn and angels trumpeting the glory of God's name? I couldn't believe in a soul, couldn't believe that any part of a person could survive once the fungus crept inside their brain. *Good thing, too,* the voice in my head said. I'd come to know it well in the months after my mother's death. *Life is nothing,* it whispered through the wind in the poplar just outside. *The earth is ruined. So are you. So are we all.*

Bad dreams woke me before sunrise. I picked my way through the pallets and down the hall, suddenly desperate for air. This yard was better tended than most, with zinnias and hostas and little bulbs of boxwood shrubs. Maud sat on a stone bench by the back fence, staring up at the sky. Her shoulders were hunched. As I came up beside her, she glanced over and straightened, smiling automatically. Her hair had broken loose from her bun and tangled against her neck. I tucked a piece behind her ear.

"You look pale," I said. "You getting enough rest?" She shrugged slightly, looking back at the sky. "I don't need rest." I looked down at my own bitten nails. The house behind us was dark and still. Keeping my eyes fixed on my hands, I asked quietly, "Do you really believe all that God stuff?" Her breathing paused. "I have to," she said at last. "This here," she waved at the fence, the town and the land beyond, "it's not enough. Not for anyone. Autumn, I drove through this state right after the Rust hit. There were children standing on street corners, just standing there, with nowhere to go. There were…." Her voice trailed off, and she shook her head. "It has to mean something. It *does* mean something. It's a sign, right there for us to read."

"All those people dying…" I started, but she cut me off. "It's not about death. It's about connection. We will forge a bond in there that will never be sundered. Think about it." She took my hand, turning to look into my eyes. "You and I, we've lost everyone, one after another. Imagine what it would be like to never lose anyone again. Never lose anything. If you make yourself pure, God will reward you. It's all this excess that pushes Him away, and in that space without Him, we create our own misery." She squeezed my hand. "That's what I'll say today," she mused, as if she hadn't already written ten versions of her speech. "Thank you." She stood, slowly. After patting my shoulder, she carefully walked back inside. I stayed on the bench, watching dawn draw itself against the sky.

Two hours later, we were in the van again, heading to the old railroad yard from which we would enter the cornfields. Tractors pulled wagons of pilgrims; others trudged along the shoulder, faces tipped to the sunlight. We drove through a sleeve of cars abandoned on both sides of the road, keys left out on dashboards; most people didn't expect to return. We slowed as we reached the yard. Someone had set up bleachers, and the stands were already packed, walkways and aisles both. People lined the tracks as far as you could see. There was just enough room left in the road for the bus to pass through, buffeted by a thicket of hands and arms reaching for Maud.

When we pulled up to the stage, everyone on the bus stood but me. Maud looked back, questioningly. "I'll stay here," I said, watching the crowd. Maud grabbed my hand and pulled me up. "You're with me," she said simply, and drew me with her down the worn steps.

I kept my head down as we walked, hiding my eyes, though I wore my biggest and darkest glasses. Hands stretched toward us from all sides, past the ropes marking our path and the broad-shouldered security guards ushering us along. The stage still smelled of sawn timbers. When we reached the top, I shrank into a corner, looking out past the blur of upturned faces to the livid bruise of the cornfields beyond. I wondered if I would make it back to the bus without being torn to pieces by these numberless hands.

Maud welcomed her followers, and their roar in return swelled like an ocean wave. One of her logistics crew walked everyone through the necessary procedures: check in, proper attachment of the combustion units, how people would file through the gates in the walls that had been hastily thrown up around the field, where to leave final belongings. Then Maud took the podium again, swaying a little as she regarded the thousands who had come to die at her word. When she spoke, her voice was low, and despite the amplification people bent forward to hear. "Friends. I am humbled that you wish to take this journey with me. Because, in the end, that is what this is: a journey among friends." She half turned, looking back at me. "A few weeks ago, I received word from a woman I had thought gone from my life forever, someone I love very dearly." She beckoned to me. The world seemed to congeal as I stepped forward, thousands of pairs of eyes now trained on me. Maud grasped my hand. "That God would send me this gift is not, I believe, a reward, for we will all have our reward soon. It is, instead, a sign, that the things we love most, the things we need most, will be restored to us." She gently removed my sunglasses and turned me toward the crowd. "There are those who look at this face, this face beloved to me, and see in it the vessel of our destruction. Those who hate the Chinese for bringing the Rust to us. But we know better, don't we?"

Thousands of heads bobbed, agreeing before they even knew why. "The Rust may have begun in China, but it was made by God. Saying it came from the Chinese is like saying an Internet message comes from the servers that relayed it along, like saying an old fashioned letter was written by the postal service rather than its sender. The Rust was God's message to China *and* to us. It is a hard lesson, undoubtedly, even a bitter one. But our redemption is equal to the hardship. Together, we shall venture into the ruin of our own greed, and offer it up, offer ourselves up. Those of us who are accepted shall be together in heaven this very day. The rest have a harder road ahead, but a greater gift of responsibility: to live in this world the way God intended, with austerity and purity, with correctness, and to spread this word. We shall take his corrections—for there will be more, do not doubt this—with thanks, for they remind us of this path we must walk. That we walk now."

She turned from the microphone and descended the stairs, drawing me along. Her hand, still clasped around mine, was very hot. Again we passed through a tunnel of hands and arms, lips whispering praises, but this time, the eyes were on me as well as Maud, and words rippled through the crowd like wind in leaves. "Bless you, bless you, bless you, bless you."

The walls loomed above us, and we were nearing the gates, but the words rose and pressed against my ears, *bless you, bless you,* and Maud's fingers tightened on mine and we were a family and we would not run from the rotten land behind the wall but reclaim it, reclaim ourselves, proclaim ourselves something more than the absences that each day chiseled into us, and I could not step away. The gates swung open and the ones who had already been checked, passes stamped on their hands like fair-goers, spilled inside, and then we were there, and I did not follow Maud in but walked beside her, into the hollow of the country's nightmares.

It was silent there, except for the wind and the rustle of our passage. Nothing lay in front of us but the churned earth stretching to the horizon. We walked maybe a mile, leaving space for the silent crowd streaming behind us, then found a place to sit. Drones whirred above us. The shadow of a hawk passed over. Somewhere, someone laughed, then stilled.

The first symptoms started after an hour or two. A few people gasped, or stared, or cried out. One or two chased ghosts. By the time others began, the first had fallen into something like a trance, twitching and spasming with their eyes closed.

The sun had slipped behind the horizon when Maud collapsed against me. I flinched and tried to prop her upright, but she slumped again. Her lips looked purple. "Maud," I hissed. "You're immune." She half closed her eyes, whispering hoarsely, "No one is immune to God. He just has different plans for us." Her body began to convulse. A stream of drool ran from her mouth, and her eyes flew open, staring at nothing, or at something I couldn't see. She extended one hand toward empty air. "Rejoice," I thought I heard her gasp through chattering teeth. I held her shoulders, trying to soothe their jerking. "Maud," I said, choking on my own tears. "Maudie." But she was gone.

I held her until her muscles stopped twitching, until her pulse stopped and her body relaxed. The air turned blue, then purple, then black. The night was strangely silent: no owls, crickets, or frogs, just the rattle of wind and the occasional scuffle of a rodent. I rubbed my arm across my eyes to clear them and looked around. There was just enough starlight to make out the shapes of bodies. The green light of a drone winked to my left. I stood unsteadily, and began shuffling back to the gate, and the long reckoning of the life beyond.

One Last Thing

Daniel Salvatore

.♠.

Beyond the cracked sidewalk, and the telephone pole with layers of flyers in a rainbow of colors, and the patch of dry brown grass there stood a ten-foot high concrete block wall, caked with dozens of coats of paint. There was a small shrine at the foot of it, with burnt out candles and dead flowers and a few soggy teddy bears. One word of graffiti filled the wall, red letters on a gold background: Rejoice!

I tried not to laugh. I'd *been* trying not to laugh since arriving at the wall, partly because I thought it was a funny thing to write, and partly because I didn't think my day could have gone this wrong. Gallows humor has always been my favorite kind of humor, but I, like so many others, thought bad things—truly bad things—only happened to other people. Was I other people? What kind of things did other people find funny?

I guess "arrive" isn't accurate. I was brought. I might even go so far as to say I was coerced. I used to argue with people, insisting everyone always did what they wanted to do most. I could frame paying bills, for example, in that way – you *want* to pay your bills because you want your lights to stay on. I don't think it's a good (or interesting) argument now, and I don't even think it was a good argument then. I didn't want to come to the wall. But I guess I could frame it – I didn't *not* want to come to the wall more.

A few days before, I went to visit the Hall. Work detail. There hadn't been a lot of assignments lately, but there weren't many folks available to take any, either. I showed up early hoping for first dibs on something interesting. I don't think I could have accurately described this one as interesting, but I got first dibs because no one else showed. The first time I took an assignment they asked me if I had any experience. Well, I owned a coat, did that count? It did. I didn't have a cudgel, though, but they let me borrow a spare.

I had needed a coat and a cudgel for this one, too. Sorry, to be clear, coats are a bonus. If it's between you, a coat owner, and some poor bastard who doesn't own a coat, it's your time to shine. At least in winter which was of late. Coat keeps you warm (and dry if you're really lucky), the cudgel is usually contextually appropriate. For example, sometimes you use it to hit folks who come into the area you've been told to keep them out of, sometimes you just need to look like you wouldn't hesitate to use it on them, and sometimes it was for rats. (Rats aren't intimidated by brandishing a weapon, so unfortunately for them and for you if you're the sensitive type, you need to go straight to bludgeoning.)

This time was just rats. This time was supposed to be just rats, anyway. I had pulled a shift guarding one of the grain stores. This store, a bank vault that had been left open, was small enough for a one-man patrol, and whenever an assignment placed me here, it had been a quiet shift. Barring another massive flood, the vault was about as waterproof as anything we could think of. The door could have been kept shut using the manual lock, which was fine so long as the power grid restoration continued to be an abject failure, but an electronically locked bank vault that no one living knew how to reopen was too much of a risk. So it stayed open with a couple dozen sixty pound bags of concrete piled up in front of it. Oh, and there was also punishment of death for anyone who closed it.

Speaking of which, lots of things are punishable by death now. Not that it matters to anyone, but I think it's crushingly ironic; an insane amount of people died in a relative instant so now remaining life is so precious we kill you if you jeopardize it. Okay, maybe it's not *that* ironic. When it came time, I voted against instituting new capital punishments for crimes that would otherwise (in some cases) not have been crimes, or at least had originally carried less severe penalties. I did agree that locking people up wasn't reasonable, mostly because we couldn't afford to designate people as guards when they could be doing more important tasks that kept everyone alive, but I didn't think killing people for things like shutting a door was a good precedent to set. But the ground on which I set my moral objection crumbled away to a sea of hands in favor of more killing to discourage more killing. Kill 'em if ya got 'em.

New world, new rules. When I first found out most (if not certainly all) of everyone I knew was dead, I was speechless. This is accurate because I wasn't capable of producing human speech for some time. I'd heard from stories about people wailing; babies, old women, evil spirits, those kinds of things. I think I was wailing. I did this until I couldn't breathe and my lungs hurt and snot and tears ran down my face and I got an abdominal cramp so bad I thought I may have shit myself but I didn't care because everyone was dead but me so what did anything matter anyway?

It's strange to think this way, but it may have been true and still may be, but I think the dogs hit me hardest. I'd gotten them before I even met Jeanie when I first moved out here years ago. Two brothers that had come to the shelter for adoption, likely from the same litter. One black, one white. I had wanted to pick out clever names for them, but after referring to them as the black one and the white one mixed in with indecisiveness, my boys became Bee and Dubs.

It was sunny on their last day and they were out in the yard and I was working from home and then they started barking like it was the end of the goddamn world. They had only done that once before that I know of. Jeanie was working nights then and had a hell of a time sleeping during the day. Reluctantly, she got some OTC sleep meds and they seemed to do the trick, except they did it so well you could dump a lake on her and she wouldn't know it until it dried up. That night Jeanie was sleeping in the bedroom on the second floor and I was in the shower post-workout and pre-work when I heard Bee and Dubs screaming hell – I nearly killed myself scrambling out of the shower, and at maximum lather point.

The meth head with a hammer later told police he was trying to rob us, but apparently attempted-rape was a bonus. The dogs scrambling at the door like they were rabid (when I knew they weren't) was an obvious tell that something horribly wrong was happening. I could barely get the doorknob to turn with all the soap on my hands while pushing the dogs out of the way at the same time, but when I did, they charged in and started trying to rip the strange man standing over my wife to pieces. He managed to stumble back out the window the way he came while only losing a bit of blood, but we were safe. They were my dogs and I loved them and I love them now. I'll think of them again during my last moments, I'm sure.

I found my dogs' remains as soon as the water receded enough for me to traipse around the yard. I'm thankful they were wearing collars. And I thought of how they had saved Jeanie as I held Dubs' wet, lifeless body in my arms, while I was looking for Bee. The rushing water had thrown Dubs through the tool shed, smashing his body. I like to think it was over before he realized it. We found Bee together, after the garage drained. He was washed inside, trapped in a corner while it filled up. The drywall was soaked and distorted, and I tried to tell myself the gouges were made by something other than Bee's claws as he fought for life. It didn't help. I laid them in a wheelbarrow and covered them with a sheet with a shovel balancing across the top and we took one last walk.

I walked my beat thinking of these things. I am always thinking of these things. It's been six months and I don't know that things are better. Everyone is still learning to live in this new landscape. And living is very literal in this sense. I thought life was unpredictable before, but after the quake and the flood and the constant bombardment of storms that followed, no one is taking bets, and everyone is too busy trying to stay alive to make a life.

I wondered if They would name it, later on, I mean. If anyone survived long enough to catalog and document again like humans like to do. Children would learn about it in schools, I'm certain. Would it have a different name in other countries? The prediction had been worldwide, and fairly accurate in my slice of the country, at least in terms of scale. The timing was off, unfortunately. By a few years, too. Can't be right about everything, I suppose. Not a big deal, though. I'm sure most people would still have died anyway.

Once enough folks in the city got their wits about them after getting KO'd by the apocalypse, we tried to form up. Food and clean water was a priority, and power was pretty important, too, so most tasks revolved around them. When you went to the Hall for an assignment, it generally wasn't skill based. Everyone had to learn how to do everything, and unless you were a doctor or a farmer or an electrical engineer, you'd likely find yourself carrying a cudgel guarding a pile of rice or canned beans. And assignments weren't mandatory by any means. Not working just meant you were on your own for supplies. Four hours of watching grain sit in an old bank vault could easily earn me a half cup of dry rice. Pretty good deal, and I didn't have much else to do. It was mostly easy, aside from the occasional rat-thumping. I didn't enjoy that part, but it was necessary, and there seemed to be plenty of the critters which didn't seem fair to me somehow. I thought about all the other animals with lower survivability and poorer proliferation. Deer, bear, turkeys, foxes, elk, racoons, possums. Cats. Dogs. I thought of my dogs again and how I missed them and I thought of companionship and how I missed that, too. Not enough to do anything about it, though.

The local rec center was in good enough shape to be used for its originally-intended purpose. Most buildings, like the bank, were repurposed for some essential function. It wasn't too common, but you could draw an assignment doing general maintenance at the rec center. The center was deemed important, a symbol. A symbol that said...what? "This planet and its people are in a brutal struggle for survival, but hey, life goes on and we have a place where you can play pool and shoot hoops when you're not busy killing the rats that are trying to eat your rice." It's long for a motto, sure, but I think it's accurate.

I only went to the rec center on assignments, which was twice at this point. A lot – relatively – of children could usually be found there. And there were also people there enjoying themselves on occasion. I had a hard time with that. Although I did miss meaningful human interaction, I wasn't coping well with my losses. Maybe with time I'd try reaching out. Maybe I'd even feel okay with feeling okay. One of the issues was that I had no way to know who was alive and who wasn't. Despair had its way with me in the beginning, and I assumed the worst. (Who would blame me?) But I had friends and family out of state. I even had a few friends who were traveling out of country at the time.

Other thoughts seized me on rotation. Were my parents alive? Was their cat, my aging childhood companion okay? With warning, would they have grabbed Jinx and his meds and headed for high ground? Was their house still standing, or were they buried in the rubble? Was Jinx buried with them, or did he escape being crushed to death, left to starvation or kidney failure without his pills or special diet? Were they alive and surviving anyway they could? Were they alive and wondering the same about me?

Travel was not an option. No one would have stopped me from leaving of course – I still had that freedom – but nearly everything was an unnavigable death-tangle or still flooded out. No one had seen a plane or a helicopter of any kind. The monthly census numbers stayed the same or went down by one or two so far, but they never went up, and everyone mostly agreed no one was coming in, at least not for a very long time. An active search for loved ones was replaced by hoping they were still alive out there and that one day we'd find each other again. Hoping helped, but hoping didn't always offset the pain I felt for the people I knew were dead. Coworkers, local friends, Bee, Dubs, and Jeanie.

Bee and Dubs are buried a few hundred yards off one of the main trails at their favorite park. I couldn't do anything for weeks at first. I was lucky enough that only the first floor of the house flooded, so I was able to ride out the death of everything I knew from the comfort of my own home. I had enough canned goods and bottled water to get by, although I had to swim through the basement to procure them. Could have been worse.

I carried these thoughts with me during my last assignment watching the rice pile at the bank. They ran through my head like a playlist set to shuffle. The songs of my life played constantly and my favorite ones could almost make me want to dance even now. My shift went on, rat-less so far, and my mind was wandering when I heard one skittering seemingly inside what used to be the manager's office. I tucked my cudgel under my arm and gave the crank on my flashlight a few rotations before setting off to investigate. I kept the light pointed low and walked slowly through the open door. I saw a pair of shoes with some feet stuck in them so I quickly ran the light up and rested it on the face of a boy, maybe seventeen or eighteen.

I'd seen him around, but didn't know his name, and it didn't matter to me. Looked like my shift relief was here. I started to say as much to him when I heard a growl behind me.

My heart beat no more than twice before I had spun on my heels, cudgel clenched, arm extending in a wide arc, and connecting with something that made a sickening wet sound followed by something heavy hitting the floor. I stumbled back, trying to make sense of what happened. The kid was screaming behind me – I think using words but I didn't understand them, and I couldn't understand why there was another kid on the floor in front me with his head bleeding severely from the temple. What did I just do? I realized I was asking that out loud and on repeat.

Turns out what I had done was pretty awful, even in the context of the hellish nightmare we all now lived. I killed the kid's brother. Caught him hard and in the right spot and he died within minutes of the strike. The kid ran for help after I figured out what planet I was on and I tried uselessly to stop the bleeding, not *knowing* what else could be done. The help, a handful of men who often held the town meetings now, listened to what happened and asked me to go with them. I needed to be isolated, confined, you could say, while things were sorted out. I was feeling a range of emotions I could barely process in the moment so I just complied quietly.

The new rule was this: if you managed to kill someone in a situation where you weren't defending yours or someone else's life, you were to die. Pretty straightforward, and not too far off from what everyone was already used to, but the new addition – after determining guilt, which they easily had since I confessed – was that the sentence was to be carried out by a representative of the deceased party. This defaulted to a relative or a friend. If no relative or friend was available or willing, the executioner was chosen by raffle. If you, as a lucky raffle winner, were unwilling to carry out the sentence, well – I can't remember but they had something for it. They'd dock your rations or reduce the amount of work assignments you could take on for some time or something like it, but don't worry – they'd find someone to do the killing. First, they asked me if I'd killed the boy. I had. Then they asked me why. I heard a growl, I said. A growl? A growl, yes. They asked the kid if someone growled. He said yes. Who growled, they asked. His brother. Why did your brother growl? He was just playing around. He was playing around by growling? Yes, he liked to sneak up on people that way – it was funny to him. (I didn't think it was funny.) They asked the kid, as the last surviving member of his family, if he thought I should die for killing his brother. Yes, he thought I should. I sighed, anticipating the proceedings to come.

The kid got up onto a milk crate and raised his hand. A murmur went through the crowd and then it fell silent, except for a few people shouting words of encouragement at him. The kid acknowledged them with a nod and a shy smile. In the full light of day, he looked less angry and more beautiful. He waited until people stopped shouting. A siren could be heard, maybe five or ten blocks away. The kid raised the bullhorn, pressed the button, and began to speak.

The siren caught my attention for a moment. Hadn't heard one go off in a bit. Maybe somebody got something working. But I let it the thought ride for the moment and interrupted the little bastard. "Oh, shut the fuck up!" I was standing next to him, so I didn't really have to shout, but it startled him enough that he almost dropped the bullhorn.

He looked at me, slack-jawed. I would have jabbed a finger into his gaping maw if my hands weren't tied. He couldn't seem to recover his composure, though, and the crowd silently echoed his shock, so it looked like I still had the floor.

I had at first felt appropriately terrible for killing the kid's brother. It was an accident, yes, but that didn't make it, or make me feel less bad. I suppose if I'd meant to do it, I probably would have felt less guilty. Funny how that works. Now, though, I was incensed. The imposition of capital punishment in this new societal grouping was (dare I say) done willy-nilly.

And I would remind interested parties that I did indeed dare say it was willy-nilly when it was voting time. It was an early meeting and there had been an issue of theft. And enough folks decided that we couldn't afford to live with any kind of thievery and then that of course led to all sorts of things folks couldn't afford to live with either. I mentioned, I don't remember my exact words at this point, but I mentioned something to the effect of maybe we, with our vastly reduced numbers, couldn't afford to live with even less of those numbers.

I held my breath as the Sea of Hands was tallied on both sides of the voting line. My side, the correct side as I saw it, was a ripple on an otherwise calm lake compared to the rogue wave who wanted harsher punishments. If people want death, people are going to well have it, gosh darn it! Maybe I imagined it, but I think I may have seen ol' Due Process walking by outside with his hands in his pockets kicking a can down the street.

That was the last time I had actually felt like there was a chance at making a difference. I think I convinced myself that people would take stock of themselves, of everything. That maybe in light of how awful things had gotten, we could decide together as one People that we would try our damnedest not to fuck it all up again.

Boy, that sure would have been super cool. Too bad, really. But… I suppose the upshot was that I could cross one more thing off my steadily shrinking list of things for which to hope. At times like these it's really important to stay positive!

So I had just told the kid what I had thought about his announcement. Check. Last words I'd ever get to say. Maybe. Probably. Was I consciously aware of the fact? Hard to tell in the moment, but might as well try to say something that counted.

My mouth was dry and letters from somewhere within crawled out of husks to form what I hoped would be words. "Go fuck yourselves." Eloquent, and no signs of stopping. "All this ceremony, and for what? More killing, more death. No one can ever get enough so long as it's someone else." I looked at the kid. "We all know what you're going to say, so you might as well save the energy and get this over with. Everyone has work to do."

My balls swelled with pride. I felt strong and brave and invincible except really I was just seconds away from becoming compost. I put some effort into trying not to think about that too much. The officiant looked at me and then he looked at the kid and shrugged and held something out to him. I put more effort into not looking at it. But that wouldn't change what it was, and it couldn't stop me from knowing what was about to happen.

This was not the first time I was convinced death was imminent, though. Not that time with the meth head hammer freak—I was too busy trying not to get hammer-murdered or let anyone else get hammer-murdered (though the dogs were the ones really handling that) to think about death as a real possibility. I also had had some control over the situation.

The *other* other near-death time, I'd had pain and cramping in my abdomen for a few days that did a little ebbing and some waning, and since going to the doctor is the last thing anyone wants to do, I decided to see how it played out.

It did not play out in my favor as something felt like it exploded inside of me while I was stirring some refried beans in a pot on my stove. I folded up on myself and slumped to the floor struggling to breathe in a way that didn't feel like sucking in fire. I didn't think about anything, though. My brain didn't jump around making connections that spanned my lifetime. I was *very* concerned I was going to die, but I thought there was a chance that I might not. So I focused everything I had on that small hope.

(Obviously I did not die from that experience.) Lucky for me, Jeanie arrived home in time to save the day and drag me to the hospital where I learned gallstones had contributed to some nasty acute pancreatitis. So there I was, afraid I was going to die, but I just kept thinking, *don't die don't die don't die* because it was hard to think of anything else. And I still had that much agency. But right now, I didn't have much of anything.

And what was happening now definitely wasn't right. But hey, what *was* right anymore? Bad things *did* happen to me! I had joined the ranks of people to whom bad things happened and made my way to the top with aplomb. A proud moment, but ah, I wished I was just about anywhere else, and I could count on my fingers the different kinds of wishes I've made throughout my life. Winning that big lotto, getting the job, and maybe even wishing to increase my luck with one or two ladies I had my eye on when I was a younger fellow. Maybe I had wasted my wishes on the trivial, but maybe wishing never makes it so.

But now the situation was very clearly this: they were about to kill me with a gunshot to the head. They were going to kill me by shooting me in the head. They were going to shoot my head until I died. They were going to shoot a bullet into my head and I was going to die from it. I was going to die because someone shot a bullet into my head. It's not the first time I tried to make sense of an incomprehensible situation by rephrasing it on loop. It didn't really help.

I was at what I had heard some folks refer to as the killing wall.

The People decided this was as good a spot as any – behind the police station. You only came here when someone was dying for some kind of bullshit, or else you came to throw some kind of paint on this monument to, as far as I saw it, human depravity. Kids or maybe angry adults would sneak over here at night and adorn this spot with a bit of painted protest or in most cases a word or string of words I couldn't make sense of. (Most graffiti I've come across is either complete nonsense or written with no regard to proper grammar. For shame.)

Another work assignment was painting over the graffiti on the wall. I avoided that one. Two people before me had come to the wall for this purpose. Did they pray for a miracle? Did they try to run? I don't know because I hadn't come to bear witness. Maybe I could have come in protest, but maybe that would have gotten me here. Heh.

Was *I* praying for a miracle? No, I don't think so. It crossed my mind, though. God always seemed to be helping football players catch touchdown passes. Maybe those starving kids in Africa weren't praying hard enough or loud enough. Is that what happened when the world descended into Hell? God's people just couldn't manage to get their shit together and pray for salvation, I guess. In any case, prayer didn't save the world, so why would it save me?

The crowd was silent now. There was no more talking to be done, nothing left to say, and only one thing left to do. I never liked ceremony, and I thought that I made myself clear to the kid and everyone else that I didn't have much patience for this one now. Patience, I feel, is a virtue for people who don't have other virtues.

I've had so much time to think these past months. And those thoughts were mostly bringing up old memories, so maybe I was remembering more than actively thinking. Am I thinking or remembering now? Do I care? I'm thinking it's too late for a miracle now, or even anything less than a miracle. I'm thinking about my life, and how nothing I've ever done could have mattered now. I'm thinking about Bee and Dubs and how they were good dogs and how I've thought about the likelihood of me thinking about them at a time like now and how I'll miss them.

I miss Jeanie. She was at work that day and she never made it home. I don't know that she even got the chance to try. She was still on nights and I had usually been asleep when she left for her shift. The crashing water woke me up and the shock scrambled my brain into near-paralysis. When I recovered enough to form thoughts of "what the fuck do I do now?" I immediately tried to figure out how to find my wife. The water was still rushing all over, slamming debris into everything. Leaving the house was death.

The short of it is, I didn't find her that night. And I still haven't. I'm sorry I can't remember the last thing I said to her and I'm sorry I didn't know our last goodbye would also be a final goodbye.

And I'm sorry for me, too. I'm sorry I'm here and I'm sorry for how people are and I'm sorry for the reasons they feel they need to do what they're about to do. I'm sorry for what the world is like now and I'm sorry for how we all got here. I'm sorry that it really seems like it's too late for me and that there's nothing I can do. But perhaps it's not too late for you, perhaps there is something you can do, and sometimes the answer stares you right in the face.

Rejoice. Because you're alive. Because you can still stand on your own two feet, unaided, defiant if you choose to be. Rejoice because it's not over. It will be, but it's not yet. And while you're here you can and may as well do something. It might not be as grand or as important as once you'd thought it could be, but in my experience, something is generally better than nothing. Rejoice. Because sometimes there's nothing else to do.

Redemption

MICHAEL SIMON

⬥

Beyond the cracked sidewalk, and the telephone pole with layers of flyers in a rainbow of colors, and the patch of dry brown grass there stood a ten-foot high concrete block wall, caked with dozens of coats of paint. There was a small shrine at the foot of it, with burnt out candles and dead flowers and a few soggy teddy bears. One word of graffiti filled the wall, red letters on a gold background: Rejoice!

The letters had been there for so long the 'o' had eroded into a 'u', turning the word into an ad for a new power drink. Graffiti covered the nearby walls and 'Rejuice' could have been the work of any number of Rembrandts that pimped and whored the east side. The candles and teddy bears were relatively new additions, lending a deeper meaning that nobody except the donor understood.

Summer had wasted into fall and the concrete step felt like a block of ice beneath my ass. The chemo made my legs cramp so I stretched out and lifted my face to the feeble rays of an October sun. Soon the first snow would arrive and sitting outside would be a bitch. On the other side of the broken sidewalk, traffic crawled in both directions. A taxi honked at Berta as she pushed her shopping cart full of worldly possessions toward some unknown destination. Five o'clock and the worker bees were heading home under thick, gray clouds that threatened rain. Across the street, two familiar faces were plying their trade, hoping for early customers. Their piece-of-shit pimp watched from a hidden doorway when he wasn't texting his druggie friends for some blow.

A gust of wind whipped up an army of plastic wrappers and

coffee cups, and sent them scurrying down the street. The sweet aroma of inner-city rot lingered, along with a trace of sulphur from the pulp and paper mill. The same chemical the company said the scuppers were supposed to eliminate. It always made my throat burn.

A door opened across the street and a skinny girl in a half-buttoned flannel shirt turned and gifted a finger to someone inside before running around the corner. Like the rest of the houses in this section of town, the windows were boarded up and the paint on the clapboard exterior reminded me of what my psoriasis looked like on bad days.

Someone slammed the door shut. *Marital problems*, I thought, and then smirked. No marriages in this neighborhood, just *arrangements*. I withdrew a hand-rolled cigarette from my shirt pocket and lit it with a beat-up butane lighter. I promised the doctors a dozen times I'd quit, however the nicotine stains on my fingers proved that cravings were more powerful than promises. I sucked in the sweet tobacco and felt some of the angst fall away. If it weren't for the panic attacks, my anxiety wouldn't be so bad. Since the operation, I can't breathe deep. Thank God I can still smoke. All things considered, it hardly compared to the addictions on the street.

I sensed his presence before he stepped out of the shadows. Something sinister and evil. I had a vision of a spreading plaque with tentacles that undulated in rhythm with his beating heart. He stopped and I shivered as one of those tentacles touched my skin.

"Hey, Mutey, how's the cancer going? Got any in your brain yet?" The pimp grinned, revealing yellow-stained teeth. At six-five, he towered over lesser mortals, his thin, greasy hair tumbling across the collar of his black coat. I stared at his pencil-thin moustache and scarred nose. The tip had been sliced off in a knife fight years ago, leaving him with a funny shaped proboscis and the nickname of

Dickface, at least when he wasn't around.

"Something wrong, Mutey?" His smile lost some of its forced humor. "Where's my favorite dirty look?" He reminded me of a volcano about to blow. I hesitated a moment longer before flashing him the finger. If I didn't respond, he was apt to pop me a few times in my surgically remodelled neck. He glanced at the finger and snickered. Then he moved off and I exhaled. Sad part was, I probably did have brain mets. Doctors suspected as much when they saw me last month but I didn't have coverage for a CT. Funny thing was, six months ago when they removed my voice box, they said they got it all.

"Dickface bothering you again, Max?" The voice came from behind and I shifted around to see a dirty blond walking up the alleyway. Charity was only in her early twenties but could be mistaken for forty. Drugs and alcohol have a way of doing that to people. She'd tried methadone a few times but said it lacked the kick of the good stuff. Once upon a time she waited tables in the nice part of town but that was before her boyfriend got her hooked.

I gave her my best fatherly smile and shook my head. Then I pointed at the departing pimp and pushed my tongue into my cheek a few times. She laughed and for a few seconds, on the street of losers, the sun came out. I reached out to touch the baby bulge in her tummy and raised my eyebrows.

She glanced down and rubbed her hand over the small basketball. It was well past the time where she could actually fasten the worn-out jeans. Instead she had scrounged some elastic bands to keep her pants up. "Soon," she said. "Doctor says I'm on the home stretch."

In that moment, she looked thoughtful, almost sad. The reason why wasn't hard to discern. Bringing a child into this cesspool was going to be a nightmare. She had managed to avoid pregnancy till now, but drug cravings will break the toughest rules. I leaned back and gave her a thumbs up. In her expression I saw a flicker of hope. I took her hand and pulled her down beside me. When things got bad, as they often do for addicts, I took care of her. I withdrew my writing pad and pencil from my pocket and wrote down a few words.

She glanced at my scribble and smiled. "My plans? How'd you know I'd been thinking about this?" She tried to find a comfortable spot on the concrete and I briefly recalled the comfy couches in my parent's living room. A thousand years ago. "Well, I've been talking to social services and they think they can get me a subsidized apartment after the baby is born. There's a bit of a wait but they promised to look into it." My smile threatened to crack so I gritted my teeth as she continued. "They say it's safe to breastfeed as long as I'm clean. Pretty cool, eh?" Her words poured out, as though she'd been saving them up on the inside. "I copied down the phone numbers for some single mother groups, and I can apply to the Y for one of the spots they keep in reserve. If I sneak him into one of the schools uptown, he'll get good grades and maybe even go to college." She looked at me, eyes bright. "He can become somebody."

A car backfired but neither of us flinched. I drew a sign on my pad followed by a question mark. A second later, she put it together. "You want to know how I know it's a boy?" Her face flushed and she quickly looked down. "I don't really. I never got the ultrasound. It's just a dream I had."

I waited as she sank back into herself. Reality has a way of pressing down, squishing all the happiness out of your flesh until there's nothing left but stark, painful reality. Her face slowly melted. Tears rolled down her boney cheeks. "I'm just fooling myself," she sniffed. "They're going to take him. There'll be no apartment, no schooling. . . I'm going to lose my kid!" I held her tight as the hope drained out of her soul.

�֍

No matter how many years I sat on this step, I've always found pigeon shit the worst. It's grimy and sticky and smells like sour milk. If it gets on your fingers or in your food, you're sick for weeks. I carefully placed my sandwich on a clean spot on the concrete. A hard rain was needed to clean the step and the street, and something stronger to sanitize the human filth.

The screen door screeched open behind me. "Is she gone?" a voice asked. I gave a thumbs up over my shoulder. Social workers made their rounds around nine. At ten they could be found in coffee shops complaining about their workload. Charity took a tentative step outside and scanned the street. Just the usual hooligans plying their trades, flesh or drugs, between the lumbering traffic. She relaxed. "It's okay, Jared. Time to go." I heard the patter of tiny shoes on concrete and savored the moment of anticipation. And suddenly he was standing beside me, all three and a half feet. In Tolkien's world, three apples tall. Skinny, with curly blonde hair, puffy cheeks and azure eyes, He looked at me before following his mother into the street.

"He's getting his last vaccine today," she said. "I'll stop by the food bank on the way home." She hesitated in mid-step, as though remembering something. "Good luck with the scan." I flicked my wrist as if it were nothing. Truth was, even after several years, the machines in the hospital still scared the hell out of me. I didn't understand them and they kept finding new cancer spots inside my body. Luckily, radiation killed them and I kept living. In oncology, they started calling me 'Miracle Max'.

More important, at least in my book, was the fact Charity found a way to keep the baby. Through no small amount of lying, faked doctor notes, and staged social work visits, she kept the kid out of their greedy clutches. For my part, I conscripted the ne're-do-wells on the street, the whores, addicts and criminals. If she or the kid needed food, we found it. If they needed medicine, we stole it. And money, well, we couldn't do everything. For the past five years, I made sure she and the kid were taken care of.

Charity turned out to be a great mom. She got back on the methadone right after the delivery and stayed clean ever since. She sacrificed everything for the kid. I marvelled at her strength, then withdrew a cigarette from my pocket. I watched a couple of street girls make a beeline for Charity and the kid while they waited at the bus stop. There was a noticeable change in the air. Somehow, the kid had infused the street with a sense of hope.

Somebody had cleaned up the shrine, repainting 'Rejoice', and leaving new flowers from time to time. There was even a new bullhorn and an egg crate that sat next to the wall. I lit the cigarette and leaned back to savor the taste. When Charity was down with the flu, she always entrusted the kid to me. It had been a lifetime since I last held a child in my arms. My hands trembled at the memory and I always sat down for fear of dropping him. Now that he's bigger I don't hold him so much. I wish he stayed small.

A crowd had formed outside the tenement building next to the shrine. Word was two addicts had taken a bad trip. By the time the ambulance arrived, one had woken up and the other had turned blue. They pronounced him on the spot. After they plied the survivor with Narcan and bundled him off to the hospital, the crowd remained behind the yellow police tape, exchanging tidbits of gossip. The shrine itself was looking worse for wear. Rats had eaten the teddy bear's innards and the most recent flowers resembled dried twigs. The flyers on the wall were frayed and tattered. Even the bullhorn was growing a coat of rust. After six years, I was amazed someone hadn't walked off with it.

Traffic came to a stop as a kid in blue jeans and a black hoodie cut across the street. Several horns signalled their irritation but the kid just raised his hand patiently. Jared didn't talk much. In fact, it was like pulling teeth to exchange more than a few words. But he was pleasant enough, and all smiles around his mother. He stepped up on the curb and I extended my hand for our ritual fist-pump. I raised my palms upward in question and he just shrugged in the usual preteen manner. It was hard not to smile. It had been a long time since I lived those rebellious years. He noticed the crowd milling around the newest crime scene and a look of sadness come over him, lines forming in the corners of his eyes. Then his features hardened, like he was angry at the waste of a life. He started walking toward the group but stopped abruptly in front of the shrine. He stared at the word 'Rejoice' for several long minutes. Several people in the crowd gave him a curious look.

The kid got up onto a milk crate and raised his hand. A murmur went through the crowd and then it fell silent, except for a few people shouting words of encouragement at him. The kid acknowledged them with a nod and a shy smile. In the full light of day, he looked less angry and more beautiful. He waited until people stopped shouting. A siren could be heard, maybe five or ten blocks away. The kid raised the bullhorn, pressed the button, and began to speak

For the life of me, I couldn't remember what he said. Charity didn't believe me—she asked me a hundred times after she got home from work—but it was the truth. I know he didn't speak for long, five minutes tops, but the effect on the crowd was palpable. The collection of addicts, vagrants and rubber-neckers stood in rapt attention. And when he finished and put down the bullhorn, they walked away silent, like they were leaving a wake. Except they had smiles on their faces.

A week later, he did it again. This time it was just after supper. There were only a handful of people around so he didn't need the bullhorn. But several cars stopped and the divers got out to listen. When he finished, everyone went back to what they were doing. No one spoke or made eye contact. It was eerie, like an apocalyptic movie before the apocalypse starts.

After that, Charity stayed home for a full week waiting. She saw him off to school and chewed her fingernails until he returned. Then she never left his side. From my perch on the step, I witnessed something strange. The street transformed. I saw new faces, many hanging around until the wee hours. Some would pace up and down the alleys like they were looking for loose change. Others would stand in the front of the shrine with heads bowed, silent. The downtrodden mixed with high society. Housewives and regular junkies. Cops started walking the beat. It was weird.

"What's he doing?" Charity asked, frustrated after a week waiting for something to happen. "Why'd he stop?" When I shrugged, she went back to chewing her nails. I silently asked Jared the same question the next morning on his way to school. His expression didn't change but his eyes sparkled. I think he was testing his mom, maybe baiting her a bit. He was the right age. But that still didn't answer the big question.

He did it again the following week. This time the crowd was bigger. Fifty, maybe sixty people. I saw cops, prostitutes, taxi drivers, and regular Joes. There was even a reporter. And Charity. I saw her tear up when he spoke, saw her shake so much she'd seemed ready to explode.

He spoke like a kid, using kid words, short and simple. He spoke about taking ownership, about sucking in all the blame that people toss around like confetti. He said responsibility starts at your heart and ends at your fingertips. He talked for less than ten minutes.

When he finished, he stepped off the crate and walked through the silent congregation. He reached out to touch the reporter on the arm. Then he went home, did his homework and went to bed.

✳

"That was freaking wonderful," Charity breathed as we stared up into the night sky. The full moon was out and the police sirens were conspicuous by their absence. "The way he talks is . . . amazing. Did you see how people hung on his every word?" I reached over and squeezed her hand. She looked at me and I pointed at my chest. It took her a second to comprehend. "Yes, he speaks to the heart," she said. "To everyone's heart." I nodded. That's why his words had the effect they did. Those that heard him were overwhelmed by the truth. I realized in that moment they weren't silent because they were coming back from a wake, they were silent because they were emotionally exhausted. Truth is a heavy burden to shoulder.

"How's he doing this?" she asked. "It doesn't make sense." She didn't bother looking at me. She knew I had no magic answers. Instead, I passed her the note I wrote five years ago. It said 'I remember you told me you had a dream about him being a boy. I want to tell you I had a dream, too. In my dream, I was supposed to leave a bull horn at the shrine.' Charity read the note several times before turning to stare at me, wide-eyed. I started to reach for a cigarette when I heard his sermon in my head. I glanced at the hand-rolled smoke in my hand before crushing it between my fingers. I felt like laughing and crying at the same time.

✳

The reporter never posted a story. And yet the crowds got bigger as his sermons became regular events. I saw a television crew show up at one point but they just stood silent like everyone else and listened to his tiny voice. The sheer number forced him to use the bullhorn. It squeaked by times and the words sounded almost gargled, but it changed nothing. The speeches were still short, fifteen minutes max, and covered the spectrum of human frailty. Traffic would seize up but not a single horn sounded. Some drivers got out of their cars to listen, some just rolled down their windows.

Charity sat front and center and wept silently. I figured this is what it felt like when your kid was the best athlete in their sport, and you get to watch every game. She quit her job and would have starved except for me supplying regular meals.

Something was happening. It felt like an earthquake in slow motion. By the third month I realized it wasn't just our street changing, it was bigger. Most of the junkies had stopped using and the whores were looking for regular jobs. Even the worst bastard on the street, Dickface had disappeared. And then the doctors told me the mass in my brain was too advanced to treat. They gave me three months.

Friday morning traffic is a bitch. The air is so thick with fumes it collects in the back of your throat like toothpaste. I did a doubletake when I spied him across the street. It had been months. Dickface looked strung out, his eyes insanely wide, his mouth agape, and his hair like a wild animal. A chill crept up my spine when I realized he was staring at Jared, waiting quietly at the school bus stop. He started walking toward the kid. Strangely, everyone on the sidewalk stopped and watched him pass. Heads swivelled but no one intervened. A cop car screeched to a halt. The driver's door sprung open and a uniform jumped out. He yelled something at Dickface, something I couldn't hear over the car engines. But the pimp had broken into a run, cutting a diagonal between cars. My heart froze when I saw the knife in his hand. I jumped up and tried to cut him off. The cop pulled out his gun. It was a useless act; he didn't have a shot. Our eyes met. Neither of us would make it in time.

Dickface slid over the hood of the last car like a movie star. Jared had his head down, reading something on his iPhone. The same iPhone I got for him for his birthday. I tried to scream a warning and felt something pop in my throat. I tasted blood. The cop fired a shot in the air. The pimp lounged, arm extended. Six inches of silver poised to end a life.

Nobody saw the taxi until it bounced over the curb and slammed into Dickface. In midair, his body seemed to twist one way, his head and legs another. He hit the pavement and rag-dolled twenty feet before stopping in front of the shrine. White bone poked out of his legs. Blood pooled in the gutter.

I stopped. The cop slowly re-holstered his gun. The taxi driver stepped out of his car. Even from twenty feet away, I could see he was shaking like an addict coming off a high. Tears flowed over his brown cheeks. Then the strangest thing happened. Jared stepped forward, took the man by the shoulders and gently directed him back into the car. The last image I had was of the bloodstain on the grill. The cop nodded at me on his way to examine the body. He took out his phone and called for an ambulance. "Hit and run," he said. "No witnesses."

That night, I didn't tell Charity about Dickface, although she could probably tell something was wrong from the way my hands trembled. If she did sense something, she was too preoccupied to ask. My attempt to scream had ripped a hole in my neck scar. Charity said she could see straight into the back of my throat. I spent a long, painful night as she hovered over me, changing dressings. I tried to tell her not to waste her time. I passed her a note with the doctor's prognosis. She gave my shoulder a squeeze and nursed me till the sun came up, and the bleeding finally stopped.

Jared didn't come home on the school bus that afternoon. In

fact, he didn't walk through the door until just before breakfast. When his panicked mother tried to inquire where he was, he simply gave her a kiss on the cheek. After he showered and left for school, I pointed to the plastic bag on the counter, a take-out container from a restaurant across town. "What's he doing way over there?" she asked. The eatery was three miles away. I touched my lips and mimicked talking. Her hand flew to her mouth but then she nodded. He was taking his sermons on tour. To a new audience. But why? Her eyes bore into mine, searching for the answers I didn't have. Whatever the hell was going on was beyond my pay grade. I leaned over the side of my cot and heaved up a bag of blood.

I was dying. For once the physicians were right about 'Miracle Max'. I could feel my life ebbing away, like Mother Earth slowly sucking the energy from my body. The pain wasn't bad, not with the injections Charity was giving me, but I was still throwing up blood. She sobbed in the chair next to my cot. A half dozen prostitutes and druggies stood in a silent vigil. No, I corrected myself, former whores and addicts. They all had jobs now. A couple had even tied the knot. Six months ago, if somebody told me how the street was going to change, I'd toss them into the loony bin.

"He's at the shrine talking," old Berta said. "The street's packed. I even saw the mayor." Charity's expression tightened and she blew her nose. I sensed her dilemma, me or her son. Her eyes flickered toward the door. She wrung her hands together.

I tried to gesture for her to go but my arm was too heavy to lift. She stared at me with tear-stained cheeks before reaching over and taking one of my skeletal hands in hers. "No," she said. "You've been there for me all these years. Now, it's my turn." I felt embarrassed. My mind started to drift. I remembered my marriage and the twins before the car accident. I remembered the small house with the white picket fence and the squirrel that wouldn't shut up.

A screen door screeched open, jerking me back to the present. Somebody stood in the doorway and the room got very quiet. I tried to see who it was but my eyes refused to focus. A small hand come to rest on Charity's. She gasped and almost let me go. But Jared held her tight as a gentle warmness seeped through her hands into mine. I felt like I was being immersed in a warm bath. The heat spread to all corners of my body, erasing my pain, filling me with energy. "Not now, Max," Jared said, staring at me with those azure eyes. "You still have work to do. For me and for you." I took a deep breath, the deepest I had taken since the operation. And yet I felt more.

"All right," I said. "What do you want from this old fart?" Three ex-call girls stumbled backward. Two fainted. One made the sign of the cross. Charity stared at me, her eyes wider than lightbulbs. I smiled at her and ignored everyone else. For the first time since my life collapsed, I had a purpose.

He pulled his hand away. It was all I could do not to reach out and grab it. "I have to go away for a while." He turned and bent down to hug his mother. "I'll come back when I'm done." Charity squeezed him hard for almost a minute before letting him go. "How will I know you're safe?" she whispered. He just smiled as he walked out. The front door slammed. I looked at Charity and realized she had lost weight. "Can I get you a sandwich?" I asked.

The step was cold under my butt but I didn't care. I reached into my shirt pocket and pulled out a stick of gum. When I shoved it into my mouth, I noticed the nicotine stains on my fingers were finally beginning to fade. Charity plopped down beside me, munching on one of my burritos. In truth, I was a shitty cook. My real job was to keep her safe until he returned. She passed me another postcard. "Baton Rouge. I think he's heading for Mexico." I glanced at the stack of postcards in her hand; Boston, Albany, Atlanta, Kansas City. He was making his way across the country. Whatever the hell was happening, was still happening. It was an underground movement. Nothing in the papers or on the news, but people could feel it. There was enthusiasm in the air and something else, anticipation. Charity elbowed me in the ribs. "You got that look," she said. "Spill it."

I shrugged. I was doing my job, the one he gave me, but I still felt a void deep inside, like I was missing something. I only now realized I still hadn't reconciled with my former life. The more I thought about it, the more I realized there was a message hidden in his last words to me. Something that stemmed from an automobile accident so many years ago. Something that needed forgiveness. "Nothing much," I said. "Just wondering if there's a church around here?"

Limboless

C. J. Worby

.♦.

Beyond the cracked sidewalk, and the telephone pole with layers of flyers in a rainbow of colors, and the patch of dry brown grass there stood a ten-foot high concrete block wall, caked with dozens of coats of paint. There was a small shrine at the foot of it, with burnt out candles and dead flowers and a few soggy teddy bears. One word of graffiti filled the wall, red letters on a gold background: Rejoice!

"Rejoice," he whispered under his breath as the car rolled on, through a splash of standing water and droplets of oil and trace amounts of nicotine from the two cigarette butts idly marinating within the puddle. His mother flashed a stern sideways glance from behind the wheel, fingers opening and splaying from the stick shift before settling down once more around the etched plastic bulb. A languid glove of flesh hanging over the map of gears. Her gaze returning to the street ahead.

Rejoice, he repeated, this time in the semi-safe haven of his mind. *Rejoice*. The word failed to compute. It may as well have been the monologue of a lion. An incomprehensible use of known language. Still, the child attempted to rationalize its meaning. As he always did when seeing something incongruous. Like continuity errors in movies. Where he would always try to explain away the impossible, regardless of how obvious it was that whatever he had noticed was a mistake. Something which simply could not be made to make sense within the world of that work of fiction. Like... maybe in that one scene she was drinking the orange juice while that other guy was talking, but then when the camera switched so we could see only him, that's when she quickly spat out all the orange juice she'd actually been holding in her cheeks, which was why the glass was more full when we cut back to her–but it was probably more juice than she could've feasibly just held in her cheeks, so she must've spat some out and regurgitated the rest, and the other character didn't react to this while we were watching him because he was so focused on what he was saying.

Dumb shit like that. So he did what he always did. Attempt to understand the inexplicable. *Perhaps the graffiti was dictated by a blind guy and the person writing it on the wall misunderstood his opening title, which was actually intended as, "Re: Joyce," and the scrawling would have continued onto the adjoining sidewalk in a fervent statement along the lines of, "She is a lovely young lady, in spite of whatever other scribblings you may have read on walls around these parts. She is not in fact a ho, or a slut, or one who 'be jumping bones' all around town. She is the very epitome of virtuous ladyhood." But the message got cut off after the erroneously transcribed "Re: Joyce" bit, because that's when they both suddenly got shot. And that's why there were candles and flowers.*

So our protagonist was, at least in this regard, a doofus. I mean... clearly. Why else would he attempt to explain a simple, glorious exaltation as the misinterpreted preamble to a sudden double homicide? Or that bit in *Jurassic Park* where Lex and Tim were in the Jeep and the T-Rex was there and the vehicle's door was open and then magically closed and then magically open again as being an act of changeably gusting wind and a faulty latching mechanism? The kid was just a goofball. Obviously. But I don't think we can blame him. Or even throw our exasperated arms skyward in mocking despair. For trying to make sense of the unintelligible. For willfully ignoring evidence and trying to square every circle.

And he *knew*. Really. Of *course* he knew. That it was all bullshit. All this rationalization. That the truth was the actress had drunk some orange juice during repeated takes and they'd edited the sequence in the wrong order. That the Jeep's door was mysteriously closed and then open because movies weren't real. That whoever had written that single word of celebration on the garishly daubed wall a half-mile back had felt an emotion that Jack could not comprehend. A sense of peace. Of joy. Of contentment.

His mother had started up her flow of sounds from behind the wheel. Her "sha-da-da-da"s and "blessa-tha-tha"s and other nonsensical utterances she was convinced were words of the Holy Spirit. Why she had to put on this maniacal performance while he was a captive audience, Jack had no idea. Although, again... he did, really. He knew. It was because, so far as she was concerned, he was her property. She could do anything around or to him. Because she had birthed him.

The only way to survive this life of grinding endurance was, in his mind, to view it as an experiment. An aloof observation of parental dysfunction under the extreme tension of mental illness. Her face grew hair. The throat, hair. Her voice, hair. Entangling and entrapping all it touched within the violent eddies of *The Jill Show*. A documentary of contemptuous ego. A study of the self-centered self and its gaping fucking maw. Emitting vines. And hair.

Through these introspections dashed a sudden whack and beep. A jolting of wheels over curb. Wheels over embankment. Wheels over car. Car-wheels-car-wheels, spinning, shrieking cartwheels. A coming to rest on the roof. At the bottom of the hill. The long, desiccated scrub cupping its new automotive statue and cradling it still. As the wheels spun and slowed. Reaching for the sky.

"Mom?" A small, self-absorbed wailing from beside him. "Mom? Are you alright?" She responded by undoing her seatbelt with some effort, slumping down onto the roof of the car, and swiveling to open the door and crawl out into the withered vegetation; all the while lamenting the cost of the insurance claim and a lack of ability to pay for it. *Guess I'll get myself out, then.* The boy attempted to follow suit–minus all the whining, that is–but found his own door inoperable and instead crawled out the driver's side after his mother. Looking up in the direction of the road they had just left showed a couple of people running down the slope toward them, shouting out their concern.

Jill sat down at the base of the hill facing the car, reached into the pocket of her battered denim shirt, and pulled out a pack of cigarettes. Her son approached and sat on the ground at her side as the bystanders looked them over and called 9-1-1. The front passenger's side wheel was the last to stop. As it did so, Jack noticed a dragonfly flit and come to rest on the balding rubber. Wings splayed. King of the wreckage. Soaking in the morning sun.

The cigarette was nearly gone when the fire department's rescue truck came trundling down a less-steep section of the hill; through the long, autumnal grasses already parched and crispy despite the preceding night's brief downpour. The pair of firefighters disembarked and asked if anyone was injured. Jack said he was fine and turned to see the hairs coming out of his mother's mouth. Reaching out for the first responders. Attempting to wrap them up in her flow of misery. Although, through the raging torrent of self-pity, she did admit to not needing any medical attention. But her words, Jack thought, were loopier than usual. And the firefighters seemed to be of a similar mind, as they asked Jack whether she seemed "to be acting normally?" Jack shrugged and answered with an uncertain refutal, for degree of normalcy was tough to pinpoint with his mother. And it was then, as she flicked her cigarette butt into the surrounding tinder, that Jill's fingers began to cramp. And curl. As she keeled over into the hillside, becoming unresponsive to shouts and pinches and sternal rubs. And then the ambulance was there, and there were paramedics and firefighters taking vitals and giving oxygen and carrying her to the waiting stretcher on a white tarp and loading and going, with Jack sat up front, belted, as the lights flashed and siren screamed, turning and craning to his left to look back into the main body of the vehicle, seeing his mother's clothes cut from her and an IV started, and they were at the hospital and in a little two-stall ambulance garage with dull concrete floor as Jack unclipped his belt and ran around to the back and followed as she was taken to the crash room, and a nurse came and ushered him out and down the hallway as he caught a last glimpse of his mother with someone about to begin intubation, through the hairs on her face; and her throat. But not her voice.

In the room. A TV set. Set. To Fox News. Talking about an outrage. A moral affront. In the hallway. An incubator of blankets. To allow the hatching of washcloths, perhaps? Who could say. And an intermittent walking of figures. And a guy in white and green who came to sit with Jack. And put his hand on his shoulder. And talk about a brain bleed. And an attempt that was still in progress. And his grandfather was on his way right now. And Jack was fourteen.

Did I mention that? I know I didn't; I'm just being chatty and approachable. Though it is hard to approach at this distance. But, yes, the kid was fourteen. And when his mother went extra doolally. A few months prior. And made Jack do uncomfortable things to her. In the bedroom. Jack had later thought: *But I'm fourteen fucking years old. Why am I obeying her orders? Why did I do what she told me to? I'm fourteen fucking years old.* And it made him feel pathetic. To be so woefully in her grasp. And show no real portrayal of outward rebellion. In the face of hideous subversion. At the age of fucking fourteen.

So as he sat, alone in the room, he was in turmoil. With a desire to get up and run outside and jump and yelp and shout at the top of his lungs with the hugest of grins that his mother was more-than-likely going to die at any moment. And also with a morose, inexplicable resignation of despair for that exact same reason.

Through this churning cognitive dissonance, there came the shouting. Not from an outpouring of his foremost urge to celebrate, but from outside the room. And down the hallway. Muffled by the big double doors separating those receiving care from the triaged-and-pending. The inpatients from the impatient. It was from out there. Amidst the tummyaches and flu symptoms and "I've just been feeling kinda dizzy these past few days"es. An angry, urgent shouting. Pretty violent-sounding, actually. The type of noise you hear which immediately sets your primate hackles to stirring. Jack stayed seated. Concerned. Eyes trained on the large, doorless opening into his room.

And then pops. Cracks. Blasts. Still somewhat subdued by the large double doors, but resounding throughout the wing with considerably more gusto than the preceding bellows. Jack leapt from his chair and to the edge of the hallway, staring down in the direction of the shots. Which was all they could have been. He recognized the sound from time spent target shooting with his dad. On one of their occasional get-togethers. Before he'd moved to Montana. And before Jack's mother had successfully completed a full course of mind-poisoning with regard to Jack's opinion of his father. Which left the target shooting memory—previously a very pleasant one—irrevocably tampered with a painted-on feeling of hatred. Toward this apparent beast of a man. Although he'd really seemed quite nice. To Jack. Despite not seeing him all that often. Though Jack had since learned he was apparently a rapist. His father. Just a fucking rapist pig. Apparently. So... That put a whole nother slant on their otherwise charming can-shooting date. In retrospect.

But it had left him knowing what gunfire sounded like.

He could see and hear panic-stricken hospital staff as they quickly and quietly headed for exits or safe rooms or anywhere but their current location, and for a moment he thought he would follow them. But then something snapped within. Something already snapped and somehow snapping even further. Like a nihilistic rubber band frantically rending itself to tiny nubbins. And he was stalking and running, down the hallway, in the direction of the commotion. Toward the propagated screams and sporadic shots. His eyes flitting everywhere, looking for a weapon, but finding only a mug containing ballpoint pens with a piece of plastic silverware incongruously taped to the end of each. So he grabbed one, snapped off the head of the little spoon, and scurried to the corner of the hallway... peering around to the right... to the double doors with small glass windows leading to the emergency department's main waiting area. And he saw him. The fucking guy. A thin little shit. Right fucking there with his back to the doors and shouting at a woman on the floor in front of him. Her shrunken, cowered form wrapping itself around some unseen blob of life within. And the guy was raising his gun once more. Slowly. Deliberately. And the rubber band that was Jack's mind gave one, final, smithereening –*SNAP*–.

He dashed. Around the corner and up to the doors, not pausing for even a moment as he picked up momentum and smashed into the crash bar, the door swinging wildly before him as he burst through, lunging at full bore toward the bewildered, swiveling shooter and engulfing him like a fucking lion on the Serengeti, knocking him to the floor and plunging the ballpoint pen down into his exposed neck in frenzied, repeated stabs. Unstopping. Unyielding. Through the attacker's fumbled attempts at defense. Stab after stab after glorious stab. Piercing one, then both carotid arteries and spraying the cold hospital floor with wild, ebullient blood. Still he plunged. Over and over and over. Even when all resistance had stopped. When all that was left was a warm, yielding body beneath. Still. Until finally, when all thought of even the slightest signs of life had been completely expelled. Only then did he drop the pen. And grip the shooter's curly, blood-matted hair on either side of his head. And violently smack his skull into the floor about a half-dozen times. Then Jack rose up. Onto his corpse-straddling knees. Up to standing. And surveyed the room. The dead and injured. The mother, still cradling her hidden little blob, now staring up at him with hero-worshiping eyes. The unscathed, peeking up from behind chairs and tables. He swayed a little in place, a lingering expression of rage still etched on his face, then finally spoke. "I got someone to see."

The crescendo of descending sirens was palpably near as the boy clambered over the counter and through the open window of the recently vacated reception area. He scooched down to the floor and walked, purposefully, back into the now-deserted hallways of the emergency department. Back down the route he'd been led just a half-hour prior. As he'd been ushered away from his mother. Turning right into the area where critical patients were taken. And then seeing her room. With the curtain left open by the staff as they had fled. He slowly approached and paused at the doorway.

There she was. Naked. With a chunk of plastic connected to corrugated tubing sticking out of her mouth. A nearby monitor showing a flat, green line and bathing the room in the solid, unwavering tone of death. Jack took a long breath, then walked to her side and found her hand with his—still sticky with blood as it was. "Hey, Mom. I guess you didn't make it, then." Her face was passive. The endotracheal tube made her look, Jack thought, like she was in a perpetual state of calling in ducks. Just without the inherently comedic sound effects. He imagined the monitor's incessant, unwavering "*beeeeeeeeeeeeé*" as instead being one long "*quaaaaaaaaaaaaaa*" and found a spontaneous smirk spreading across his face. "Well... I know we've had a tough time, you and I. Although, I think *my* side's probably been a bit fucking tougher. But, anyways, I just wanted to tell you that I love you." His words brushed across Jill's ears. Curling into her cochlea and round its coils. Gently tingling the lingering nerve cells as they carried the last messages of a world turned dark to a brain turning off. And she knew she was loved.

Even though it was just lip service. As it turned out. For, as the boy left the room, he felt the wave function collapse. Seeing his mother gone had opened up Schrödinger's Box of Unresolved Emotion™, and it turned out the kitty-cat inside was thoroughly joyful and looking forward to a future of dangling wool and liver-flavored kibble. So he marched, head held high and smile on his face, back toward the main entrance. Back through the double doors to where the police were now swarming, amidst doctors and nurses and paramedics scampering, as the uninjured and walking wounded gasped at Jack's reappearance and pointed and shouted out variations on the theme of, "That's him! That's the kid who saved us!"

Several officers immediately surrounded Jack and escorted him, past the pulpy-necked body of the shooter, out to the refulgent midday glare of the parking lot. Where he squinted and saw a good couple-hundred people–police, patients, staff, gawkers, even a few fleet-footed reporters–gathered and milling amidst the still-flashing squads and ambulances. As they were leading him out, the cops were showering Jack with praise and questions. "Great fuckin' job, kid!" "You injured?" "You got some balls, kid..." "What's your name, son?" "We could use a few more guys like you!" "You know how many lives you saved today?"

As they reached the edge of the crowd, Jack stopped. He turned to address the oldest-looking of his entourage and straightened himself up. "You're gonna take me away for questioning and shit, aren't you?" "Well... Yeah, kid. We kinda gotta get your story." Jack paused, then gestured toward the large crowd of people before them. "Can you let me talk to 'em? Before we go?" The mustachioed officer smiled and winked, slapping the boy on his shoulder. "You bet." Then he turned and shouted off to the side. "Hey, Sarge! Can I get that megaphone? Our young hero's got a few words for these survivors, here!" The police quickly prepared a small area at the head of the crowd and the sergeant conveyed a few words of highly flattering–yet understandably impersonal–introduction through his bullhorn before handing it over.

The kid got up onto a milk crate and raised his hand. A murmur went through the crowd and then it fell silent, except for a few people shouting words of encouragement at him. The kid acknowledged them with a nod and a shy smile. In the full light of day, he looked less angry and more beautiful. He waited until people stopped shouting. A siren could be heard, maybe five or ten blocks away. The kid raised the bullhorn, pressed the button, and began to speak.

"Hey. So... I just wanted to say a couple things, if that's cool." He paused, almost seeming as if he were waiting for any potential protests at this notion. None came, and he continued. "First off, I want to say how sorry I am to all the friends and family of those that got shot in there today. I have no clue what that douchebag was thinking, but, well... at least we know he ain't thinking *shit* no more." A slight ripple of irrepressible laughter rose from the assembled, in spite of the somber atmosphere, and there were several yells of support for the boy's dismissively irreverent attitude toward the dead shooter. Jack had rested the megaphone down by his side and seemed about to step off the impromptu podium when he hesitated, squared up to the crowd, and raised the bullhorn once more to his lips.

"There was just one more thing." The crowd hushed. "Seeing as we all know this shit is gonna go viral..." There were a couple of small chuckles from the many people holding their smartphones aloft. The kid smiled again. Just a little. He stalled and seemed unsure of himself. Then his features solidified into a look of resolute determination as an almost statesmanlike demeanor came over him and, through the softly distorted booming of the bullhorn, he continued.

"I've always thought—especially in the past few years—that I was a fuckin' pussy. My mother, God rest her soul, had got me on fuckin' lock. She got away with treating me like I was subhuman. And I took it. And I hated myself for it. Because I thought I was weak. I thought I had no control over my destiny." The crowd stood, transfixed. The words swirled out of the boy's mouth. Not as vines. Or as hair. But as doves. Flying out from the milk crate. Through the parking lot. Through the live streams. To far-flung reaches.

"But the events of this morning have forced me to reevaluate. I'm not trying to sound like I'm bragging or anything... but a pussy doesn't attack a deranged, armed man with a little ballpoint pen. That ain't gonna happen. So why—if I wasn't, actually, a dickless piece of shit—did I put up with years of abuse?" He paused. "I think I know now. It's because it was the status quo. It was just what life was. It's so easy to put up with what already exists, that I never did shit about it. I just figured that was my life. But now I see I was just looking at it in the wrong way. And that's what I want to tell all you kids watching this... and, shit, probably a bunch of you adults, too... Don't look at abuse as a continuation of what's normal. Look at it like it's a fucking active shooter walking into your day. Any fresh act of sickness or violence toward you... that's your fucking shooter, right there. I'm tellin' ya; chances are, you're actually a really strong person just trapped in the status quo. Look at that shit with fresh eyes. Do what you need to–right fucking now–to get out of that situation. Because you can do it. Alright... Enough with the 'motivational speaker' bullshit. That's all I got."

The crowd stared, dumbstruck, at the child before them. As he stepped down to the tarmac, handed off the bullhorn, and was whisked away by police–who recommenced enthusiastic back-patting as soon as his feet left the milk crate. As Jack was taken from the scene, the doves were still soaring in his wake. Disappearing beyond the neighboring buildings. And towns. The routers and servers. Spreading ever outwards.

Of *course* it went viral. How could it not have? A fourteen-year-old kid, fresh from heroically stabbing a murderous psychopath to death with a slim stick of plastic, standing out in front of a large group of people and spilling his guts about being brave in the face of everyday challenges? Yeah. That shit spread like wildfire.

Before school had even let out that day, countless children around the country–and, for that matter, other countries–had shared and watched his speech. In hallways. Under desks. In bathroom stalls. His impassioned oratory burning from behind a blood-soaked T-shirt, softly browning in the midday sun. And it wasn't like they'd never heard anyone talking about abuse before. Plenty of people had talked to them while they were growing up. About inappropriate contact. Good and bad touches. All that stuff. But it had always been *adults* doing the talking. Purportedly well-intentioned adults. Kids always seemed to be "protected" from speaking about it. In the classroom. In whatever media form. Presumably to save them from exploitation. Like the exploitation of talking about abuse would somehow be worse than living through it, day in and day out.

Dipshits.

But now Jack had opened that door all by himself. As the footage was already out there and being watched by everyone anyway, the news networks figured they could just go ahead and show it, too—in a heavily bleeped-out format, of course. And once he'd been shown in the news talking so openly about abuse, well by extension that just seemed to give *everyone* in the media a green light to talk with him about it. In skipping the middleman, he'd made the middleman available. It's a funny old world.

So it was that Jack became the toast of the town. If "town" were replaced with "nation." But I'm getting ahead of myself by a couple of paragraphs, here. Bear with me a moment. So, yes... After leaving the hospital Jack was taken to the police station, where he gave his official recount of what had transpired during the shooting. His grandfather met him there. Pretty much in tatters. He was, from my admittedly subjective viewpoint, a kindly old soul. A widower since four years prior. Now he'd suddenly lost his only daughter... who, according to the officers' talk he was picking up on, had just had her memory very publicly trashed by his only grandchild. A grandchild he would now have to somehow raise all on his own without any prior warning. That's a shitty day.

As they left the precinct, in Jerry's well-maintained 2005 Park Avenue, they had a heart-to-heart. About what had really been going on in Jack's home life. Behind the veneer. It didn't come as a huge surprise to his grandfather. Not really. He'd just been guilty of some excessively wishful thinking. After Jill had left the asylum. Where she had been involuntarily committed for three months, back when Jack was eight years old. After suicidal ideations and stabbing couches and shaking out a large crucifix on the living room floor with three five-pound tubs of hot cocoa mix. Jack had lived with his grandparents during his mother's spell of psychiatric internment, and it was with some sadness and trepidation they relinquished him. When the state was done with her brain-fixing. Back into the clutches of unverified suspicion. But they had wanted to believe. Of course. That their daughter was just troubled. That her cross was hers alone. Again... I don't know if we can really blame them for that. Though, naturally, it's not my place to judge.

What I can say for sure is that Jack liked his grandfather. As they pulled into the driveway of his little suburban home, an old Orrin Thompson rambler, Jack felt a warm fuzz come over him. Anticipating the orderly calm of what lay inside. The tick of the heirloom cuckoo clock, brought over by his great-grandparents when they'd immigrated from Norway. The cherrywood curio cabinet, filled with figures and yellowed documents and military regalia. The clean tables and countertops, uncluttered with the mounds-upon-mounds of inconsequential trinkets and bullshit his mother simply could not dispose of back home. And the guest room. Which was *his* room. Whenever he stayed over. And now. Until he grew up and moved out.

It was the following morning they got the first call from a television network wanting Jack to appear on a talk show; the request clearly prompted by the extensive coverage on the previous night's news and Jack lighting up social media like some stupid simile. What shall we go with? A blowtorched cotton ball factory? Sure.

Jack said he'd call them back and then chatted for a while with his grandfather before going to his room to think alone. He was unsure whether the limelight was what he needed at this point. Whether he even *wanted* a platform. During yesterday's speech, he'd been soaring high on the jittery euphoria of his sympathetic nervous system. Now he felt like what he essentially was. A fragile, bedraggled lepidopteran, finally free from his prison and frantically pumping meconium, dreaming of flight. As he sat, almost meditative in his contemplation, he dared to envisage. What he could actually be. And as he did so, he became aware of his wings unfurling. Hardening. He stared out the window; at the backyard; at the sky. At length he shook off his reverie and returned the call.

Jack's first televised interview appearance was on a popular, late-afternoon talk show with a highly affable female presenter. Although, for the life of me, I can't think of a popular television talk show which *doesn't* feature an affable presenter. I guess I just wanted to let you know that Jack was in kind hands. This definitely wasn't Frost vs Nixon territory. The show had a reputation for being mostly lighthearted, with occasional fleeting forays into the elusive world of broadcast sincerity. Just a *touch* of sincerity. Not enough to lose viewers, but enough to retain a pretense of having a heart. And Jack would be that heart.

Or so they thought. And indeed he *was* that heart, but he was also so much more. It turned out he could flit from serious to frothy in the flick of a frame. But I suppose you could judge that for yourself if I included a brief excerpt of that first interview. Let me just find the right bit, here. Ahh yes, here we go...

"...*must have been very hard for you*." "Well, yeah... It was. But like I was saying outside the hospital, there... I really just felt like that was my lot in life and there wasn't anything I could do about it. I didn't realize I actually had the power to stand up to her all along." "*You talked very movingly about the danger of the status quo. That we let things happen because it's a continuation rather than something new.*" "Yeah, I absolutely believe that. But I've been thinking a lot more about it since then, and I've realized that when it's your own parent, there's extra challenges involved, y'know? The way I see it, they start off with three extra powers they can rely on. Trust, love, and family. When you're a little kid, they've got all of those over you. Then, as you get older and you realize something isn't right, they lose that first one. You don't trust them anymore. You know they're not all on your side. But they've still got those other two special moves. Then you get even older. And you question your love. You realize that you don't love the person who's doing this to you. But then there's that final kicker. They've still got that ace up their sleeve. Family. And that's kind of *like* love, because it's ingrained within you. I've come to see it as like a love hallucination. And whatever they do to you, there's this love hallucination you keep on seeing. It's like this obligation that never leaves you. Even though my mother's gone and I'm happy to be free, there's this fallacy still there in my mind. It's why I told her I loved her when she was already gone in the hospital bed. And I know it can't be real. My rational mind can't make peace with it. I don't even want to acknowledge it. But it's there. You can feel it. That's your abuser's biggest tool. Even after they've burned up your trust and genuine love. Family. And those are the three powers an active shooter doesn't have over you. Which I guess is why standing up to *him* felt so much easier." (*There are a couple of seconds of silence.*) "*You say you're only fourteen?*" "Yeah... They tell me that, but I've never seen my birth certificate, so..." (*Jack and the host laugh, and the audience joins in.*) "*And now here you are, a national hero, a national inspiration, on national television.*" "Yep. And, really, it's all thanks to my first-grade teacher, Miss Moen." (*There is a brief, puzzled pause before the host follows this up.*) "*It's thanks to your first-grade teacher?*" "Oh, absolutely. You see, she taught me the best way to hold a pen." (*Jack winks and grins, and the studio erupts with laughter.*)

OK, so... I didn't actually get the network's permission to show you that clip, so I'd better write a quick review to explain away its inclusion under "fair use" practices. They're horrifically litigious, you see. Hang on a moment; it'll just be a quick one. Ahem... "This was a great episode of the show. Jack proved himself to be a very smart and likable individual." There; that'll probably do it. I hope this brief interruption didn't disrupt the flow of the narrative for you. Although I would assume it probably did. My apologies. Back to it, then.

Before this appearance, it would be fair to say that most TV execs secretly harbored fears that Jack would turn out to be an awkward, profanity-laden freak of a child who was wholly unsuitable for television. However, after acquitting himself with such exceptional aplomb, the floodgates were officially opened. And Jack, it transpired, was happy to oblige the torrent. For he had forged a tentative plan of great aspiration.

Five days after the incident at the hospital—and one day after his mother's interminable interment—Jack was standing on the North Lawn of the White House, receiving the Presidential Citizens Medal. For, as his internal monologue described it, "Outstanding Use of Stationery in the Face of Calamitous Peril." The president, however, waived this definition in favor of "a truly heroic act of selfless bravery." Which was essentially, Jack mused, a slightly less entertaining way of saying the same thing. The glowing fall foliage on the grounds cast a spell on the boy. Yellowed as his grandfather's war journals. Ruddy like his shirt as he'd marched from the hospital. Rippling in sepia invitation. *I'll be back.*

It had dawned on Jack—fairly early on, in fact—that Hollywood would be likely to attempt a cinematic immortalization of his last day with his dear, departed mother. What he had not even *remotely* pondered, however, was that *he* would be called upon to play the lead role. A grizzled old Hollywood actor-turned-director had seen Jack's speech and subsequent television appearances and evidently felt that Jack was the only person qualified to really portray *Jack*. Despite his initial surprise, the boy was, upon reflection, willing to concur. If method acting really is a solid way of getting a good performance, well then, heck, he should have had that shit dialed in after fourteen-some years of practice. *Plus, I did do that barbershop performance with my school that one time. Geesh... I may as well be a fuckin' Juilliard alumnus already.*

When *Redemption* finally hit the cinemas around a year-and-a-half later, the really surprising thing about Jack's acting was that, well... it was actually *good.* Like, *really* good. *Tearjerkingly* good, even. Of course, in reality he'd been acting nearly all his life, so it probably shouldn't have come as a shock. Still, the praise rolled in, from critics and audiences alike.

Just as a little aside... Jack had actually considered a far better title for the film to be *All the King's Horses...* What with all the action essentially starting with Jack and Jill falling down a hill. But he realized this was really a pretty silly idea and sensibly kept it to himself.

Whilst our real-life protagonist had been enjoying his newfound fame and success, he was seemingly suffering from something akin to survivor's guilt. Regarding not the hospital attack, but rather his freedom from parental tyranny. He knew how commonplace his scenario must still have been across the state. Across the nation. The world. And he felt the need to do something. Which was really his long-term goal. He looked at all this celebrity fanfare as mainly a means to an end. A way to gain a well-known position of likability and respect within the public eye. With a view to public office. In the meantime, he put his wealth and profile to good use by becoming actively involved with initiatives to tackle domestic violence. Which meant that, what with school, homework, additional acting opportunities, media appearances, and working with various charities... he was lucky if he found enough energy to spank the monkey even *once* before succumbing to sleepytime somnulence. I would think that anyone who is—or has at some point been, or, I guess, has even *lived with*—a sixteen-year-old male will appreciate just how hard this would mean he was pushing himself.

But, anyways... I suppose it's really time for me to wrap this tale up. Young Jack's formative years have been addressed, and I wouldn't want to outstay my welcome. I hope you wish him well. I know *I* do. The charming little fuckup that he is. I don't want to flash too far ahead, but I would like to indulge in one brief sputter to the future. To one of my favorite moments of his remarkable life. Five years hence.

Jack is driving along a road he seldom travels, though it's just a few miles from home. The rich, earthy scent of late fall blowing through the cracked windows of his sensible, nondescript sedan. He yawns and wipes the tiny remaining bits of sleep from his eyes. Though he only actually slept for an hour and a half. On the floor. In a corner of his tiny campaign headquarters. Where he had joined his team in watching the results roll in and realized, in due course, that he was going to be the youngest legislator in the history of the state. Now he is taking the shortest way home, as the early morning sun glitters in the haphazardly scattered puddles left by the overnight rain. Across the central median, he sees the embankment which ended his mother's life and began his own, seven years ago. As he drives, he thinks back to his childhood. The insecurity. The resignation. Though he rarely calls it to mind anymore, he briefly flashes back to that moment in the hospital. Bursting through the door and lunging. The unbottling of so much rage held within. Then, just as quickly as the memory had come, it is gone again. Replaced with thoughts of his new appointment and all he will be working to achieve. Glancing once more across to the other side of the road, he sees that same wall from his childhood. Where the little shrine had been placed. The once-resplendent gold background now flaked and weathered to merely splotchy patches of bronze. Adorned with new scribblings and patterns; drawings and proclamations. But behind them, in the faint traces of huge, red letters, Jack can still make out that lingering sentiment of an unknown artist. He mouths the word, gently mulling it over as he does so. Then, through his exhaustion, a smile begins to spread across his face–wider and wider–and he finds himself repeating the word with renewed excitement as a fire engulfs his heart. "Rejoice. Rejoice! Fuckin' A, right!"

ABOUT THE AUTHORS

Andrea Avery is a teacher and writer who lives in Phoenix, Arizona. She is the author of *Sonata: A Memoir of Pain and the Piano* (Pegasus Books). Her short work has appeared in *Real Simple*, *Ploughshares*, and *The Oxford American*. She is currently at work on a novel.

Virginia Brackett's 15 books have been cited by the New York Public Library; the Pennsylvania School Librarians Association; Tri-state Books of Note; the American Library Association, Amelia Bloomer Project; and *Booklist* (Editor's Choice, Reference Sources, 2008). She has published more than 150 articles and stories for children and adults, and her electronic books include *Angela and the Gray Mare* (children) and *Girl Murders*, a time-travel mystery. Her memoir focusing on her father's death in the Korean Conflict and its effect on her family, *In the Company of Patriots*, is under contract to Sunbury Press. (https://www.virginiabrackett.com).

Dominic Breiter, 28, is a mailman living with his wife in southeast Wisconsin. His other works have been published by *Orange Hat, Great Lakes Review,* and *Eunoia Review*. He has been writing fiction more or less daily since before he could spell, and despite his better logic, doesn't appear to be shaking this compulsion anytime soon.

Aramis Calderon earned his MFA in Creative Writing from the University of Tampa. Every week he participates in the DD-214 Writers' Workshop, a writing community for active duty service members, veterans, and their families. He currently resides in Safety Harbor, Florida with his wife and three children.

Kyle Caldwell is a writer and musician from Hamilton, Ontario, Canada. He is currently working on a collection of short stories and a crime novel and has released several albums under the pseudonym The Cold Atomic. Follow @thecoldatomic.

Travis Dahlke is a writer from Connecticut with work appearing in *Structo, Sporklet, Bridge Eight Press, SAND Journal, Apt.* and *The Longleaf Review,* among other literary journals and collections. He also has a novella available from Otherwhere Publishing. Find him at deffbridges.com.

Helen Dent currently resides in Texas. She holds an MA in English from the University of Virginia and is an active member of the DFW Writer's group.

Katherine Doar grew up in Oklahoma but has since moved to Virginia, where she is an adjunct instructor of writing at a small college. She has a B.A. from Sewanee: The University of the South and M.A. in English from Boston College. Her favorite short story writers are Eudora Welty and Kelly Link.

Kelsey Wollin Dunn is a Wisconsin native who works in a bindery that has not yet bound one of her books, is a part-time secretary for the little white church on the hill in Cooksville, and does her writing with the aid of her blind pigeon named Spot who sits on her shoulder, as all good muses do.

Daniel Earl lives in Michigan with his wife and their six children. That's not a typo, there are six of them. Last he checked. He is working on his first novel. When he is not writing, he is a professional genealogical speaker and researcher and a substitute teacher. You can learn more about his other works at http://www.danielearl.com

Lila Evans is an occasional teacher and full-time writer with a degree in English Literature and a Bachelor of Education. She has had work published both online and in print and would love to turn fiction writing into a career. Lila lives in Ontario, Canada with her husband and two cats and enjoys wildlife, the great outdoors, and the first few weeks of winter until it drags on too long!

Scott Adam Gordon is a British journalist living in Berlin, Germany. He writes news for mobile technology website www.androidauthority.com and tweets from @scottadamgordon.

Kelly Griffiths lives with her family in Northeast Ohio and is a 2019 nominee for Best Small Fictions. Her recent work is published in *The Forge Literary Magazine, Ellipsis Zine,* and *Reflex Fiction.*

Katherine Kendig lives in Champaign, Illinois, with her husband, her novel-in-progress, and a consistent craving for brownies. Her work has received awards from Dartmouth College and the University of Illinois and has been featured in *The Cincinnati Review* , *PodCastle,* and *Shimmer Magazine.*

Autumn Mabry. As a small-town girl from Texas, Autumn grew up in a world of her own imagination. She enjoys dabbling in various forms of creative arts, professionally and otherwise, such as fine art, design, writing and music. This is her first published short story of fiction.

Nancy Moir grew up on both Canadian coasts, and now lives near Ottawa with her husband and five cats. When not rolling through the countryside on a bicycle, she can be found with her hands in the earth, tending her vegetable—and story—plots.

R.Tim Morris is a Vancouver author who writes in a variety of genres. To date, he's written four novels of suspense/thriller, literary fiction, speculative fiction, and adult humour categories. Find out more at rtimmorris.com

Alissa Jones Nelson grew up in Southern California and has spent the last fifteen winters wondering why she ever left. Since abandoning meteorological paradise, she has traveled widely and lived in Spain, the Czech Republic, Japan, Scotland, and Germany. Her short stories have appeared in the anthology *Home Is Elsewhere* and been shortlisted for several international prizes, including the Berlin Writing Prize, the Fish Short Story Prize, and the Half and One Prize. She lives in Berlin.g

Zackary Pierce is currently an exchange student in northern Germany. At twenty-one, he has been writing for four or five years, and tries more and more to publish his work. Though he admittedly enjoys improving on the craft infinitely more than exposing it to criticism and rejection, he believes it's an important part of becoming a better writer.

James Potter lives at the foot of the Blue Ridge Mountains in Upperville, VA. His writing for young and old has appeared in The Portland Review as well as various science fiction and steampunk anthologies. Last year his YA graphic novel series *The Glimmer Society*, co-created with New York artist Plaid Klaus, had its debut by Image Comics. When he's not writing fiction he loves making music with his wife Amy in their Americana band The Crooked Angels.

Rob Rowntree, lives in Nottinghamshire, England, with his wife and two boys. He took up writing fiction over ten years ago and has had some success with short stories, notably, Armadillo, in issue two of the short-lived professional magazine, *Farthing*. More recently his work has appeared in the *Transtories Anthology*, from Aeon Press, and the anthology *Colinthology* (in memory of the SF writer Colin Harvey), from Wizards Tower Press. *Unbound Brothers*, his first novel, was self published and gained good reviews. He is currently working on his second, *Oumuamua's Children*.

Erin Ruble's work has appeared or is forthcoming in *Fugue*, *Green Mountains Review*, *Midway Journal*, *Tahoma Literary Review*, *The Tishman Review*, and elsewhere. A native of Montana, she now lives in Vermont with her husband and children and the occasional flock of chickens.

Donald Ryan's words appear or are forthcoming in *Cleaver*, *Hobart*, *Fiction Southeast*, *Soft Cartel*, and elsewhere. He's a full-time part-time librarian in the GA Pines. (www.donaldryanswords.com)

Daniel Salvatore loves to write, read when he's not writing, and draw when writing and reading become frustrating. He lives in Portland, Or, where he currently works in IT for some reason, and can often be found drinking too much coffee.

Michael Simon lives in New Brunswick, Canada, where he works in the health care field to support his writing addiction. Previous science fiction stories have appeared in *Apex: Science Fiction and Horror*, *Andromeda Spaceways Inflight Magazine*, and several anthologies. Non-fiction articles have appeared in *Stitches Magazine*, *The Medical Post* and *Hockey Net*. He has a weekly radio show.

Rita Sommers-Flanagan is an irreverent clinical psychologist who recently escaped the confines of academia and has resumed pursuing her earlier callings--happily publishing poetry, essays, short stories, and so far, one novel. She's a blogger and an activist, furious with the way the world is drifting, and determined to make her words matter.

C. J. Worby was born in England, moved to Japan for a spell, & now lives in sunny Minnesota with his wonderful wife and son. He considers himself exceptionally fortunate to be a firefighter & even *more* fortunate to be a B-shifter! He once bludgeoned an innocent pig to death with the blunt side of an axe at the behest of remote Papua New Guinean tribespeople, though that is probably a story for another day.

JUDGES

OWL CANYON PRESS SHORT STORY
HACKATHON No. 2 CHALLENGE

DAVID GREENSON

David Greenson grew up in Oakland, California, before it was hip, and then spent
twenty-seven years in New York City, many of them living in an intentional community
and working as a grassroots political organizer. He now lives in Asheville, North Carolina,
in spite of his disinterest in beer, dogs, and hiking. He was ordained by the
CHI Interfaith Community as an Interstitial Chaplain in March 2019
and is currently working on his first novel.

JULIE HALL

Julie Hall grew up on various Air Force bases across the U.S. and one in Japan.
After retiring from the position of military brat she attended college, raised a child,
and had a career in computer programming in Las Vegas, Nevada. She has been
published in the *Rio Review* and *The Jellyfish Review*. Julie currently resides
in Austin, Texas with her partner, musician Christine Cochrane.

LORAIN URBAN

Lorain Urban's work has appeared in the *Kenyon Review*, *Narrative*, *CALYX Journal*,
Tahoma Literary Review, the *Midwest Review*, and the inaugural issue of the *Hong Kong Review*.
Her short story, "Half of What You See," is included in Owl Canyon Press'
anthology of its Summer 2018 Hackathon, as the second place winner.

CPSIA information can be obtained
at www.ICGtesting.com
Printed in the USA
FFHW022014290419
52156511-57519FF